# The Blue Talon

## By S. T. Kesler

Published 2019
Kesler & Associates
978-1-7334257-0-4

'

# BOOK I Sergei's Story: I Do Not Die

## The Beginning: A Family's Burden

"Do I have to repeat myself?" I asked the stony-faced persons facing me. Drawing my body up, I added, "Both of you agreed six months ago you would not attempt to enlist Jeanne and me for at least three years. Is your word of no value? "

My two eldest children stood shoulder to shoulder in the middle of the entryway. "But Papa…,"  the taller and male half of the duo began.

My answering scowl silenced him in mid-word, but his companion continued unfazed. "You know we wouldn't be here under ordinary circumstances, but what we face now is a disturbing, frightening situation. Our computer model at HQ shows Jeanne as the most ideal for addressing it—our best hope to avert a potential and disastrous chain of events."

"Valentina," I said, trying to be patient with my oldest living offspring, "No. No not now. Unearth someone else. That gigantic computer network identifies more possible volunteers than ever we could in times past. Do a new search. Jeanne is too young and lacks the knowledge even the greenest family member in the field possesses. Did you both forget I was already sixteen when I first encountered the Blue? No one less mature is ready to face the challenge fate has tasked us to do."

"But, Papa," she began.

"No. I agreed many times with your regimen of pulling our young ones into training camps. I've joined you in the field when you called and given advice when asked. My answer is no."

Valentina responded much as I expected. Her uncompromising stance conveyed her opinion of my unequivocal answer. On this occasion, she showed more than simple reproach. She radiated disapproval mixed with disrespect. They'd come assuming my capitulation despite my often ungracious and often reluctant acquiescence in the past. They'd been wrong this time.

"I mean to hold you to your word," I said.

Met with their silence and trampling down my inner sadness, I opened my arms and embraced both. I did love them. They did not ask to be what they were. Nor did I. I grasped both their shoulders and turned them around toward the street. I smiled as I motioned them to their car. For now, I had prevailed.

"Until we return then, Papa, do svidaniya," she said.

They turned and left without another word. Afterward, my eyes were moist, and my spirits sank. The pleasant afternoon was only a wistful memory.

Yet, I recognized one day soon I'd have no alternative. My youngest, well beloved, and talented daughter, Jeanne would face a challenge as her siblings had before her. When that day arrived, I must lay on another of my children a burden imposed on me and mine so long ago.

On some future day, one I had dreaded since her birth, my carefree daughter would enter a world her friends would never know. My head sagged as unbidden images of her flooded my mind. The mental picture of my chubby toddler holding my hand,  the same as a gangly tomboy, and an inconsolable daughter sobbing for her lost mother

I was twice sad because I was the person most responsible for the way she was, the way she must become. When Jeanne was small, she said, "Daddy, some of my friends say you talk funny? Like somebody from an old book? They sometimes giggle when you talk."

5

I had made her no answer. How could I tell her I was over three hundred years old?

## Sixteenth Century Imperial Russia

I watched the two drive away and entered my now too quiet house. My pleasant living room now seemed oppressive. Even as my mind slipped back to the day when this chain of events began, as surely as if she stood in front of me, I could hear Jeanne's sassy response to my future revelation.

"Oh, right, Dad. Like that'd happen. Promise me this isn't another of the how hard things were for you in the old days and how I should appreciate how easy a life I lead compared to what you had."

Unlikely perhaps, but true.

The day I died began as any other crisp autumn day. The afternoon was late when Sasha and I encountered a troop of marauding Cossacks. Shouting, they raised their swords and played with us as if we were pawns in some game they invented on the spot. For what seemed like hours, the devils had chased us on horseback, inflicting searing slices over most of our bodies. The memory of my terror remains with me, an acrid taste in my mouth.

The next thing I remember was stirring to the thought, "If I am dead, why am I still so cold and wet?"

I lay, not daring to move, afraid to open my eyes, afraid the heartless bastards still lurked nearby. I strained for any movement, any hint of another person. No one. The forest mocked me.

I heard only silence. Nothing, except the thudding, beating of my heart. Yet, when I turned onto one shoulder and lifted my head, I discovered Sasha slumped by my side.

His lax face tilted toward me. His clothes reeked of copper, soaked by deep wounds. I'd seen him run through by their commander's gilt-edged shashka.

That Cossack bastard must have gutted him like game.

An excrement stench drifted from the coils of Misha's intestines. They covered the ground, and ants crawled on the mass. My tunic and cloak were ragged and equally bloody, but I was still alive. No marks marred my skin. My injuries seemed healed. I had no explanation why, and my confusion was epic. I looked away, rolled over, and peered into the blank eyes of a dead Cossack soldier staring back at me. My stomach lurched again, and I spewed bile onto the dirt.

How did that bastard die? Not by my dead friend or me.

I sat up and spotted yet two more bodies on the ground nearby. I didn't care how they died. Not when my family and my village were close by. The Cossack band might still be near. I leaped up shouting,  "You whoresons can rot. I must reach my village before the likes of you can murder the rest of my family."

After running, racing, hoping to warn my family of the Cossacks. I arrived staggering down the lone street to my house, breathing in raspy gasps. Too late. I found my father impaled on a wall, nailed there by the iron head of a soldier's lance buried in his chest. The shaft must have broken off. The man who murdered Misha was an officer,  but a low-ranking commoner's lance slew my beloved Abba.

Pools of blood were everywhere—so much blood. No one but me left alive in my entire village. Even Sasha, my mongrel dog, lay sliced nose to tail. The swine murdered and mutilated everyone. We'd missed the carnage because Misha and I had left home early to sell vegetables on market day. For all the good that did— they killed us anyway.

Sixteen, not much older than Jeanne now, I was alone in the world, bereft of family and friends.  My eyes burned as I struggled against unmanly tears. I crouched and threw my head back groaning with the sorrow of my loss and despair at my solitary future. I realized dressed in tatters caked with my own blood. I made a perfect target if any Cossacks still roamed the area. Frantic, I returned to where Misha died to strip off the clothes of the dead cavalryman beside him. Perhaps dressed thus, I might better blend in, acquire a new identity, and not be marked as a fugitive boy from the shtetl.

As I slipped on his smock, the fine cloth seemed too soft, unnatural. I'd never worn such fine clothes. The well-to-do of my village did not dress as well as the lowest of military men. The thought I being a ghoul to strip the body of a dead man and put on his garments, did not cross my mind. I took the trousers, the shirt, and his heavy coat. Anything more military I left in the mud. I hesitated overlong with his boots. Of all his fine clothes, I coveted them above all. They were so fine, so much better than my crude shoes. Alas, too small. Except for my feet, I'd morphed from what seemed a ghastly corpse to a pseudo-soldier.

Lost in my thoughts, I asked myself  "Why are you alive?  Who—or what—stepped in to give me life? Why? For what purpose?"

I asked myself in every way I could imagine. No answer came.

I used one Cossack's entrenching tool to bury two of the bodies and to hide the evidence of my theft. I covered the mound of loose dirt with stones—not out of respect or to hide his nakedness. Only to deter the wolves from revealing the body and revealing one still lived.

I walked away and threw those beautiful boots in the river. I still regret having to discard such fine leather.

## My First Family

My rational self-understood that was then and now was now and I must push aside the echoes of long ago and concentrate on my role as a twenty-first-century father. Jeanne would soon return from her day at school, and we would resume our familiar routine, a close rapport between father and daughter.

My youngest and I were closer than I'd been with my other children—and not simply because of the expanded role, I found myself in as a father of today. Since her mother's death, I'd served as the fulcrum of her life and she of mine. We laughed together, talked together, and shared each other's interests. I bandaged her knees, and her smile uplifted my spirits. I ran alongside her as she took her first wobbly trip without training wheels. I was the proud parent in the audience when she played Wendy in the grade school performance of Peter Pan. When she left for her first time on the bus to school, I experienced that odd mixture of parental pride and worry when a child reaches a milestone.

Would our closeness survive after I shared the sordid details of my life and my admission I am the one responsible for the fate from which she would have no escape? When I finally explained to her, what I was, and how I came to be unlike other fathers, how Would she react? How should I respond? How could I make real to her such an unread legacy? Would she reject me along with my wild and impossible story? I'd lost my old life, my identity while lying with the dead on that field so long ago.

I sagged on the couch staring into space, trapped by my memories. Scenes of my past traveled in their inevitable sequence again. My chest heaved as my dream-self panted, racing to gain as much distance away from the Cossacks as possible.

I saw again the first sun of morning appear, and I remembered slipping from under the shrub where I'd hidden and racing away, far from my birthplace. Autumn days were short in Russia. At night, wolves and other predators roamed. Each evening when the light faded, I needed to secure a safe place to hide, where I might sleep. How far I traveled, I'm still not sure, but after many days, I drew up enough courage to enter instead of avoiding the next village. I was young, strong, and, I'm told, handsome. Village scenes swirled as I recalled my life there.

For over a year my fear of the Cossacks ruled me. What if someone recognized me as a fugitive from the shtetl? I lived, drained of energy, and I froze at the sound of every hoof beat. I shook whenever I heard an unfamiliar voice. The panic, the deep fear I lived in became such a part of me I wove a wide band of privacy around me. Even after I married and Alexei and Valentina joined us, I remained secretive. My unapproachable attitude, my aloofness undermined my relationship with this first family. We all suffered for it. I admit I slighted these two little ones. I never dared share who I was or where I came from with them. For their safety, I hid my origins, mimicking the villagers around me.

Nevertheless, I nurtured a fierce love for my wife Katya and both children. The two, Alexi, my strong, handsome son, and my first daughter, Valentina, gave me hope. I called her my *lyubimaya*, my angel. I shocked my wife when I quipped, "She merits an icon."

"Shhh," she told me. "The priest may overhear you."

I wanted to lift my little girl in a bundle, protect her, and smother her with love. When she was a toddler, I'd say to her, "Valentina, give Batya a hug."

She'd run to me, arms out for an embrace. "Why must Russian fathers act so stern, so autocratic?" I'd ask.

As our children grew older, I didn't trust myself even this small pleasure. If I'd thought more or been more open with Alexei and Valentina, I would have been able to delay abandoning them so soon. Alexei was barely sixteen when I left. We never held each other. Russian men embrace each other, but not their sons.

Almost from the first, I realized I stood apart from other men. I grew aware I'd changed in a profound way on that October day. A deep-set uneasiness separated me from others, even those closest and most dear to me. I lived with loneliness as my constant companion. I longed for the sense of belonging I'd had back in the shtetl. While I appeared to live a normal village life, inwardly, I spent my days dwelling on the why and how I came to be so alien. For a long time, I had no answers.  Active knowing came later, much later and in a different country.

Vodka gave me a clue. The memory of the first time I encountered the Blue, I blamed the alcohol for the ghostly sly-colored glow swirling up my body. I clung to this belief until one midday when I had no drink I encountered the mysterious phenomenon a sober man. The same greedy mist enveloped me. My peasant mind lacked even the words to describe the ebb and flow of alien energy in my body, even less to articulate the why or what of the manifestation.  My world seemed darker with a newfound the ability to recognize evil intent in men improved. On those times, a dark malevolent red exposed their true nature.

I wanted to reject my newfound ability to recognize their foul taint, to sense their cheating, their plans to rob or murder. I grew to realize that when the shimmering Blue rose and encircled me. Some unspeakable act occurred nearby. I began also attribute the Blue with changes in my body. I grew stronger, seemed healthier, fitter, younger, and more alive.

The hue and solidity of the Blue varied. The wicked lived and did their dirty work in many places, but I learned the intensity of the nourishing glow faded quickly with distance. What the priest called sins somehow strengthened me. One day laboring at the foundry, I wrenched my back carrying the heavy bells—no longer a problem because the cure lay in a detour to pass by the usual location of one my habitual malfeasants. This would be where I'd find the healing Blue.

In the beginning, I considered these effects accidental. But once I began to plan my use of the Blue,  I developed a routine:  "Stop" where I stood, still with hands stretched out to the side, palms up;  "get ready," then I would breathe deep two or three times to focus and "inhale." At inhale, my entire body seemed to open up and seize the power of the spiraling force around me. In my mind's eye, I visualized the Blue emerging from the gleaming cluster at the core of the phenomenon to rise then dive into my center.'

Despite its origin, the corruption spawning the shimmer didn't infect me. Quite the opposite. I grew compassionate, more concerned. The Blue appeared to be part of the unused portion of the doer's intent that might have halted the act. On occasion I sensed scarlet reaching out from the cloud, and I'd pull back. I told no one in my town or my first family of this. Would they have called me a witch? Perhaps, Russia was not a tolerant place to live in those days.

The Blue seemed something miraculous then. Hangovers disappeared, something handy for a Russian man. How could such a thing not be good? I told myself the sense of well-being must be a blessing, and I'd have nothing to fear. An error in judgment, I soon found. My craving for what I thought of as the Blue grew greater. The colorful mist held a hidden danger. If I took too much, I was, heady, exhilarated and became too willful. My scars faded, my cheeks seemed less weather-beaten and visibly younger as the result of the wicked actions of a few. Villagers began to eye me with suspicion.

I'm not sure why, but, worried by the reaction of neighbors, I speculated on a way to lessen the apparent effect—if an excess made me young, might not sharing a portion reverse or change the effect.  Perhaps I could use the Blue to help others. Many of my friends were the victim of the same despicable acts which produced my well-being. My father-in-law, Lev, was one such.  Once aware of his suffering, I recognized my selfish attitude. Gradually I grew aware of the 'inhale,  as I termed my drawing in of The Blue, must serve the needs of others, not just me.

"But how?" I asked myself, then answered my own unspoken question as the images of two faces appear in my mind's eye—those who shed most of the Blue. I still can picture them both even after all this time. Images of past events marched through my mind.

The first was Maxim, dark-skinned, burly, and bearded, the local moneylender. The demands of Maxim's loan reduced Lev, my wife's father, to a shadow of himself.  My second chosen target was the arrogant Baron who owned the lands and people outside the village. His history of rape, beatings without cause, and extortion of his serfs and villagers chronicled heinous deeds, unforgivable regardless of his rank. I tried first to help Lev, and then deal with the Baron.

I picked my way through the pig shit and up the lane to the larger-than-most cottage where Maxim did his dealings. The cries of ecstasy in the hut, audible in the street, revealed he entertained a local courtesan. He steals from the poor and squanders the money on a whore. All around me, I sensed the energy I drew on.

My plan was simple, what would happen if instead of "inhaling," I "exhaled"  Today I planned to test my idea to direct the power I leeched from the evil at a target. Why I thought this possible, I can't say, but my first try proved me correct. The energy bursting from my body created a sudden and powerful unseen effect. I aimed through the air across the cobblestones and beyond to the cottage. A single heartbeat later, a terrible scream echoed in the street. The whore came running out, a terrified expression on her face, whimpering. I sauntered off.

A neighbor stopped by in the morning sharing the gossip about Maxim.

"You should have heard him, Sergei, screaming like a hysterical woman. He raced around, twisting and turning as if he  were under attack by a swarm of black flies."

"You don't say," I answered. We both smiled, relishing the thought of the moneylender getting his just deserts.

I didn't need to add anything. After all, I was there as he screamed, acting as if the devil himself pursued him, and, after his mind was gone, he collapsed.

Later I returned to the moneylender's house and feasted on energy until I was sated, overfull, gluttonous. Real evil gave off an intoxicating Blue. Savoring his downfall was glorious, and I'd helped my father-in-law besides. How should life be better?

While I worked at my job, I spent hours thinking, concocting schemes to bring down the Baron. No chance I might confront him at his dacha. No commoner dared enter the estate without an invitation and proper papers. Mine, being forgeries, wouldn't give me access. Only a summons from the man himself would suffice. No, I needed to find him in the countryside or in the village. I stalked him and mapped out his usual haunts.

My meticulous plan fell apart before it began. Dusk fell over the village when I neared my home. At the gate, Katya came running, sobbing, and saying, "Sergei, he took her. He took our Valentina, scooped her up and threw her over the back of his horse, carried her off to his estate."

"Valentina? She is just a child," I said, trying to placate my wife.

" Sergei, she is twelve, almost a woman. Does a father never notice?" Katya's bleak voice cut into me.

I hadn't. To me, she remained my little angel. We stood in the street, My Katya and I. Katya sobbing against my shoulder, her tears soaking my shirt. Peasants were powerless to confront the aristocracy.

Even to comfort Katya, I could not reveal I possessed the power to revenge the wrong done to our Valentina. I pushed my wife away, "I need to go to the estate. I must find a way."

"'No, Sergei," she wailed. "No, I don't want to lose you, too!"

Anger robbed me of any gentleness. I walked outside the village toward the state of the Baron, carrying a stout ash staff. The closer I got, the stronger the flashing Blue became. Good, plenty to use on a philandering bastard. In a week, I might not use all this.

By the time I arrived, the darkness of autumn night masked me lingering outside his gate. The pulsating Blue only I could see hovered and enveloped me. They crushed me, a welcome pressure. My body quivered and shone with the energy I digested. "How far will this go? Far enough," 'I answered myself. "I will accept nothing less."

I sent a silent message to my angel, "Come out, Valentina, come to Batya." The usual sounds of the night stopped, ceased, and left a foreboding silence. I paid little heed to the wind rising to scream and beat at the trees. The shutters of the room where evil lived banged against the house. A dark mist streamed through the second story windows, and they flung open. At last, the sound I waited for. The scream of the damned, the shriek that wavered on and on. The sound gladdened my heart, soothed me more than the sweetest lullaby.

I disgorged it all, vomiting Blue through the gardens, penetrating the walls leading to the bedroom where he misused my child, my Valentina. I strained to peer through the profound darkness into the mansion at the end of the drive. At first, I thought night creatures were making the faint sound, the sweet sound of Valentina's "'Batya, Batya, I'm coming, Batya."

A small form in the white chemise fell into my arms, and we shared our tears. The moon shone overhead, and I could see I had arrived too late. A telltale red on the back of the shift confirmed my worst fears. The Baron had abused my baby, "I'm sorry, Sweetheart. I'm sorry."

She patted my back to comfort me. I clutched her, and she became my anchor against the swell of emotions sweeping over me…hate, anger, regret, shame at my failure to protect her.

Cradling her sweet body, I carried her up the long road back to our cottage in the village. Wolves howled in the distance, and I sensed their eyes scrutinizing us. No matter—we arrived home safely. In an instant, Katya smothered Valentina against her breast. I stood back, became once more the stoic Russian father. A small hand emerged and grasped my sleeve, pulling me into a warm, comforting circle of family togetherness.

The love in the embrace fed my soul and gladdened my heart, but my body suffered from the lack of my unique nourishment. I had drained all my inner reserves. Before dawn, my craving demanded I return to the gate outside the Baron's dacha. The substance I craved—required—must still linger.

When I reached the dacha, I inhaled, once, then again. The fatigue retreated, my eyesight sharpened, my hearing amplified. I stood intent on the conversation of the authorities, the Oprichnina, in the garden. "Not dead yet, but the doctor says he won't last long. No explanation for what happened to the Baron. The servants claim not to have seen anyone. God knows we questioned them hard enough."

The laugh that followed put ice in my heart. I inhaled again, so much power, so rich, so satisfying. I laughed along with the police.

Let the bastard go to hell. He'll not molest others in my village.

I spun, gleeful and with my revenge. On the way to my home, I paused at a rain barrel to wash the dirt and grime off my face. When I glanced down at the shiny surface of the water, I saw a stranger's face. No, not a stranger's, a much younger me. I understood in that instant Sergei would never go home. I was sixteen again. No one will believe who I was. What should I do?

Stealing a shirt from a clothesline, I continued into the village. I stopped at my home, but no one recognized me. Not Katya, not Alexi, no one.

"They arrested him, Katya," the younger Sergei said. "The Oprichnina, they took him. He was all bloody and beaten."

She collapsed, tears running down her cheeks, my Katya. I, the boy she thought a stranger, caught her when she fell and held her while she shed tears for me, her dead husband. Everyone knew no one taken by the authorities of the Czar ever returned. Alexi knelt by her, and Valentina's arm lay on her shoulder. Their faces were bleak. Dying seemed easier than walking away from my family and my life with them. What choice did I have? Their father Sergei no longer existed. Sergei the boy departed alone to an uncertain future.

Leaving the village I'd called home, I was a lost soul. At the memory, I shuddered violently, bowled over by the sense of loss and utter despair I had experienced that long ago afternoon. My breathing grew ragged.

## The Present

### Sergei

I sat frozen until the front door slammed. "Dad, I'm home. Who were those guys I saw leaving the house? I didn't recognize either of them."

She came clattering into the room where I sat. " Dad, are you ok? You look really weird—like you'd seen a ghost or something," she added with a laugh.

"They were …some folks I knew a long time ago. Our relatives in a way. You'll meet them someday."

"So why didn't you ask them to stay for dinner like you always do when someone stops by?"

"Not a good time—maybe on another visit," I said. "Today they had to leave."

"Okay. What have we got to eat? I'm starved. Coach had us running lines."

I put my arm around her shoulder, and we headed to search the kitchen for teen-worthy snacks. I was thankful for teen priorities, food comes first, and anything else comes next. The knowledge on some future day the life of my youngest would change forever. Something caught my attention and I looked up. How long had I been lost in thought?

### Jeanne

What's with Dad? He's just sitting there staring into space. He didn't even notice when I came in and sprawled across the room from him, munching on my fourth cookie.

"Well, Dad, come on, you can't just leave me hanging. Something happened today—did the guys I saw leaving do something bad?"

"You're sure you don't have things you'd rather be doing?" he said, not even attempting to answer my question.

"Not really".

He was trying to blow me off. I can tell. Whatever he'd been thinking must have been ugly. He looked like he did the day Mom died.

"Dad, you can tell me. I'm not a little kid anymore. "

"Maybe later. I've got a lot to do, and you want to go on a hike Saturday. And you must have homework. "

He thinks I'll forget how weird he was acting. Nope, I don't think so, not when he's such a basket case.

"Oh, Dad, before I forget, I have a humorous essay due next week. How about you share some funny stories about your patients. They'd give me some ideas."

When he didn't object, I knew for sure something nasty had happened.

**Sergei is Alone**

**Sergei**

After she left, I did not rise from my comfortable chair. I allowed my mind to sink back once more into the past. I entered that space where dream and reality blend and lived once more a life I'd lived before. I stared into space, silent, filled with my customary melancholy. Will I ever be free of the desolation? Why, on one of those times when nothing I seemed worth living for, could I not die as others did?

I've asked myself this question so often; a reasonable man would realize no answer existed. Countless times, I questioned why the Blue revived me, an unproven youth, and only me. Would I ever escape the guilt I carried in forcing my family to follow the same path? When Jeanne learned what I had been, what I had done, the life of my youngest would change forever.

I lost my family the day I took my first step away from my adopted village.. Downcast and discouraged, I'd trudged west across the vast lap of Mother Russia. As I look back now, venturing on such a trek bordered on naïve. I was provincial, unaware of the world outside my small village, or how far the Czar's domain stretched. As I passed through each hamlet, the village elders welcomed me to do any work requiring muscle and strength.

The young girls admired my strong and comely body. The men seemed jealous— amazed because I never seemed to tire. My dejected expression when I paused to watch their children run and play with their friends confused them. The Blue kept me fit, but to my dismay, I discovered few villages were free of its presence. How sad that human beings and evil appeared to co-exist everywhere and be my constant companions.

I went from village to village. I'd linger in those where I found little Blue, staving off my need for as long as my hunger would allow. For months, perhaps years, I wandered and worked. My scant earnings sufficed to feed me and replace my worn out shoes. I carried my meager possessions, a ragged blanket to cover me at night, a battered wooden plate and cup, knife and spoon in a pouch hanging from my belt. I cut myself off from friendships.   I admonished myself, 'Don't get close to them. Not again. Never. I will just hurt them as I did Katya and the others in my family.

How long I'd plodded thus detached, I was unsure, but in time, I realized I'd wandered far from my home in the Pale of Settlement. I'd paid little attention to how long or how far I traveled between villages. I'd avoided larger centers of population where the Czars men might be present to check my papers. They wouldn't pass scrutiny, and I did not fancy the pain I'd earn from members of the local garrison of the Czar's Special Guard. I'd witnessed their beatings. The unlucky bastards favored by their special attention were almost unrecognizable as men—if by good fortune they earned their release.

I wondered if any other in this world were like me. Did the Blue choose others? Why did the Blue nourish me, make me heal, make me young? Why me? And, I'd encountered no one else? What canceled my death at seventeen? Countless questions intruded into my subconscious, but no answers appeared. Answers count—believe me. I've learned their value.

I was more fortunate than other boys of the time because I knew how to read a little, write my name, and do simple sums. The elders of my home village served the shtetl boys well with by insisting we master these lessons. "If you learn these skills, no scoundrels will cheat you," they said.

Any advantage I possessed over the illiterate existed because of their foresight. I journeyed at will when few enjoyed the right to leave the land of their lord. Most of all, I had the experience of my earlier lifetime to draw upon to make wiser choices.

The mountains lay further behind each day, the forest less dense, the land more open. The language of the villagers I encountered seemed subtly different, less easy for me to understand. Sometimes I grasped nothing of what the person had said. I realized I would need to listen carefully to learn their speech.

"Please, sir, can you repeat what you said. I didn't quite understand," I say. Or "I have a different word for this, what do you call this thing?"

I'd point at the object when I asked. By this time, my head contained at least two names for most common tools, foods, and the other things of everyday life. Sometimes the words seemed familiar and other times, not at all. The farther I got from my home village, the greater the differences in the words used. Although I was unaware then, the skill for language I acquired roaming the steppes prepared me for my future lives. Few ventured so far from their home in those days.

For years I drifted, an outsider in the world, a lone observer. My world, the world of my heart lay far away with my daughter, my son, and my wife, those dear ones who mourned my death. I did not marry in this life or the next. I could not. I chose to live as a nomad, clinging to my self-imposed isolation.

I encased myself in the armor of isolation, a shroud on a living man. Villagers sensed something about me that made them uneasy. My strong shoulders were still welcome, but I was not. My stays in each village were shorter, and I needed to unfurl my ragged blanket next to the animals rather than in a private home or inn. I'd learned a valuable lesson in this life. People always blame the outsider. One night, I lay sound asleep and curled up in an opening of a nearby copse.  I'd awakened to torches and men yelling, "There he is, the thieving bastard."

I ran. What crime they considered me guilty of didn't matter. I needed to make a move. I raced blindly up the hill with the mob in close pursuit. My legs strained with the effort needed to cover the steep incline. My Blue-fostered strength served me well. The men fell behind and never caught up. At the moment I thought I was free, my feet thrashed in e space. I fell from the cliff invisible in the starless night. I bounced once, banged my side on a rock, scraped my legs, hit, my shoulder, and cracked my head. Battered and verging on unconsciousness, I rolled like a cadaver down the final distance and came to rest in a depression by a large boulder.

How long I lay with my nose jammed against the rock I never knew. A gradual awareness of my surroundings caused me to stir. The clamor of highwaymen rousted me to full consciousness. They were robbing an imperial mail coach traveling a winding road through the middle of the valley. Horses whinnied, and a warning shot rang out from the gun of their leader. The driver used his whip to urge the team forward, but the brigands caught up and shot him, then the others. One slung the royal pouch over the horn of his saddle, and the gang galloped away.

The Blue cast off by the act blasted me, sending slivers of icy pain up my legs to my heart. My wounds sealed, my bones knit, my thoughts cleared. I fought against the ache and raised one hand above my face. What I saw was not my hand, but once again a young hand. I was a boy again. I cried.

Some years of lonely wandering passed before the Czar's men scooped me up and forced me, along with so many of my countrymen, into the Imperial army. I fought my way through most of this life finding blood everywhere, mine or other men's, on one battleground or another. Nowhere did I find any shortage of The Blue.

My wounds at Azov in the south against the Ottomans earned me a promotion. Ironic. When our turn came to defend the same fortress, I left the front line unscathed but, as we retreated, the Turks captured and sold me as a slave. I never made a good slave. Slavery thrives on pain and the fear of death. I dreaded neither. The iron shackle closed on my ankle had been the only thing keeping me from an escape.

The Blue gave me the strength and ability to bear my master's violence and kept me alive. I'd toiled summer and winter, performing backbreaking work, urged on by abuse. Nothing I did pleased him. Looking back, my death at his hand was inevitable. My fearlessness robbed him of a weapon over me, which infuriated him. He often whipped me, hanging me up and striking my feet over and over with a heavy cane. Were it not for The Blue, I would not have walked again from the damage he inflicted. My unexplained ability to recover enraged him.

His cruel punishment left me in excruciating pain. He took care to leave no visible marks to reveal his vicious nature to his neighbors. Over time, I feigned a lameness, which seemed to satisfy him for a while, but not for long. I used the Blue to heal myself and thus dull the joy he got from his pitiless abuse. He satisfied his perverted pleasure with more severe battering.  I suffered longer lashings more often. His bearded face loomed over me after each blow. He screamed,  "Cursed infidel,"  and worse. I'd stare back at him, stoic, which maddened him more.'

"Bastard."

On the last day of this miserable life, he no longer cared about marks and used his bullwhip across my back, my face, wherever he could land a blow.

"'Son of a whore,"  he grunted, bringing his whip down on my back. The agony took my breath. I stifled the groan rising in my throat.

"'Disobedient excuse of an infidel slave"  drew more blood. Every nerve in my body throbbed.

I never gave him the pleasure of a scream, goading him to strike me until my bloody body sagged, and ceased moving. He kicked my ribs one last time and threw my carcass into the river. His final delight was denying me the burial as Ottoman custom dictated. Then, angry with himself for destroying his own property, not my death, he cursed even more.

My body must have drifted with the current because I did not see him ride away. How long I'd drifted as the river dragged me, I can't say. My reanimation had been slow and painful, more so because the force of the water had slammed me against floating logs and submerged rocks jutting from under the surface. When I grew aware of the agony in my body once more, these many injuries added to my misery. Coughing and sputtering, I emerged painfully, crawling from the water and up the bank, not sure where I was. I lay, struggling to inhale, but soon I drew in the energy of the Blue and renewed my inner strength, ignoring the icy pain of coming alive. Ironic, my new vitality came from the residue of his cruel act. Well, perhaps not his, then from someone as brutal as he. It pleased me to think my master's act gave me life and youth once more.

After some days, I came upon a village. Familiar with the customs of Islam, I imposed on the hospitality of a local official, the Bey who governed the district, for clothing and food.

"Assalamu alaikum, Ertan Bey, I am a humble traveler begging the hospitality the Prophet doth command."

"In the name of the Prophet, you are welcome," he told me.

His religion obliged him to care for the needs of his visitors, and so he did. Thus, I ate well and wore clothing given to me to replace my torn garments. His faith did not require him to provide me with coins, jewels, and a mount, but I left with them anyway. Had his countryman not used me without mercy, to steal from the devout man would have been unthinkable. I chose to answer to my conscience another day.

Such a foolhardy act spurred me to flee north at full gallop for as long as my horse could keep the pace.

**Jeanne**

"Earth to Dad, come in, Dad."

I'd never seen Dad so spaced—staring into space with that weird blank expression on his face.

"Sorry, Jeanne, did you say something?" he asked.

"Are you sick or what? I've only said it three times now."

"Sorry, Jeanne, I've had a lot on my mind lately."

29

                                                    

I didn't buy that answer for a second. Dad and I have always been buds, and I don't remember him ever acting so weird before. I'd worm out the real reason from him, but for now, I said, "Okay, Dad. I just wanted to tell you I'm going to bike over to Sandy's."

"No problem. I've got reports I need to review before my meeting Monday."

"I'll be back by dinner," I said and took off. Talk about a lame excuse—this was the first time he'd mentioned any meeting.

**Seeking Answers Then and Now**

**The Present**

Later that night, after dinner and she'd gone upstairs to bed, I lapsed into thought

once more. She'd caught me, as I was obsessing over a part of my story I hesitated to

share. The violence, the cruelty, the disregard for others. Still, the recollection of my

unsavory act brought an unpleasant smirk to my face. The more the world changes, the

more it remains the same. This may sound like a cliché today, but the truth of it still

resonates. The unconscionable act of one Ottoman Muslim brought retaliation on an

innocent, a worthy member of the same faith.

I shook my head and sat up with a start, not sure where or when I was. I glanced at

the clock above the mantel. Two o'clock. I did it again. Where had the time gone? I still

needed to complete the reports I brought home. With the hour late, I, too, dragged

myself up the stairs to bed.

My mood was dour at the thought Valentina and Friedrich would soon appear to

shatter the cozy life I shared with my youngest child and steal from her the naivety of

childhood. I owed her an explanation of who they were and what their relationship to her

was before they came again. She'd asked me once how come I didn't talk about my

parents or what I did when I was growing up. She was too young then, and so I

distracted her and changed the subject. I still thought she was not ready, but their visit

trumped my timing.

The next morning I stood in front of the mirror shaving and daubing a tissue at the

small wound I'd inflicted on myself.

31

"Morning, Dad,"  a too cheerful voice behind me piped.

"You startled me, Love. You're lucky I didn't slice my throat clean through."

"Come on—you nick yourself all the time. You're a doctor and should know how to stop the bleeding."

I gave her a wry look.  "Doctors hurt, too."

She shrugged.  "You didn't forget we're going on a hike today and taking a picnic lunch, did you, Dad?"

"No, how could I? You've reminded me so many times," I said, thinking as I did that the trail would be a good place for me to relate more of her family history. When you mix some fun into a task, no one notices the work.

"Good, because I've already made the sandwiches and put them in our backpacks. You didn't forget you were going to share stories about a few of your patients while we walk, did you ? I still need a good hook to use for my English class."

This might be my opening.

"The  bright side of a hot dusty hike is I'm always glad to spend time with my little girl,"  I said, swallowing the lump in my throat. Every bit of my life I shared would put me closer to losing her.

"Breakfast first," she said dismissing my sentimental words with a wave of dismissal.

After we finished eating, I put on my hiking shoes, and we walked to the car. Bending to unlock the driver's door, I noticed a stranger lounging on the other side of the street. He waved in a neighborly fashion, and I waved back. I thought no more of him as we drove to the few miles to the county wilderness park, a huge area where the only concession to civilization was the many groomed trails. Each time we came, I remembered similar untamed areas from my youth.

Jeanne trudged alongside me on the trail, uncharacteristically quiet. Instead of her usual expectant expression, from the set of her body and occasional glances my way, I sensed something was bothering her.

I plunged in before I would put off this necessary, but repugnant, task. "I have a better idea for your English composition. How about an old family story you might be able to use. Sound good?"

She nodded, although with little enthusiasm I noted.

"This is about a fellow named Sergei."

"Weird name," she said as I began.

We were nearly to the fork, which split the path at the four-mile mark. One narrow trail led toward the sea, the other toward the foothills. I related Sergei's story, from the shtetl, to his first family and daughter Valentina, and finishing with his exit from the Ottoman Empire. I spoke without pausing and couldn't see her reaction as we moved single file on the rough surface. When I spotted the large log at the fork, I said, "We can sit there and eat our sandwiches. If I keep talking and walking, I'll have no voice left."

Anxious to hear her impressions, I turned toward her, and the expression of disgust and the condemnation of my thievery on the face of my rule-following daughter was unmistakable.

"Dad, I know you're making up a story when you said Sergei didn't die, but,…that bit about Sergei stealing from t

he what-ever-you-called-him, that was for real? "

I didn't answer her question straight away. Her words brought my slave years into full focus. The phantom pain of my tortured slave body returned for a few moments, and I limped, dragging one leg.

"Yes, Love. Sergei was a thief. He convinced himself they owed him for taking years of freedom from him."

Her young mind weighed the merits of an act of theft against the character of the father who loved his children. Her shoulders straightened and she said.  "What else, Dad? You're messing up our family image with stuff like this. Do you need a time out?"

"No, Jeanne. I'll be good. No more tales about family thieves, and, if we had cattle rustlers, no one ever told me about them."

We both laughed at the ludicrousness of a timeout imposed on a grown-up doctor.

I didn't want such a dark cloud to linger. I had so much more I must tell. As much as I didn't want to share much more of my slave life with her, she needed to learn what shaped me. Those years molded me as much as                  any preceding or following them. To dwell on the time when another controlled my every action weighed on me. I hope she will never need to experience the loss of self that complete submission to the will of another imposes. No person should control another, be able to force a person to serve their needs, or submit to their whims. Even today, food and wine tasted all the better for the freedom to drink it.

"Would you like me to tell you something maybe a little happier?"

"Only if you promise not to tell more horse-thief stories."

"You got it, girl," I said, forming a fist to bump hers. I adjusted my backpack to take some of the strain off my shoulders and began. "I found this story at the bottom of an old trunk I inherited. I unearthed a handwritten diary under a jumble of papers. I would guess the book was old almost to be around during the time of Sergei. The writer was a lot like me—a doctor, Ignacy was his name—except he lived in Poland hundreds of years ago. His journal described his life in Krakow. I'll play the part of Ignacy and  try to that relate his story more or less as he did in his history."

**..At** University of Krakow

The crisp voice of a bugle greeted me when I approached the walled city. I'd reached my goal, Krakow, the home of Polish kings. During my many months of travel, I'd met many men who spoke of this town. I decided this elegant place would be my destination, no more aimless wandering. I hoped an explanation for why death's release eluded some would be here in this university town. Krakow's university was a prestigious institution, the oldest in all of Europe, and was one of the few medical faculties of the time.

My ill-gotten wealth in hand, I had, occasionally, enjoyed the luxury of traveling aboard a riverboat on the Vistula. However, most days, I rode or walked until I collapsed into an exhausted sleep. The clear high notes of music high above me halted as my horse nosed through the gate, the melody cut off at mid-tone. I recalled the legend represented by the broken notes. The bugler played each day in memory of a sentinel who manned the tall tower of the church. From his high vantage point, he sounded the call to arms warning the Turks about to attack. His life ended on the point of an Ottoman arrow through his throat. Who better than I to understand the uncanny accuracy of the Turkish archers? The haunting sound seemed to welcome me, another victim of the brutal treatment of the Sultan's men. The music seemed to signal I belonged.

I didn't enter the city through the main gate. The lesson from my past lives taught me to be cautious and careful in unfamiliar situations. Before I crossed through the gate, I divided my valuables and, secreted portions in several caches outside the wall. The balance I stashed in various parts of my body and in my clothing. My upscale appearance together with my new set of forged papers and a letter of recommendation from a dead nobleman made me confident they would admit me to the University. I hoped studying medicine would give me some answers about what I was.

I tried to mask the awe I experienced as I walked the streets of this grand city. I arrived a country boy, unfamiliar with urban sights and sounds. The enormous central square with its many merchants, street magicians, and other townsfolk overwhelmed me with aromas, clatter, confusion, and constant movement. Realizing I was hungry, I squandered my only Polish coin and sat by one of the food stalls watching, absorbing the ebb and flow of daily life. I had two immediate tasks—to approach the university and to find lodging.

I asked a street vendor where a student might find housing. He studied my face and then said, 'You strike me as foreign, although I admit you speak our language well. Have you enough money to pay for a room?"

I wondered why he took so long to answer. Why did he give my face such scrutiny? Did he see something wrong with me, something distasteful?

"Yes, but not a great deal," I answered, wishing not to seem either too poor or too wealthy. "I have simple needs.  My belongings are few for I traveled a long way to reach your fine city and excellent university."

"I think you should try in Kazimierz," the vender said. "The Kazimierzi housewives are always looking for a way to put extra coins in their purse, and the neighborhood is close by to the university."

"How do I get there?" I asked.

He made a vague gesture with his hand at a street leading between the buildings surrounding the open area and dismissed me. He turned away without another word.

When I arrived, I noticed many of the homes still showed damage from the invasion by the Swedes years before, and something about the residents of the district set them apart from the majority of Krakow Poles. Maybe something differed in how they dressed. Color of their hair? Was I so obvious an outsider they avoided eye contact? I grew uneasy. Spying a sweet shop, I followed the aroma to the open door. Everyone buys pastries—the owner must know who accepted tenants.

The merchant pointed me toward a two-story house not so far away. "Look for a big red flowering plant by the front door."

I munched on one of the odd pastries he sold, twisted circles of crispy semi-0sweet dough, strung like beads on a string.  Peculiar, but tasty I decided. I glimpsed the bright red potted geranium the shopkeeper had mentioned and knocked. The door opened to a small woman, dark-haired, wiping her hands on her apron.

"Good afternoon," I greeted her. 'My name is Ignacy, and I seek lodgings.  I used the Polish assumed name showing on my papers I'd purchased. I explained my situation to her and earned a short nod.

She tapped her finger to her chest, "Rachel."

A motion of her hand bade me follow. She led me up winding, narrow stairs round and round until we reached the attic on the top floor. She pulled aside a curtain and showed me a tiny room fashioned out of the open area. A single cot, a small table, a chamber pot, and pitcher—no more—furnished the small space. She announced the cost, one that seemed minuscule to me. I nodded, and we made a deal. I gave her the smallest of my Turkish coin, and the frown on her face surprised me.

"Such a large coin, Ignacy. I cannot make up the difference."

"How long might I stay with this coin?"   I asked.

She looked confused for a moment, then counted on her fingers, "Ten months, half that if you board with us."

"You board as well? I asked, thinking who in their right mind would not jump at the chance for home cooked meals. My decision to purchase both room and board ended up one of my best. Rachel proved to be an exceptional cook, and her husband, Itzak, a burly mass of a man, reminded me of my father, only twice his size. Housing for me and my horse thus secured, I hauled the last of my meager possessions to my loft. The good fortune of that one coin providing my housing and meals for two terms of the university and another small coin bought my sturdy mare food and shelter for the next year I hoped my luck would hold when I applied.

Acceptance by the university proved no problem. Perhaps, they accepted the outstanding person described in my bogus papers. As I possessed sufficient funds to cover tuition and housing, the faculty welcomed me. No matter. I was in. The university curriculum grew out of the study of alchemy and expanded into medicine. Over the years the quality of education offered attracted an exceptional medical faculty.

I wasn't sure what to expect from my studies. My gown purchased, I attended my first class and discovered all my classes were in Latin and held six days a week. I drew down my purse again when I realized I would need a tutor to teach me this strange tongue and help me read the medical journals. Understanding the lectures, conducted also in Latin, proved a challenge. Every professor had a different accent. Still, the days spent during my travels to learn ways to acquire other tongues on my travels served me well.

When classes began, I filled my days with learning the proper technique of bleeding with leeches to rid the body of villainous humors, using herbals, and administering clysters, what we call enemas today. My professors showed us how to use forceps to deliver babies and as well as other implements necessary for a career in medicine. I remember well the day the professor allowed us to watch an actual delivery.

I'd heard him through the screams of the woman, racked with the spasms of labor, but his gestures showed me where my attention should be. I nodded. The presiding doctor opened the curved blades of the forceps, "What you need to do is wiggle one blade into the opening and over the head of the infant, like this,' he said, demonstrating the movements.

"Yes, Doktor," I said, trying to imitate his movements,

"Then the other blade goes here. Close the blades like scissors and lock into place. Now you take hold of the instrument, Ignacy, with care until you're more used to the feel."

"Using this implement speeds the process if the birth is difficult because the woman is exhausted," he said.

My professor was enlightened for his time. He advocated for quick and easy a far better than hours of painful labor even if more intervention was necessary from the physician. I didn't know then, but the crude forceps of the time damaged delicate parts of many mothers and infants.

The medical profession—and the church—wanted men to handle medicine. Male doctors preferred the ease of the clamps around the head. Women and midwives cared more for the mother than saving time. The authorities often called the midwives witches, accusing them of dabbling in the black arts. This charge often resulted in their death by burning at the stake. No witch burning occurred while I lived in Krakow. In other parts of Europe, however, some still lost their lives trying to help their neighbors using traditional remedies. I'm not sure who wanted women in medicine less, the Church or the doctors. That's how things were then.

I soon realized much of what the university taught must be incorrect. If malignant vapors upsetting the balance of blood, bile, and phlegm caused illness, shouldn't I be able to detect them with the Blue? For a long while, I tried to convince myself the professors were correct and the invisible gases caused disease. I'd used the Blue to heal, but no gases appeared leaving the site of the infection. My doubts grew.

**Picnic Interlude**

Jeanne interrupted. "All of that sounds yucky. Doctoring must have been an icky job back then."

"A healthy baby makes the doctor proud in any era. Almost as proud and happy as when the baby is your own, like you Love,"  I said, giving her a squeeze. I smiled, but I wondered how doctors of three hundred years from now might see our current practices.

"Did Mom…" She hesitated, her expression pensive and her voice dropping off, but I knew the unspoken conclusion of her sentence,  "after she died."

"Your mom was special, Jeanne. When she learned how sick she was, she wanted me to be prepared for when I would need to take care of you. Goodness knows I was inept. She even had to show me how to turn on the stove."

"You weren't quite that bad, Dad."

"No, I suppose not," I said. "Close, though."

Sometimes I needed to remind myself, today's children grew up too soon, more so than those of past centuries. A more onerous tragedy for those of my line whose childhoods always seem too often cut short.

I heard the sound of a fellow hiker behind us and half-turned.

"Dad, I think that's the guy I saw by our house a couple days ago."

We stopped and waiting for the man to reach us. I nodded and waved him by. I noted his appearance, short brown hair, blue eyes, pale skin. He stood taller than I. We waited until he was out of sight before picking up our conversation.

## Beginning the Long Path to the Future

**The Present**

" Why did Sergei stay in Krakow? Wasn't he afraid they'd find out he was a fraud?" Jeanne asked.

Jeanne acts as if she's sure this was another of my tall tales-- but belief began to creep in, too.

"The papers were fraudulent, but I was genuine," I said, stressing the I.

"You know what I meant, Dad," she answered. "But keep on pretending as if you were Sergei if that floats your boat."

"Uh huh, well, I guess I didn't worry much. I was too happy. Happiness was an emotion I'd not enjoyed for many years. I was still careful, but I was comfortable in Krakow. The more so because I met a woman. A beautiful woman, Jeanne, loving and intelligent. In no time, I was smitten. Don't let anyone tell you love at first sight isn't real."

"Dad, this sounds really weird-- you talking about another woman instead of Mom being your wife."

I glanced over at my youngest and my eyes watered .  "I miss her, too, Love."

"Doesn't sound like it when you make up stories about you falling love with someone else."

"Yes, but in another time."

"Umm, sure, Dad."

My heart echoed her plaintive tone.

I cleared my throat and continued. I thought to distract her, turn her attention in a different direction.

## Wedding in Krakow

"In my second year, Pan Professor Ochman invited several students to a gathering at his home."

"Pan?" Jeanne asked.

"Sorry, Jeanne, they used 'Pan back then to indicate a high rank like Sir or Lord—understand?"

She nodded, so I went on.

"Where was I? Oh yes, Professor Ochman. His niece Bozena visited from Warsaw during the spring. I spent every waking minute thinking up excuses to see her, to visit her uncle because she was there, whatever would work to spend time with her. I showered her with sweets and flower and fine words. When she returned to Warsaw, I resorted to letters. To my relief, she humored me with replies. Encouraged, I journeyed across Poland to ask her father for his permission to marry. He seemed less than impressed. "You don't show the best countenance, but, if you love her, I agree."

The weight of my purse may have testified to my worth. With his blessing in hand, I asked her on bent knee. The silence following seemed endless, but at last, she said in a faint voice, "Yes."

After an appropriate time had passed, we posted the bans and set the date for our wedding. Those who received an invitation for the wedding of an extremely wealthy and influential man's daughter to an unknown student were the envy of those who did not. To attend was a social coup. With a few words, plain Ignacy **Kowalski no longer existed and Pan Ignacy Kowalski took his place. We bought a house in Krakow near the central square and settled in. When I finished my studies, Pan Doktor Kowalski shared the home with her.** Those days in that house made my life seem so full, so glorious. Like most doctors of the time, I set up an office in the front room of the house where I treated patients

In due time, our first child arrived and seemed a signal for a second chance at happiness.

When the last patient left, my son Aleksander would race in, "Tata, ride, Tata!"

"Oh, so you think I am your horsie, do you"

"Yes, yes," he'd shout, and I'd fling him up on my shoulders and race around the house, both of us laughing and Alek shrieking with excitement.'

I found my family again. The empty void I carried since I left Magda, Valentina and Alexis filled. We lived the good life. Life on our street seemed like that of the minor nobility, comfortable, quiet. Pawel, our second, came along, and finally Gizela. Gizela, my baby. She seemed so like Valentina I almost believed my sweet *lyubimaya* returned to me.

Our family differed from others in our circle in ways our neighbors found strange.

"Pan Doktor, why do you call a midwife for Bozena? Surely you are better prepared?"

"Women experience birthing babies than we learn in centuries of study at the University." I answered, "And besides, she chose to call Kaska."

"Oh, now I understand. Wives need to be happy," my questioner would say with a knowing nod. "Of course, we make the decisions…after they tell us what we must decide."

We decided to ignore the usual conventions, choosing to educate all our children, not just our sons.  No matter to me that Gizela was a girl. I remembered the advantages I enjoyed lifetimes over others my age because the Elders of my village insisted we educate ourselves, to learn, and become literate. Why should Gizela not enjoy the same?

Pretending, even to myself, I was like other men, I lived with Bozena and my family as if I were.  I remained ever aware evil haunted our city. Remnants of the Blue tainted even my neighborhood. Some might say enlightened self-interest motivated me to act thus. I depended on the Blue to remain vigilant. I sought out the dishonest merchants whose dishonest dealings spun Blue when my need grew strong. Thus, I protected my loved ones and steered them away from priests misusing their power or corrupt soldiers garrisoned in the city.

I began to experiment with sending small amounts of the Blue at persons I found apt to commit a dishonest act. Often I succeeded in making them forget what they planned to do, but occasionally I was too heavy-handed. Some ended up mixed up mentally permanently. No loss in the big picture.

Bozena and I walked with the children in good weather, chatting with others in the neighborhood. Alek, at fourteen, seemed almost a man. I pretended not to notice when he slipped off to walk with a neighbor girl who'd caught his fancy. Later that spring was when I first became aware of occasional small startle reactions by Alek or Gizela. I'd notice him jerk suddenly and glance over to stare at empty air. Gizela sniffed and smiled as if she smelled the sweetest scent. Pawel, in contrast, wandered back and forth, never exhibiting the same kind of behavior.

"It can't be," I kept telling myself. "Only a coincidence. Not like me."

Thereafter, I kept a close watch on the two and jotted notes those times when and where they behaved strangely. I wanted to be wrong. My children did not deserve to inherit my affliction. My heart said no, but my mind admitted the evidence was clear. My children shared the same trait as I…the peculiar ability to be aware of the Blue.

My thoughts drifted back to the children of my first family. I did not share the same closeness with them as those in Krakow. Did I miss the same signs in them? Did they now feed on the Blue somewhere in my motherland? Were they careful not to take too much, monitor the amount absorbed so their need did now grow and overcome them?

"How like me were they?" I asked myself, an honest question at last.

Thereafter, when I spotted an odd movement or quizzical expression, I'd ask, "You flinched, Alek. Why? Something you saw?"

"Something strange, Tata. Like fire in the air only not. Lots of bluish-white flames but nothing nearby burns."

"Gizela, Angel, why the funny look?"

" I saw a silvery blue-white ball with different colors around it, Tata, bluish-white mostly, but sometimes a gruesome red. The Blue always makes me feel better when I see the glow or smell the scent surrounding the light."

Sure, now, whatever infected me dwelt in them. How would I explain to them what this meant? Guilt hit me hard. Tomorrow. I promised myself. No more delays, but dawn arrived accompanied by shelling from the Russian and Austrian armies intent on dividing the last of Poland between them.

"We need to go," I yelled at my family. "We must escape, leave now, go out into the countryside, and so we do not become part of a battle not ours."

They threw on clothes, and we slipped down the street and out of the city. Many of our friends cowered in their homes, but we melted into the forest, hiding whenever we heard movement. We'd hunker down when a stray shell landed nearby. A day later, after a search of the area, I located a cave large enough to shelter us where we slept for the night. We'd carried no food with us, but I'd had the presence of mind to grab the moneybag I kept in the house as we left. I gave Alek the bag where I put  the coins.

"I don't .want to take it all with me in case…. In case, I need to go for food for us. Berries and weeds will not long suffice for our needs. If something happens to me, the contents will provide you the means to survive."

"I'll come, too, Tata," he said. "I can help carry our food and drink."

"No, Son, you must be the man here while I am gone."

As soon as I left the woods, some soldiers spotted me. With a gun aimed at my heart, the taller cracked his weapon against the back of my head.  Stunned, I dropped to my knees. They shoved me to the ground, took my money, and then beat me hoping I would reveal whatever I might know. I had no knowledge of any importance to hide from them—except where my family might be. I didn't resist, said nothing, fearing for the safety of my wife, my sons, and my little Gizela. I angered them with my sullen silence, and in frustration, they shot me in the chest.

How long my body lay there, I can't say, but the smoke from the desperate fighting blanketed the battlefield.  To me the haze was Blue. I revived and returned once more to life, alive, and a boy of seventeen. My reanimation came with pain. An ache spread across my back laid open by the sharp rock under me. My cheek twitched and my nostrils flared open to the soft breeze blowing over me. Feeling returned, and my teeth chattered from the icy surges invading my body. Chilled and with extreme effort, I roused to begin the search for my family.

I returned to the cave in a roundabout way, but they were long gone. Whether they still lived or were already dead, I had no idea. I didn't even know how long  or what year it might be. How many days or weeks had I lain a cadaver on the ground? Overwhelming regret and guilt swept over me. Guilt at my abandonment, more guilt because I told my two children most like me what they needed to know. What the Blue would do for them and to them.

### Lunch Time In the Present

"All those are so bloody,"  Jeanne said, interrupting.  "They're not kid stuff anymore. I'm not sure my teacher would want me to use this one."

"You decide. You're the kid in the class."

She made a face at me. "You're talking about that Blue stuff again, aren't you?"

"Ah, once again you surprise me. You noticed."

In response, the face, the eye roll, and a leg scratch.

"You hungry, Love? How about we find a log and take a break. After we eat, we can make the ridgeline before we need to get back to the car."

She nodded, and said, "Good idea. I'm famished. "

I perched on one end the log and she on the other. We split the chips. I managed to snag one of the cookies before they disappeared. We ate in silence, enjoying the forest and the day.

When the last cookie was gone, she reached in her bag, pulled out a bird book, and said, "I bet I can identify more than you can."

I let her win, but the competition lasted until we returned to the lot where I'd parked my car. I assessed our day. I was happy, exhausted, and aware she referred to Sergei and to me interchangeably. What she needs to learn is a huge challenge, and I was happy to see she'd taken the first step. I'd made progress.

### *Convincing Jeanne*

Tina and I trailed the others on the way to my house. I smiled at the silhouettes of the three in front, Friedrich walked with his arm around Jeanne, and Dmitri  leaned over and would appear to the entire world to be an older brother graciously attending to his younger sibling.

"Sort of a Kodak moment, that is if Kodaks were still around, wouldn't you say, *Lyubimaya*? She's hanging on his every word."

"Uh huh, one thing Dmitri doesn't need is more feeding for his ego. He thought well of himself, even when he was a boy, a real boy, back in our village," she said, giving me a small smile when I used her pet name.

I didn't respond at once. All who lived with the Blue remembered when they were real. A condition we no longer enjoyed, destiny having decided otherwise. I chose not to pursue her sad train of thought, "Agreed. No need to repair her self-image! I'm concerned about your youngest sister. She matured even in the short time since you three arrived. The change happened in the time you shared more of what she always called "Dad's fairy tales."

"I don't disagree, Papa. Surely, you've noticed the signs she'd become aware of the Blue, even if she doesn't recognize the sensation yet. I remember how unsettled I was when I began to sense the mist and the unseen force around me."

She grew quiet. I was sure she was reliving those first few years when she was alone with the Blue

I was around to pull Friedrich back from the brink–she needed to battle the Blue alone, no one to help her, no one to ask what was happening. "Pretty rough for you wasn't it?"

She nodded, and we walked in silence until the front of my adobe colored bungalow came into view. Then she surprised me when she burst into a run, passed the three, and threw a challenge back over her shoulder at her brother. "Come on, Ricky. What's the point of a young body if I can't beat my kid brother in a race?'

"Think so, Sis? Not a chance."

They ran full speed past the others laughing and whooping.

Jeanne must think the entire family was deranged.

Jeanne slipped back and took my hand. "Dad, are they always this crazy? Both of them are like really old, and now they are acting like little kids."

"Believe me, Love, I'm as amazed as you. I can't remember the last time I heard Friedrich hoot and holler."

Their lead feet hit the front step at nearly the same instant. Hers might have touched a tad sooner, but no way would her brother admit she bested him.

"You're lucky I decided to let the old folks have their fun," Dmitri jibed.

"We'll have to compare actual birthdates one of these days, Nephew, see who's the geezer here."

We shed our wraps and hung them in the hall closet, then trooped into the main room. Jeanne giggled at something Dmitri said under his breath, a pointed gaze directed toward Friedrich.

What lies are you telling her about him now, Grandson?

Tina cleared her throat to ward off another of my yet unspoken flood of reminiscences. "Ricky, I think we're some seventy or eighty years behind schedule, I assume you have more to share with Jeanne. You do realize we need to move on with this so we deal with the real reason we are here?"

"Jeanne, meet Simone Legree," Dmitri said.

They all tittered, but my son acted as if he were the main attraction at a hanging.

"You'll be up to speed—as much as we have time for—soon. When the war ended, we learned how, despite the efforts of every operative, the Nazis committed unspeakable acts of brutality. Other missions met with more success. The family saved lives, stopped battles from happening, and assisted soldiers from both sides trapped behind their enemy's lines. The information we gathered helped the fighting to end sooner."

He looked up, and the faces of the others reflected the grim pride a warrior brings home. "My contribution seemed so slight; I couldn't share their pride in what they'd accomplished. My life seemed a constant "If only I'd found out sooner, I might have been able...."

"What do you mean, Ricky?" Jeanne asked.

"I never digested the intelligence quickly enough, never gained sufficient lead time to place Blue Talon agents at the right place soon enough," he answered. "Close but no cigar, as they say, I'm not sure how much of this you study these days; I drilled history into my son, Mark. I knew experienced the events as I did; he needed to learn from his books. No matter. Where was I? Okay so far?"

She nodded.

Was I ever that eager to learn?

"OK, let me share something about us trying to use Dmitri's grandson Malcolm as an aide on Winston Churchill's staff."

Jeanne shot one eyebrow up, questioning. "Is this going to take a long time? I don't want to miss practice. You've been talking…like forever. Aren't you done yet?"

He chose to ignore her and kept talking to forestall further questions. Considering the current situation, I understood why he wanted her to understand family history, but

"Having one of our own with Churchill seemed a smart move. Malcolm possessed the right qualifications—he'd handled diplomatic assignments before. Not that his experience did much good, in the end, our efforts came to nothing.

Neither Churchill nor Roosevelt believed what we knew to be true. They refused to accept the existence of slave labor camps. Nor the murder of Polish officers…any of the atrocities. From our perspective, the Yalta conference was an unmitigated disaster. Stalin forced the others to hold the meeting in his own back yard, and he set the agenda.

"Despite all our efforts, he gobbled up Poland, Czechoslovakia and a bunch more besides. True, he annexed some while his treaty with Hitler and the Germans was still in force, but the rest…my fault. To this day, I am amazed the British and Americans allowed him to keep his gains as an ally of the Reich. They say the enemy of my enemy is my friend, but Uncle Joe Stalin never was anyone's friend except Joe Stalin's."

Hundreds of thousands of residents from Bohemia and the Balkans became refugees, driven from the only home they knew. The other allies attending yielded to his pressure. They re-adjusted the boundaries of their sphere of influence to give the Soviets an even bigger slice. Soon a tall wall split Papa and my home city of Berlin. My fault. I should have convinced a confidant of Roosevelt's to persuade him. The world ended up divided in two for decades from my incompetence."

"The world's not like that now."

"You're right, not as much, anyway. Warring factions Russia plays tough guy, old frictions still divide China and Korea. Even after all this time, I'm still short of operatives in those areas."

"I don't understand, Ricky. How come? When you say, you've got the Blue and all that."

By the expression on her face, I realized I needed to break in to explain. "Friedrich did as well as he could with what he had to work with in those days. The thing is, Love, the Blue has rules. We were able to use the power to confuse, to make the target witless or easily persuadable, but the Blue refused to be a killing device. We found this out when a few of us tried to use it to kill in the trenches in the first Great War. Instead of taking out the enemy, our efforts neutralized the Blue. To say we found the stuff tricky to handle would be an understatement. The rays persisted in being fussy and peculiar about how and how much they allowed us to do."

"Papa is right. To use the Blue, we needed to avoid a direct attack and sidestep the restrictions. The best we could do was to infiltrate someone else's plan. We planted a seed; listed alternatives for them, and then waited for the others plotters to develop. Alek just happened to mention botulism poisoning to someone else in the kitchen some weeks before Stalin died of botulism-like symptoms. If we remained on site during an attempt, the Blue let us spread confusion. We short circuited the resistance and allowed the perpetrators to make an escape."

"You act like the Blue is alive. You're kidding, right/" Jeanne asked, glancing over at me.

"Not alive, but whatever gave me, gave us, the ability to recognize and use the Blue, did so with strings attached. I think of this power, this force as an inwit, an intelligent conscience. Decades passed before I realized something born of unused good intentions would be unable to do the unconscionable. I've tried to make sense of the inwit for a long time now. My best guess would be somehow the world got out of balance. Remember, we talked about the action and reaction thing? Unquestionably, we've drawn on that power to heal, to reanimate, to confuse and stupefy.

"The closest to a violent action I remember was when I threw the Blue at the snake that harmed my Valentina. Even so, the Blue did not kill him. The witless bastard jumped out his own window. We've learned to cope with the limits placed on us, but what gnawed at me for centuries. Still frustrates me as a doctor, not understanding what happened to us. What made us this way? In my first lives, when I was still an ignorant peasant, I never doubted some obscure magic touched me, leaving behind…something, a gift or perhaps a curse, I worried because weren't  the same as the short-timers. Their lives have a pattern. Not ours. The only constant I believe was we never grew younger in new lives than we were when we first sensed the Blue—for me, the age was seventeen.

"Try as I might, despite all my centuries of scientific and medical knowledge, I can't explain, can't pinpoint the why or the how. I examine and compare the DNA of the long-lived with the others countless times and come up blank. If a mutation is involved, the thing must be so subtle, as to be invisible. I'm hoping my failure is only because our equipment is too crude to handle the task."

Jeanne's face reflected her confused reaction. Dmitri listened to my attempt to explain with a thoughtful expression on his face, "I've never been a doctor, Papa. Doubt if I ever will. I'm more into what I'm aware of around me, like the waves of blue-black surrounding the killing camps. This Blue appeared almost as if something gelled, grew nearly solid. Some of us went from men to boys in an instant."

"The frightening thing was how much evil is necessary to create such a dense fog," Valentina put in.

Jeanne piped up, "Does any of this matter, the why, I mean? What's wrong with magic? Like who cares what makes an airplane fly as long as it does? Isn't what you are, what we are, what you do, and the most important?"

My daughter is bloody well brilliant!

### Alone again

### Twenty-first Century

Jeanne went up to bed shortly after we got home. The phone rang, and I wondered who would be calling me this late? I was tired from today's physical demands and didn't want to talk to anyone. I cringed at the second ring, fearing I might hear the voice of my eldest daughter.   "Hello?"

I enjoyed instant relief at hearing the voice.   "Hello…"No, we aren't interested in any solar panels…and why are you bothering me in the middle of the night?"

I hung up happy. Despite my apparent irritation, any phone call other than one from Valentina or Friedrich was preferable. Each time relief followed apprehension when the caller did not announce they were on their way.  I turned off the lights thinking, " A m*atter of time, Sergei, matter of time. Deal with it."*

Fate's call waits on no one, but why so soon for my Jeanne?

My least relished duty was serving as the primary person initiating a young and innocent member about their future with the family and Blue Talon. I hated more having to share these cruel facts with one as young as Jeanne. Hours must have passed before I slipped into a troubled slumber marred by dark dreams percolating up from my subconscious. A stranger's sinister face lurked in the deep recesses of my mind. I woke exhausted the next morning, doubly glad for another weekend day when I wasn't on call.

I slept poorly, but late. Patches of blue sky peeked between the clouds before I hauled myself out of bed to start the day. I joined Jeanne clearing the dishes after breakfast. How mature she seemed. Only two years into her teens, not old enough to drive or vote, and yet, mature before her time and as responsible as an adult. After Kim died, the two of us shared the loss of a wife and a mother.

"What's on for today, Dad?" she asked me.

"Must not be much going on in your social life if you're asking me. Are you willing to spend more lazy time with me?" I asked half-teasing.

"Most weekends you're on call or gone. Other kids have dads who aren't doctors. They can coach and do other things with their kids. Sometimes…maybe if Mom…Well, I kinda liked just being together, even if we don't do anything—just you talking and me listening is kinda cool, too/"

Her words thrust a knife through my heart. How much longer would we enjoy this?

"Okay, what did you want to talk about?"

"Tell me more about that Polish guy."

"Okay."

I settled down on our comfortable maroon recliner, and Jeanne took the couch facing me.

"I'll try to make this as close to the journal as I can."

I found a few blank pages, then began again.


### After the Battle

I'd never faced such a dark depression in all my years. Alone, a boy again, cut off from those I loved, and stripped of anything I had of value by the soldiers. I was obsessed with one thought, a stark realization that for me, no matter how bad things were, no matter how dire my situation, I'd lost the ability to die. Again, death was a temporary respite—a complete escape no longer existed. I envied the dead their peace. I spent the first day of my new life sitting on a log, hands laced over my knees, rocking back and forth in misery and thinking that old world prophet Job's problems were paltry compared to what I went through.

By the second day, I had accepted my fate. I was alive. This meant I needed to move on. I struggled to find something to motivate me. *"At least I'm not penniless this time, providing some Russian or Austrian soldier didn't find my hidden coins and jewel,"* I thought.

Even one intact cache would be enough to support me. I was grateful for the advice of many in Kazimierz telling me to send some money out of Poland for safekeeping. They spoke of a fall back in case…in case a pogrom or…I entered another life. A close trader friend in Kazimierz had given me the names of several bankers. "You never know what might happen, how bad things might get. My advice, Ignacy, be prepared for the worst, always."

To my amazement, no one ransacked any of my hidey-holes.  At dusk, I returned to the city to find my horse still in her stall, content, and well fed and groomed by the stable master I hired. Why no one stole her, I can't say.

My spirits sank when I discovered many of my old friends were dead or missing. No one seemed to be able to tell me if any members of my family survived or where they might have gone. My adopted city fell into the hands of the royal house of Austria in the latest round of fighting. Not good,  I gathered. Friends described how the Empress Maria Theresa, a single-minded fanatic, ruled with a heavy hand and a bigoted view of life.

A looter had ransacked the contents of my home, paradoxically providing me an easy cover story. If someone spotted the youthful me inside, I'd appear to be another thief searching for anything worth toting away. I retrieved my letters of credit, useless items to the illiterate. Blessings on the elders of my home village.

I dragged myself up the stairs to the bedroom I'd shared with Bozena and paused by the window where I once stood with her to enjoy the sights on the street below. The full-force of my loneliness hit e then, and I said good-by, too close to tears to linger. Perhaps my cheeks were wet.

No matter, I'd set a new goal, the only one left. With nothing remaining here for me, I needed a new start, a new city, a new country. If I followed my money, with any luck, I'd retrieve what I sent to the banking families in Frankfurt and Berlin. My friend in Kazimierz suggested their names, although I had only a vague idea where the two were located. I suspected I had at least one more language to learn.

I kept my eyes forward as I quit the house. I couldn't bear to look back. I mounted my mare and kept my eyes averted away from where I'd spent so many happy years. I pulled the reins over her mane, clucked at her, and bid a silent farewell to Krakow.

### Seed of Belief

When I spoke of my yearning to die, by chance I'd glanced up and saw the horror reflected in Jeanne's eyes, and her anguished expression gave me pause.

I sat back, my head full of conflicting thoughts. Pride, sadness, regret, hope. Her expression reminded me I needed to be careful how I told my story. She was still too fragile after losing her mother. Yet understanding this part of me, the not-dying, was a necessary part of what she needed to learn. I was the reluctant messenger, the bearer of bad news. She said you, not Ignacy. She was beginning to believe.

"You okay, Love?"

She sat back, "I guess, but sometimes when you say things like that … she paused, drew a breath. "I'll get over it. What did y…he do after he left Krakow?'

### The Monastery and the Road to Berlin

Of the two cities to send funds, they told me Berlin was the closer. I set out for the city, not stopping. I did tarry a bit with an order of monks who fed and housed me but asked me no questions. I shared their hospitality for a while, perhaps a decade, two at most.

After losing my family twice, I was world-weary. The high stone tower of the monastery seemed a beacon calling me. The monks proved trusting souls. The monastery walls stood unfortified, offering no barrier to any with evil intent. I simply rode in, and they welcomed me without reservation. The bed they assigned me was hard, the cell small, the food less than adequate, but I welcomed the solitude, the silence. At first, the set routine, the times for prayer and meditation nurtured me, but after a while, the rote repetitions made any entreaties empty of meaning—even if I'd chosen to invoke any. Religion became one more dead-end in my search for self. I accepted the reality. God didn't harbor an interest in me, and the monks expressed disapproval when I hinted at the multiple lives of my past.

"God gives us but one life to lead. No man except our blessed savior lives more than once," they said. When I decided to depart, they seemed uncertain with their directions. "To reach Berlin all you need do was follow the Spree."

Good advice had they known how to get to the river. "North, maybe a bit west." Fair enough, I had all the time in the world, after all.

I hefted my coin-heavy purse from its hidey-hole nearly as full as when I came. Due to the generosity of the brothers, the pouch would cover my needs until I reached Berlin. The monks made the sign of the cross and sent me off with a  "God be with you."

I purchased a new mount soon after I left. My faithful mare had succumbed to old age during my stay at the monastery. I set off, first on foot and later, mounted on a fine gelding I bought. In each  village, I'd seek a person able to point me in the direction I needed to go.

I finally found the Spree near Budyšin. Looking down at the river from the Ortenburg Castle, I was sure my destination must be quite near. Not the last error I made to be sure, but to this day, I have no idea of the actual distance. At that time, every town had its own measure of the distance of a Landmeile. The same sort of silly contest Americans have with the metric system. I suppose I should have checked how far someday, but somehow I never seemed to find time.

As I followed the river, I realized how poorly I understood the local languages, and soon I reverted to asking, 'What do you call… as I pointed to an object. Many I met spoke Polish, but as I went further upstream, the more difficult I found it to decipher what they said. Conversations appeared to be in a crossbred tongue, a difficult to understand blend of Polish and German. Many of the German words seemed similar to the dialect of my home village, which eased my task. I couldn't pop into one place today and another the next day. The slow pace of travel became an advantage, giving me more time to adjust to a new language and a new identity.

According to the papers in my Geldbeutel– that's purse for you—I'd bought off a forger Herr Doktor Gustav Kellner rode astride the grey gelding Ignacy purchased. I'd hoped for a life with the same social status as I'd enjoyed in Krakow. I toyed with the idea of becoming a royal von Kellner, but decided the risk was too great. With documents less reliable, I faced more severe punishment if an official found my identity false. I determined to become fluent in my new adopted language, and I'd stopped on my travels to chat with the locals to practice.

I'm sorry folks today have nothing, which compares to the pleasure of riding into a hamlet at the end of a day. The anticipation for the first sight of the local pub and ordering a stein of the marvelous beers made along the Spree. Sheer ambrosia. My opinion of my fellow men improved with the many fine people I met along the Spree. I still picture in my mind's eye some of the villages. Happy memories. My healing which begun at the monastery continued, and my spirits improved.

"Guten Tag, Mein Herr," I'd say if the owner were German-speaking or "Dobrý den, Hostinský," if he greeted me in a Slavic dialect. Without asking, the innkeeper would slam down a mug, and the first swallow slid down my throat as easily as honey down a bear. The heavy malt filled my mouth and assaulted my nose. Cool from the cellar, the beer was the perfect way to end a day's journey. I sipped the rest of the stein more slowly and chatted with the men in the taproom.

"How are things here?" I asked the innkeeper.

"Ach, mein Herr, not so fine these days. Our village is part of Austria now, instead of like before, part of Prussia. Our taxes are higher, and because of that, my business suffers. Many here weren't Catholic and left after the rumor circulated that Maria Theresa considered non-Catholics to be heretics, and expected her soldiers to force them to convert or kill them."

"Good thing I won't be staying long. I'm on my way to Berlin."

"Not your problem anyway. That our village is half the size it was before is my concern. Another beer?"

"Thought you'd never ask," I said at once. "I'm hungry enough to eat a whole cow. Have you food and a room where I can spend the night?"

"We've got a couple rooms upstairs if you don't mind sharing. My wife cooks the goulash. Her Vanočka is the best around."

"Give me some of the bread and the stew. Is there a stall in your stable for my horse?"

"Round back, sir."

He was a friendly sort, making even such banal conversation welcome. That night, I shared my room with five other men, and all but one snored. None of them washed. Not ideal quarters, but, at least, I was warm and out of the rain. I left after a breakfast of kolacky pastries. "My wife bakes them every morning… and I've got tea as well."

When I left, the overcast sky threatened with a heavy drizzle. I pulled my collar up and my hat down to keep the water from soaking my back and tched- tched my mount forward to reach Leibsch. There I planned to book boat passage for my horse and me to travel up the Spree to Berlin. I trotted off, scrunched down against the rain, cold and uncomfortable.


### Rising to the Defense of Others

0.

Had I turned as soon as I heard the sound of gunshots, the village would  have been still be in sight, but the cries of men shouting, and the screams from the children brought me to a halt. To make myself less of a target, I dismounted and inched my mare into some thick brush at the edge of the forest.  I debated if I should remain hidden even when the gunfire smoke grew denser and the number of shots increased. I froze, paralyzed by memories of our flight from Krakow.

Soon wisps of the Blue radiated in waves coming from the direction of the commotion. The smiling face of the innkeeper's wife as she ladled her stew onto my plate, urging me to eat more because I was too thin, seemed to appear, pleading for my help. Bozena would have laughed at anyone calling me thin considering the round belly I carried, and I heard her voice coming from nowhere, "You need to help those people, Ignacy. Others helped us."

In that moment, my conviction that the family I'd left in Krakow survived. Lost to me, but alive. Questions. Questions. Did Bozena remarry? Was I a grandfather? I shook my head. No time for such now.

Assisting the villagers ceased to be a choice. The Blue compelled me to help. Instead of running or hiding, by tracking the quantity and intensity of the Blue, I was able to creep closer to the carnage. At first, I advanced with stealth, inhaling the Blue as I went. When the Blue I inhaled was sufficient, I 'threw  gleaming clots into the knot of uniformed men.  I stalked the village, marching down the road as if I were leading an army.

With each additional volley of the Blue, the advance of the soldiers—for such the attackers were—became more unsure. Some pulled up their horses and turned in the opposite direction. My efforts clouded their urge to attack. Their horses milled about carrying their confused and uncertain riders.

I shouted at the village men who were still upright. "Take your women and children into the forest. I will hold the others here until you leave."

They seemed as confused as the soldiers, but hastened to do so, dragging their wounded with them.

"Gleichzeitig müssen Sie ausgehe," I shouted, acting as though I possessed the authority to give them the order.

The men of the village stared at me; not believing one person would dare to defy an armed squadron of soldiers. I gathered more Blue and redirected a beam at their commander. His face slacked as though his intelligence had leaked from his body. Once more, I yelled, "Leave, you bastards. Leave this village now!"

The senior officer appeared to shake himself and then ordered his men in mechanical tones. "Hab  ab, mach schnell.".

As if they were one man, the squad turned and galloped back the way they came. I breathed a sigh a relief. Even with The Blue, I hadn't been sure my bluff would work. When you can't die, you do crazy things.

I continued up the lane to the Inn. I passed by the dead, but stopped to bathe the wounded in Blue—thinking to ease their pain, perhaps to heal them. When I entered the inn, I found the innkeeper's wife holding her husband's head in her lap, tears on her face. "Why did they attack us? We are all Catholics, Mein Herr. I overheard a soldier saying someone informed them we were apostates. Not true, Mein Herr. Still, they set upon us."

'I nodded as if to comfort and said, "Let me examine your husband, good lady. I am a doctor."

Using my medical skills was futile I knew, but I hoped a taste of the Blue I still held within me might allow him to live.

"Care for him, Frau Gastwirtin. I will attend him and then see to the others. Perhaps I will discover who betrayed you."

When I emerged from the Inn, the villagers rushed to me, trying to kiss my hand or the hem of my tunic. I stopped them with a wave of my hand, "I did as God directed. Nothing more."

I realized appealing to their superstition would be most effective. Doing so may have been cynical, yet I realized such an explanation would best serve the simple folk of the village, "No need to thank me. You need to care for the injured and discover who told the lies which led to this."

A grim voice from the edge of the square said, "I know who the bastard is, Mein Herr. Not satisfied to take all the land from the lutherischen after they left, he wanted ours as well. Good thing for us his greed kept him here to watch."

The speaker and two others moved through the crowd, dragging a burly man twice his size of any of them. "This is the son of a bitch."

"How say you, my Lord?" a local asked me.

"I am not your lord. I have no authority to judge here."

"More than any other man," he insisted, bowing.

Looking at the face of a person driven by greed, I nodded slowly realizing this was my responsibility, no different than using the Blue when I encountered a dishonest citizen in Krakow. I fought off my sense of inadequacy. How should I do this? I struggled with what to say and then told the crowd "His lands shall be forfeit to the village, to be worked by all. The scoundrel shall labor one year for each family who lost a loved one. A fair verdict, say you?" I asked, directing the question to the man in front of me.

He glanced about the hostile faces of his neighbors, nodded with reluctance and croaked, "Fair, my Lord."

I gazed down on the gathering, many bloody or battered, and said, "May your prayers and blessings as I continue my journey. Heed well this—should another person need your assistance, you do so without question, regardless of his religion."

The men nodded with such solemnity, the square seemed a sacred place. Their prayers would do little for me, but their aid for another who needed assistance would. I did not doubt they would fail at the charge I gave them.

### *Raw Emotions Jeanne*

I hesitated and glanced up at my listener as I spoke to her. "Jeanne, I left with the raw emotions of the village hanging in the air so thick, I found it hard to breathe. As remote and poor, wounded, and hurting as this tiny town might appear, I had no doubt I'd left those who lived there in a better place. You probably are thinking I acted  like a sentimental sap, but…"

"No, Dad, no way.  You were just ahead of your time, you know, like with the idea of pay it forward."

"Thanks, Love. What I'm trying to share is, on that day I realized I'd acted purely from good will. This was the first time I used the Blue to do something which did not benefit me in some way.. Until that, if I used the Blue, when I did not gain anything directly, I did so indirectly. What I did earned nothing except personal satisfaction. I remember thinking perhaps this is the way the Blue expects me to act—without thanks or without reward."

"Dad, you hardly ever think about yourself. You think about your patients, the doctors you work with, and me, once in a while."

69

"More than once in a while, Love."

"You stopped in the middle of a trip. Then what happened? Did you get to Berlin?

I was glad for her question. "Eventually, I did— but not without some delays. "

### *On to the Bustle of Berlin*

### *The Voyage*

The fierce winter complicated my journey. Little of the fall season remained, and few vessels would embark for the voyage as far as Berlin. Booking was impossible. A few hardy captains plied short runs up and down portions of the river, but most remained in port for the winter. I did not fancy braving the icy winds howling the steppes on horseback and sought lodging in the village. I secured a room until the spring thaw arrived, and, when the boats returned to the water, I was on the first one to Berlin.

Life on board was austere, but enjoyable nonetheless. The good river captain maneuvered his craft north through the wild areas of Spree Wald and past small villages with tall brick buildings flanking the shore. Often level fields of wheat and mustard stroked by the wind rippled in the distance resembling the water beneath the boat. We put ashore to off-load or on-load cargo. Most locals were poor and lacked the means to afford to travel as I did, in relative luxury aboard ship. With few passengers, the captain and I became surprisingly good friends, chatting together as companions.

"Mein Herr, one day more, maybe two, and we shall reach the point where the Havel flows into our river, and we'll see more traffic. We all use the ample docks of the Spree. The piers are like a village with so many boats—some working vessels like mine, but pleasure boats for the rich and idle as well," he said with a small sly smile.

I took no offense at his little poke at me. His subtle jibe included me as a man rich enough for boat travel. We both dismissed the words for the friendly spirit underlying them, "Not for me, Gottlieb, as pleasant as you make sailing, once we arrive, I'll be a dedicated landlubber. Once I'm back where I belong, I will need lodgings, a place to set up my clinic. Have you any suggestions?"

"We'll be docking not so far from the Yacht Club where the water is deep enough to pull up to the wharf. I'd advise you to get off there. Friends tell me the area around is a good neighborhood with a generous supply or rental houses, and the Bierstube –ach, best in the city, or so they say. Find yourself something temporary and explore the area for rooms which meet your needs."

"I'll take your word for it, Gottlieb, you've gotten me this far."

We said goodbye, actually auf wiedersehn and spoke of plans to share a beer or two when he was in port, which we did often during the time I lived there.

### *Koepenick*

The advice Gottlieb gave was sound, and I settled in Koepenick, a small village near Berlin, the fast-growing Prussian capital. I suspected its aggressive neighbor might target Koepenick in a future expansion—an ultimate advantage for a growing practice.

I leased the bottom two floors of a home close to the river. My top floor fell on the middle floor of the house. The upper floor I used for sleeping and leisure time. The first floor, opening onto the street, neatly solved my clinic needs. The kitchen doubled as a place for the cook and a lab for concocting my medicinal herb mixtures. The journal of the herbal remedies I collected in Krakow together with medicinal recipes I gleaned during my stay at the monastery became an important part of my practice. The two tiny rooms at the back housed my housekeeper.

The small clinic outfitted to my satisfaction, I ventured into the heart of Berlin for a meeting with my representative at Mendelsohn & Co, banking house. Kazimierz friends recommended them as successful and honest. Their offices shouted their success. Marble floors and dark rich woods testified to their reputation as prestige bankers to the kings. A great contrast from where I conducted my usual business with the moneylenders of Krakow. I hesitated, wondering if they'd want to bother with a simple country doctor.

A bank employee met me at the door, "Guten Morgen, Mein Herr. How may I direct you?"

Hoping they would accept my fraudulent documents and cover story, I mumbled my name and the name I'd been told to contact. A brief frown crossed his face, and then cleared. He motioned for me to accompany him. "Follow me, Herr Doktor Kellner."

He led me to a lushly appointed office at the rear, "Herr Mendelsohn, this is Herr Doktor Kellner. He asked after Herr Jakobson." Mendelsohn's eyebrow went up when he introduced me thus, and I wondered what was wrong.

The stocky gentleman behind the desk stood and extended his hand, "Unfortunately Herr Jakobson is no longer with us. He passed eight years ago, I believe."

"I am sorry to hear that, Herr Mendelsohn. My grandfather spoke highly of him, although he never met the man in person. After the partition and the fighting subsided, my parents returned to Krakow. My mother, Gizela, married an Austrian officer, Herman Kellner. They moved to his estate in Silesia where I spent my youth. Unhappily, they both died young in an epidemic while I was studying medicine in Krakow."

What a liar I was. Glibly I improvised, using my children to manufacture my history to facilitate collecting on the letter of credit I held. I shamelessly spun what I hoped would be a credible falsehood. "The friend who arranged the transfers for me told me it might be sold at a discount and transferred to another person if I needed money sooner."

I hadn't done so, but I did not want any difference in name to arouse suspicion. Even knowing Germans seldom questioned the statements of a titled person—such as my Doktor designation made me. I stifled my relieved sigh when they appeared to find no fault with my explanation.

"So sorry, Herr Doktor Kellner. How can we help you?"

After I pulled the paper from the pouch on my belt, I placed the letter on his desk and said, "I would like to take one thousand of the total in thalers and keep the balance with you, verified by a new credit document I can take with me."

Their respect level climbed considerably when they read the amount shown on my document. "I am not sure if we have on hand the necessary numbers of thalers. Would you find it acceptable if we rounded out the sum in guilders?"

"Of course," I answered, having no idea what either was—or what the real value of the letter might be after so many years."

After I left, I did a quick calculation and realized if one factored not dying into the time span to earn interest, you end up with a tidy sum. I left the bank with my thousand thalers and a note for more than my original deposit. I felt somehow I'd cheated the bankers— performing no work for the extra funds— but my friends in **Kazimierz** had assured me, "If the market thrives,  you may experience considerable growth."

They called this process investing and providing the bank stays solvent, the depositor is paid interest. I walked out thinking how fortunate I was. Already well to do, a professional, now I would be wealthy and likely to remain so in the future.

The Blue gave me a longer time than an average man to generate earnings.  I put deposits in more than one place and, to be prudent, I  spread out future funds even more.

In that moment, I recognized, in addition to my strange gift, the Blue mandated I use my wealth to help others. The weight of the power money conferred was daunting. At that moment I understood why evil men valued power above all else. In the next instant, I grasped how discreet I must become. Better that few learned the extent of my newfound wealth.

Doors opened to me after my visit to Mendelsohn & Co.; Herr Mendelsohn himself put out the word about the wealthy new doctor in town and introduced me around to men of influence. . Prussia at that time revolved around culture, music, art, and discussion salons. I soon found myself with a diverse group of friends. Some were Prussian, some Saxon, many assimilated Jews, and a few like me saddled with completely phony lineages. Several of my fellow doctors came from Jewish families, although many now were Christian or secular. I struck up friendships with many attorneys.  Living in Berlin was rich and full in my "set."

Rich Berliners filled their drawing rooms with music and readings in the afternoon and early evening. The gentry welcomed me to join them in their diversions. I spent pleasant hours listening to wonderful musicians, even an exceptional female pianist somehow related to that famous composer Felix Mendelsohn, Often the ballrooms filled to capacity with people, so many I found little opportunity to meet or speak with all attending.

In time, I grew bored with my self-indulgent life. Filling my time with pleasant but empty gatherings grew unsatisfying. I sought a diversion of higher value. I decided to put some of my money to work providing medical care for the children of the poor. A friend told me of an existing clinic sponsored by the Lutherans, which might be a promising place to support. I scheduled a visit to decide if the center merited my support. To be honest, when my friend told me a woman did the oversight and directed the operation, nothing would have kept me from checking the place out.  Such a rare thing intrigued me.

When I explained my errand, the clerk in the front office left to fetch the director. A beautiful woman emerged from the back, and, in that instant, I was as smitten as any schoolboy.

Did I dare marry again? Even if she would have me? I had abandoned two wives, sired children who might be like me. How could I risk inflicting this curse on others? I thought back on the long years of my past, the friends lost, the families scattered. How much longer must I endure this life? Doubts swept over me like a wave over the dike.

She recognized me immediately, although I could not place her.

"Guten Tag, Frau…? … Fräulein…?"

"Guten Tag, Herr Doktor. I am Frieda Herzog. How can I help you?"

"Frau Herzog, how unexpected."

"Fräulein, Herr Doktor. Fräulein Herzog. I remember you. You sat across the aisle from me at a concert in the salon of Gräfin Grünstat. You left to answer a call from a patient, and we were never officially introduced."

"Fräulein Geschäftsführerin, I…uh…?  Wh…wh…?" I stuttered, as much shocked to find the clinic header by one of her social status as her gender

"Why is an upper-class woman like me doing in a place like this, Herr Doktor?"

"I didn't mean…"

"Of course you did. Many men including my father do not approve of a woman working. Papa forbids any mention of my 'foolishness', as he calls it, in our home. Are you another who thinks a woman is not capable of running such a place, that we should be embroidering tea towels or lingering in the garden painting bad landscapes?"

"Not at all, Fräulein…uh… "

"Then perhaps we have something to talk about, Herr Doktor Kellner," she said, smiling for the first time. "We shall see if we can work together."


### *Present Day Questions from Jeanne*

"Don't let them tell you love at first sight isn't possible, Jeanne. I am living proof. I was that day in Berlin, and I seem to have made it a habit."

"Were you just as silly when you met Mom, too?"

"Yes," I said nodding, "but look how well that turned out"

"Dad, I don't get what the big deal is with having money. When you were talking about the after you left that bank—why would it matter? Jane's dad is mega-rich and has a bunch of money.  What her dad does is no big deal  to us."

"In those days, I'd be a target. Folks living in poverty do desperate things to eat. Rich and powerful men would scheme to rob me, manipulate me, and lie to do their dirty work.  The Blue became at once both my friend and my enemy. If I tapped the Blue too heavily for self-protection, the rebound effect—an overwhelming craving—drained me. I realized when I left Mendelsohn's I would need to be discrete, then and now."

"Even now, Dad? "

"Human nature hasn't improved much, Love, and may be worse, in fact, considering the internet has made information so available and so unreliable. Little old ladies being scammed by gentlemen claiming to be from Nigeria would have been impossible back then."

77

"Good point."

Jeanne had laughed at my weak attempt to bring some humor into our discussion. I smiled, but underneath my mood remained grim. Everyone in my family needed to be watchful and alert. I thought back to the times I'd felt someone was watching me. As Jeanne would say, "Stuff happens."

### *Family Time in Berlin*

I had a hard time straightening out my thoughts after I left the clinic. Whoever said lightning couldn't strike twice, or in my case thrice must be wrong. Had my luck turned? Once again, could I hope to be again a man with hearth and home? I scarcely dared dwell on the thought. I usually proceeded with caution, took my time, planned ahead. Instead, I plied Frieda with flowers and candy, salons and concerts. We soon became an item in Berlin society. Most thought I was aiming well above my station. An obscure newcomer pursuing a local woman of wealth and influence, one with a family tree traced back centuries.

Not long after our first encounter at the clinic Frieda and I wed. The Kaiser accepted our invitation to attend our wedding, a rare honor, and a clue to the position my new in-laws occupied in the power structure. We chose One Seventy Six Unter den Linden as our new home—not for its fashion or prestige, but for the beauty of the tree-lined boulevard. We paid far too much for one of the smaller homes, but no matter. Frieda's wealthy family provided well for her, and gladly gave us the amount we lacked for the purchase. I didn't want to reveal my hidden wealth, and I was uneasy at accepting. For Frieda's sake, I agreed.

My practice thrived as a stream of wealthy patients, many friends on my wife's family or referred by my well-meaning bankers, flocked to my offices. In time, I suspected Herr Herzog did more than cast a big shadow in financial and social circles. He dabbled in governmental intrigue. I wondered if fear, not influenza, motivated some of the eager ailing who flocked to my office.

I did nothing to confirm my suspicions. Frieda and I lived in what we called our tranquility bubble. Many of our neighbors sons fought first with, then against Napoleon in the forces of the new German coalition. Frieda deplored bloodshed, and my past encounters more than convinced me to agree with her. Let others concern themselves with political and military affairs. We had each other.

We threw ourselves into the clinic, expanding to treat poor women as well as treat their children. Frieda spent long hours, tireless, and shameless in her mission to relieve our comfortable circle of their money and support the clinic's effort. Having skilled physicians on staff, (mostly me) made our facility unique, a fact Frieda used when extracting cash from potential donors. We did not ask our patients to pay, but did require a member of their family to assist with their care, usually cleaning or cooking, during the stay of their family member. When they regained their health, we asked them to promise to help others if they were able.

### Life Begins Again

After ten years of marriage and no children, I believed we would be childless. Although I longed for a little one, I reconciled myself to having no children. At least, I comforted myself, and I'd sire no others who shared my curse.

One balmy May afternoon, when I arrived home, Frieda met me at the door. My patience was thin. I was tired after a long day dealing with the paying—and more demanding—patients of my practice. "Good evening, Gustav," she said. "I see you've had a hard day? Come, Cook has dinner ready for us."

Never in our wedded life had my wife met me at the door. Unsure what the reason might be for Frieda's unexpected welcome, I dutifully followed her into the dining salon for our evening meal. When we finished eating, she dabbed her napkin on her lips, and said, ""Gustav, I've been thinking we ought to redecorate the south wing bedrooms. We could start with the one over the garden."

I stared at her. "Frieda, you've never shown the slightest interest in decorating. Why now?'

"I don't believe the rooms as they are would be suitable," she answered with an inscrutable grin.

I humored her, "Na ja, Liebchen, unsuitable because…?"

"The maroon would be much too stodgy for a nursery, don't you think?'

When I realized what she'd said, I raced around the table overjoyed, embraced her, scooping her up from her chair, and kissing her soundly. "Frieda, my love, this is wonderful news. You decorate to your heart's content."

The next few months were anxious days for us. Frieda, at nearly thirty, was old to be having her first child. The prospect of a child pleased me, but worry sent an icy feeling floating around in my heart.

Fortunately, all went well. Young Friedrich arrived just as autumn arrived to decorate our street with a wash of orange and rust, appropriately highlighted by heart-shaped bright yellow leaves. Frieda took a personal interest in our son4105 and chose not to leave him in the charge of a nanny as most in our set did. She even toted him to the clinic with her— where everyone doted on him.

Our unconventional lifestyle continued, and I spent more time with my son than other fathers. His close resemblance to Alexei, my first son, unnerved me. I treated our days together as a second chance. My doctor self was frantic when Frieda announced she was

                    *Claws of the Blue*

pregnant again. At her advanced age, the risk was considerable, yet she refused any pennyroyal.

"I'll be fine, Gustav. You see, I have such a fine doctor...."

Her mischievous grin warned me no argument I wielded would bring success. In due time, Heinrich joined his older brother and finally, their sister, Hilde, arrived to complete our family at Unter den Linden. With Hilde, Frieda suffered complications during the birth and suffered through the enforced idleness of a long convalescence, but we were again a whole family, playing games in the garden, riding in the Tiergarten, taking tea at the café. Even after years of frequenting the sidewalk cafés of Berlin, the scene still charmed me. The open air was welcoming, inviting friends and acquaintances to stop by our table for a chat over a pastry.

### Chance Encounter

One day while Frieda and the children lingered with me over the remnants of strudel, sipping our tea, and enjoying the late September sun, I saw someone who logic said ought not be there. She seemed about my own ostensible age, tall and regal in appearance, but her resemblance to Valentina, my first daughter, the one I called home centuries before, the small village In Imperial Russia. The resemblance was uncanny. Impossible, yet I had no doubt the figure was from another time, another place. This woman was Valentina. I continued to stare at the beautiful young woman I'd called my angel when she was a child.

I stood up, incredulous, and burst out a spontaneous, '*Lyubimaya?*'

The woman spun when I spoke and seemed about to speak, but, instead, she shook her head and put her finger over her mouth. She mouthed, "Not here, not now," and disappeared into the crowd. I gazed bleakly after her.'

"Gustav, that woman, do you know her?' asked Frieda.

"I'm not sure, Liebling. Probably not, but she…" My voice trailed off.

Frieda's voice had an odd tone when she commented, staring at our Hilde, "Incredible, they're so alike, Hilde could be her daughter. The hair, the eyes, and the way she walks. Perhaps that woman is a distant cousin or an apparition of Hilde as an adult. **Eine Erscheinung.** I usually don't accept such nonsense, such non-scientific explanations, but, Gustav, I was chilled to my depths when she turned toward us."

"Na ja, Liebling, you're not subject to flights of fancy. Clearly, I must have been mistaken. Such things are the stuff of children's tales." Privately I wondered why not now, not here?'

We finished our tea, collected the children, and returned home.

### *Second Encounter*

When winter arrived, the café's sidewalk seating closed. I fretted until the first frail signs of spring. I haunted the cafes, hoping for a glimpse Valentina once more. The solstice lacked only a week or two when she strode proudly along the boulevard, not mincing as many women did. An elaborate hat shadowed her face, but she was unmistakable.

I remembered not to call out aloud, but instead slipped in behind her, trying to be inconspicuous. I murmured under my breath, "Valentina, *Lyubimaya*, please tell me if you are who I think you to be.

Her head swung instantly in my direction, "Batya? Is it really you? I couldn't believe… I convinced myself I didn't see you. We all thought you'd died in Russia."

"And I, you, Sweetheart."

We looked at each other, not saying a word for a long time, for what seemed like hours. My eyes poured over her face and hers over mine. I noted our noses were alike, our lips identical, and our habit of raising a single eyebrow the same.

"How?" she asked at last.

I shrugged, "You are here which means you must feed on the Blue?"

"Da, Batya, but I call it cold fire— but, yes. Not when you still lived with us, later."

"Did you discover the cause of what you call cold fire, Valentina?"

"Da," she said, slipping back again into the language we spoke so long ago, "I concluded when an accident or a crime occurred, somehow the criminal's good intentions were discarded, lingering in the air nearby afterward."

"I described what happened differently, but the truth is the same," I said, "Did you seek out the flames? Wanting more?"

The stricken expression on her face told me what I needed to know. She suffered the same craving, the fierce desire that stole my inner thoughts and clawed deep at my soul. I hesitated, unsure of how to proceed, but she anticipated me and spoke without self-consciousness.

"I didn't at first, but I soon realized cold fire was most often present near the homes of certain people. If I were tired or ill, I wandered by their houses. At first, I took only enough to cure my ills, but over time I took in more and more. I craved the fire. I shook with need. Only after I grew conscious of the odd looks in the village, did I realize the Blue affected me in other ways. I learned the energy did more than simply refreshing me. The icy flashes made me well…and younger."

I nodded, "And so it was with me. When I returned to the Baron's estate, the Blue was so plentiful, so strong. I didn't hesitate but gorged myself until I sat sated on the ground. Only an image of myself reflected in the rain barrel revealed the result of my gluttony. My body had regressed back into one of a youth—an unwelcome stranger."

Silence prevailed for a time, and then both of us commenced talking at once, "How…? When…? Are there…? Did you…?"

We laughed, "You first, Sweetheart."

"No one else ever called me sweetheart, *Lyubimaya.* I always felt sad when I heard when others called their daughter …that simple word reminded me I had lost you, lost you to the Oprichnina. Only I didn't, as I now discover."

"Valentina, do you remember the young boy who brought the news of my capture?"

"Vaguely. We were so distraught."

"I was that boy. The loneliness I experienced that night, surrounded by my family and my friends was the worse I'd ever felt."

"I understand, Batya, the same sense of being utterly alone has haunted me often."

"For decades I tried to live a solitary life, Valentina, but sometimes certain women drew me to them, and I would become part of a new family. The children with me before at the café are those of my current family. I must have grandchildren I never knew existed, great-grandchildren. In time I recognized the signs I needed to prepare for the day when I must 'die  or suffer abduction, disappear. I contrived some other explanation ready for the day when others began to notice I did not age—and they did. Too many questions for that long ago age of superstition. I would drop hints or complain of new pains. Each new life I lived granted me better control over my appearance and more understanding of how create an apparent aging for a while."

"How long did it take before you learned to control the craving, the hunger? I struggled to rein in the desire. Nothing sapped my will more than the Blue flame. I was a moth to candle until one day a village child called me a witch because I stayed young. Each time the temptation to stay and feed grew stronger, I remembered the boy and what might happen to my loved ones if I were accused and burned."

"Powerful incentives—love and the family," I agreed. " I sensed the  force of the dark allure the night by the Baron's estate, but many years passed before I mastered my hunger for the Blue  by aiding the victims of wrong doing and taking only enough to give me energy and fight off illness."

"I thought I was the only one of my kind, Batya. I never considered the possibility of others, nor of you being the way I was."

"I feared, no—I realized, two of my children in Krakow might share my…our condition. The Austrians attacked before I was able to speak with them, tell them what they need to know to prepare them for the type of life we face. I died a true death and came back, but they were gone before I revived. I carry my failure to prepare them with regret deep in my heart."

"A true death?"

"A violent death at another's hands. Not a lasting death. My body lay lifeless to all around me until the Blue generated by the battle reached me, permeated my body, and I lived once more. Life did not return easily, only after a long and lonely pain."

"I did not die as you did, but I feigned death once, allowing my husband to place me in the family crypt. I was never as cold as in there."

"What can we do? Being alone and alive so long is hard. What if there are still more like us?"

"If there are, it is our obligation to locate them. I have money, Valentina. I can send men back to the village we shared, to Krakow to find my children, my grandchildren, if there are such."

"Perhaps—men are not so free to talk as we do here and now. I doubt there are written records," she answered.

"I remember the priest in our village was able to read and write. Perhaps he kept a journal to record births and deaths. Possibly his successors were literate as well. At least we'd have a place to start. As for my life in Poland—my wife's family was prominent in Krakow. Someone may remember us. I do think we need to keep our search discrete, not attract attention. We cannot meet often. I do not want to upset Frieda, and she would not understand. Our children are young. In ten years  time, they will be older, more involved, and more knowledgeable. Age makes us less likely to be judgmental, and more able to accept the truth of what we are."

"I understand, Batya. Knowing you live comforts me."

" In ten years  time the, *Lyubimaya*, on the same day as today at the café. Send a messenger if you cannot come, and I will do the same. Agreed?"

"Agreed, Batya. Not long for such as we, but time enough for us to seek the answers we need in faraway places."

We kissed on both cheeks in the usual way, hugged in a tight grip normally frowned up, and took our leave. We embraced with our eyes and went our separate ways. I stopped in the shadow of a building and watched her walk away—so short a time. I clenched my fists. Was this emptiness, this desolation what others felt at my deaths?

Instead, I slipped behind the trunk of a large tree and kept her in view until she was out of sight. I dare not ask her the question, which haunted me since I left her in the village.

### Jeanne: Questioning Customs of the time

"Didn't you at least give her a hug?"

"We didn't hug again, Jeanne—as much as I wanted to hold her longer. Public displays of affection were considered improper by the Prussians."

"No hugs? No kisses? Not ever?"

I shook my head. "Attitudes were different then. Being so huggy-kissy as you say, would never happen. We lived in more formal times. Today I can reach over and hug you anytime."

I gave her a squeeze, and she did the eye thing again but didn't push me away. She stared into space, her head tipped to one side.

"Dad, you can't be seriously talking about Valentina in all this?" Jeanne interrupted. "She'd have to be two hundred years old."

"You realize, then, how old I must have been as well, don't you?"

She didn't answer, and I didn't press her. Interesting, she was open to me being lifetimes old, but for another to do the same was harder to accept.

My hands clenched as I thought. *"I told Valentina and Friedrich she was too young. Why didn't they listen?"*

Jeanne's voice interrupted my thoughts.  "I think having to say good bye to made this Sergei guy really sad. Why do you give all your stories such unhappy endings?"

"Sergei guy?"

"Isn't Sergei the name you gave the dude in your stories?"

"Oh, yes, of course."

*What will she think when she must accept Sergei and I were one and the same?*

"Did Sergei…did… you…cry after Valentina left?"

A hint of progress.

"Jeanne, remember, didn't I tell you Russian men don't cry."

"Right, Dad," she said, giggling at our standing inside joke. Question posed and the expected answer given.

"You up for more?" I asked.

"More of your tall tales? Umm, I guess."

**Berlin Saga Continues**

### *New Expectations for Fathers*

When I returned to Unter den Linden, my heart still ached at the memory of parting with Valentina. I grappled with the sorrow of the loss of a shared life, but  the knowledge she still lived gave me some comfort. To be this happy in my current life, and yet so sad in the same minute for my past loved ones, might have  been unbearable were it not for Frieda and the boisterous three waiting for me at home each day.

Evenings Frieda and I encouraged lively chatter over our usual evening meal of bread, cheese, dry sausages, and spring fruits. Many families still clung to the children should be seen and not heard  maxim, but we were not one of them. Frieda delighted in igniting spirited debates. Friedrich excelled in razor-sharp repartee, yet Heinrich and Hilde often bested him. At other times, unfortunately, they subjected us to typical brother-sister bickering.

"Vati, may I attend the recital next week at the Schmitt's? Augie tells me Herr Schmitt hired a fine quartet."

"Of course, I'm glad to see you are taking an interest in music. I didn't realize you enjoyed the music of Herr Bach."

"He doesn't!" Hilde snipped. "What he enjoys is the company of Gertrude Schmitt."

"Haven't you ever heard of respecting your elders? The one about children being seen and not heard? We adults are better able to judge?" Friedrich retorted.

"If you're an elder, I'm an imperial Czarina."

I broke in, "Enough, children. If you can't conduct a civil conversation, you must be silent and tend to your dinner. Your mother and I have earned some blessed quiet."

Dinner done, Hilde often played the pianoforte until Frieda or I called for the books to come out for study. They'd groan and complain, but not long because they understood we expected them—Hilde included—to enter the university on merit, not family connections. With new opportunities opening up for girls' schooling and even being allowed to enroll in some selected universities, the world would be more open to Hilde than my other daughters. At times, Frieda or I would help them over a difficult patch, a task most parents in our set left to the tutor they'd hired or to a household servant. On a few occasions, when we were out of the house, I enlisted my secretary Karl to assist them. Ours was a happy life, richer for each other than most. No man could be more proud of his children than I. Perhaps love and happiness improve with practice, but my complacency over my parenting skills was about to be tested.

When Friedrich turned seventeen, he began his university study. At no surprise to me, he chose to pursue the law. Brash and opinionated, he was convinced a bright mind and a quick tongue comprised the sole ingredients necessary for success in law. Secretly, I wondered if the high ethical standards we expected might prove to be a hindrance to our headstrong son, but I left my doubts unspoken.

My other fear also went unvoiced. My son had scarcely begun his second year when the first hint he might take after me in more than eye color and stature appeared. I became aware he seemed never to need sleep, arrived home late after nights drinking with well-heeled Junker youths, but never seemed to tire. Not yawning, never napping—only school and play, with more of the latter rather than the former. He seemed less and less the boy I raised— coarser, uncaring, and more arrogant. I had no choice but to confront him.

Since then I've replayed the scene often enough in my mind to be convinced I did the right thing.

I slept in the parlor to ambush him when he returned. I'd dozed off, but the stench of pipe and stale beer woke me.

"Friedrich," I growled, "*Komm her zu mir… jetzt.*"

"*Guten Abend, Vater*, "he slurred.

"*Guten Morgen*," I corrected as no part of the evening remained. The blush of the sun was strong through the etched glass at the door.

He'd obeyed and hung his head. I guessed deep down he realized he acted badly. Or, perhaps he exhibited the respect for elders drilled into the heads of youth of the day.

"Sorry, Vati.'

"Sorry is not good enough. Tell me how do you go night after night with that bunch of aristocratic hooligans and still manage to stay awake for your classes? Before you answer,  I have spoken with your professors."

At least I'd sat down with the two who were former patients of mine. They told me Friedrich did well, although…The although   I discovered, meant the growing arrogance he showed toward others, especially with students of little means.

"Not only are you upsetting your mother and me, Friedrich, you set a bad example for your younger brother and sister."

He sagged further. Whether from shame or fatigue I didn't know.

"How do you do it, son? I suspect there is something you are not telling me."

His head flew up at my word, mouth hanging open, reeking from the beer he'd consumed, "What do you mean? Did someone tell you? What did they say about me?" he asked, an angry tone in his voice.


### Learning the Ways of the Blue

"Do not make excuses. I know full well what you are doing because I did the same thing myself. I have fed on the Blue. I partook often enough to realize its force is both a gift and a danger."

"What do you mean? What danger could there be? '

"I think you can guess, Son. The hunger, your craving growing and driving you fiercely each day. I recognize the ache in your eyes, the dulled expression on your face, and how your nostrils flared to catch the distinct scent generated by the Blue. Not all the confusion in your thoughts has been due to your lack of sleep. Consider the pain in your body leading from your skin down to the bone, the driving urge to satisfy a need you can't identify. '

"You've seen that Blue…shimmer?"

"Not only seen, but I understand the cause, though the why I still do not comprehend. The Blue eases the fatigue of your body, Friedrich, but not your mind. Your irritability, your arrogance, and the uncaring attitude you've been exhibiting stems from lack of sleep. If you persist, I fear for your sanity."

We sat down together, and I shared the ways the Blue changed my body and my life. His rebellion softened to disbelief. Disbelief sank into denial and ultimately into a measure of acceptance.

"But, Vati, what you experienced was a long time ago. Times have changed. Why should the same thing happen with me? Haven't I always been the good son, not like Heinrich," he added in a petulant tone.'

His hand trembled, and a tic marred the expression on his face. "Friedrich, think about how you feel, the changes in your appearance, the belligerence you show your mother. Can you honestly believe you are different from me and won't pay the price of the Blue? That you somehow are invincible and immune?"

He hung his head.

The next night he did not go with the Junkers. Instead, the two of us walked some distance to the house of a well-known government official, a  sort of fellow certain to provide us with the Blue. I knew well how power  corrupted – at least for government officials. I showed Friedrich how to select the less vibrant portions of the Blue, those less likely to encourage heavy feeding. On those occasions, if he started to take in too much or inhale the essence too quickly, I stopped him. He shuddered. He breathed deep, but only once.

" Enough now, Son," I'd say. "You must learn when you have taken enough to satisfy your need."

Weeks passed before he understood the safe amount and when to stop before the hunger took hold. We grew closer than we were before as he struggled with addiction. Sometimes the wild antics of his Junker friends grew attractive, and he relapsed. I swung between happy and sad, proud and impatient. Not happy weeks for either of us.

Once Friedrich learned to control and conquer his dependence on The Blue, I regained my talented son, the old Friedrich returning. He continued to attend the

94

university during the day, but at twilight, the two of us prowled the streets, seeking the Blue, not to consume, but to identify the person responsible. He started to be able to anticipate the beginning of an action by one of our "regulars,"  and copied my efforts to frustrate their activities. I'd tell Frieda we were going for a walk, but privately confided to her I wanted to keep an eye on Friedrich so he did not take up with his old crowd again. "Irresponsible rakes, all."

If the Blue shone bright and solid, we kept an extended watch on the offender to uncover what he was doing. If his actions harmed innocents, we'd use the Blue to discourage an action in progress. In this way, we accomplished two goals. We balanced how much Blue filled our bodies, and we kept a record to report his actions to the proper authorities. The report provided Friedrich good practice preparing in a brief. He often used the language of law to describe the act. I remember our first night of training.

"Where did you go most often, Son, when the hunger was strong?"

"Near the Tiergarten, Herr Kruger lives there, I think."

"What does he do to attract the Blue?"

"I never tried to find out, Vati."

"Now you try, Son. The Blue demands diligence from us for the rewards given."

One other evening, we happened on a young man intent on robbing us. "Let him get close to us, Friedrich, so close he thinks he already has our money and watch what I do."

He eyed the thief creeping from one alleyway to the next, looking for the best place to make his move.

"Now, Vati?"

"Not yet. Watch closely now. Open yourself so you can sense what I am doing."

"Yes, Vati,"   he whispered back.

I drew on the small supply of Blue in my body and directed a flow toward the young man. He stopped, seemed to try to avoid an unseen threat. His confusion grew evident, yet I continued to transmit brief bursts of the Blue. A short time passed before I turned to face him, "What is it you need, young man? What are you doing?"

"I...I...I'm not sure, Mein Herr."

"Why would you be following us? Are you in need?"

"I am very hungry, Mein Herr. I can't find work. I care for my little sister— our parents are dead, and we are all alone."

"Are you are willing to earn your keep? Well, now. Take this card. Tell the woman in charge at this address you are there to work. She will feed you and, if you do well, you may have a job."

"Danke, Mein Herr, Danke, Danke."

He was still thanking us as we left.   "Sometimes, Friedrich, stopping a crime before it happens is best. Do you understand what I did?"

"I think so, Vati. I must practice. What a wonderful trick."

The young man did as I asked and came to the clinic. He proved to be a loyal and diligent worker, earning what he and his sister needed to live. A much better outcome than jailing such a young person.

We grew so close, my son and me. I think we both realized the value of our close bond. Our closeness was an extraordinary gift I valued more than my wealth. I decided to enlist his help should I need assistance with his younger brother and sister.

"I think there is a possibility Heinrich and Hilde may also be attracted to the Blue," I said to him. "When the time comes, if the time comes, you can help them learn to use the Blue and deal with its effect on them.'

Once again, the good son I'd known nodded solemnly. "To do less would shame me, Vati. I lost too much of myself. I do not want the same to happen to Heinrich or Hilde."

Sometimes my relationship with Friedrich seemed such a blessing. I started to worry something might happen to destroy what we had built. The loss of my prior families left me I untrusting and I grew wary, worried something would go wrong, with good reason, as it turned out.

### Cholera Strikes

The epidemic started in India, swept north, and continued across Europe on its way to North America. The Asiatic Cholera Pandemic wiped out hundreds of thousands of lives. Cholera did not discriminate on victims but attacked anyone who drank the contaminated water containing it.

Two of those who died were my Frieda and son Heinrich. As a doctor, I realized their chances to survive such a devastating illness were nearly infinitesimal, but I labored day and night in an attempt to save them. Friedrich and I remained untouched, of course, and Hilde seemed able to fight the sickness. Friedrich boiled the water and did everything but use a funnel to pour it down the throats of my stricken family as dehydration was a lethal symptom. In one of the few times, the Blue failed me and had little effect on them. When the light left Heinrich's eyes as it had Frieda's, the heightened frustration of a thwarted doctor made my sorrow greater.

I'd neglected some of my other patients those last days and, and after the deaths, I threw myself into their care to extinguish my inner anguish. Hilde thrived with her brother's attention. Nothing helped me. I was seldom far from tears. All around me were reminders of my Frieda–her scent, her trinkets on the bedside table, her favorite chair.

"Friedrich, I don't think Hilde remain here. She's too weak and a reinfection would be more than she could handle.  Book passage to one the north countries, or even England where the sickness is not so widespread. When you locate a place, get word to me, and I will try to rid myself of my practice and join you.

I'd never been the one left behind. I'd always been the one who left and initiated the day and time of my partings...or the Blue did. I wasn't dealing well with the ghastly deaths of my wife and son. I was angry. Wasn't the clinic enough, weren't the ones we saved sufficient to balance the books? Why did they have to die? *Frieda, Liebchen, I miss you so...*

### *Grief Spans the Centuries*

My sad memories must have shown in my dejected manner.

"You look so sad, like you did when Mom died."

"Yes, the same,"  I answered, wiping my eyes.

Jeanne seemed to sense my mood and tried to direct my thoughts to something more pleasant. She said,  "So if you didn't use the Blue ...uh...stuff the right way, bad things might happen?"

Unfortunately, yes.

"What did this Herr Kruger do—the guy you and Friedrich found?"

He called what he did 'dabbling  in the slave trade. This was unlawful in Prussia, and evil in itself.

"And you made sure the good guys got him?"

"We reported what we'd learned to the officials.  In almost every case, the official we notified conducted his own investigation and an arrest soon followed. Occasionally the perpetrator proved to be too well connected making him virtually untouchable. On those few occasions, we projected an increased amount of the Blue in his direction, leaving his mind bent, with no memory of prior acts and little ability to do them again."

"I get it. Basically, you two were like Batman and Robin."

"Jeanne, you possess a remarkable talent to link everything to some comic book hero."

"What's wrong with that? You understood what I was trying to say, didn't you?"

I sighed and sent her the look parents use when they want to tell their offspring how much patience they need to draw upon to deal with them.

After a brief silence, she said,  "That thing Friedrich did for Hilde, to help her with the Blue, that was great.  If I had a brother or a sister, I'd try to help them, too."

I stare at her thinking, she does, many brothers and sisters, and she's never met any of them.  My account of Valentina seems an abstract for her, not personal. *Too soon yet*? Aloud I answer,  "I'm pleased to hear you say that, Jeanne, many wouldn't, you know."

"If you say so, Dad, but I don't understand why. You know what, I wish your stories were real. They're so cool."

Does she really think I'm only storytelling?

"Dad, what do you mean when you said the Blue rewards, but also punishes? I thought the  Blue was supposed to be good."

"Yes, Love, but the Blue comes with consequences. By this time, I'd learned the price for long life and health. Too much taking, too much self-satisfaction leaves a void—a psychic void—which must be replenished. "

"I guess that's fair...sort of,"  she said, doubt showing in every word.

"Off to bed now, Love. The little hand is on the eleven."

She shot me a disgusted look. "Dad, I'm not a little kid anymore."

"Granted, Love, but fathers never want their little girls to grow up. I guess  you'll have to live with it."

"Uh huh. I guess I will."

"Night, Dad."

My thoughts drifted back to the day I'd shared with Friedrich how the Blue changed my body and my life. He was older than Jeanne, almost an adult. We used the Blue in limited ways. No longer. She is so much younger than to find herself in the center of a changed world. The family planned to place a heavy burden on her young shoulders. I must convince her to accept what I am, what she is, and our role in the future.

## Valentina Returns with the Mission

### *Stranger in the Neighborhood*

A harsh spike of sunlight struck my eyes, forcing me awake. I'd always been an early riser—probably a habit left over  from my youth when we rose at dawn. The past few days I'd clung to sleep, putting off the day. Both of us seemed to be making sleeping late a habit.

I yawned and slowly stumbled to the kitchen, following a trail of coffee fumes. Jeanne grinned and handed me a cup when I arrived.

"This make it  better, Dad?" she asked.

"Oh, yeah. Thanks, Love,"  I said, noticing she was by the front window staring across the street.

"Your boyfriend out there?"  I teased.

"Get real, Dad, you know I don't have a boyfriend right now. Besides, that's an old guy out there—he looks like the same guy I saw a few days ago."

I joined her.  "That's odd,"  I said, "I don't recognize him either." A stranger loitering in the neighborhood put me on edge, and I turned away.

Later, after we finished putting the breakfast dishes from breakfast into the dishwasher, I refilled my mug of potent black coffee, doused the contents with milk, and led the way into the living room. Dog-tired, I leaned back in my favorite easy chair while Jeanne perched on the couch. I turned my wrist to check the time – nine o'clock. She had four hours more--hours, not years. I hope the organization is doing the right thing. Jeanne needs to accept what I am telling her as real.

### *Leaving Berlin and Another Reunion with Valentina*

The two years I lived alone were lonely. The days were beginning to feel crisp when I received a message from two young doctors eager to establish their practice approached me. They bought everything. Better still, their wealthy father fronted the cash needed to complete the transaction. Money held little value for me, but the finality of the sale did. I deposited most of the proceeds with the Mendelsohn bank who'd treated me well. I directed them to transfer a portion to their correspondent bank in Stockholm.

I was glad to leave Berlin. I didn't regret leaving Prussia where reminders of my lost loved ones loomed in every room and on every corner. Moreover, the new Kaiser Wilhelm struck me less worthy of a man than his father. My adopted country would suffer from Bismarck's  bad advice and influence on the Kaiser. The attitude of the court hardened and began to stifle the openness and  damper the pleasant atmosphere of the city. Only the anticipation of my reunion with Valentina held me in my home on Unter Den Linden waiting for a buyer.

Friedrich and I wrote each other frequently. As quick of pen as he was of tongue, the vivid pictures he penned of Sweden's capital made my destination more real. I wrote often and tried to hide the melancholy, which filled my vacant house. After I wrote a letter, I set it aside until the next day. The following morning, I would reread what I'd written and delete any hint of self-pity before putting the envelope in the post. Through his letters, he shared the news that Hilde had enrolled in the Academy of the Arts and pursued her painting. I did not hesitate to respond with congratulations. My son hinted at other developments --her talent and proclivity in using Blues in her palette, tasting new food and the like. A casual reader might take what he said at face value, but not I. I fretted, understanding well his veiled references.

When the day came, Valentina and I were again face-to-face, I was able to purge my soul and tell her of my changed circumstances, to recount how Frieda and Heinrich died, and share the news both Friedrich and Hilde shared our strange proclivity—and no doubt long life.

"I am so sorry, Batya. Once I lost a child… before I… had to leave, but to lose two of your loved ones at the same time. How tragic."

"Thank you, Sweetheart," I said thinking her loss taught gave her understanding of those moments, those short gaps in daily life, the pause between the first word or gesture and the realization the person is no longer. "At first, every evening I would leave my clinic filled with news of the day, anxious to share—only to be jolted once again with the realization Frieda was no more."

"I did the same, for many weeks, even months, after Gregor died."

"We are two of a kind, Sweetheart. How many times more? How many deaths must we face?"

She didn't answer, and our mutual sadness hung in the air.　"What is, is; we cannot change what is not ours to change. Batya, I do have happier news to share with you. With the money you gave me, I hired a man to conduct our search. One of the reports he sent induced me to visit our home village. A miracle happened—I found my son, Dmitri. He resembled in every way the young man I left one hundred years before. He recognized me at once. We embraced. Such joy we shared. We talked for hours at a café and again over breakfast at the inn where I'd booked a room. Like me, when his time came, he left the village for another life. He'd returned after five years posing as his young "cousin" from Kiev."

"How much did you tell him, Valentina?"

"He was my youngest. The others died normal deaths. I disappeared before his adolescence. I did not suspect he shared out affliction. I found out when we reunited, the Blue entered his life during his teen years. He struggled, Papa. How he struggled. The Blue held him in a firm grip for a long time before he crashed and came to terms with the hunger."

"So, I'm Papa now?"

"Ah, a custom I adopted when I lived in Hungary, and, for a time later, in Italy as well."

"We must move and adapt, mustn't we? I've used many names and been called many things. I'm sure you have, too."

She nodded, and added, "Papa, I need to show you something."

She turned and gestured to the table behind us, motioning a tall blond young man to join us. "'Dmitri, come here, please."

"Dmitri?" I asked.

"Meet your grandson, Papa. Dmitri, this is your grandfather."

We kissed on the cheeks following Russian custom, and I leaned back to scrutinize his face closely. "He might pass for your brother Alexi, Valentina. The resemblance is uncanny."

"Truly, he is unmistakably ours."

At her words, a shiver went up my spine. Ours seemed to have such a special ring, an aura, a beyond mere words. More remarkable because we were gazing at one another after a two hundred year separation."

Dmitri acted shy with me, quite out of character for him as I discovered later. Definitely a manner quite out of character. He sat in silence, making sidelong glances my way. In the end, he thawed, and we achieved a tentative rapport. I must not be as intimidating as I thought. Life seemed brighter that table in the café, but Valentina soon quashed my happiness at being surrounded by my newly revealed extended family.

"Papa, we must return again to Kiev. Dmitri tells me his son, Alexi, has exhibited hints he shared our peculiar…curse. Dmitri departed before he was able to confirm this fully. We must locate him. If we are successful, you will meet at least one great-grandson and perhaps a great-granddaughter as well.'

"So soon, Valentina? Would a day or two make a difference?"

"Winter is on us in less than a month, Papa, and the distance is great."

Strained minutes followed while we worked out how we would correspond regularly and more often. We agreed to meet again at the cafe in ten years' time. Should one of us be too far from Berlin, we would telegraph to set a new date and place. They disappeared in the crowd, and I struggled to contain my tears. In the following months, I'm ashamed to say I abused my body with alcohol. Friedrich's letters kept me going.

Leaving at last, I traveled overland across to Denmark, which I found a friendly place, if unbelievably flat. I took passage across what the Vikings, Sweden's most infamous voyagers, called the Eastern Lake to Stockholm. A winter storm sprung up and tossed the ship about, but I arrived thankful to be safe, if a bit seasick, as the ship docked.

105

Friedrich and Hilde stood on the pier to greet me. Our usual old world reserve shed, we embraced each other, holding tight, no one moving, our shoulders shaking.

Friedrich had leased a comfortable place in Västerort, in western Stockholm. The house sat on a quiet street, and the fetching city with its trees and canals impressed me. My son and I often talked long into the night, after Hilde said good night and headed to her bedroom. Not just the first night, but often all of us, both at home and in the street as we three stalked The Blue we needed. Not much lingered, and over time I agreed the Swedes appeared to have abandoned their warlike ways. The sparseness of the Blue said they'd become a peace-loving people and honest for the most part.

However, somehow we didn't connect with Stockholm, and none of us understood why. This Venice of the North should have satisfied anyone--even had the population not been composed largely of blond, blunt-speaking, and ethical people. A growing unease seemed to encourage us to move on, but the where remained an issue.

One day Hilde sat, curled up reading the newspaper when she emitted a little yip. She read aloud an article describing an organization in America called Pinkerton Security. 'Their employees, called Pinkertons. They usually work with law enforcement, but employers often hire them to break strikes or put pressure on competitors.

Excited at her find, she proposed a new course for us. "What if we organized a group along the same lines? With everything we've learned over the years--especially you, Vati." She glanced over at me with a grin, '"If we add organization to what we to the advantage we gain from the Blue, we could create something positive—something to dampen criminal intimidation and stop corruption. If we are able to react sooner, before the less desirable have the upper hand of the average citizen, we'd be able to neutralize the damage from folks like greedy lenders who prey on the poor. Wouldn't this ease the addictive overload we fight? We all have some special abilities. Organizing in this way would maximize and make the more positive effect greater…"

The idea seemed just bizarre enough to make sense.

"Where?" I asked.

"Why in America where the 'other Pinkerton's heavy-handed activities have caused so much turmoil."

Hilde convinced us to come to America.


### Just Like That?

"Just like that? One talk, and you dropped everything to come to a place you'd never even seen? Why do I have to talk forever before you agree to do something I want?

I didn't bother to respond to her comment. She didn't seem to expect an answer and moved on. "How could that Dmitri guy still be a boy, after so long—like over a hundred years later?"

"For the same reason, I appear the same age as your friends' fathers."

She tipped her head, "Sure, Dad, whatever."

Her doubt notwithstanding, I must go on. A knock on the door would come soon, too soon.

## Establishing Blue Talon in America

### *Landing in the New World*

"Ooh, cool! Ellis Island, I'll bet. We just read about Ellis Island in American History."

"When we arrived, Ellis Island hadn't opened yet, Jeanne. For that matter, in the early nineteenth century, ships, ships caught in storms often ended up blown off course. When that happened, the ship's captain might demand an additional fare to take them to their original destination. If they couldn't afford to pay, he put them ashore at the nearest port. My Berlin neighbor's son settled for Brazil."

"That's not fair. The captain should take them where he said he would."

"Perhaps not fair, but the captain would need to restock the ship, take on water, and pay the crew. The money had to come from somewhere."

"I guess. So if you didn't land at Ellis, then where?"

"We disembarked at the Hudson River port in New York. Gratefully disembarked. Believe me. Leaving the Montana was a happy even for everyone on board. Our entire voyage, even in first class, I wouldn't call the accommodations pleasant. The poor devils in steerage traveled six to a bunk, ate half-rotten food, and had to deal with lice and who knows what else. Those completing the trip proved themselves a hardy bunch. Being in first class was a favor, ironically, funded by a Bey in the Ottoman Empire."

"Completed?"

"Not everyone made it, Jeanne. Many died. Nothing came easily in those days. Grab us a couple soft drinks, and I'll tell you about our first introduction to the New World. Goodness, ten thirty already."

"Ok, Dad."

"Hilde suggested we try to find a German-speaking community. Friedrich and I agreed. English was new to us. While in Germany, I'd encountered a few travelers from England, but we spoke French as most educated persons did. We met some helpful Americans we met at the port described many cities and even some larger areas they called states where the residents spoke German. Having little English hampered us. Besides French, we were fluent in Russian, Polish, German, even Swedish, plus the dialect of my home village, but not English. We hoped casual, simpler conversations might result in a better command of our new language.

"We eliminated Wisconsin, Minnesota, and Texas. Besides being too far, as immigrants, we'd have to travel in uncomfortable second-class cars. Apparently, Americans of the day thought all immigrants were dirty and ignorant. The closer part of Pennsylvania in the west better suited our needs. Although Hilde stared wistfully at New York's German neighborhoods, containing the sites of art and culture, we decided on Pennsylvania. She was unhappy having to turn her back on an urbane city for an unknown rural corner of a state with an outlandish name. Still the copious amounts of Blue we encountered in some parts of lower Manhattan, such as Five Points or the Bowery, convinced her our plan was sound. A couple of weeks later, we took a ferry to Jersey City and boarded the train for the "Dutch" country.

"On the train, we welded Russian and Polish onto our normal speed, thinking we would less likely be overheard by others sitting nearby. Families in the car were speaking German, Swedish, and even some Italian. When they heard our strange garbled conversation, they ignored us—as we'd hoped."

### *Adapting to the New World*

"I remember sitting across from each other on the narrowest, least comfortable seats I think I ever rode on before or since. I sensed eyes on me. I turned away from the landscape and caught Friedrich staring at me with an odd set to his face.  "Vati, we look more like brothers than father and son."

Gazing at my reflection in the window, I realized we did indeed. "'So that makes me again Gustav? I must look more like your brother and not your father. Too much of the Blue  makes a person appear young again."

"Probably, but Hilde and I also appear younger than we did before as well. Perhaps this is simply anticipation."

"Gustav it is, Son... **egad**…brother," I corrected.

"You'd pass for someone old enough to establish a medical practice," Friedrich said. "People expect German from a doctor, but I likely will need to attend university again for a while, partly to learn the laws in the States, partly to improve my language skills. My credentials require a credible command of English."

"This might be a new beginning. I could attend  Conservatory again," said Hilde.

"Good ideas all, but let's wait until we have a clearer idea of our new surroundings and discover the unforeseen opportunities they offer."

Once again as the old saying goes, the best-laid plans often go astray. A tightly knit, closed communities of Amish, Moravians, and Anabaptists populated the German-speaking area we chose. Neighbors convinced in their firm belief they controlled the only true path to the gates of heaven proved not so comfortable place for us. I'd lived long enough by then to realize no group holds the exclusive right for access to the soul of the universe.

We retreated to Pittsburgh, a thriving community with neighborhoods where English shared equal time with my current language. We found the city's diverse population far more attractive, but we stayed less than a year because the soot and grime thrown off by the countless steel mills sickened Hilde. She needed to spend too many nights wandering about in the dark seeking the Blue in an effort to stay healthy. Many of our neighbors suffered from racking coughs and shortness of breath.

By now, we'd mastered enough English to get by. We discovered useful similarities to German, which allowed us to gain fluency quickly. Still, I must say, I never encountered such an inconsistent mishmash in all my lives as the English language.

In the center of the state a university offered the law courses Friedrich required. To my delight, the curriculum not only offered law, but also a school, open to women seeking to study medicine. The news thrilled Hilde, "I'll study nursing this time, and in my next life become a doctor like you, Gustav," she said with a mischievous grin at the use of my most current proper name.

"Why wait, Hilde? Take your time and study hard. Another fine physician in my practice to do the work so I can relax more would suit me just fine."

She wrinkled her nose,  one eyebrow lifted, and she flung her hair back. "Is that a challenge?"

I shook my head, "No, not even a prediction. With such a beautiful woman in my office, more likely I'll become incredibly wealthy what with all the young men flocking in to consult with the beautiful lady doctor about  any and all of their imagined illnesses!"

She giggled, but achieving her goal proved not as easy as we first thought. Before she could enroll at Penn, they insisted she prepare for her medical education at the Women's Medical College of Pennsylvania. I thought this might be a ploy by Penn to keep women out. If so, they failed. By 1896, we had a second doctor in the family. Friedrich and I opted for Philadelphia as the best city for him to establish his practice. I set up my new two-doctor clinic.

We made such a team, she and I. Her smile directed toward me each morning brought up my spirits and seemed to lighten the load for the tasks we planned.

From now on, we would lead two lives. By day, we'd be stalwart residents of the community; by night, with luck and good planning, we'd serve as a force to soften the damage to our fellow citizens from crime and cruelty.

The knowledge we gleaned from neighborhood gossip and newspaper accounts of Pinkerton exploits gave us some concern that spending too much too close to their office might be inadvisable. No doubt their activities attracted heavy concentrations of The Blue, which might trigger our addiction posing the danger of overexposure for us.

Friedrich, using his contacts in the legal community, assembled quite a file on the group. Although he uncovered evidence the Pinkerton often acted as responsible detectives in providing corroboration against criminals, their actions on behalf of employers as union busting thugs unfortunately also proved correct.

Either way—if the Pinkerton operatives emitted the Blue personally or if the presence of the bank robbers and murderers they tracked. How they added to the supply mattered little. The Blue aura hung around them. Nosing around them or a current crime scene they were investigating presented a problem for us. How did we learn what we needed to know without endangering ourselves was a dilemma?

"They're extremely meticulous, Vati," Friedrich said. "Over the years they've assembled photos and filed newspaper stories so they get a clear idea of how a particular gang operates. We need to inspect their offices, see how they do it, figure out ways we might improve their methods."

"I doubt any of us would have an opportunity," Hilde objected.

"She's right, Vati. We are all too well known. Too many might recognize Friedrich, the hot-shot attorney with the atrocious accent, or Hilde the beautiful lady doctor, even Gustav, the oh-so-respected doctor at the city's best hospital."

"Then how?" asked Hilde.

### The Doorbell Rings

I glanced up. Jeanne sat intent. "Jeanne, what would you do?"

My youngest daughter threw me an expression of total disbelief, "What do you think I would do…break in?"

"No break-ins, Jeanne, a real solution, a workable one."

"You'd all be too conspicuous. I guess I'd find someone else to go undercover like in one of those detective novels, put someone in their local office."

"Exactly right, Love, our method was a bit more complex, but pretty much you got it right."

Although I was set to continue, the sound of the doorbell at the front door interrupted me. My heart sank.

"Why don't you get that, Jeanne? I'm going to refill my cup."

She hopped up and headed to the door. When she opened it, three very tall, very blond young people stood on the entry. "You must be Jeanne," the woman said. "I am your sister Valentina, your brother, Friedrich, is behind me, and the laggard back there is Dmitri, my son and your nephew."

*Jeanne spun around, disbelief on her face, "You mean this fairy tale you've been spinning for me the past couple days is for real? Not just another of the wild tales you used to tell me when I was a little kid? I mean,* like *were you… like* serious? *Dad?"*

Book II: Enter the Family

### *Family reunion*

Surprise didn't come close to describing my youngest's face when the three visitors strolled through the front door. Bewildered, unbelieving, disappointed or all of the above. Her head swiveled from me to Valentina and back again.

"Who did you say you are?"

"Not so easy the first time, is it?" Valentina answered.

"First time?"

The two behind my eldest smiled with a knowing nod at the question Jeanne had blurted out.

"The first time you meet the rest of us from the extended family," Valentina answered.

She  turned to give me a firm hug and asked in a tone I knew only too well, "How much have you shared with her?"

I delayed having to respond by stepping to one side for Friedrich and Dmitri to give the dumbfounded Jeanne a brotherly hug.  "I've told her everything…well, at least up to the time Hilde joined my practice in Philadelphia—around 1890, wasn't it."

"Papa, that's not  enough. Surely, you understand how important a role she'll need to play. Why hamper her, not tell her what she needs to know? What took you so long? I'll wager you didn't tell her how we built on the Pinkerton model to form  our Blue Talon organization."

"Fraid not, Sweetheart."

As I watched Jeanne's baffled expression, a vision of Reki, the small mongrel dog I'd once had, flashed through my mind. His cringing image when I had scolded him spoke to how I viewed myself in that moment. Valentina wasted no time in scolding me. "Papa, that's not fair. You agreed you'd complete briefing her by today. You promised to make sure she understood what she is, how she fits in and why she is one of us and different from everyone around her. Without complete knowledge and understanding of her family's origin and history, she won't be prepared to accept her assignment."

"Sorry, *Lyubimaya*," I said and sighed at the accusation. She softened a little when I used at my special pet name for her, my 300-year-old name from long ago, the one only I used with her. She was no stranger to my shortcomings and reluctance to surrender another child to The Blue. Her lack of patience with my delaying tactics came from her past experiences with me. I prepared for a louder reiteration of my failings, a lecture she had delivered often.

"Why do I even scold you? When have you been anything other than a sentimental father? Only every time you sat down to share stories about your past lives, your other children with one of your current family. You manage to stretch out the tale as long as you can. For you to leave out a detail or two wouldn't weaken the tale you have to tell. Without doubt leaving out a detail or two would shorten the time, but still convey what is necessary in something less than forever. Reminiscing is fine, but must you always dwell on minute events until you choke up and need to stop for fear the tears welling up in your eyes be discovered? Tears, by the way, you never admit to having."

"To describe a man's life story as a briefing isn't reasonable, Valentina. Jeanne interrupted me constantly with questions, and I'm getting old, you know. I've been around longer than the rest of you."

"Your body's age is no older than mine or Friedrich's or any Eight if you want to be fair. Your memories might start before ours, but none of our bodies wear out. Too old? Sorry excuse."

I was sure Valentina would soon discover my portrayal of Jeanne and her constant questioning to be well founded. My first feeble attempts fighting the internet began in an effort to answer her constant whys. On cue, Jeanne proved my point as she burst in once more, "What's an Eight?"

I opened my mouth to answer her. "Papa," Valentina said frowning. "My turn now."

A long time ago, I forget how long, most of my children had agreed among themselves to call me Papa. True, some, Jeanne, for example, called me Dad. Others used different names, different languages, and different centuries, but this proved too confusing for family members of different centuries. Thus, within the family I am Papa. My descendants always used a form of their first given name, no matter how many names used in other eras or how outsiders might address them. I answered to Sergei. Valentina—Tina now—was Valentina only in her first 'life  and had used many names since. Friedrich went by Ricky today— to all except me. I've never been fond of nicknames.

"We really don't have time to listen to one of your overlong explanations," she countered. "Jeanne, an Eight is our short hand for one of Papa's great-great-great-great-great-great-great-great-grandchildren," she said counting the greats on her fingers as she said them. "Saying all those greats is too time-consuming and, if we leave out one, others might be confused about who we are talking about. The current crop of young people your age generally would be Fifth Rung on the Family Tree."

Dumbfounded yet again, Jeanne shot me an incredulous glance. "Dad, is this for real? All this she's telling me, I mean? Or is she nuts?"

"Every bit is true; Love, describing a family became confusing when most did not die. We didn't always have a long-lived in each life, and, on occasion, none. I guess only the Eights and a few Sevens are at their first family. Not all of our children see The Blue, but enough do—which makes the family uncommonly large. By now, we are scattered around the globe."

My mouth opened to add more, but once you spend three centuries together with someone, you begin to anticipate what they would do. I was certain Valentina would break in before I got uttered a single word.

"Papa, you didn't tell her anything about how we began Blue Talon? Nothing on what we did in the twentieth century? At least show the grace to try to appear chagrined."

In Valentina's mind, their plan to introduce my youngest to the rest of the family solidified months ago. No excuse from me would be adequate satisfy her. Deep down she might be as sensitive about the pain of 'giving up  a child to the family, but she had managed to maintain a business as usual attitude every time. For me, the sadness grew more intense with each new separation. The Brits did their stiff upper lip thing, but my lip lacked any starch at all. Valentina shot an accusing stare at me. Our mutual glare held steady a moment before I sensed my body sagging and gave in.

"Jeanne, Valentina is right. I always have taken too long–but in all fairness, Sweetheart, I lived the longest…gave up more of my children."

Again a nod, but a reluctant one and only barely perceptible.

"The thing is, Jeanne, I wanted to keep you with me longer than circumstances allow. When your mother died, you were not much more than a toddler. Never in all my centuries had had I faced the responsibility of being both Mom and Dad to such a wee mite. Our life was you and me against the world for a long time."

"Not all that little, Dad, I was eight–well almost."

"Na ja, you've always thought you were all grown up, Love."

"Papa…,"Valentina said with an edge to her voice.

"Valentina, Friedrich, and Dmitri came when the Blue generally shows itself. Being the way I am, the way Valentina or any of the others are isn't a certainty. In one family, all my children lived and died as normal people do. Secretly I almost hoped you would be the same, but, as much as I would like to, I am unable to deny your nature anymore."

"You want me to die?"

"Never. That's not what I meant. You know I love you…but, if the day the Blue claimed you were delayed, you'd be mine longer—I'd keep our team together. I'd learned to control somewhat how the Blue affected me and used cosmetic tricks to create an appearance of aging. A few contrived wrinkles allowed me to spend more time in a life before people noticed how young I seemed. To me, being able to live with my children longer, to grow older as they matured into adults, not forced to abandon them or lose them to the family meant a great deal to me, something more priceless than long life."

"I'm not leaving you, Dad."

"I wish that were true."

"Papa, be fair, we always came back, didn't we? None of your children truly abandoned you," Valentine said.

I gave her a reluctant, barely perceptible, nod and put my arm over the shoulder of my youngest before I said, "Jeanne, you need to listen to your brother and sister. Valentina is correct. I tend to reminisce too much."

"Thanks, Papa. Ricky and I will work hard to make up the slack. Jeanne. What I tell you will not be as detailed as Papa—not that any possibility of this might exist. We accomplished more in the twentieth century than we were able to do in the hundreds of years before. Ricky says this is true in part…

"Ricky?"

"Friedrich's modern name," Valentina said her irritation at the interruption apparent. "Partly because we use more efficient methods. Life, in general,  has become faster— swifter transportation, instant communications, twitter. I'll let him fill you in more about Blue Talon later. My job now—she shot me a disgusted look—is to fill in some important highpoints you must understand.  I'll give you some hints of how and where we fit into what the short-lived commonly call history, the less-than-complete accounting of what happened taught in school."

"Blue Talon?" Jeanne burst in again.

"The youngest always asks the questions."

"Our family organization," she explained, holding up her hand to fend off another question from Jeanne. "Why don't you hold your questions until later? This let us will use our time more productively," she said as she sent me another accusing glare, as clear as if she were saying the words aloud. "I'll pick up where Papa left off and give you a quick rundown. We can go back to storytelling later."

The expression on Jeanne's face reflected well her opinion of her sister's efficiency idea. I'd seen the same twisted lip on other of my children, especially on the one standing behind me with the knowing grin No need to turn around to be sure.

Valentina ignored her and began again. "You won't read about us in the history books— if you do, chances are you'll never realize the connection to the family. We prefer to work behind the scenes, although…"

Not yet, *Lyubimaya* a. Too soon.

"…newbies struggle more to understand where they fit in if they pick up only little bits and pieces of what they need to know instead of an organized step by step explanation. For many years, both our day and nighttime activities operated in and out of Philadelphia. Everyone in the Philadelphia knew Papa as the much-in-demand Doctor Kellner; Friedrich gained a reputation as a Main Line attorney, and Hilde, the renowned and rare lady physician, was recognized everywhere in the city. Local citizens saw us as stalwart and respectable citizens. Friedrich served for a time on the city council. His  city government service makes a tale in itself, what with corruption rampant and the oversight of Boss Vare. You can ask him about this later."

"We decided to take on bigger criminals—swindlers, con men, double-dealers—using the Blue proactively, as they would say today. They uncovered, and, I believe, the current term is busted countless illegal or immoral operations. Nights grew fuller, busier, and more intense. The increased effort grew burdensome and, at Papa's invitation, I joined them in the new world to assist the organization and direct a concentrated search for other long-lived members of the family.

"Papa and I devised early search methods to try to locate other family members and offer help to them in dealing with The Blue. Frankly, our techniques likely might seem disorganized or less effective compared to those of today. We had differing goals—Papa wanted to shelter them from the loneliness and isolation he and I had suffered when we thought no others besides the two of us existed while  Friedrich and I, wanted more bodies for what he called his 'Valiant Band of Crime Fighters'."

"So what did you call what you were doing? Lonely Hearts United? The Orphan Army?" Friedrich interrupted.

"Ricky, get serious," Valentina snapped at her brother. "You'll have your turn later. Be fair, we all wanted to find the lost members of our family. Even you would admit we were doing more than simple genealogical research and digging in dusty old documents to make marks on a chart."

"No, you did your digging to make more work for us tracking down them so we wouldn't have time to do our real job."

"You're going to give Jeanne the wrong impression of us."

Then he grinned and laughed. "Tina, you are so bloody gullible. Have been for centuries. I would have thought you'd catch on to me by now."

"Why are you two fighting? And why are you calling each other Tina and Ricky?"

"Ah, Jeannie, we're just playing around. That's what brothers and sisters do. And Friedrich and Valentina seem too long and too stuffy to use today."

"Jeanne, you'll find some brothers never seem to grow up," my eldest huffed, ending the off-track detour.

"Jeanne, my work back then progressed slowly, painfully slow. Remember, no internet existed, no databases, no computers, and no television–nothing we used today. With word of mouth as our only tool, our good intentions led only to frustration. I arrived as one of many emigrating to the United States or Canada from Europe. Papa and I lived in many places, but I couldn't count on family members being anywhere Papa or I remembered."

She stopped for breath stop, and Ricky broke in, "How about we put this on hold for a bit and get a bite to eat? Something to drink? We had a long flight, and all we got was stale peanuts."

"I am a terrible host. Jeanne, will you help me in the kitchen?"

"Sure, Dad."

"You wouldn't by any chance have some good German beer, would you? Americans make excellent coffee, but lousy beer," Ricky said.

### How Blue Talon Worked Before Computers

### Too Soon, Too Fast

I kept my negative thoughts to myself. If they'd let me proceed at my own pace, I would have been able to introduce the events of the past centuries in more manageable bites. Jeanne has what it takes to absorb it all, but with six months more, I would have had those opportune moments  to slip in what my eldest intended to slam into her in hours.

Jeanne's sly glances from the corner of her eye toward the newcomers revealed her curiosity, an intense fascination laced with a few questioning grimaces directed toward me. We lingered over our sandwiches and soda and sat opposite the others at the table. Pushing away her plate, my youngest said to Valentina, "I don't understand how anyone could find anything before the internet, before television."

"Not just finding, keeping in touch was difficult. Even telephones were rare in the early days, and you couldn't put much into a telegram."

"Telegram?"

"Kind of like e-mail, short, but delivered in code, translated and printed."

"Wow, that's cool," Jeanne said.

"Cool or not," Valentina answered. "Remember, back then discovering one of our kind meant long hours of tedious work and volumes paper. Perhaps the best way for me to explain would be to take a page from Papa's book and recount how I conducted one of my successful searches."

"Umm," Jeanne muttered—her disbelief in anything Valentina might say quite clear.

"With what I had to use my connection with Mario was more by accident than intent. I subscribed to all the newspapers I could in order to review the passenger manifests for ships docking in New York. I subscribed to a theory an off chance existed for the lists to be productive. I might recognize a name, or a village, or perhaps a street name from our shared past might appear. I scanned the 'New York Daily" often, checking current and past issues. Staying awake was a hazard I faced reading the dry-as-dust materials. One day I spotted an old list printed in tiny type detailing passengers on the SS Mura and sporting a familiar name, Top of the page: Mario Angelici, father Pietro, final destination San Francisco.

"My heart stopped. Was this Mario, my Mario, the eldest grandson from my Italian family? In 1901, he'd have been twenty-four. Was it possible he'd emigrated  to settle in San Francisco? Without another thought, I packed a satchel and took the next train west."


"You just left? Without knowing for sure if he  was your guy? Without calling or anything? Why didn't you try one of those telegraph code things first?" Jeanne asked, incredulous.

"Sad to say, no, I acted only on impulse," Valentina said, shaking her head. "Directories which contained phone numbers or addresses from other cities weren't plentiful. I took a chance. Five days later, I knocked on his apartment door and recognized him at once. I introduced myself. "Good evening, Mario. My name is Valentina. Perhaps you remember me? May I come in?"

Valentina hesitated, took a deep breath and a sip of water before she continued. After my marathon storytelling with Jeanne, I understood the pause was not about thirst but for her to garner time to gather her thoughts.

"At first, our conversation was awkward," Valentina began.

"No sh…kidding," Jeanne said with rising eyebrows. Valentina ignored her.

"Grandmama, you're dead," he gasped at me.

"Papa, you remember I told you he'd barely entered his teens when I 'died  and joined you all in Philadelphia?"

I smiled my agreement. Valentina had spent hours boasting about her brilliant grandson.

"Once his initial shock at seeing his dead grandmother in his doorway disappeared, I was able to spend time advising him on we deal with the Blue. I shared Friedrich's plans for Blue Talon, explaining why we decided to fight crime on all levels, how an offense became our best defense against Blue addiction. I described how much more we accomplished after we organized the family. He was full of questions, but kept coming back to the way we used the Blue."

"You've experienced how the Blue heals and understand the trigger for these cravings?" he asked, reframing the question each time.

"I answered him, "We think if we take too much of the Blue and do not act against the source, we create an imbalance in purpose. This unstable state  generates our craving and hunger. Why we are the way we are remains a mystery, but, however it happened, whatever caused our…uh…'condition', we all feed on the Blue. Papa thinks we must act to generate an equal and opposite reaction to balance the effect of the emissions. He says the laws of metaphysics must be similar to the laws of physics. I can't say."

"We talked far into the night. I took pity on him and cooked dinner every night. Poor thing, so skinny and no idea of how to prepare a meal—and the street food was frightful. I stayed two weeks with him, and we explored San Francisco together. We spent hours sharing what happened since we parted, updating each other about people and places of his past and mine."

"In those days, the community was one part wealthy entrepreneurs, one part bawdy sea town, and the rest hard-working men and women from all parts of the globe. Full of questions about Blue Talon's work in Philadelphia, he seemed eager to sign on. Telling me, 'perhaps I can do the same thing for Blue Talon right here."

"Before you ask why I choose this story to tell you, Jeanne. I'll ask the question for you. Because not long after my visit the disastrous earthquake of 1906 occurred. Mario had been acting as the arm for Blue Talon in San Francisco. He wrote me frequent and long letters sharing news of events of his chosen city."

Valentina reached into that huge bag she calls her purse, the one that I suspected would hold half of my wardrobe, and pulled out her tablet. She flicked down and began reading. I was not as eager to adopt many of the twenty-first-century gadgets as my children. Valentina prided herself on being up to date.


"Dear Nana, you must know by now of the disaster we suffered in this city. I was up all night roaming the streets trying to pull people out from the rubble. I couldn't tell until I uncovered them if they were dead or alive. I grappled with greedy looters intent on stealing from the injured. I had some close calls, Nana, tangling with armed robbers to stop murders.

'Get your ass off that poor man, you son of the devil.  Don't be shocked. Those days this was often my usual greeting. I spent a week throwing the Blue at ruffians as I tried to help innocent folks. The Blue lingered everywhere, but, with crime everywhere, it posed no problem for me, dissipating as fast as I inhaled the energy I needed. Sad to say, I lived off the hurt of others to keep myself going and prevent additional harm. After eight days of no sleep, I could do no more and collapsed. I slept for a day and a half before I rose to go out again.

My neighbors made me into a sort of local hero. I smiled but inside all I thought of was how many I didn't reach. Thinking back, I realize the extent of what I did. What we do is never enough with things that bad, Nana."


Dmitri spoke up then "What he proved to us was how effective even one person might be in such a huge disaster. I left Philadelphia when the news came across the telegraph and planned to join him. I wanted to help where I could. The streets of San Francisco remained blocked with collapsed homes, bodies, and an enormous fire was burning. I didn't connect with him until weeks later. Both of us temporarily located to San Rafael, a small town to the north. We recognized each other immediately. Auntie, I think, when you meet him, you'd agree, we're hard to miss—seeing him each was kind of like looking in a mirror at myself."

"Auntie?" Jeanne asked. "Who's she?"

"Why you, of course, Great Auntie," he shot back with a smirk.

She sputtered for a while, but fell silent at Valentina's impatient, "Let Dmitri finish, Child."

I registered her about to protest at the reference to her as the 'child', but caught her attention and shook my head slightly at her. "Just listen," I mouthed silently.

"Afterwards, my 'cousin  and I lived together–or near each other – for years until our friends became aware we weren't aging, and they were. The two of us had set up the official West Coast branch of Blue Talon. When we needed to move on, we'd swap. Mario stayed in San Francisco, and I went south to Los Angeles—or vice versa. We'd swap places about every twenty-five years. Later after Valentina and Papa reconnected with Karl in Seattle, we recruited him to cover the rest of the coast.

"Wow, that's cool," came from Jeanne, "I read about the earthqua…?"

Valentina cut her off, too harshly I thought, but appreciated her fear we'd never complete Jeanne's indoctrination.

"Thanks, Dmitri, for stealing some of my thunder," Friedrich put in.

"You're entirely welcome, Uncle," Dmitri mocked with a bow.

"Enough, all of you," I said to Valentina's approving nod. "Let's get back on track. One of you needs to tell her about the idea Hilde had to 'go undercover', as we say now, in the Pinkerton organization. I was about to when you arrived," I added keeping a straight face. My ploy didn't work.

Instead, Valentina shot me the look I'd discovered all my children employed and began her narration again. "We discovered the Pinkerton detectives to be as their press as competent as the press portrayed them, and the agency's strong-arm tactics with

130

unions and public demonstrations reputation equally earned. Hilde proposed planting one of us as a spy into their main office. The mission was to find out more about how they ran their operation. The person we assigned the task needed to provide a detailed picture of their past cases, how they organized their files, who hired them. At that point, only Dmitri and Hector worked with us at Blue Talon. We voted to send Hector. His English might still have a hint of an English accent, although he had over eighty years to practice the American accent, should intrigue the person hiring. He possessed a skill the rest of us lacked. He studied bookkeeping so he'd understand their finances better."

"Hector and my son Alexi are on the same rung on the family tree," explained Dmitri.

"Too many names all at once," my eldest said, cutting him off. "You'll simply confuse her. She'll have plenty of time for all that later. Where are we? The way I found Mario was typical. When a newfound family member discovered others also lived with The Blue, a weight lifted from them. Knowing others enjoyed the same good health and long life and fought its addiction made them seemed like coming home. Learning what they were, how they belonged  freed  them from loneliness, freed them from the fear of being unlike everyone around them. Those I was able to locate in those early days are active members of Blue Talon today."

"Pat yourself on the back often, Sis?  Friedrich teased.

She ignored him. "I didn't find many in the beginning. Too much time and distance separated us, providing few clues to point me in the right direction. Today, I have computer models, trend studies, and a trained, dedicated group of savvy folks on board to help me."

"How does that help?" Jeanne interrupted. "It's not like you've got a name to search by. How many different names did you have? Dad said he had a bunch so I suppose you and everybody else did, too."

"Exactly right, Jeanne," she said, giving me an approving nod.

Sometimes a parent surprises you, Eldest. "I think I've done all right as a single parent, encouraged her to think and question. Heaven knows, she'll need to be able to do this," I said in response.

"Names and places don't help much in finding new family members. Once we identify a person, we can use his or her personal history to point our search toward others. We add what we discover to show trends in the traits we've identified—things like appearance, personality, intelligence, aptitudes. We feed it all into a computer model we put together to display likely candidates," Valentina sighed, shrugging. "Unfortunately, without some reliable genealogy, even with all that, we find one in five hundred if we're lucky; one in a thousand if we're not, who sees the Blue."

"Which means what the geeks give us is only slightly better than garbage," Friedrich put in.

"We need to put an agent on every lead, and most of them don't pan out, Short-timers do most of the legwork, but one of us must follow up on anything promising."

"Short-timers?" Jeanne asked.

"People with one life. We can't say mortals. Who knows, perhaps we're mortals, too. A time may come for us when the Blue's support will no longer be as effective or as available, and we die."

"Some hope that is so," I whisper, thinking no one would hear.

They all pretended they didn't.

### *A full Family Event*

The room filled with a hum as Jeanne's newly discovered family jousted for the flood. One after another, they tested an introductory sentence, but another drowned the person out. In time, Friedrich moved in to dominate the conversation, preening like the stud he fancied himself to be. "Finally, my turn, little sister," he announced. "Kidding aside, Tina does an impressive job at what she does, even though she probably gets too puffed up over it."

"Pot and kettle, younger brother," his sister answered. "Perhaps in another hundred years, your ego will shrink enough to allow someone else into the spotlight."

"Touché, my ever-so-much-older sister."

I sighed. The two came from different families, different times, appeared to be adults, yet they wrangled as if they were cradle mates. Time for me to intervene. "If you persist with this silliness, you'll give Jeanne the wrong impression. Your bickering children charade doesn't paint a proper picture of the responsible persons you are…and you only acting this way because…because I didn't quite finish…"

Two heads spun, two faces incredulous.

"Quite finish? Valentina broke in. "Quite finish—more like almost began."

"Yes, that," my son chimed in. "Papa, Tina wins this round. Let's get on with it. I'll be the adult and take over for a while. Jeanne. Let me ask, you play a sport, right?"

"Uh huh, basketball. I'm a forward."

"Ok, any good basketball coach knows her players know a right and a wrong time to run a pick and roll. Be where you are supposed to be at the right time and you should score, right?"

"Coach says so. She's got this drill we have to do. Like over and over and over.

"The same way we picked the right time to run our infiltration play. Not only the timing but also the referee, meaning the government, was at the other end of the court, letting the players commit all kinds of fouls. No one stopped the robber barons of the time do, as they liked— free throws for the opposing side. Nothing stood between to keep us from zeroing in on the inner workings at Pinkerton. Their operation set the standard for the time making them the real deal. Some modern detectives, police and private, still use techniques they pioneered. Spies, too, by the way. When we began implementing our plan, their practice was to assign agents out to a huge number of cases, different types of cases, different areas. You should be interested to know they were the first to use a woman detective.

"With Hector inside enjoying free access to their confidential files, we learned the strategies used when they investigated crimes or business corruption. Even better, from our perspective, we discovered how they'd branched out into areas outside of crime— more for us to learn. We mastered their field tactics, improved them, and, best of all, they paid Hector to pass on the information to us. A perfect pick and roll, as you basketball players might say."

"I don't get it—why would they pay…?"

"Not literally pay us, Little Sister, Hector got paid for doing a job, and he shared what he learned while working. We learned about when their agents worked for companies and persons meddling in national affairs, who they represented, and a broad picture what was going on behind the scenes in America. The stock market crashed a couple times. Pinkerton's fingerprints turned up on investigations of stock manipulation schemes.

135

Hector found files on the speculators who connived and schemed in the mining, railroad, and various other industries. We duplicated many of their files and kept notes on those we didn't.

"Ironically, the partners loved Hector. They called him a natural. Hector acted as their lead agent on many of their heavy-duty assignments. Jeanne, we got it all."

"I'd call what you did stealing," Jeanne said.

"Today, Jeanne, they'd call what we did industrial espionage. When we started, we called Hector's time in the Pinkerton offices research.  Hector, by the way, is Tina's grandson from her Hungarian family. Her son Ambrus moved his family to England, and Hector grew up in Oxford."

"All this is starting to be too much for me to swallow, Dad,"" she said glancing over at me.

"Na ja, Love. Won't be much longer. This'll make perfect sense to you," I replied, realizing I'd used an expression she'd never heard before, one from my Berlin days. Must be because Friedrich is here. Probably the first time for many unintentional anachronisms.

"Back then folks played by different rules, Jeanne. If they didn't find the goods on you, you were innocent. Companies planted spies in their competitor's businesses often. We even handled one of the spy jobs contracted by our 'boss  at the agency."

"Doesn't sound too nice to me."

Damn, she's managed to make me feel guilty. And, heaven help me, most likely Friedrich as well. He's tried to be ethical, one of the good guys. There've been time when he allowed criticism to bother him too much—his own the worst. Self-doubt turns him into Mr. Doom and Gloom.

136

"The Robber Barons of the 1890's set the rules, Jeanne. We played the game the same as everyone else. Still, you're right. The nineteenth was a tough century in which to live. The poor often starved. Laborers didn't get paid, and children your age and younger worked 12 hours a day if they wanted to eat. From what we learned in our questionable research, we acquired the skills to make us more effective in our efforts to help them. The how seemed less important. We improved on their techniques, at any rate. Partly because we take a longer view on events, much longer."

"What do you mean 'longer view?'" Jeanne asked.

"Besides the obvious, I assume?"

She didn't like everything Friedrich was telling her—didn't believe much—but to her credit, she listened avidly.

"Pinkerton kept files on each individual gang outlining how they operated. Jesse James, Butch Cassidy, the Younger Gang, each had its own file. We analyzed how they committed their crimes. We called what we called their "style" and set up "style" categories. We classified the most common situations by who, when, where, and how crimes were committed.

Today Valentina uses computer simulations to do the same thing in less time than we took to put down a plan. Even with our original paper methods, our reputation rested on our high rate of success in predicting when or where a particular style of crime might occur. So much so some police departments suspected us of planning the particularly outrageous capers"

"What's a caper? Isn't that a word, like from a comic strip?"

"Caper is an old word for a crime. In those days, when we still worked for outsiders, we advised our clients what measures to take to lessen their risk. We used our criminal style categories as a tool and kept meticulous records on our observations of a successful crime. Then, if they didn't listen, they needed to hire my law firm more often and my practice became successful and prospered.

"So what you did was kind of like setting up system to give them less chance of being robbed or whatever—like being a sort of firewall?"

"Not a bad comparison, Little Sis. We advised them on schedules, exits, and entrances, banking, all the different actions a person takes when running a business. If they followed our instructions, they blocked the number of ways someone might use to slip off with the goods to a minimum."

"Did it work?"

"Must have, we're still here. We are still our best client for taking our own advice. Given our special circumstances, we needed to stay out of the spotlight as much as possible, still do. I'll share some of our better cases with you when I have more time."

She nodded, but said, "Whatever."

I'm impressed. Jeanne was hanging on his every word. She would definitely be a major player with Blue Talon.

"After Blue Talon came out in the open," Friedrich continued, "and the headlines of our success from some early clients hit the papers, our business grew rapidly. Hector left the Pinkertons to set up our London office. Hilde's son Augie came on board and staffed Berlin. By 1912, we had offices on both coasts in the US, in Paris, and Toronto as well.

Tina kept uncovering new family members, so I added offices to keep them employed. We hired competent and dedicated short-timers in our locations, as well."

"Blaming me for your employee problems, are you, Ricky? Seems to me I remember you hanging around my desk asking if I'd turned up another family member," Valentina jibed.

"Ja, well, I needed to keep you on point," Friedrich answered. "When the twentieth century arrived, we found our resources stretched thin. When rumors of war began to swirl around, we realized we needed all the experience of the Blue Talon operatives…and hoped we'd have enough.

"War broke out in Europe in 1914. Conspirators from a Serbian independence plot used a guy already dying of TB to shoot the Austrian Archduke. With a single shot, he set Europe off on a war that leaped the continent pitting one group obligated by treaty to defend against another. Those were dark days, Jeanne. I can still picture Papa, standing over his examination table at his clinic,   saying "They're at it again, those egotists in France and Germany. Won't they ever learn? Who can we put in place to help the average citizens of those countries?"

"Not many, Papa," I answered him. "We've got a few, Philippe who's French and Dominik, in the Austro-Hungarian Empire and Charles from Great Britain."

Perfect, we've got both sides covered. Looks like we take a trip back to Europe. Can't leave my grandkids to do this alone, not after the training we perfected here."

"Hilde will step up and coordinate Blue Talon."

"All right then. We go. With little more thought, we committed to give assistance where needed."

Jeanne's head was swiveling back and forth as she took in all the names and place. What I saw was skepticism.

"Our training program was less sophisticated in those days, nothing like what you'll get today, Jeanne, but effective, none the less," I added.

"I'll get?" she asked, a challenge in her tone.

Friedrich ignored her and kept on as if she'd not spoken.

"Lots more effective than most soldiers in the trenches came with. Off we went. Papa who hated war and despised violence and I, who never faced the horror before, headed straight into hell. In time with luck, we found Charles and Philippe. I needed a long time to find Dominik, and, by that time, the trenches were in place. You know about the trenches, don't you, Jeanne? They still teach about those in the schools, don't they?"

Seeing her doubtful expression and remembering the horrors I'd found in France, I interrupted to explain. "Reality dwarfs by ten times the worst of anything you might read, Love. The history books shortchange that war. Picture rats eating decaying bodies, poison gas searing lungs, soldiers executing senseless orders, and men committing suicide."

"Yuk

"The long-lived from Blue Talon patrolled the warrens, dazing soldiers to prevent their intention to release mustard or chlorine gas. We flung waves of Blue to confuse at officers known for their disregard for human life. We moved by ones or twos through areas no one else could survive to drag the wounded to safety and give them a chance for adequate medical attention. More times than I care to remember, we were drained and stole away to heal our bodies in The Blue. We crept across no man's land the next day to the next trench to do the same again. What encountered took all my medical skills. I used everything I'd learned in almost a hundred years. I recall conversation along the lines of "Doctor, thank God you are here. We took a direct hit. Half my men are dead, and most of us are wounded."

"OK, soldier. You help me move the living away from the dead, and I'll do my best. Friedrich, bring the bandages and the iodine. Some morphine if we have any left."

"You remember, Friedrich?"

He nodded and rubbed his eyes. He began to speak again in a husky voice. I guess partly to regain control. "None of us discriminated about who to treat. Good men from both sides inhabited those filthy passages. Papa and I communicated in German when we needed to, English at other times. Others in the family worked with those sharing the language they spoke in their youth. Philippe worked mainly with the French and the Canadians who spoke French. Much of the war happened in Dominik's back yard in Silesia and Poland, in Krakow, where Papa once lived. He watched children from his childhood neighborhood die from stray bullets, but was able to locate some of our family there, Papa's son Aleksander returned, although with a new name, of course. On those times our paths crossed, he passed on news of our sister Gizela efforts as well."

"Who...? Who's she?"

"Hold that thought, I'll deal with that later—we tried to prevent attacks as well as assist the wounded. The German High Command realized a two-front war would involve a long supply line, making a shortage of vital resources likely. To make sure they didn't run short, they deployed huge numbers of soldiers east to resupply what they needed. The loss of life was horrendous. The Russians alone lost over a million men.

The Blue overwhelmed Dominik, Alek, and the others with the intensity and the quantity hanging in the air. Despite their best efforts, the energy seeped into their bodies, and many lost so many years, regressed to young teens. This left them no choice but to leave the area, not sure how much more Blue might be safe for them."

Jeanne's eyes were beginning to glaze over again at all the unfamiliar names and places. When I'd spoke of any of this, she thought she'd been listening to grown-up fairy tales.

"Yeah, well if this is for real, why didn't all of you turn back into teenagers?

I opened my mouth to answer her, but Friedrich spoke more quickly. "I did, some more than others, Jeanne. Only Papa didn't regress."

She spun to face me, "Why not?"

Again, Friedrich answered for me. "Because he used every bit of the Blue he took in. Doctors always treat critical patients as a battle with death. When a doctor loses the fight, he or she forfeits a part of themselves as well. The scene in the trenches was so dire; the wounds so extreme, Papa squandered his own Blue as well as the energy around him trying to save the dying. Night after night, he'd return, drained, exhausted. That's why."

I thought I'd hid my body-numbing fatigue from him. I realized now I didn't.

"Really?" she asked, an open question to us all.

No answer was her answer.

The room lapsed into silence, each of us remembering those days. I finally broke the silence, "Sometimes I can still smell the stench. Hear the screams. Worst was what the gas did to men, left them gasping, coughing up their lungs. None of us were prepared for what we encountered in that hellhole."

Jeanne comes round the table and put her arm around me, comforting me, "But you helped, Dad. That has to mean something."

Jeanne seems to be as sensitive as I am. I always tried to shield her. I know how much harder our life is, will be for her, for someone who is sensitive, who suffers the pain of others.

Friedrich sighed, "We all did what we could, but when the war ended and the ocean was safe to travel again, our mood was dark, discouraged. One fact seemed obvious, in the end, our contribution made little difference. If we were to succeed with our given mission, we needed to bulk up Blue Talon. We were too few, stretched too thin for the job at hand."

"We had our work cut out for us, Jeanne," I said.

"Yeah, but..."

### *Good Try, But...*

"But Dad, that's not fair. How does he come off saying you failed? What's failing about saving lives and helping guys with wounds?"

"We did, but only a few thousand, Love. I'm sure this may sound like a lot to you, but millions lost their lives in that war. Over eight million soldiers died, and, to my knowledge, no one ever made an accurate count of how many civilians were lost. Considering the staggering size of the numbers, our contribution mattered little."

Recognizing the obstinate expression of the face of my youngest, I added, "Granted we did what we could to save many and, in many cases, we made the quality of life more bearable, especially for those who were gassed. In truth, we lacked organization and spread our efforts too thin. Most of all, our numbers were too few. With the conflict so widespread, stretching over many battlefields in as many countries, sheer distance limited our effectiveness. The "cloud" of the Blue we directed toward a neighboring trench might halt the close by shelling, but farther down the line, the artillery shells fell on target. Some of us died more than once just trying to reach the next bunker."

"I remember," said Friedrich. "Papa died twice—being a doctor, he drove himself too hard. Many families welcomed home their son or brother because he was there to treat them. He often operated in places no normal physician would risk going. This not-dying of ours gave us a big advantage. After the war ended though, what did we had we accomplished? With no strategy, no game plan, as they say today, we didn't make much of a difference, except..."

"Except what, Ricky?...Wait—did you say Dad died?" She looked at me. "No way. He's here. He didn't die."

I simply smiled and held up a hand to fend off her comment. She'd understand why later.

"Except…one of the gassed men we aided in Belgium was an Austrian corporal," Friedrich continued, avoiding a response to her outburst. "Philippe to this day has not forgiven himself for using the Blue one  windy October day."

"What's wrong with that? Didn't you do this all the time?" Jeanne asked.

"Without knowing what we had done, we saved the life of a man destined to lead the world into another brutal war."

"Oops."

This was bringing back too many painful memories. I wasn't back in the trenches physically, but emotionally I'd returned. The stench of decaying bodies filled my nostrils and the thunder of distant artillery interfered with my hearing what the others were saying. I swayed and shook myself back to the present.

"Moving on, back in Philadelphia, Hilde welcomed our return," I said, my voice shaky as I picked up the story. "While I was gone she'd hired another physician to cover the workload of the practice I'd abandoned. The doctor agreed to stay on for as long as she wanted because, according to the government, officially I was among the missing. The War Department reported Herr Doktor Kellner MIA in Europe.

"When Friedrich, returned, he came home appearing to be a boy in his early teens and too young to practice law. He slipped into the post a boy of his age might be able to secure—as an office boy. A younger slimmer version of me took his place. Our resemblance proved fortuitous. The real Friedrich practiced law. I only pretended to. He wrote the briefs and authored the legal documents. I acted knowledgeable. To cover for

145

my complete lack of courtroom experience, we hired an up and coming attorney, named Rawle, Mawle, something like that, to handle litigation in court. I pretty much sucked at arguing a case."

"**Whatever**," said Friedrich. "Being office gopher during the day and coordinating the work of the family members of Blue Talon at night, kept me more than busy. I hate to admit an uncomfortable truth, but Tina's good work in unearthing of Papa's descendants swelled our ranks sufficiently to allow me to place at least one company representative on every continent. By the way, Jeanne, in some places, like Southeast Asia, we still make do with one family representative and a few short-timers.

"My head understood, even fortified by our growing numbers, Blue Talon would find our tasks a challenge and a strain to be effective. In in my heart, I hung to the hope if we got enough advance warning, we might succeed," Friedrich added. "But for the first few weeks and still moored in the horror I'd endured in Europe, each night of my new life as an office operative, I treated myself  to my own private pity party. In addition, I so disgusted myself with my poor planning, my lack of organization, and my lousy coordination that I spent every evening after work at the neighborhood pub. Fortunately, Papa pulled me out of the bottle once again. "Pull yourself together, Son," he'd say, "What is done is done. We can't change what happened –you can't alter history."

"Uh huh," said Jeanne, stifling a yawn.

She's too young for an all-day marathon. I tried to signal we needed a break, but Valentina plowed on. "You did," said Valentina. "I'm not so sure others did."

"Maybe not," her brother answered, "but I needed to try if I wanted to stay same. Sober at last, I decided to do what lawyers do best. I called a meeting. Not one of those

146

where everyone argues over how to divide property or the proper way to negotiate a settlement, but a group to decide the future direction of Blue Talon. I sent cables to every ranking family member in our overseas offices and telegrams to the same in North America asking them to come to Philadelphia the following month. Even back then the first law of Big Business as "Schedule a Meeting." Or is that government? Oh well, not important. Not too different, anyway."

"Twenty long-lived attended, representing many rungs of the family. Our conversation shifted between one shared language and another until I called the room to order. I paused and, a voice sang out, "Hey, Sonny, pretty young to be chairing this important a meeting, aren't you?"

"I looked around the table for my heckler and the big grin on the face of Dmitri's son Alexi—far down the family tree from me—gave him away."

Jeanne quickly glanced at Dmitri and got a wink and a grin back.

"I played along and said, "Quiet, kid, or I'll have my sister Valentina spank your butt. You need to show some respect for your elders." I'd expected the wise guy to be Dmitri. Once you get to know him, you'll understand why."

Dmitri smirked. Jeanne grinned back.

"The group howled with laughter at Friedrich's expense," I said turning toward my youngest. "I felt sorry for him—standing there, looking like a kid of 14. Fortunately for him, his voice still sounded like an adult. Alexi appeared to be more like thirty or thirty-five would still be laughing if Friedrich's voice piped in treble.

"Alexi got both the first and the last laugh of our session. The room settled down quickly, Friedrich said. "Everyone understood actual and apparent age meant little in our

147

family. Eight million reasons existed for us to be better prepared for next time…and none doubted another tragic event lay in the future."

"Then, Auntie," interrupted Dmitri pointing into his open mouth, "he actually hung a chart on the wall, lines and triangles to show and illustrate our successes and failures. I thought we'd take more casualties from sheer boredom than we had in the war. He kept droning on and pointing at his bloody chart." He pointed at his mouth again. "Gag me."

My grandson and my youngest shared an understanding look—identical head tips by the twenty-first-century-girl and her eighteenth-century-nephew. Those two will be a pair to contend with in a few years.

Friedrich ignored him. "Once the laughter at my expense died down, I totaled up the results of our efforts. On the plus side, individually we saved several thousand lives by direct intervention, perhaps several thousand more by dulling the enemy's senses to stop the shelling or gas canisters. The times we managed to thoroughly, if temporarily, fry the minds of the attackers, fewer suffered. We influenced field commanders to call for short truces to remove the wounded. Most of you took part, including some newly identified members.

"However, let's face it; we can't describe the operation in any other way than as a poorly planned and executed disaster. We failed to apply even the most basic of our usual techniques for crime. In my opinion, Blue Talon came late to the party and others suffered. To be blunt, we didn't anticipate a conflict of this size. We overlooked groups or individuals who might push a nation to war. We kept files on gangster guns, but nothing on military weapons, or how and who might use them. Our less-than-complete analysis of what made an attractive "haul" from a national or military point of view was deficient. I took—and still take—full responsibility."

I recognized, at that moment, he was reliving Blue Talon's first meeting as he was describing what happened to Jeanne much as I had just returned to the trenches. I remembered the meeting well, not because of an overwhelming sense of guilt and failure by my son, but sympathy for him because he did.

"Ricky always plays the martyr card," said Dmitri. "You don't have to beat yourself up Unc. You stepped to the plate, got us all together to plan. None of us came off without mud on our boots. Papa, as usual, sat in to offer advice."

I smiled. He said advice like it was something rather obnoxious. The way I remembered the day, the meeting had been lively, everyone chiming in. "We need to learn more from history, that's for sure.  Suggestions like, 'We need to find out which countries are always getting into it, which ones have interlocking treaties. National agreements can't all be secret, and, even if they are, we need someone in place to find out.''

"I was glad Papa made the meeting. He's always been able to quiet a room," said Valentina. "Everyone respected him. A wave of his hand and the noise of everybody talking on top of each other ended. He didn't need to raise his voice. He pointed out the issues we needed to consider. If we were able to accumulate files on every country, become knowledgeable about their economy, their history, their loves, and hates, who would read and interpret the file contents. Who'd update them? What triggers do we recognize feed a disaster like the one just ended?"

"They all agreed. "You're right. At least from where I sat, I'd say starting a war took more than one disgruntled Serb," from a voice at the end of the table.

"However, Tina didn't agree," said Friedrich.

Her comment was, "Perhaps not, well, most likely not one, but, perhaps all it takes for one country is one man to put events in motion, I doubt Princip intended to ignite a worldwide war, but the killings still happened. What scares me would be a scenario where someone intentionally maneuvers to cause a war or take over a whole continent."

"She had support from Hilde and Cossette, but I didn't buy her theory. I argued, "How the hell do you expect us to do that, Tina?"

She came back with, "I don't know, but I think we need to try."

"A thick silence followed. With the sheer size of the problem, the demands on my family to influence any action needed more resources, where should we start? I was flummoxed," Friedrich trailed off."

"Dad always tells me when you've got a problem; the best place to start is at the beginning."

Friedrich glanced over at me, "Still using that old saw, huh?"

"Good advice for a long time now, Son."

"The best as we found out later."

"So what did you do?" Jeanne asked.

"Believe it or not, Little Sis, the first thing we did was to buy a warehouse on Cuthbert Street in Philly."

"Why?"

In the next little while, we shared our recollection of the discussion at that meeting and explained the importance the building played for Blue Talon.

"If we're going to attempt this, we need a plan," Hilde began.

"Of course, that's a given. We must remember though, no matter how we decide to map out our strategy, the sheer volume of the paper will be so great with the size of our office , we won't be able to house even a tiny portion."

"Fine, fine, I hear you, but let's not get bogged down with mundane details, strategy needs to come first."

"No argument, Hilde."

"Before you ask, Jeanne,  remember we had no computers, Telephones for international calls wouldn't happen for over a decade. Any of the family outside of North America faced at least a week-long voyage to reach either of our coasts," Friedrich said.

"I don't understand...."

"Wait a bit. I'll tell you. We put down what we needed to monitor: the type of government, the educational level of its citizens, everything we could think of with the economy..."

"Why?"

Count on Jeanne to ask questions.

"We need to know what they manufactured. If they made any significant changes. For example, a factory making women's shoes converting to heavy men's boots. Not too many soldiers go out in sling back sandals, but many march in boots."

"I get it," she said with another yawn.

Tina chimed in, "We needed a department doing nothing but track crop output by region and by country. Note if the harvest failed and folks might need to draw on reserves. When times are tough, people start peering over the fence to check for something to take from a neighbor. We decided to collect records of the weather to see if a certain type of day was better or worse for an attack. Everything on a particular country goes into their folder, ditto a larger territory. Friedrich got out some of his graphs showing where long time hostilities exist between regions, countries, and people of one religion versus another."

Jeanne yawned in unison with Dmitri.

"I told them, 'Don't forget the psychological part of the mix," Tina added. "The attitudes of the people, how they feel, what worries them. I'm sure how people perceive their situation is the key. Of course, they came up with some objections, but, finally agreed I had a point. We added Sigmund Freud's ideas in the mix. After this heated meeting, in the end, we agreed everyone should assume the responsibility for monitoring their own area and making reports. They were all in, enthusiastic.".

Then Friedrich said, "Ok, I'll go along. I think we are biting off more than we can chew, cliché or not. Good thing we have a thieving scoundrel for a father so at least we should have enough money," he joked, trying to lighten the mood."

"I took offense at that, Son," Papa said with a smile, "True as it may be. The Bey not only didn't know I'd made off with his stash, by how he's too long gone for him to object how we use  it.

Tina permitted herself an uncharacteristic giggle, "The thought of you in curved toe slippers flinching his goodies still makes me laugh. I think Papa has more than repaid the debt since."

Jeanne spun toward me with an upset expression. "Dad—"

She was not so amused.

### *Too Little Too Late = Disaster*

Jeanne leaned over closer to me and asked, "Dad, did you really steal that Bey guy's stuff?

"Guilty as charged, Love," I whispered. My reply remained unheard by anyone else, drowned out by Friedrich plowing on detail after detail. I tried to catch his eye. My bleary-eyed daughter showed clear signs of boredom.

"Jeanne, most of the paper shuffling stayed on Cuthbert Street, but the head of each office recruited short-timers to assist with more thorough investigations in their area," Friedrich said. "Of course, officially, we expected our clients to assume we'd branched out and were offering our services for research investigations for universities or companies wanting to do business in a region.

"The "Research" angle provided a good cover for us to tell our short-timers. For securities sake, agents used couriers to deliver monthly-encrypted reports. Alek, Papa's son from his Polish family, turned out to be a bloody genius. He devised this gadget, a code machine, if you like, with a randomized set of gears. We installed one in every office. Whenever a steno typed a report, the machine changed her words into encrypted gibberish. The key setting making the contents readable lay hidden in the date of the dispatch."

"What's a steno?" Jeanne asked.

I stifled a mental chuckle. Of all my children, Friedrich was the slowest to admit women were as capable, more capable in my opinion, as a man—family members excepted, of course.

"Um…steno is an old word for what they call executive assistant these days. Back then women held mostly steno jobs."

"Why? Couldn't any men handle the work?"

"Gender isn't as important as the job getting done," my son said in a defensive tone. His body language broadcast his impatience with her question. He continued, "We set a date to meet once a year. After the first meeting, we changed our location each year so the wrong people wouldn't notice. We put together a better organization than the government—better organized and better informed. We tried to be discrete, but meeting seemed worth the risk because good ideas surfaced. "

"And did your bright ideas work?" she managed, stifling another yawn.

"Somewhat, sometimes, for a while."

"A while?"

"Don't get me wrong, Little Sis, we had our successes."

"Don't call me Little Sis. I don't like it. I'm nearly 15 and lots taller than Tina."

"Fair enough," Friedrich answered. "Let me answer your question. We realized this mass of information gives us a heads up in predicting an event well in advance. Every office kept a detailed record of significate events in their region and sent in reports at least four times a year."

I tried once more to catch Friedrich's attention. Jeanne was showing signs of more than simple boredom. In her words, "Enough already." He shifted on his chair and ignored my signal.

"Most of the time," he admitted. "Not long after we put our system into place, our analysis indicated the possibility of an imminent showdown between unemployed

155

veterans and the government. The trends we'd identified proved spot on. We sent family members to Washington DC hoping the Blue would calm the crowd. Public sympathy lay with the veterans. The agents mingled with the crowds, chatted with the veteran using clouds of calming Blue in an effort to avert major violence.

"What we didn't anticipate was the President ordering up troops or a rogue general mounting an unauthorized attack on his own. Without our actions, the mob may have turned to more intense violence. We deal with a higher death toll I'm sure, but in the world of woulda-couldas, how many dead? Who knows. We realized predicting was easier than preventing a disaster. Frankly, we didn't have the strategy or the tools to be proactive."

"Like knowing the team you coach would be playing in Thursday night's basketball game but not the plays you need to win the game?"

"Pretty much, Jeanne, pretty much."

Jeanne bent over and whispered in my ear, "Dad, how much longer is this going to take? This is getting boring, capital B boring—and besides I've got homework to do."

"Only a little longer, Love."

Dmitri took over, "After that, it seemed overnight the whole world turned into one big overfilled septic tank. Shi—-stuff all over. The worldwide economy pretty much tanked. All over the globe, people were out of work. Inflation made things worse. In Germany, for example, housewives needed a wheelbarrow to carry enough money to buy a week's groceries."

"You're kidding, right?"

"Nope, real story. No work meant no food. Kids went hungry, families lost their homes, and their anger grew. Think about what happens at your school, Auntie. When folks get mad, they look for someone to blame."

"All bullies at my school do."

"Yup, same thing with countries, and we sat, watching from the cheap seats when all hell broke loose."

The room fell silent for several minutes, then Tina caught my nod toward Jeanne and said, "Ricky, want to take five?"

"Thanks, Tina, sounds good. We all need to get out and stretch a bit."

"Dmitri, how about you and I take Jeanne for a walk? I saw a place to pick up a latte down the street? For old time's sake? Like in Berlin?" she suggested.

"I'd like that."

"Can I have some of that nummy hot chocolate?" my youngest asked as they headed out the door. I'd love to be a mouse and see how she dealt with people she'd never met who claimed to be related to her.

After their voices died out, Friedrich sagged back in the recliner with weariness. His hands shook, and he braced them against his knee to stop the tremor. We sat together silent for what seemed an intolerable length of time. My son's distress was evident, but neither of us broke the hush. Instead, we both drifted in our own thoughts.

I'd seen him in this morose frame of mind before n the times I'd gone with Friedrich to assist him in his role as head of Blue Talon. Every time he needed to relate those operations where he played a major role, he relived his past and beat himself up for what he didn't do. I suppose I'm as guilty at times, so I understand his self-reproach. He could only do so much. If only he would consider his successes as well. Too late now, but I wish I'd told Jeanne more of Blue Talon story and spent less time sharing my earlier memories.

Friedrich handled administration, analysis, and the law far better than most, but when he took on the task of sitting down with newly discovered family members or meeting the young uninitiated children when they came with Mom or Dad to HQ, this took a toll. As the head of Blue Talon, he needed to deliver the "speech." The speech when kids learned their lives were not theirs to direct, and they must suffer frustrations only others of their kind will experience and understand. Too often, we both detected the innocence of childhood fade from young eyes when they realized they were forever different. Only those sudden glimmers of hope in one who lived in isolation made the process tolerable. Lately, nearly all the audience for Friedrich's speeches had been children. He's appointed himself messenger. I wondered if he was trying to assuage his guilt.  His rational was, if these unwitting family members met the head of the organization and learned how important their task would be, their fears at encountering their destiny might be more tolerable.

After centuries, I should be able to be dispassionate, more objective. He had always found this difficult. Most days he's born the weight of his position well. Efficient, too, God knows. Why did I dawdle with Jeanne? I should have shared more of the Blue Talon story and spent less time with my earlier memories. I left the burden for Friedrich. Maybe because…

Friedrich's voice interrupted my thoughts. "What is wrong with me today, Papa? Maybe it's the dreams I've been having lately about those dark days in the first part of the twentieth century."

He sighed, "I keep dreaming over and over what happened around us, and how we spent our time when our country seemed in a lead-up to war. I spent last evening with painful, frustrating scenes infiltrating my sleep and robbing me of any rest. I've shared this with you before, but in past weeks they've plagued me more often."

He leaned back in the recliner, closed his eyes, and rubbed his forehead. "It's like I'm time traveling, back in the past, sitting as I used to do at my desk reading reports, giving orders."

His voice trailed off. I wished I could join him, but a person's thoughts and memories remain their own. Still, for me to conjure up the sight of him sitting in his cubbyhole of an office wasn't difficult.

"Tell me about last night, Son."

"This time the dream was so real, Papa. As if I were watching part of an old movie on TV."

"So tell me what took place."

"I was sitting in my office. I fingered the texture of the ink blotter on my desk; saw the black smudge on my index finger from the carbons I'd been reading. Mary, my short-timer steno came in and placed a pot of jonquils next to the tin inkwell. She said, "You never seem to get out of the office, Bossman, Today is such a beautiful spring day, I thought I should bring a bit of spring in to you, so I stopped at the flower stall and picked these up."

"Thank you, Mary. This place needs a little cheer."

"She smiled and left. I retrieved the cover letter from Hector's London report from the stack in front of me and began reading. I read the letter aloud. I was right there, Papa. Everything seemed so new and so real."

159

Greetings Uncle from the land of fine pubs and foul food, (Just kidding.) The big buzz here is our wouldn't-be-king, the Duke of Winsor, and his doxy are visiting in Germany hobnobbing with Hitler and his ilk. Good riddance to bad rubbish, although Nazi sympathizers are becoming more open. Half the people think war will never come and the other half fears it will. Overall, the economy still shows an upward trend. I've attached all the charts and graphs you and your minions could hope for.

However, two things continue to be worrisome from our point of view: Chamberlain continues his policy of appeasement with Adolf. Money remains too scarce to mount an adequate defense should we need to do so. Can't fire a bullet from a broomstick. Chamberlain's course of action is popular with the people, especially those with their heads in the sand and their ass in the air. I tried, am trying, to arrange to have one of our agents close enough to him, partly to influence him if we can and partly to gather our particular brand of secret intelligence. So far no luck. We believe we need to get our kind into the public school tie set to be imperative.

My concern with the direction of the country grows now. Chamberlain tied his political fortune to a lunatic on the continent. However, Winston Churchill that mixed breed fellow—he's American and British—comes on strong trumpeting his misgivings about the current regime in Germany. He's starting to get followers despite his conservative economic views.

Things must be getting worse in Germany itself because huge numbers of Jews immigrating to our island. Immigrants need a guaranteed job waiting for them. For anyone to find work can be a problem with our high unemployment. My next-door neighbor has an attorney for his yard boy. Many of the jobless see them as a threat.

On the hopeful side, agricultural production is up. I've attached a chart listed by type of crop. I worry, however, because the country imports nearly half of what it needs.

(Sg) Hector.


"I put the paper down and called Mary in, "Mary, can you ask Filip to stop by?"

"Sure, Bossman."

"In my dream I saw Filip, one of Gizela's twins, bound in, "What can I do for you, Uncle?"

"I glanced right and left to check if Mary were still in earshot, Short-timers would not understand our family relationships, where the uncle clearly appeared younger than the nephew.  Show a little good sense, Filip. Low profile, remember?"

"Sorry."

"I handed him Hector's note. "  I'm worried. How many were we able to slip into the bowels of the Third Reich? We got one on General Rommel's staff, one with the unenviable task of housekeeper for Himmler. Papa and Hilde are coordinating miscellaneous folks in Munich and Berlin. No luck in getting anyone with the big guy. He doesn't seem to care much for women. One lives with him, but, so say the rumors, they aren't 'together" so to speak. We tried placing one of our agents as her maid, but Eva, I think her name is, doesn't make any of the important meetings."

"I run my hands through my hair, "We've got to do better somehow…I hope we're there soon enough this time."

"He nods. He left, and I saw myself picking up the next report on the stack."

"My memories of those days are no happier, Son, but what done is done. We need to move on."

Friedrich said nothing as if I had not spoken.

April 5, 1938, Hong Kong

"Esteemed Uncle, I send greeting with a most-heavy heart, News has been slow to reach us, so I am sure by now you know Japan attacked us here in China, We now possess reports, verified reports, of unbelievable acts committed against the inhabitants of Nanking. Thousands are dead. Women, in particular, suffer attacks and disappear to an unknown fate. Bodies line the streets. One man who fled to Hong Kong, seeking British protection, tells me Japanese soldiers are using living Chinese for bayonet practice or simply for sport. Young medical students came to China to use fresh cadavers for anatomy training. Some say, too fresh, still living.

"Over 40,000 bodies now rest in mass graves. Most businesses no longer exist. The Japanese burned or looted many. My brother Da Kang will send future reports when he can. The horrific treatment of women leads me to the decision to leave home and seek refuge for me and my daughter with my grandfather William in London.

"I must admit the statistics and other information attached seem far less detailed that what I usually send you. Much I obtained came from local businessmen who now are dead or fearful and leaving Hong Kong.

Sg: Ai Lee"

Friedrich's eyes moved back and forth as if he were reading an unseen paper.

"September 30, 1939,  Warsaw

"Friedrich, I fear this may be my last report for a long time. I hope not forever. Even to send a coded message courts danger. I cannot jeopardize the life of a courier in the future. The Germans overrun our homes and our country. They commandeer all the big houses to serve as barracks for their officers leaving the more modest ones to barrack their men.

Women are afraid to go out in the street. The soldiers force our Jewish citizens to sweep the streets, clean the cesspools. If any resist or complain, they shoot them. Looting of Jewish shops and homes is widespread, and I am ashamed to say some Polish men participate.

"Rumors fly German SS commandos herd the Jews together and march them off to who knows what fate. My contact in the countryside near Krakow reports they shot hundreds of Jews. In Chelmo, they drove mental hospital patients out into the garden and killed them all.

"The Soviets took over the eastern portions of our country. Those who know say their soldiers are more brutal and greedy than the Germans.

"I'm told the Germans killed or captured most soldiers of the Polish army. They join the Jews in performing undesirable tasks. The SS (a monstrous and brutal division of the German forces) target intellectuals, and thus I, too, must go into hiding when I finish this communication. I plan to create a new identity and assist in the underground resistance. We are in total 10, this being all the family members in the area of Poland and Czechoslovakia. We will attempt to obtain radios and send short bursts of intelligence when we can.

"I attach what we have assembled to date.

"I know you are no believer, my brother, but pray for us

anyway.

Gizela"

I could barely pick out what he said, his whisper was so faint.

"For you, Sweet Sister, I'll make an exception. Not sure where our kind fits in—the

dark side or the light, but a prayer even from a non-believer can't hurt.

'May 9, 1940, Munich

You would not know your countrymen, Friedrich, Every night I listen to hate-filled speeches at Munich rallies. What they say, and how the crowds applaud and fling that ridiculous Nazi stiff-armed salute sickens me. No more tarrying at sidewalk cafes these days. I am ashamed to say I cannot get near to this place called Dachau. The Blue is too strong. Remember how we fought its effects in the trenches. You cannot imagine how much stronger, more intense the cloud surrounding the compound appears to be. I sense a primitive, animal malignancy mingling with the Blue.

I fear I might not be able to resist its lure and become as confused as those we target. I take what I can handle and try to stop as soon as possible. Today I happened upon a brown shirt beating on a young man. I stopped him, using the Blue, and sent him on his way. I did all I could to heal the man, so young, no more than a year or two out of his teens. I believe the wound may result in the permanent loss of one arm.

He told me, 'Thank you, Mein Herr, but I am a socialist. All you did for me may be undone tomorrow if I am found out again. I need to leave this country. At least, thanks to you, I have today. Nearly all members of my party were taken early on, and few still live, if any.'

He struck me as honest, so I took a chance and gave him a contact name. Any who oppose the regime are already in SS custody or afraid to say anything. The most horrendous things often begin with the kids. All young people are required to join the Hitler Youth, and many become such fanatics. The son of a pharmacist with whom I struck up an acquaintance turned in his father. No one says anything, but I suspect he is dead.

Every day, more Slavic speaking men and women appear on the streets cleaning and doing what the Germans no longer will do. Some are being "rented" to factories as workers. I routinely pummel their guards with The Blue. On occasion, I have gained access to do the same from within. They treat them no better than slaves. I understand well the life of a slave.

More and more troops are massing and marching west. I must say, although I wish it were not so this army is impressive, mechanized, well trained, and well-armed. I believe France and the Low Countries will not be free much longer.

As you requested, I make every effort to place our people with high-ranking members of the SS and the Wehrmacht. Some are promising to be good sources of information.

Read over the troop counts, inventories of long-range artillery attached.

With all my love,

Papa


"16 June 1940 Paris

Today Marshall Petain addressed the nation. France is no more. In its place is a puppet regime headed by someone we mistakenly called a hero. Anything he does is at the direction of our occupiers. The swaggering troops of bosche march freely in the streets, and rumors fly Der Führer himself will come to gloat. Already French girls are making eyes at the newcomers.

More Blue swirls through the neighborhoods, densest around the black uniforms of the SS. I personally observed French citizens taken from their apartments to Gestapo headquarters. My neighbor counted himself fortunate to return home. Most, I understand, do not.

I do not wish to give you the impression our citizens are reconciled to the occupation and accept an inferior status. They are not. Already a resistance is forming and I, of course, will do all I can to assist. Uncle, if you strive to place people who can influence the states to enter the war, I urge you, press hard. Britain is all that stands between Hitler and his plan to rule all of Europe. I will no longer provide anything in writing to you, so please monitor the transmissions in the high-frequency range of 3100 MHz coming from France. I've attached my routine, double coded.

Intelligence gathering is increasingly hazardous, and the bastards don't care if they take women and children if some asshole collaborator betrays them. They use little kids to carry messages with the hope they will seem too innocent to be part of the resistance. The hardest thing now is you can trust no one. The Bosch pay well, and we've got our own supply of anti-Semites who infiltrate resistance groups.

Au revoir, Philippe"


"When I finished, Phillipe's report, I awoke with a start, Papa. Got to get more sleep. I'm useless like this. The worst thing is I feel the guilt all over again. I put every family member I sent into danger. I, and only I, was responsible. I sent them into danger, while I still lived comfortably, in a land free of war. Well fed. Safe."

I remembered that letter I sent so long ago from Munich. The revulsion and shame for one of my adopted countries were as fresh as when I sealed the envelope. Poor Friedrich.

"You can't take hold everything, Son. You need to let the hurt, what I'd call unfounded, guilt go away. Remember, I'm always available whenever you need to talk."

"I will, Papa," he said, his eyes seeing something visible to no one else.

### *Jeanne Learns about her Family*

*Having a serious talk at a coffee shop seems wrong to me, but then, what the heck, why not?*

"Tina, why does Ricky act so whacked? I don't get it. Aren't old people the ones who should be losing it or getting tired? I supposed he is over thirty and all that, but still. Is he sick or something?" I asked sipping my hot chocolate.

Dmitri chuckled, sat back, and waited for Tina to answer.

"No, Jeanne. He's not sick. He just let his job overwhelm him again. Being the head of Blue Talon is a huge responsibility. He's been in charge for over 100 years, and sometimes, he loses his cool—if that's the right expression. He doesn't sleep, sometimes for days, and relies on the Blue to keep going, even though Papa drummed into him the danger he faced misusing by doing this. You wouldn't know, but Dmitri and I expected today to be a bad day for him. His son died one year ago. Mark was fifty-five."

"Ricky had a kid who's older than Dad? That's crazy. Are you all nuts?"

"No, Auntie, we're not," Dmitri said, "although Tina might may seem a little weird. She's older, lots older than Ricky."

"You all seem nuts to me," I said and gave him what Dad calls 'my evil eye.'"

Dmitri sorta smirked, but Tina didn't even smile. *Gag me, she is just too serious.*

"Ricky and I were working at our new western headquarters in Santa Barbara when the accident happened," she said as if I didn't say a word. "His son worked as an underwriter for one of the international insurance companies and lived in London at the time. An idiot American with too much to drink forgot what side of the road he should be on and hit Mark's car head-on. He died on impact. Ricky took the news hard. We all

*Claws of the Blue*

understood Mark, being a short-timer, would die eventually, but Ricky counted on him being around lots longer."

"The funny thing was… they hadn't seen each other for over ten years. Ricky kept in touch with his son by phone or webcam. He kept the clarity level low and assumed Mark wouldn't notice how young he looked. Uncle Ricky set the camera for long shots, walked around the room, always wore a baseball hat shadowing his face," Dmitri explained.

"Everything you're telling me—this whole deal seems so unreal. I'll ask Dad. He'll give me the real answer. At least *he'll* tell me the truth."

"No one finds accepting what being part of the family means at first, Jeanne," said Dmitri. "I stumbled around like an idiot for a long time, trying to make sense of my life, the Blue, what happened to me. The fact is, until my mother, Tina, found me and explained what our kind is like, I didn't have a clue."

"Other than no way do I buy Tina is your mother, I kind of get that part. What I don't get is the "our kind" part. Well, not really, but I'll go along. I get that Ricky's son dying made him sad, but why's his job so hard? From what I heard, he just sits behind a desk and drinks coffee most of the time. Am I wrong?"

They both laughed but got serious again almost at once. "Physically, Jeanne, you're right, most of the time his butt is planted in his chair. Not that he never carried his weight in the field, but each time, we soon realized he needed to be where the family needed him most—in the office at headquarters. In the early years of Blue Talon, his, the way his mind worked was the only tool we had to analyze the mounds of reports and the newspaper clippings pouring in from around the world. Now, of course, we use computers, but back then, we relied on Ricky to identify trends and spot patterns. He excelled at it far more anyone else—and, in many ways, we still do."

"My dad does things like that all the time."

"He does, Jeanne," said Tina, "but none of us match Ricky's skill at making sense of a jumble. The pieces in the puzzle always seem to fall in place for him, and he did—does, the same thing with places and events. He puts a great deal of thought into his decisions. Everything from when and where family members go on a mission to making sure we keep sufficient funds on hand to do what he asks. Every agent can count on a complete package for an assignment. Our father would rather be a doctor. Doctors, as a rule, make poor businessmen, and worse computer nerds, I'm afraid."

*Yeah, right, our father. Ha!* Aloud I asked, "Package?"

"Names, place, background information, the purpose of their mission. Everything they need in detail."

"If you'll pay attention, Tina is trying to tell you every calamity, every unspeakable deed, and every horrendous action happening anywhere in the world passed over his desk. This hasn't changed in the last hundred years since we formed Blue Talon. He can't escape from reality. He collects facts and statistics, analyzes them, and decides the action to take. All the hard stuff, the things no one else wants to touch is his. We count on short-timers to interpret food supply or similar events. Ricky's job is to record and dissect the way people interact, how they respond to a shortage or to an event generating Blue—always involving bad people, worse acts. As for me...I find confronting the dark side of humankind easier—and more fun."

"Why's that, Dmitri?"

"Remember the story Ricky shared with you this morning about the soldiers' march? Poor guy, he never catches a break. Most of the crap he deals with is far worse."

"What would be…?"

"What would be worse? Okay, my turn to share. I might get you to understand if I share one of my nastier experiences. Hang onto your hat. Auntie, and come with me to wartime Leningrad."


"No one ever called winter in Leningrad a picnic, but we'd been there on this mission for a while, and I should've gotten used to the cold. The interior of the building we'd chosen did little more than shield us from the wind—we'd burned the floorboards and furniture in our hut to keep warm. The Germans the city surrounded for months. I consoled myself with the smug knowledge the SS SOBs outside the walls still wore summer uniforms. Papa and I…"

"Dad was there, too? Come on—get real. No way"

"Hush, children should be seen and not heard," he said.

I shot him the 'look', but his story sounded a whole lot more interesting than Ricky's, and I shut up and let him talk. He's a better storyteller, for sure.

"Papa and I wore so many layers we resembled barrels with legs. Our two outer layers we'd borrowed from residents who starved to death. Some so-called enforcers threw the dead bodies into mass graves and left them naked in a heap. Even ordinary citizens stripped the shirts and shoes off  of a corpse figuring the dead didn't need them. Sergei and I could understand the needy trying to survive, but the hoodlums who robbed the dead to sell their belongings on the black-market, nope. "

Tina broke in, "Jeanne when we are on assignment, we always use only first names, not a relationship. Better that way for the short-timers."

"Ok"

"Can I talk now, Auntie?"

I wanted to stick my tongue out at him, but I just nodded.

"Okay, back to Leningrad, Auntie. No more questions—your job is to listen"

Dmitri was a world-class storyteller. He painted such a good picture with words I was there with them.


"I don't understand why this city hasn't been overrun, Sergei. The local cadre is no better than the commissars who shipped nearly everything back to those bastards in Moscow."

"Papa sighed. "In my opinion, we are at least somewhat responsible. The quantity of Blue we've floated over them day after day affected them, made them indecisive and less likely to attack. We've slowed them down and stopped their advance, but now we face a stalemate. The soldiers' orders are they are not to retreat no matter how cold or hungry they were or how dire the situation. If they do, they face summary execution. Those Nazi troopers have little more food than we do. We can thank Moscow for the order to destroy anything, which might help the Germans. Bridges are down; most of the grain burned. My guess is they're out of gasoline, if the numbers of idle machinery are any clue. Those panzers don't run well without fuel."

"True enough, but the people inside live on less. Every day when I go out, I step over the bodies in the street. Half the time men are fighting to scavenge their ration cards. Why anyone would want to eat what they call bread is a mystery to me. Sawdust and rat crap—

less poop lately, they're eating the rats. You know how careful we need to be when we

go out. Half the population is wonky from hunger. Some of the bodies we stepped over

weren't whole—missing big pieces as if a butcher had carved the carcass for food."

"Not everyone can be nourished by the Blue, Dmitri."

"I guess, but what they can get barely keeps them alive. Pisses me off when I spot

someone selling black market stuff. Food they've hoarded and not shared. No idea where

they expect to spend the money they get. Even the black marketers don't have an appetite

for sex anymore."

"Worse than the trenches, Dmitri. At least there, one could count on your mates to

back you up. Here they turn on each other, and the Red Army kills as many civilians as

the Germans."

"At least some food is coming in. Since the lake froze, trucks can travel over the ice."

"Not much, I'm afraid, and most get snapped up by the black market dealers. The

people don't see much."

"Terrible, what has happened to our country, Papa. Our days under the Czar seem

better in comparison."

"What's sad is we can use the Blue to ease their pain, but, without enough to eat, all

we do is blunt their hunger and pain."

"If the Nazis hadn't been so brutal, we might not be witness to this siege. Shooting

whole villages, shipping the Jews off to prison camps, taking their food and their animals.

If they'd been a bit more civilized, the people would have rallied to fight with them against

the Red Army. Individual soldiers shared their rations with families, bandaged a wound,

175

but the orders from Berlin were clear. Consider Slavs of no consequence, subhuman and fit only to serve the superior race."

"Look, Papa, the sun is rising. We've got six hours until sunset and the temperature drops."

"Grab the knapsack. I'll check the street."

"I followed Papa, stepping into his footprints from the last night's snow. I'll switch places with you when you get tired."

"He nodded, and we rounded the corner, following our usual route to keep a distance from the party officials. We avoided neighborhoods where the Germans would gain a clear shot and stopped at those buildings where we used Blue the day before.

"How goes it, Maxim? Feeling any better?"

"A little, Doktor, the herb tea you gave me seemed to work."

"Good news, Maxim. Take care."

"We went in building after building, checking on those from yesterday, stopping to bathe others in the Blue, this was our world. The sun began to sink by mid-afternoon when we moved toward the illicit market on the outskirts to replenish our Blue. In the distance, we heard thunder.

"Thunder? In the middle of winter?" I asked Sergei.

"Artillery, Dmitri. Telling us, we must die soon and slip out during the night. If the Red Army arrives and finds us looking this healthy, they'll shoot us. Shooting is all right. We've both dealt with this before. I worry more they'd decide to burn our corpses. I'm not so certain we'd come alive again, even with endless amounts of the Blue—if our bodies no longer exist."

"What do we do, Papa? I'm not keen on being toasted like a marshmallow."

"With as thin as you are, you'd be more like a slice of toast."

"I glanced at him, incredulous, and asked myself, "Did he actually just make a joke about us becoming crispy critters?"

"Papa kept on talking, not waiting for my reaction, but I spotted the smirk he tried to hide. " I think now we go back to our cellar, take stock of what we have. I'm not excited about being first in line to volunteer for the burn unit."

"And then?"

"Then we'll see."

"I followed him retracing our footsteps in the snow. When we neared our cellar, I took up a nearby board and used the edge to brush off any sign we'd been there. Predators lived inside the city as well as outside. Better be overcautious than a brave casualty."

"You tell much more exciting stories than Dad. You almost make me believe. 'Course you ruin it by calling Dad Sergei. That's not his name."

I didn't like the way Dmitri grinned at me with such an 'I've-got-all-the-answers" expression. Did he really think I'd buy into all this?

"Auntie" he began.

"Really, Dmitri? We studied European history last year and nothing in the book was even close to what you said. "

"I'm not surprised, Jeanne. The victors write the story of what happened. Even to hint the Germans were not worse in every way than the Allies meant not everyone fighting for

Germany wasn't responsible for the atrocities committed. Believe me, there was enough wrong-doing on both sides in that war. In most wars, as a matter of fact."

"Hmm."

"Can I finish my story of what a big hero I was now?"

Tina snickered behind me. "I guess," I said.

"Okay, then. Listen up. We're getting to the good part."

### *The Good Part*

"Leningrad sounds really yucky, Dmitri. Why were you there anyway, assuming I believe you, which I don't, at least I don't think I do."

"Not to sound all high and mighty, Auntie, but Blue Talon agents go where they're assigned. Our first language, well almost first for Papa, was Russian, so duh"

"You speak Russian?"

"Deed I do, Auntie. I'm not just unbelievably handsome. I'm talented. I'm smart. In short, I am a man of many talents."

I crossed my eyes. He was so full of himself. "That's it? The whole story?

"Not hardly."

Dmitri had this funny look on his face, and he acted as if he were back there. Like Dad says, some folks let their imagination run away from them.

"Back in our hut, I sat working on a scrap of pigskin I'd found the day and was attempting to cover the hole in my shoe. Leather was getting harder and harder to come by. Many boiled the shoes of the dead to make soup. Nothing I would recommend. The taste, as I remember, was foul and disgusting. Nothing to keep on the menu.

"I watched Grandfather Sergei, scratching again with a stick on the dirt floor. After a while, curiosity overcame me, and I squatted down beside him.

"What are you doing with that stick?" I asked him.

"Diagnosing our problem."

"I don't see any sick people around here, Sergei."

"Ha ha. No, but old speech habits die hard," he said, his smile rueful.

"I moved alongside him to have a better view of his sketching on the packed earthen surface. Near the top of the crude design lay a white pebble, visible even in the dim light. What he drew made no sense to me.

"What is this? Are you trying to show me something?"

"We've gotten ourselves in a bit of a pickle, Dmitri. We must leave before the German and Soviet armies start shooting again.  Otherwise, we'll make prime targets for both sides. One set of soldiers considers us the enemy, the other, deserters. Our mission for Blue Talon is to report what we found in Leningrad. We've done that. No more to do here."

He paused, and then picked up, "I think bodies burning in mass graves is more than possible if we believe the rumors Gizela and others reported. I remember once I stood nearby when someone burned, believe me, this is a memory that makes me disinclined to test my incineration theory. We may not die, but the pain of the sword or the bullet would be real. I don't much fancy drowning  ... but being burnt alive? Uh uh. No, I've treated burn patients, and their agony disturbed me a great deal. I'd rather not have a direct experience, even a non-fatal one."

"No argument from me on that." I said sensing burning must be more of worry for him than he let on.

"If we are to escape, my thought is, once we leave the city, to find a way to blend in with one side or the other. Dress like the natives, talk the way they do."

He picked up his stick again and jabbed the ground by the oval stone. "We're here. At the extreme edge of Mother Russia. This land is vast. I've walked or rode on horseback the length and breadth of her. The odds of evading capture and surviving the crossing such huge expanses aren't good enough. Distance is too far and takes too long, even in peacetime, No, Dmitri, we must head here."

"He poked at a fingerlike shape at the top of the drawing, "Here. West to Sweden. We need to go to Sweden."

"Sergei, are you serious? I've not lived enough lifetimes to learn to swim well enough to paddle across the Baltic, even in summer."

"We must choose the nearest unoccupied neutral country, without doubt Sweden is the best destination for us. Hold on," he said, holding up a hand palm toward me, "I realize we might run into some problems. Other issues come first, long before you need to improve your swimming skills. Before we borrow trouble, we face a trek across a couple of countries with impossible languages—a different one in every country. Making ourselves understood will pose a problem. Still, I believe my plan is workable."

"What plan?"

"Simple, we become Nazi soldiers, preferably officers."

I stared at him, not able to voice a single word. He'd lost it for sure.

Dmitri glanced up at Jeanne, "Our father does some weird shit sometimes."

"Dmitri!" Tina scolded, but Dmitri started talking again.

"The first thing we have to do is slip out of the city tonight. I'll wager most sentries are more interested in keeping from freezing than keeping watch. We navigate with the stars. We both learned the night skies in our youth. We spent our childhoods without streetlights."

He moved the stick across the dirt. "We follow the coastline through Latvia to Lithuania. With luck, we should be able to make ourselves understood if we need to because the Russians forced the Latvians to learn to speak Russian. Hopefully, we avoid any close contact."

"His stick wandered along the line beneath the finger shape on the crude map. I guessed he meant to show the sea's edge.

"Once we reach the border, we find ourselves some German soldiers and swap clothes with them. Germany controls the country so the local will assume we are German and leave us alone. We pass along the coast to the warm water port of Klaipėda. When we arrive, we should be able to convince a local fisherman to take us across if we pay him enough."

Mama always told me to respect my elders, so I didn't argue. We left the same night.

"Soon I began to wonder how much my reanimation might hurt after I froze solid. Not that I had any tools to judge the cold, but  the ice that formed inside the cloth I put over my face to leave only my eyes uncovered was a clue. We crawled on our bellies past the German sentries. Sergei made the right call on their vigilance. Once we were well out of the city and we thought we'd gone far enough to be safe, we hunkered down and huddled together to keep warm. We cut blocks of the hard snow and built a shelter.

"We found a few sturdy branches sticking up through the snow and sharpen the ends to help keep our balance while we make our way on top of the crusty white top layer. I worried about breaking through —who knew how deep the snow the drift-covered might be? Good thing our family always seems to land on their feet, and the family luck held for us. After some days— how many I can't say—we did little except endure the cold, crossing a layer of white broken with patches of black ice.

"We must be nearing the coastline, Dmitri. Much of the area is swampy and difficult to navigate in summer. More passable at this time of year and, thankfully, no black flies. From now on, we keep our eyes open for our quarry."

"Are you certain we are still alive? I am so cold I feel almost nothing," I complained.

"If you eat, Dmitri, you are alive," he responded in a dry tone. "Rations are short, but every time we stop, your mouth moves."

"After a couple hundred years, Sergei seemed to possess uncanny luck carrying out his plans. We didn't go far since crawling out of the night's snow shelter when we heard the whap, whap, whap of axes off in the distance.

"Promising sound that, Grandson."

"We moved toward the chopping with stealth, moving from tree to tree toward the source of the noise. A squad of German soldiers loitered in the clearing four or five occasionally wielding axes, and the two officers passing a flask back, forth, reeling a bit.

"Shove the Blue toward them. This will confuse them and make them more suggestible," Sergei whispered. "We can draw what we need at will. I sense an ample supply all around us. These men must have done something which would not make their mothers proud for this much Blue to fill wilderness air."

"What are we going to try to do? Walk up and say '*Wie Gehts*. That doesn't seem too smart considering the guns stacked near the men with the axes."

"That's why we use The Blue. Come on."

"Sergei strolled out from behind the tree with a big smile on his face. " *Wie Gehts, mein Herren. Bitte, teilen Sie eine Schwalbe aus Ihrer Flasche?*"

The two officers showed a lax expression on their faces as they spun to confront us. "Why should we share an excellent schnapps with strangers?"

"When men share schnapps, they cannot remain strangers for long, my friends."

"The two hesitated and then smiled stupidly. *"Das Stimmt."*

"We moved forward, swapped the flask back and forth. Bit by bit we steered the officers out of the line of sight of their men. I overheard one with an ax grouse, "Them, they give the schnapps. For us, less than nothing."

"We took only tiny tastes of the fiery liquid but pretended to drink heartily. Sergei sat down on a log and motioned for the two to join him. We were all giggling by now—singing *Bierstube Liede*. We clapped one another on the back and shared silly laughs. Schnapps friends in arms, "What fine wool in those uniforms. *Ach,* if only I might wear such cloth. Can I interest you in a trade?"

They didn't need much persuasion after an additional coating of Blue. My skin took on the same color as the two Germans, and we shed the clothes we were wearing. We all laughed and pointed at each other as we redressed in changed clothes. Sergei "suggested" the two to rest on the log for a while. As we slipped back in the woods, we wafted Blue over their squad to befuddle the men enough not to question why their officers sat patently out of uniform. We took care to put as much distance between the Germans and ourselves as we could.

Once clear, we practiced clicking our heels and giving the stiff-armed salute, a skill we soon need when we encounter other unformed men toting MG 42 automatic weapons.

Good thing, too. We passed a number of patrols on the way. I spotted a guy on a motorcycle with a sidecar and wanted to "borrow" the thing. Sergei was all over me, but I decided after the war was over; I'd make sure to give a motorbike a go.

"I've got nothing against thieves, Dmitri. I was one myself once. This time though, calling attention to ourselves would not be a smart thing to do. Better the feet be sore, than the whole body from an encounter with someone's baton. If I remember correctly, the train track we passed will take us where we want to go. Taken for officers, we should be entitled to ride."

He was right again, and we trained all the way to Klaipėda. When the train left the station, we braced ourselves against the wind and started down the cobblestone street. We wanted a clothing store to purchase civilian dress. Our chances of persuading some fisherman to take us across to Sweden were slim to none dressed as Nazi officers. The Germans might control the town, but no love was lost between them and the townsfolk.

The shops didn't stock much for us to pick from, but we managed to buy something at only ten times what they were worth. We trudged down to the wharf area and, wonder of wonders, a ferry. Sailings for Sweden left twice a day. I decided that day anytime I pull a field assignment, I'd request Sergei as my partner. We booked passage for the morning departure. While we waited, we found an inn and tavern with some well-prepared fish.

"Ashore in Sweden, we stopped at the first public bathhouse. Later, clean and appearing to be two Swedish workers. Sergei remembered the tram routes and handled the transfers to the house in Västerort, which Ricky owned at that time. Owns still, I think. Blue Talon housed an operative there for the duration. Once we arrived, we sank into our first warm sleep in a long time. "No rest for the good guys either," I groused to Sergei when we landed in Denmark.

"Finally, I'd thawed. Believe me, Auntie, warm can be a relative term. The fire warmed my outsides, and the Aquavit burned my insides. Unfortunately, Sergei, too prompt as usual, got word to Ricky we were safe and in Stockholm, Two days later— no more— Ricky Legree got his whip out and sent us on another mission, assigning us to work with the Dutch resistance."

I tried not to, but my eyes did the roll thing. This was too much. "Sure, Sergei, whatever you say."

Then a familiar voice behind me said, "Hey Nephew, don't you go giving my sister the wrong impression. I'm no Simon Legree."

"Sure seemed like one at the time, Uncle, "Dmitri shot back.

Dad and he had come up from behind and surprised us. Ricky sat down at our table, latte in hand clutching a blueberry scone. Taking a bite, he added, "The temperature has dropped. What say we go back to Papa's house? I don't fancy freezing when I could be warm."

"Uncle, you have no bloody idea what cold is like."

Ricky was whispering something to Dad. I'm exceptional at eavesdropping and moved closer to them.

"He's right, Papa, damn him. I don't know what real cold is. I wasn't at Leningrad with him. I wasn't in Manchuria with Mario. I wasn't with the men I sent with the D-Day troops either. I sat on my ass, in my office warm and dry.

Oh boy, Ricky is one big gloomy Gus, one big pity party. These guys must be improv actors. No way their story is for real.

### *What We Are*

At that, all eyes fixed on Jeanne. Friedrich reacted first, "You wouldn't be trying to say what I think you were going to say, would you, Papa? What you used to say to us when we were children."

"Say what, Friedrich?"

"Out of the mouths of…"

"Don't you even think about calling me a baby," came loud and clear from the youngest in the group less than a second later.

The "Sorry, Little Sis" from him scarcely uttered when Jeanne ground out between her teeth, "And D O N 'T call me Little Sis!"

She needn't bother. Valentina squelched us all with a look and nodded at Ricky to go on.

He wriggled his neck, squared his shoulders, and started. "I know you think enough is enough, but this is the piece of the story you need to know, Jeanne, I promise. Once we put the parts together, we'll be able to show you where you fit in. Bear with me, and I'll even act out the roles—if that'd make this more interesting."

My youngest was not impressed. Her only reaction was a sideways twist of her mouth. Thus, when Friedrich noticed her squirming, when he fell back on his courtroom experience with a jury. No surprise for me. He struck a melodramatic pose and dropped his voice a full octave. Jeanne sat up straighter, her attention no longer lagging.

"Jeanne, Karl speaks in a deep voice any network announcer would envy," Friedrich explained in the tone he used when testifying in court. "Even when he spouted complete nonsense, he sounded knowledgeable. "

I managed to stifle my chuckle at the sight of my dignified attorney son performing like a high school thespian. Sentence by sentence—first in one voice, then the other.

I will enjoy this performance.

Friedrich assumed a stance and made a dramatic gesture to his audience of one. Jeanne giggled. Instead of "Ladies and Gentlemen of the Jury," he began with "This whole thing began one day with a casual chat."


"Bossman, this will serve our needs for centuries."

"Karl, for what we're paying for this heap of rocks, I expect this to be the last time I need to allocate funds for something like this."

"We can afford it, Ricky. You're the one who insists on a low profile. Look at it this way, once we finish the build out, no one will know we're around, Talk about self-sufficient and under the radar...heat pump, pure water aquifer underneath, on-site natural gas source to run our generator, no problem tagging onto the government's secure internet. Perfect, even for one as paranoid as you."

"You call hollowing out a mountain a build-out? We're not talking about adding a deck or updating a bathroom here."

"That is what makes this site ideal. Remember, you won't need to build exterior walls or do any painting in the future—forever."

"And that's supposed to justify the expense because...?"

"In all seriousness, Bossman, setting up a self-contained operation, centralized and under the radar is what we need. You're the one who's always ragging me about not rubbing some big shot the wrong way or having anyone think we're trying to take over. If

189

we're not discrete, we'll end up as a target for Homeland Security or some nut case will throw a bomb at us screaming obscenities and ranting about the Protocols. "

"Getting people in and out may pose a problem."

"Uh uh, we've got title to the area around the mountain; the rail line is not too far away. We can pass almost anything off as supplies for the ranch. "

"What ranch?"

"The one we'll start on the land. Grow wheat or start a cattle business. Bring in a little extra cash on the side. Trust me on this one, Ricky. We found the ideal location. Isolated and Canadians are too polite to ask what we're doing. We'll just be more landed immigrants. "

"Perfect when it's complete, but…"

"I've already put most the mining equipment in place, Came in pieces and our people will be able to assemble them. The plan is for self-stabilizing excavation. You must admit we've got somewhat of an advantage with two engineers with over 150 years of experience. They don't need to learn any of the basics, so they move on to the latest and greatest without a hitch. We're using ablative laser techniques. "

"Like the pointers?"

"Right, Ricky, trust a lawyer to not appreciate technical expertise. No, not like the pointers. The equipment we use is a team of robots with continuous wave lasers. We can take out large amounts of dense rock in a short while with little environmental damage. Costs a tad more than conventional methods, but…"

"Define a tad…how much more expensive? Two times? Ten Times? "

"I don't think you want to know, Ricky, You're good for it. We're already done with Phase 1 and part way through Phase 2. "

"Which means?"

"We've got six forty square meters, ten meter high rooms carved out and a similar number in phase two. They'll mirror, except a portion in the second to serve for water, ventilation, and sanitary facilities. Phase 3 is the farm. Natural light comes in to at least two of the floors in each room. We've kept the depth at around one kilometer, that's about a half mile to our American associates who persist in using their old measures. We want to make sure the temperature stays cool enough for the size of our computer banks. Even with as small as the chips are now, we've filled the bottom half of Phase 1. "

"I get claustrophobic just thinking about living half a mile down inside a rock."

"I think you'll be pleased when it's all done…the sketches show a complex resembling a luxury hotel."

"What's max capacity when Phase 2 is complete?"

"We won't need many bodies besides my geeks in IT and instructors. I doubt most of our regular operatives will spend more than a few days."

"I suppose you're right—this is our best option. With the amount of data, we lift from the computers of most nations added to the observations of Blue Talon agents around the world discretion is imperative. We're no super humans or psychic wizards; the only aces up our collective sleeves would be the Blue—plus the collected memoirs and the experience of all our lifetimes. Two tools to assist us in doing what we need to do. Once we are operational, we house our third tool, technical know-how. The computer is our other tool to anticipate and stop the killing sprees, individual or national, before they start.

"

"Exactly as I see it, Bossman."

"The only way I can justify the cost of what we are building, what we're doing, is because this mountain safehold is Blue Talon's insurance policy. You, I, and the others in the family can't be sure we'll live forever. There's a chance we may face death like any short-timer. Every death, if they happen, represents an enormous loss of memories. I'm hoping we can incorporate our combined experiences in our database with the other information we've collected and will collect. "

Jeanne threw herself back and blurted, "Hold on, come o-o-on—I don't believe this. I was starting to buy in with the not-dying thing, but a bat-cave carved in a mountain? What comic book did you find that craziness? How about you get real? Come clean with me why you're really here. Dad, tell them they need to shape up."

I gave Friedrich a too-much-too-soon glare. These last few intense hours crammed with everything new for her, overloaded Jeanne. She needed a break, and I wanted to tell her everything was okay. I wanted to postpone the day when she must confront her destiny. Something is wrong with a world where we let computers set the agenda.

Friedrich answered instead. He sat down straighter, faced her, and folded his face into a somber, earnest expression, "Everything we've told you is true,  laced with a little exaggeration from Dmitri. What we are, what we do, all of it, is not a comic book, not a tale dreamed up by some loony fantasy or science fiction writer, simple fact."

"So prove you're the real deal. Dad and I are doing just fine without you."

I said nothing, but my head moved in a reluctant nod.

Tina jumped in to help Friedrich. "Do you remember when Ricky and I talked about using computer models to locate family members and predict trends?"

Jeanne didn't object, which gave Friedrich an opening, "Thanks, Tina. I told you about all the times we tried to intervene, to stop a war, to prevent death and failed because we didn't do what we needed to do soon enough. I wish we were some of those comic book heroes with superpowers. Our only so-called special abilities come from lifetimes of accumulated family experiences and remarkable memories. We don't need to start at the beginning like the short-timers. We pick up where we left off. Most of us attend classes to keep up with new methods or new technology. We're better than most because we've encountered the same or similar events some other time, some other place. What works and what doesn't in not new to us."

"We've learned life repeats itself, exists in a series of patterns," Valentina added. "Relying on our brainpower, we anticipated some events, but the big picture escaped us. The patterns were too complex. The computer system—I won't even guess how many zettabytes—can. Using the computer models our data jockeys put together, we predict earthquakes, when a dike might fail, and so on. More importantly, we can forecast those persons who may become serial killers, the one able to invent a device to replace eyes. Our model exposed those who might be catalysts for another war. If we are prompt in placing an agent, we fulfill what we're called by the Blue to do."

"The trick is acting soon enough to influence the person we call the 'fudoer', the future doer, before he or she takes the first step or invents the machine, which will cause a significant change to take place. Most of these "in-fills" one of us can do, but on occasion, we need to recruit a person who is a first-lifer. We search for one whose view of the world

193

mirrors the fudoers, not the view of someone who's lived multiple lives. In a normal situation, we have time to find the right person as macro patterns seem to evolve slowly. Once in a while, the potential event is so dire we must move at once. Like now, when I must tell you, you are the infill operative we've chosen," said Friedrich.

I watched a stunned expression fill her face as Friedrich paused and waited for the explosion I expected I didn't wait long.

"Dad, tell these people to leave. I don't know them, and I don't want to listen to any more of their goofy stories. I've got comic books for that."

I sounded as sad as I felt when I answered, "Love, with all my heart, I wish Friedrich were not right, that things were not as they are. You are so young for such a responsibility. If he hadn't been so right before, I'd say no, but…"

"Well, from what I've heard, he's full of bullpucky. Mostly he whined about how rotten he was at his job. Well, this is your answer, Mr. Big Shot. Forget it. I won't do it."

"Jeanne, before you decide, at least let me tell you why we are here, making what must seem to be an unheard of demand for one your age, someone who has not yet experienced the hand of the Blue."

"Dad?"

"Pay attention, Jeanne, The facts he laid out for me earlier convince me the importance for you to learn what he is telling you now."

"You want me to listen to more of this…this baloney?"

"I do, Love."

"OK, I will— but only for you. And I don't have to believe any of it, she added, looking in Friedrich's direction."

Mein Gott, was I ever that pig-headed?

"Thanks, Papa. Jeanne, those cubic meters of computers we stowed in the mountain revealed a boy, in your same grade with the potential to change our future. If we don't somehow nudge him onto a positive course, the world will be a worse place. Right now, he is bright, driven to study, but without contact, he may become a serial killer such as few have seen before—a sociopathic leader with the wit to drive others to do perverse things. If we don't act, he may obtain a position of power, well, the wars we've lived through in past centuries would seem insignificant."

"You are such a drama king," she answered. "If he's this bad, what gives you the idea a kid like me would make a difference?"

"With Papa, you've lived as children should. I know. He's my father, too. This boy, Rob is his name, lives in fear at home. His stepfather drinks, then abuses him, beats him, and beats his mother. He forced Rob to sleep on the floor and go to bed hungry as punishment for some imagined infraction.

"Rob's withdrawn into himself, ashamed of how he lives. He has no friends at school. You'd expect his teachers would see his intelligence, his potential, but his defense has been to act sullen so they view him as uncooperative instead. He drives off everyone who tries to get close to him or help him. His life demonstrates the classic recipe for creating a monster.

"In short, he needs a friend he can depend on, someone to talk to. Teens need approval from their peers."

"And you want me to be this clown's friend?"

"Yes."

"No way."

"Jeanne, hear him out. There's more," I said.

Nothing in her body language said yes, but the two pressed on anyway, "We think from our analysis, this coming year is the critical one for Rob. If you agree to act as a positive influence in his life, to be someone to confide in, he will use his potential to do as much good for society as he would do evil without your intervention."

"That's way too much to swallow, Ricky."

"Uh huh, from your perspective I'd agree. From ours, we know to a 93% certainty if the current trend continues, we're all in for big trouble. If you step in, we expect an 80% probability Rob will be in the running for a Nobel Prize."

"And you expect me, a kid, to make all this difference. A kid with no clue about what to do or when or how to do it?"

He nodded. She hesitated so long; we all grew concerned their mission was a failure.

"OK, I'll do it, but on one condition."

They looked at each other, everyone but me amazed she dared to lie down conditions. No one ever said no to Blue Talon. The organization expected anyone in the family to accept their assignment without question. "What condition?" Friedrich asked, trying not to sound too taken back.

"That Dad is my partner and goes with me. Dmitri told me Dad's the best one to partner with."

My smile must have been wide enough to warm the Arctic.

### *Sergei's Bargains*

The dumbfounded expressions of Friedrich and Valentina gave me unseemly glee, and I was tempted to join Jeanne and Dmitri in their high five. The two were soul siblings, two of a kind despite the span of years separating them.

I had realized long before today my youngest was unique within our family, a modern woman in the making since her toddler days. I believe everyone in the room that day, Jeanne excepted, sensed Blue Talon dynamics changed when she made her mission her choice. Did she foreshadow others to come?

Differing emotions warred within me, elation and gratitude at being able to keep my daughter as my daughter for a while longer and regret at her loss of innocence soon to come. A familiar sense of loss filled me as I began preparations to implement stage one of our joint mission which called for us to relocate from the only home Jeanne had known to one acquired by Blue Talon, far away in the  vast interior or my adopted country, to the wilds of Minnesota.

I negotiated my own concession—a delay until the end of the school year. This concession, of which I made much to Jeanne, tempered her dismay at leaving her friends and favorite teachers. She did her best to mask general unhappiness and defiant attitude. I did not learn her true feelings until years later when she left for her first Blue Talon assignment as an adult.

**Jeanne's Role**

### *Sergei: A Father's Concern*

As a father, accepting Friedrich's demand for this much from a first timer this young, was painful. Until that day, I'd stayed as removed from the missions of my children and grandchildren as from my many far-flung great-grandchildren. Allowing them to pursue their obligations without my oversight at least gave them a semblance of free will. Friedrich prided himself on being circumspect when he paired partners. Having this initiative taken from him left him disoriented.

As for me, taking on such an active role in my young daughter's mission was also new. Blue Talon  practice was to put first-time agents in a support role, behind the lines. Yet here we were, a worried father and a resentful teen, taking on a vital, but unlikely, unsung and unrewarding task. Never reticent about sharing her thoughts about our relocation, Jeanne complained about her "subject," Blue Talon in general and Friedrich, in particular.

We settled into a far too large house, picked up the pieces of our new life, and changed identities. Quite soon, my role became apparent. My primary function was to serve as a listening post for her frustrations and an animate source of information and advice. She seemed content to accept the arrangement—as long as we remained partners.

Less satisfying was my role as snitch where I kept Friedrich updated on her progress. Jeanne, on the other hand, limited her contact to the weekly—she tried for monthly—reports. She attempted to hand off this task to me, but I refused. Whether she realized or accepted the fact, her link with Blue Talon lay inextricably as a part of her future. I simply hoped eventually a sense of family would develop. At times, distinguishing who was more unwelcome," the unformed future Rob or the present Friedrich was difficult. She was not happy with the change in school or having to try out to secure her spot on a new basketball team.

Still, I was proud to see her basic good nature come out as she pursued her relationship with Rob. Each evening we set aside a few minutes to go over any new impressions or developments she considered relevant. The enforced communication strengthened our relationship. Was it possible we might avoid the dreaded teen-parent alienation?

Something about being her partner as well as her parent eased the generation gap. In my prior lives, my parental role was more distant, shared by my wives, dictated by the norms of the time.

This was better.

### *I Ask Why Me While Living In Minnesota Winter*

I kept trying to tell Dad trying to mix reports and middle-of-the-mountain briefings short-circuited any chance I might score a normal teen's gig. "Can't they dig up someone else? "

"I wish they had, Love, as much for my sake as yours. The thing is, you didn't choose your ancestors very well," Dad told me with a wry grin slipping to one side of his mouth.

I punched him—a love punch, not a real one. "So I'm stuck, huh? That's what you're trying to tell me?"

"The Blue shapes our lives, Jeanne, for you, for me, and for us all, as it has the family since the day I didn't die."

I didn't like his answer but decided I had to live with it. Meanwhile, I dragged along a known and unliked nerd with a strange face everywhere I went –making my social life take a dive a sure thing. Think hawk after a rabbit-type dive. Not so fun, let me tell you. If it weren't for the end of the world business, Id'a told Ricky to stuff it a long time ago. Tell him something like, "See how it goes for you, Big Shot."

The weird thing was, once I got to know Rob the Nerd, I actually liked him—not like I'd date him or anything like that even if he weren't the 'subject  of my investigation. He didn't seem like a monster about to destroy the world.

After he clued into the fact  I didn't classify him as a hopeless freak through his thick head, unlike the rest of the kids at school, he warmed up and began to trust me. He let loose with a wicked sense of humor and an amazing knowledge of every profanity known to man as he shared stories about some of the BMOC. Even though he limited the more colorful terms to only English, I was sure he'd be adding more. "This one guy," he said, "apparently took one too many tackles wearing a defective helmet."

I won't say I didn't resent squandering all my New Girl capital on getting him included once in a while because I'd be lying. I had to keep reminding myself Dad—Sergei—put up with the same thing for centuries. On the plus side—I enjoyed telling off a few of the bullies who'd been on his case since middle school.

One day at lunch, I used some of Rob's choice vocabulary, which worked well with Warren, the bully-in-chief, and his bunch of trolls. The word got around to leave Rob alone and don't mess with Jeanne. I remembered a friend from my old town, the one before we came here. In most ways, he was kind of a jerk, but he always made one of his childhood playmates part of his group, even though his adoptive buddy definitely didn't make the in-crowd. One time he took one of the 'special  kids under his wing and dared the jocks to do anything. I figured he got a pass for the other stuff. I used him as my role model in dealing with Rob. Just the good points, of course, not the arrogance and all the self-love.

Rob was no dummy. He understood where he fit into the pecking order with and without me. He admitted, on his own, his chances of being included in my crowd were located somewhere between a snowball's chance and none. Most of my friends were okay with my inconvenient special project and didn't object…much…when I dragged him along. I gotta give them points for that. I included him in anything going on at my house. Bjorn, the studly guy I was dating,  thought I was nuts but dealing with Rob was no biggie for him. The whole thing seemed kinda cool  anyway. I considered myself like, well, noble for doing what I did. Dad told me to drop the self-congratulations just for doing what I was supposed to do.

The public me slipped into the same 'A crowd I'd enjoyed back home, and Rob and I were in a lot of classes together. Kids at that school considered science and math 'cool subjects. Probably because so many of the kid's parents were doctors or their mom or dad worked for one of the labs at one of the hospitals.

The Blue Talon me hated being such a phony.

One thing I didn't plan on was Rob talking smack to a couple his old computer geek friends. Maybe hanging with me made him think he was hot stuff and might explain the snarky comments, but I called him out, "How did you like it when Warren or one of the other a-holes in his posse did the same thing to you?"

He didn't say much, but he backed off, mostly. I think I got through to him with, "What if one of them has an asshole father like yours?"

My assignment meant writing Ricky's bloody reports. Of course, Ricky insisted on weekly-encrypted accounts of my week transmitted to his minions in the mountain, which cut into my free time like in a major way. Dad helped me with the first few despite my arguing his explanation would be 'better than mine. So why do I need to do any almost leaves my mouth before I think better of it? This living two lives gig sucked, needing to treat Rob as a friend and a 'subject of interest at the same time like tore me up. Talon operative Jeanne hung around every time hometown buddy Jeanne spent time with Rob. When Blue Talon hotshot outlined her positive and negative thoughts, actions, whatever, the other me asked, "What's wrong with you? I do the same thing myself once in a while."

How did they do it? Every one of them, the Blue Talon and other family members, living split apart for centuries. For that matter, what the hell did I have to look forward to?

I started cutting Dad some slack, remembering how sad he'd seemed when Tina and Ricky showed up. His kids seem to be his lifeline to normality. In a way, I almost envied the others who had to spend their summers in a cave. They must learn how to deal with this kind of thing.

To admit to being a bitch, even to yourself, was a real downer. My noble plan to make it up to him went down in flames big time. I put him through about a week of me smiling all the time, laughing at his more than lame jokes. Finally, after I turned down tickets to a concert at the auditorium, he scuttled the whole deal. The screen on my cell barely started to display my apps when he took hold of my shoulders and spun me around. "Out with it, Alien, where did you hide her? I want my daughter back Aye Ess Oh Pea."

"Funny, Dad. That line was old before I was born."

"Come on, I'm entitled. Would you rather I used Russian? What's been going on with you, Love? What's happened to your comebacks, the protests at having to be home early? I miss the old Jeanne."

I lost it. Like a flipping little kid, I bawled into his shoulder. "I've been such a shit. Giving you a hard time when compared to the stuff you deal with, my quote quote assignment is small potatoes."

He didn't say anything, kept his arm across my back as I slimed his shirt. After a while, I calmed down. "You didn't buy the Stepford daughter act at all, did you?"

"Not for a minute I've lived a couple centuries. Why the stories I could tell about daughters past…"

I slugged him, Right in the gut. Not hard, more like with affection.

"I think Ricky got the wrong person for the job. Sometimes I resent Rob. Screw him, making varsity or being homecoming queen or some other typical high school goal seems more important, What if the computer is off base, and my life is all effed up for nothing? And, and why do I need to do it at twenty below?"

"No one is right all the time, Love, but this time I'm sure, or as sure as one can be about something which hasn't happened yet. I am more and more amazed at how accurate the Blue Talon computer analyses have become. Friedrich called me last week to share they'd stopped a suicide bomber from boarding a cruise ship, for example. Once or twice, my long view spin on event adjusts the handling of an operation, that human factor we talked about before. Remember?"

I nodded. "And my view is so special?"

"When Dmitri first floated the idea the assignment for you, quite a few on the board objected…saying they thought he was, to use your term, nuts. This might be a little strong, but close. Valentina, on the other hand, seemed to understand why almost immediately."

This surprised me. She always seemed such a stick in the mud.

"Valentina told them, "We've never encountered a problem which required such an early intervention. I doubt we'd find much success if the individual doesn't come across as real. Anytime the police attempt to infiltrate a narc into the high school, the kids pick up on the imposter within hours, never days."

"Friedrich added, "She has a point, folks. Remember what we tried in Marseilles? Not what I'd call a sterling success."

"There was some grumbling about trusting punk kid and spy kid yada yada, but they went along. Dmitri is a real fan of yours, Jeanne Bond. He enjoys crowing over how he has to save the day once more. Ricky threw a pen at him."

I laughed, picturing my dignified brother nailing Dmitri with his pen. Still, perhaps I grew up a little in the past few minutes.

"In the meantime, be my Jeanne, My bright, mouthy, caring, beautiful Jeanne."

"Damn, you'll have me all weepy again."

"We need to grab all the family time we can. Ironic, the short-timers seem to be granted more."

He trailed off and allowed silence to prevail for a few moments. "Fact is, Jeanne, let's enjoy what's left of the week. Ricky wants us in the cave, as you call headquarters, next week."

"Daaaad, that's Prom week."

### *Jeanne: Dad Tries for a Positive Spin*

Deep down I realized Dad was as unhappy over the move as I was. He tried so hard to make our life seem normal the next few months.

"Great game, Love. You'll start next year for sure."

This just made things worse. What next year? I might not even make the team at my new school.

Of course, I tried to make nice back. "Thanks, Dad. I hope so. I felt good about this one, too."

Who was kidding whom? Whom? What I was sure of was, from now on, my life would totally suck. In a way, I was mad at Dad, too—which didn't make much sense because he was as unhappy as I was.

After they left, we talked. He tried to explain to me what just happened. Turns out, I was too dumb that day to realize what a bomb I'd set off when I told them the only way I would agree to do what they wanted was if Dad would be my partner.

"Jeanne, you left them both speechless—and Friedrich is almost never at a loss for words. Since those two organized Blue Talon, no one else ever considered they might have an option to decide if they wanted to take an assignment or insisted on a particular partner. You set them back on their heels. Friedrich or Valentina might pose their mission as an invitation, but no one ever said no or put conditions on their participating."

"Serves them right, butting into our lives."

"Being part of our family has never been something one would choose. Fate has a strange sense of humor, Love. Like taking a left-footed jump shot."

"Daad."

Later, I found out, well, I found out two things. First, he was right. Family members **never** decided who their partner would be on an assignment. Ever since Ricky and his minions put together the database of all time, the smarter-than-anything supercomputer did. Second, until they drafted me, the last time Blue Talon tapped a real first-timer teenager for a mission of this size, or any meaningful task, for that matter, was fifty years before.

By the time the movers came, I'd begun to believe this three hundred year crap. Not that the stories they told weren't interesting. They were just ancient history that didn't seem to apply to me. The whole thing got to me. My friends started asking me if something was wrong. I learned to fake happy.

Dad did all he could to support me, but my "siblings" kept telling me how lucky I'd been—usually family teens needed to pay their dues at boot camp before their first job. Lucky was not the way I would describe this mess. Letting my team down did a number on me.

Dad explained Blue Talon instructors didn't call the training boot camp, something more like Talon Talent Training School. When the others got as old as I was the day Ricky and Tina showed up at our house, the other kids started three summers of Blue School. Instead of the beach and pizzas, their parents sent them to study inside a mountain, Classes in family history, coping with the Blue, how to use and adapt to the Blue radiation, Blue Talon methodology. When class dismissed, the knows-all computer decided if, when, and where they'd go to college or trade school. Ricky's crew whipped them into shape, buffed, and shined them into fully credentialed Blue Talon agents. After that, their lives began.

209

Gosh, I didn't realize how deprived I'd been to miss all that— NOT!—Obviously the ones who did wouldn't make the cut to qualify for this assignment because the brainwashed little  munchkins were already marching lock-step in tune with Blue Talon think. I figured I'd fit some of this oh-so-valuable information in—in my next life. I got so flipping sick of hearing, "We realize you weren't able to attend Talon Training, but…"

When I was younger, I loved saying something out-and-out outrageous just to watch them sneak a peek at each other. A one-second glance at their faces told me exactly what they were thinking. Did they forget the reason the PTB handed me the assignment was so I'd act like a short-timer would expect me to act? Duh!

As for Dad and me, our lives took a new turn when school ended in the spring. The change took some getting used to. New town, new school, new job, new everything. We'd no sooner arrived than some geek at Blue Talon pulled strings for Dad with this big clinic to give him a job. Dad, the doctor part of him anyway, seemed excited. Officially, his 'consulting physician  job' involved a 'worldwide consulting practice'.  How Ricky managed to convince the board they needed a person to make house calls, like in the olden days, blew me away. The difference--his 'patients' were other doctors around the globe who needed assistance diagnosing and treating some mysterious condition.

Supposedly, Dad was awesome at coming up with novel treatments for folks who needed help. Part of the problem the gaping holes in most folks' medical insurance, exceptions so restrictive they wouldn't pay for new treatments. Dad's boss made sure medical schools were eligible to call on the Consulting Country Doctor, too. Dad explained how this was supposed to work, I didn't understand then, and I still don't. Wonderful cover for him though. Everyone said so.

I grew up with a doctor, so I was used to him being 'on call," but here Dad was on two call lists, the one from the clinic and the other from Ricky Legree at Blue Talon. Of course, nothing ever appeared on either one they didn't classify as an 'emergency. With less than a moment's notice, Dad would shoot out of town to deal with the latest crisis. He kept a list of families he could park me with while he was gone. This wasn't all bad. At least there were kids. After a while I insisted, threw a tantrum actually, saying if he had to be out saving the world somewhere. Anytime, I didn't have school, I got to tag along. I visited some really cool spots. I never tried to play the diva, but considering how much they wanted me, I generally got what I wanted. If I wanted to be honest about it, which I don't, I admit I relished playing a prima donna.

Not that everything turned into cupcakes and candy canes for me when he was home. I'd drawn a tough assignment. My first year seemed like every teenager's nightmare. I suppose I should have guessed right away. For one thing, the house. Why such an enormous, five bedrooms, living room, dining room, and get this, a breakfast nook for two? How about the big hole underneath the house? I wasn't used to having an empty space under the floor. Well, not really empty because someone who owned the place before us had turned it into an apartment kind of thing. Come on, folks. The only ones living in this McMansion were Dad and I.

Considering the size of the thing, when we moved in, I wondered why the backyard didn't have a pool. My guess was the land was too steep, what with sitting on a hill and all. Five months later, I discovered the reason– snow, up to my knees snow, right outside the door. Not sitting on a mountain where it belonged. The sparkling white stuff fascinated me…for about three days.

Rob—aka "the subject"— lived two doors from me down in another humongous house. Everything on the street was big, somewhere between sixty and seventy years old, but they seemed old to me after growing up in California. The day we met, I mean physically met, because I'd already spent hours reading over what Ricky calls my "briefing synopsis"—the thing I thought I'd never finish. Dry as dust and longer than Crime and Punishment. Every time I paused or tried to reread something, the machine faded into a more into a complete description of what I'd been on whenever I hesitated. I never did learn how to disguise my reactions. What Blue Talon did with computer interface goes way beyond an app.

I must have inherited the family memory because I remember the exact day Rob and I first set eyes on one another. Dad was impressed with my minute-by-minute report. I was jogging down our driveway when I literally ran into the "subject."

"Hi there. I'm Jeanne," I said after I caught my breath. "My dad and I just moved in. We must be like neighbors." I said all bright and perky, smile, smile.

"Yeah."

"Um, do you have a name?"

"Why do you want to know?"

He didn't seem nearly as nerdy in person as his picture, but the rest of his dossier seemed right on. Hostile, surly, eyes on the ground not looking at you, wearing long sleeves even in the swelter of a hot, muggy summer day.

"I don't know anyone here yet, and you're convenient. You seem about my age— chances are we'll go to the same school. You could fill me in."

"Yeah, well, I'm sure you'll find someone soon enough. I don't see why I should waste my time with you. The day after tomorrow fall quarter starts, you'll never talk to me again anyway. Why don't you have that high powered doctor father of yours take you out to the country club so you can meet some of your own kind?"

"Look, Buff Boy, I pick my own friends and my daddy does not dump me off to find them. I guess from the big house, your dad is up the rungs himself."

"Stepfather," he snarled in a bitter way.

"Whatever."

"Not really"

"What do you mean?"

He didn't tell me then naturally. Later he shared more with me. Off-loaded a lot, even coming close to tears a couple of times. How many days we sat on the top of the hill overlooking the hospital talking, I'm not sure. I mostly listened anyway.

"Want to come over to my house? I can crack a soda? Fill me in on the school; tell me what there is to do around here."

"Soda? Oh, you mean pop. Soda is something my mom uses when she makes Irish quick bread. I've heard the word used on TV, though."

We shared the drink in the breakfast nook. He got up and peered into the adjoining rooms. "I've never been in here before. Neither of the old owners spent much time at home. The guy hired someone for the yard and the sidewalks, so they didn't hang around on week-ends."

"Well, we're around, at least I am. I'm not sure how much time Dad has to work yet."

He nodded, so I asked him, "So what do you and your friends do? Like for fun. Anything special?"

"What friends?" His chuckle lacked any humor.

The briefings I had read filled me in on the facts. The bleak tone of his answer and the expression on his face connected the dots. His stepfather bullied him, and Rob lived as an outsider in teen society. What I read didn't mention something apparent once I'd had our face-to-face chat. Score one for Dad. The reason Rob's face seemed off-sides to me was because one half didn't move right. If he smiled, his lips struck me as lopsided. Something about his eye or maybe his forehead seemed off. Why I kept my mouth shut and didn't stare, I don't know. Dad told me later one of the tricks of undercover work was not to react at the unexpected. Maybe I was a natural. He avoided focusing people in the eye because he wanted to hide his face. A messed up face like his was more than enough to cull him from the pack in high school.

I told Dad about what Rob when he got home that night. Our cook—would you believe it, had dinner ready when he walked in. Our own cook, plus a yardman. Three cheers, I lived liberated from kitchen clean up. She lived in the basement, and he came once a week. The best part of the cover act called for someone to clean our house twice a week. No more having to pick up my room.

"Dad. Seeing as we've got a maid, what happened to our chauffeur?" I asked.

He sent me a pained look. "Love, I haven't had live-in help since, well since Philadelphia. The only reason she's here is for image. I'm not used to having outsiders live in anymore. We must take care what we say when she is around."

"You think Martha is some kind of spy?"

When he finished laughing, he took a deep breath. "No, Jeanne Bond, I don't. Back in the day though, I wouldn't laugh. Competitors placed spies on each other's household staff quite often. Our problem lies when Blue Talon operatives stop by. Supposedly, they'll be in the medical profession. We need to make sure any overheard conversations do not drift beyond medicine or trivialities. I've sound-proofed my den, the room behind the living room, for this reason."

Ok, so I forgot to include the den or mention the workout room upstairs or the attic, which Dad turned into a huge library. Half the books were in languages I didn't understand. Not that there was anything I was interested in. Nothing good to read, no novels, no fun stuff. Anyway, I told him about Rob's face and how I thought his social life probably tanked because he looked funny.

"The most likely cause would be some form of Bell's. I can't imagine his parents don't bring him in to be treated. Nothing much shows in his medical history. Of course, in this case, history seems likely an exaggeration. Not much there. Only when the school nurse initiates a consult."

"Maybe his step-father doesn't want anyone to examine him."

"Possibly, Love. Bell symptom sometimes appear after an injury to the head or face, I'll let … no … you'll let Ricky know."

I stare at him. "For real?"

"Time to get to work. You'll need to draft your first report as an operative, Jeanne Bond."

### *Minnesota Years, a Look Back*

Looking back, I realized I totally missed some things in the fine print when Ricky pitched me to sign up. I'm smarter now and probably would make more thorough read, but I was a kid back then and dumb enough to think I could trust Big Blue to keep the promise Ricky made that Dad would be my partner. In the small print I didn't read, I overlooked the section where they "reserved the right" to make our partnership a non-exclusive arrangement. I didn't count on Ricky expecting Dad to "confer with operatives assigned nearby"—nearby being within 24 hours flight time. Ricky considered Sergei's centuries of experience far too valuable to squander on one smart mouth teen like me.

Sometimes Ricky's henchmen only stuck around long enough to score a free meal, but every six or eight weeks, another set would show up. I halfway suspected Martha's excellent cooking delayed their leaving. Dad tried to tell me they only stayed long enough to ask for his advice on the best strategy for whatever-it-was, but I suspected the savory smell from the kitchen created additional questions. Occasionally the 'Bossman" himself showed up accompanied with what seemed like the entire cast for a musical. Well, not a musical, more like a debate team tournament or a melodrama.

Dad tried, tried  hard in fact, to keep the visits during the time I would be in school. He wanted the two of us to be able to live the way we used to before the hordes of pushy relatives invaded our space. He set evenings aside for father-daughter time. Nice try, Sergei. One out of ten ain't bad, I guess, but when the conversation droned, he would invite them to stay for a meal. I don't need to guess how often the dinnertime talk slipped from the current hit moving into their problem of the day.  All of them. So much for sharing what happened to me at school.

They used code words and half-baked work-a-rounds to try to keep me in the dark. They thought they were being so blinkin' clever. Did they actually think I wouldn't eavesdrop or set up a web cam feeding into my laptop from the den? Sometimes the Blue Talon agents showed their age big-time. I think Dmitri half-suspected me. The geeks didn't do a thorough job—they only swept the rest of the house. I mean, really, when someone my age lived here? I used the house wiring to set my system up, so I was good to go unless they dug around in the bookcase looking for wires, which they didn't, of course.

Most of the time Ricky's minions would show up after I left for school. Martha scurrying around in the kitchen was a sure-fire sign a tip-off company was coming. Apparently, her reputation with Blue Talon folks as a great cook meant most tried to pick lunchtime for their meeting in an effort to comply with Dad's limit to school hours . Every day, before I left for school, I'd head upstairs to get my backpack and practice stuff and set the webcam to record, usually from ten to four.

Unless I had a shitload of homework or something better came up, when I got home I checked out what happened while I was gone. Mostly I'd scan the display and pause on what seemed to be interesting stuff and in English. Dad was forever ragging on me to learn another language. I started Spanish to humor him  but didn't find many opportunities to practice outside of class. Dad spoke maybe six or seven, so I guess they picked the one most of them shared.

What I did tune in on gave me a lot of ammunition on Blue Talon I used later. I got a better idea of what the organization was all about than I had from Ricky or Tina's explanations. I was no big fan of history class, but being on the inside was different. Not that some stuff wasn't just as boring, but the ideas and events they discussed were happening now, not a hundred or more years ago. I loved hearing about something an agent I met was working on, then reading about the same thing in the papers weeks later. I didn't quite put all the pieces together yet, but the Blue—that I got.

This one morning, early, before I was even out of my pajamas, the doorbell rang.

"I'll get it," Dad said and waved me to sit back down.

"Good morning, Friedrich, Karl. So nice you could visit. You are the first. I'll have Martha bring in coffee and sweet rolls into the den."

"Good morning, Sergei, Jeanne," Karl said.

"Sounds good, Papa. Morning, Jeanne. You're up early," Ricky said, moving down the hall past me.

I didn't have a chance to answer. They whipped on back to the den and shut the door. Then the bell rang again, and Martha hurried to open the door.

"Good morning, sir. They are back in the den. Do you know the way?"

"Indeed I do. Morning, Jeanne."

I searched my memory for the guy's name. Filip. I was almost sure. He was some kind of big shot back east. Then a woman I'd never met appeared in the entryway.

"Good morning. You must be Jean. I'm Anna. Where are we meeting? She asked in a German accent. "Oh, never mind. I see them now."

"We're down the hall—in the den.  Dad called. He must have heard her voice.

The door closed, and I hurried upstairs and set my webcam for an all-day session. No way was I going to miss this, sure as snow in Minnesota, something juicy this time would be on my recording.

That night when I clicked on my laptop, I high-fived the air. "Damn, I'm good!"

Even a quick scan showed this was no run of the mill get together. All the big wigs sat around Dad's cluttered desk, and I heard other voices so Karl must have set up a teleconference for who rated high enough to be included. Didn't they have a cave for stuff like this? Did they have to bother us? Invade my space?

I wondered who- was minding the store back in their mountain. Dad told me they use some short-timers. But from the sound of things, everyone who mattered was here. Ricky laid it on thick.

"I needed an update on current cases," Ricky said. He sounded worried.

"You're yawning, Uncle?" asked Filip. "Long night?"

"In a way, a long trip and bad news don't make for much sleep. Karl, would you bring up the spreadsheet with our current items of concern?"

"Sure, Bossman."

I peered in close to the screen. Well, thank goodness not one of his bloody pie charts.

"Ladies first?"

"Of course. What's our top priority?"

Ricky simply shrugged, but Dad said, "You've shown yourself to have a remarkable understanding of what's important, Annie. Start with that."

The way he said this made me a little jealous. Didn't he remember I was his daughter and his partner?

"Of course, Sergei. Do you all remember the job we picked up tracking money laundering in Turkey?"

The heads on my screen moved up and down. Seeing the nods, she continued. "Turns out, their dirty money scheme is—what's your expression— the tail wagging the dog. The real money is in drugs. Our sniffer tracked the fund back to heroin sales. Heroin, apparently, is back on the list of in-drugs. We're at the point where we need to make a decision. Do we stick with the scope of the original contract or expand our efforts in an attempt to curb sales.

"My issue is this, I'm afraid if we decide to pursue the traders and embed anyone outside the family, we put our short-timer at too great a risk. These jokers are nasty. The traffickers range from Mafia-like strongmen to Kurds raising money for their cause to persons in the government of damn near every country on the continent. Billions of Euros, over a half million addicts, and that's only heroin, no other drugs. To top it off, the business appears to be expanding in an effort to compensate for the loss in revenue caused by a couple of decades of Gulf Wars.

"I'd love to take down at least a few of the bigger players, but I'm not sure we've enough agents on hand to cover all the routes out of Ankara. They'd be hi-jacking Lorries carrying the stuff, and I mean a lot of Lorries since the cache on each is only around 20 to 50 kilos, I'll need to strip half the family from the rest of Europe—a worry because our ability to take on new cases would be compromised. And did I mention the bribery and violence at the end of the money trail? Suggestions?"

Wow, looks like Dad wasn't kidding when he said Blue Talon was still involved in some important stuff all over the world. If I were older, I might even...

"I'm glad you didn't bring us a big problem, Annie," Ricky said. "Snap of the fingers, some creative cloning and we're done. Poof. All solved."

"I realize you're joking, Ricky, but trade is a thousand-year-tradition in the area—only now the goods are nastier. We tried deflection. We fogged the customers in known shooting galleries with Blue to counteract their addiction, the effects appear short term, Bottom line—we simply do not have enough family in place to blanket every community in Europe, or even all the major cities. Because only those who see the blue are able to direct its use, we're limited. As big as the family has become, we're too few. The addicts are short-timers. They've only one life, and they're throwing it away. Tough for us to watch young people squandering what they've so little of."

Dad's head drooped and his shoulders sagged. The sadness in his face made me sad, too. You'd think he'd be able to handle this kind of thing better after all this time. Maybe the Blue didn't let him. I turned back to the screen, not wanting to miss anything.

"You're right, Annie. Men I met in the trenches began smoking opium, and they died before their heart stopped beating. Let's brainstorm for another approach. Create some cancers in the organization so they turn on each other. Karl, do you think you can hack into the various suppliers and lay down false information? Get the drug lords snarling and snapping internally?

"Piece of cake, Bossman.

"Seems to me we tried something similar in Mexico a year or so ago?"

"You're correct, close enough to use to construct a model. Annie, you're here…hmm…three days? We can get back to Ricky before you leave. Sound good?"

She nodded.

"I'll need to take time to analyze possible scenarios. I'll be able to tell how good the data is," Karl added.

"On the other hand, I believe we can arrange immediate back-up for you. You used our money laundering stuff before. Tell us who you think are involved? We'll hack in and keep tabs."

"Definitely useful, Karl."

"You're up, Filip."

"Thanks, Uncle Bossman," he said.

My dignified brother must love it when they call him that. Too bad, Big Bad Bro.

"My office currently is juggling a couple hot potatoes. We have our own drug cases. The US_DEA bloody well loves us. When we're involved, they've no need to notify the local PTB, or need an order for extradition.

"Anyway, our two drug-related investigations...the first one is a DEA case dealing with a possible new connection between the Colombian traffickers and the Mexican cartel. The DEA narcs jumped up and down with joy when our prelim showed 90% confined to Colombia and Peru. On the other hand, certain high placed officials of the government don't exactly have clean hands. I placed a few family agents along the trade routes from South America north to the US and Canada. Annie has no exclusive on spread thin; let me tell you. Either we start having more kids with the trait, or Tina needs to dig up a few more. I threw in some short-timers to track the money. Annie, you and I need to compare notes on this.

"The other DEA job involves a ring peddling designer drugs to pro-athletes. I put Feliks back into baseball, and fortunately, I found a long-lifer who used to play college football. He younged, and the Niners picked him up. Got others in tennis and MLS, but that's all for now. They slung Blue around in the sport they drew hoping for more on how they peddle the stuff in the locker rooms. We're down to two possibilities—a known criminal ring, and one that passes for legitimate. I'd need at least one family operative in each outfit."

You're kidding. Someone in our family is undercover in the NFL? Bjorn'd go nuts. I gotta find out from Dad what name he's using and how good he is. If he's up there, selling autographs should cover the cost of the outfit I want.

"If you can spare some time, Papa. We'd like you to do some tests on the drugs we confiscate and track down their effects. You're still the best for anything medical, even after all these years. If you can't, then maybe Hilde? From you, Karl, I need a matrix showing who we send to butter up and infiltrate the gang. What the feds pay us isn't enough to cover what we need until we pile up enough evidence to get a conviction. I'm not greedy, but the cash helps to take care of my short-timers with spouses to support or kids to educate if things go wrong."

"I'll make time, Filip, "Dad said.

I thought short timers only worked in the office doing routine stuff. Guess not. I paused the recording thinking I heard Dad outside my bedroom door. False alarm. I clicked resume.

"Of course, if the king pin ends up outside DEA jurisdiction, we'll need to arrange to boost the bodies and drop them off on their steps."

An involuntary gasp from the crowd in the room and a shocked look on Ricky's face followed.

"Relax, Uncle, not literally. We generally set up an inconspicuous drop site."

Way to go, Filip. Twist the Bossman's tail.

"Not funny, Filip, but I see no problem with getting what you need. Sounds like the DEA business is moving along. What's the status on the corporate job?"

"We're working with a multi-national. Of course, they always try to keep us at arm's length with their need-to-know crap. Our contact on a major ring peddling knock-offs of their big line is reliable. Unfortunately, for us, the fakes appear virtually identical to the genuine article. Unless you're in on the scam, the phonies appear legit. They suspect at least two of their subcontractors are supplying parts for the counterfeits, but suspect more may be involved.

"Karl, we need the original design and specs, to understand what we're tearing apart. Without them, we're just as much in the dark as the average buyer. This company is hurting. Sales are down because others can undercut their prices by a lot. Either we signed with the world's dumbest client or someone supposedly working with us is double-dealing, Dealing with these clowns leaves a foul taste in my mouth. And, five'll get you ten, they try to stiff us on the agreed fee.

"Little do they realize; our short-timer accountant found entries where they forgot for pay taxes on some off-book income. They cooked the books for their financials and siphoned off dividends due their stockholders. One penny under the amount on our contract, and we approach Treasury. They can pay us for what we dig out. And I'll personally Blue the company bastards to make them forget they hired us."

Oohh, this was getting good.

"Not sure if you can, Feliks. Get too close to doing excess harm, and the Blue may balk."

Balk? The Blue's alive?

"Don't think so, Uncle, I happen to know Papa and Dmitri pulled the same trick on their Leningrad gig. They play fair, so do we. If they don't, well…"

"Remember what we do, Feliks," Dad said. "Since that first autumn day, we've been the good guys."

The room was silent for a minute, and then Ricky asked, "Anything else?"

"Yeah, a consumer protection group asked…:

Damn. What happened to my recording? Did a power outage blitz the rest? I did a fast forward and found nothing more. Figures, my luck. Oh well, I've got homework to do anyway.

**Blue Talon Operative**

### First Timer

I suppose I should've been impressed with the invite to HQ, lowly first timer that I was, since I got to sit in with all the family bigwigs, but sorry, Charlie, I wasn't. Let any of them try to balance being a teen-ager with saving the world from death and destruction and see how they like it. Most of them lived normal lives— most of the time. Teens worry about things like acne and a date for the prom, but no, not me. I was the one drafted for a life of danger and intrigue, plus the Blue Talon big wigs, meaning Ricky, made me move half-way across the country plus switch to a new high school—all of which really sucked.

"Earth to Jeanne, Earth calling Jeanne, come in Jeanne."

"All right, all right, Dmitri. What do you want?"

"The debriefing starts in five. You got everything you need? You know how they are."

"Of course, this is my fifth time at HQ. I'm an old hand by now. I wish they'd schedule these dumb meetings over a break though, so I don't miss classes. Especially since Advanced Calc is giving me fits."

"Better you than I, Auntie."

"'I don't know which annoys me more—you calling me 'Auntie' or Friedrich's 'Little Sis'. I may be a first lifer, but I pull my weight…and don't you forget it, Buddy boy.'"

"Here comes Papa. I think you're on now. Good luck."

Luck didn't matter unless you counted Ricky giving in when I'd insisted Papa be my partner. Poor guy, dealing with my hormone-induced crisis at the same time he needs my mind clear for our mission. If I ever have a kid, I hope she's not like me.

"Why do they insist on these meetings when practically everything we do is keyed into the computer?" I said, falling into step beside Dad.

"You've got to cut us old folks some slack, Love. We're old school—we like to look someone in the eye, get a reaction. Ask for some subjective opinions—they don't fit well into a computer model."

"I thought this latest one did think. I heard it understood and analyzed what people said, facial expressions—all that stuff?"

"From what Karl tells me, no. Apparently, our brain houses more memory banks and synapses than they are able to construct in a machine. The fact we are able to draw on our past lives, build on them, especially for long-timers like me. The memories and experience of the short-lived die with them. We need to keep them intact, even though a reanimation. Gives us five aces in a four ace game. I suppose someday the machine will come closer, but giving a computer the ability to recognize effect a connection between family, friends, and lovers colors our recollections. Emotions like love, hate, grief, joy all influence what we do. The rapport with others aspect is why you qualified as the girl of the hour for this assignment."

"The first time living through the teen years is the most spontaneous. Our reactions are more genuine than any we have later. The mood swings, the defiance, the excitement of seeing something for the first time is real. After that, even though the Blue resets our physical and hormone clock, we experience only comparisons after our first go-around. When a similar event happens, the best we get are only subtle reactions, no more than nuances. The angst is familiar but unfelt. All this makes us unfit to act like a genuine adolescent."

"Wow, Dad, that's deep. You plan to be a psychiatrist in your next life?"

All right, perhaps I was being a teensy bit sarcastic, but come on. I'm entitled to play a drama queen once in a while without one of the long-timers chalking up everything to hormones and nothing more. Whatever happened to individuality?

"You're on deck now. The business part of the board meeting is almost over," announced Feliks, Filip's twin brother.

"What are you planning to do now you've retired from the Cubs?" Papa asked. "Any plans?"

"I'm thinking about coaching for a while. Working for the family in the off-season, of course, like I've been doing."

"I've heard good things about you on the field and off, Grandson."

Feliks bowed his head shyly at the praise. "Thank you, sir."

"And in the future?"

"I'm hoping I can do the same thing in my next life. I love the sport. There's a Zen to it, you know."

Zen in baseball? He's got to be kidding.

"As long as you fulfill your obligation to the family, I don't see any reason why you shouldn't do what satisfies you."

For someone as old as he is, Feliks is such a child. How many more centuries before he decides to grow up and stop chasing a ball?

"Sergei? Jeanne? Can you come in please?"

They always, well, almost always, call him Sergei when he's on a field assignment. This family works in such weird ways. Go figure.

Tina turned around and re-entered the room. Dad and I followed, and she waved us to sit down in the chairs. I smiled at Dmitri as I passed and gave Ricky at the head of the table a nod. "Sergei and Jeanne are handling this operation," my sister told the others as she introduced us to a couple new faces, new to me that is.

They respond with nods and hello's and hi's to me in a bunch of different languages.

When the group quieted down, everyone picked up the packet and opened to the final page, which Tina read aloud. "Case 7345, North American Region, Destiny Diversion, Subject Rob McLean, Operatives on site, Peter McCormick and Jeanne McCormick. Or, as we call, them Papa and Jeanne. Your floor," she said nodding at the two of us.

"Why don't you take lead, Jeanne, and I'll jump in if I have anything to add."

I nodded and began a rather rambling account of the past year with Rob, my next-door neighbor, best friend, potential mass murderer, and villain of comic book proportions. "Overall things turned out well——at least after Rob won his scholarship, that is— thanks to Ricky's…"

"We call it the Talon Talent Search The board just voted to make the award an annual event."

"Hey, that's great, Rob was thrilled. He'd never been able to afford college on his own. His stepdad wouldn't have given him a dime. Dad, on the other hand, was stuck with my tuition and stuff. After we got settled on campus, Rob seemed happier than I'd ever seen him. Getting away from his stepfather, leaving the mess at home and far enough away so he didn't need to worry they'd stop by made him much happier. Even the way he walked was different. We enrolled at the same university. I may have influenced his choice a teeny-tiny bit. I figured if I'm stuck spending my college years babysitting the guy next door, I deserved to go to the one I wanted.

"When we both got acceptances last spring, I did the jumping around thing with him, even though  Ricky'd already told me we'd been skidded. "

I glanced up and gave a big grin to my audience. "What's not to like about a place closer to where I lived pre-Minnesota, one with weather a whole lot warmer. I don't think I ever got used to those winters. How do you people stand it, out in the boonies in the middle of a mountain, with outside temperatures too cold to guess? Worse even than Minnesota.""

Crikey, even thinking about winter weather makes me cold. I shivered, flipped my shoulders, and picked up the pages of our report.

"They assigned us to the same dorm. His room was three doors down which made us like neighbors, same as home. He chose his major, bioengineering with an emphasis on genetics. Me, I elected for pre-law although I kind of enjoyed my intro psych course and thought about a concentration in behavioral studies as well. To be honest, both Ricky and Tina are my role models occupation-wise, but Dad would rather I'd chosen pre-med."

"The world always needs doctors, Love. Take it from me, I should know."

"Sure, sure. Aaanyway, I can tell he's living better in his own skin because I don't need the Blue to calm him down as often, plus, when I do, I use less. Dad taught me some cool techniques to control the effect. I've gotten good at how much, how often, how to spot the signs things were going sour for him. Sometimes I still feel like a double-crosser treating him as a lab rat, even though he didn't realize what I've done to influence him."

231

"Jeanne…"

"Ok, Dad. I get it. I'm off track again. I set things up to ease our transition for the first few weeks. Concentrating on Rob turned out to be a good thing. I stayed so focused and busy, I didn't get a chance to be homesick. Now I've been on campus long enough to move in mentally. I missed having Dad around all the time, but we talk a lot. We've got a boatload of minutes each month, so I consult him almost as much the guys who hang around our house all the time."

I threw a smirk at Ricky.

"We're still partners, but we're less obvious about it," Dad said. "You should see my phone bill the first couple months. We decided if I were on campus too frequently, instead of back in the snow, Rob might begin to wonder why—and it didn't take her long before she was comfortable acting on her own. My input was more affirmation of what she'd done rather than advice on what to do.  He smiled over at me, and I smiled back at his implied praise.

"I stepped the first week and Blued a few of the guys into becoming his best buddies, but he made some good friends on his own, too. He's over the top gradewise. Socially, too—he doesn't have to work like hell to connect like the way he did in high school. I may have overdone it. This one guy always seemed to be hanging around. Can't be positive, but I suspect this weirdo might be gay and putting the make on him. Rob acted funny with me when he was around—not his usual geeky-self. Like I might think he was gay, too, and would've liked him less if I thought they were more than friends. Like that would happen, after all this time, even if he weren't, like, you know, him being my responsibility and all."

232

Karl, the computer guru, chimed in, "Our model shows a mild possibility for a slight tendency in that direction. We picked where he fell in the spectrum when he was around eight. His stepfather seemed to sense something and abused him more. Our analysis showed a positive prognosis for him if he were to come out, statistically little difference. We've placed the greater influence on him being able to leave the unaccepting, somewhat brutal environment he grew up in."

"Somewhat brutal? Don't those spies of yours have eyes? Where did they think the welts came from? His kitten?"

"What's your take on this friend of Rob's?" asked Ricky, ignoring the snipe I'd shot at them.

"Um, well, he's like different, you know. Something about him seems off to me, but I'm not sure what makes me distrust him."

"Can you add anything, Sergei? Did you have an opportunity to observe this person?"

"No, when I came on campus publically, I've played doting Dad. I never met him. I will say this though. If she senses he might be a problem, she's been right in the past. If she says he's squirrelly, hide your peanuts."

"Think we need to put some time into this. What did you say his name is?"

"I didn't. His name is Walt Anderson, and he's from Idaho if I remember right."

"Got a town? Idaho is a big place to hunt for someone blind and knowing the city would narrow the search quite a bit."

"No, but when I get back to campus, I can find out and contact you."

"Not sure where you stand on this, Ricky, but I'd be more comfortable knowing you'll take a closer look at this guy," Dad said.

I'm with him. Can't hurt to find out more anyway. Might as well give the geeks something to do.

### High Five?

Ricky chucked a torpedo into my life—sooner than I expected. My last round of finals wasn't dry when he dropped in and "suggested" I attend some other classes—at Blue School. Great, just when I was beginning to think things couldn't get worse, they did. Dad and I were sitting over breakfast when Ricky lowered the boom on me.

"I think you might find much of the content Blue Talon offers helpful. I understand Papa and Dmitri shared a lot with you, but you undoubtedly have holes in your knowledge. And yes, I also am aware you planned to do this "in your next life," but why not prepare in this one?" Ricky said in a smarmy tone, the way adults act when addressing a child.

Why not? How'd you like to be the only one in a class of kids not even half your age? I didn't say this aloud, of course, by this time I'd learned the drill. Whatever Ricky wanted, Ricky got. Good of the world, family obligations, yada yada, all that other crap. Everyone in the family was brainwashed into thinking the party line. O M G, I'm getting waaay ahead of the story. I need to fill in some missing pieces.

Ricky was right about one thing when he dropped the Blue School bomb on me. Dmitri and I were buds. He seemed cool since Day One.

I remember the night he showed up at Brewco where Rob and I were nursing a beer and watching the Bears-Bruins game. He'd gone young, but as soon as I caught the sound of his voice, I recognized him. What's he doing here?

"Jeanne? Jeanne McCormick? Do you remember me? Steve, Steve Smith?" he said.

I put on a lukewarm smile and a blank stare. I'd been around Blue Talon enough to hesitate long enough to paste a phony OMG expression on my face. "Steve, how long has it been? What are you doing here?"

"Watching the game, same as you. Duh."

I waved at Dmitri and the line of my friends at the bar. Suspicious I wanted prep time. "Rob, guys, this is Steve Smith. We went to grade school together. What are the chances we'd end up together here?"

None of them moved their eyes off the screen, although Marcia, an old dorm friend of mine, smiled, leisurely looked him up and down, taking stock of his well-built body and tight abs. The men deigned to notice him and pushed out a disinterested, "Hi, Steve, glad ta meetcha."

"Sit down. Tell me all about yourself. What's happening with you these days?" I said.

"Second year here. I'm in Finance."

"You're in school here? How come we never ran into each other before?"

"The fact is, until an old dude in San Simeon took pity on me and decided to set me up with a scholarship, I needed to work whenever I wasn't in class. I didn't often find time for such decadent pastimes as beer and Bruin's football."

"No loss this season. My high school team had a better record—although today may be a miracle, and we pull off a W."

I stared at him, reading his face. Chance meeting, my ass!

"Bring your beer over and join us for the game. I don't think we'll be able to talk much over the noise though. Let's shoot for coffee tomorrow? At Kerckoff?"

"It's a date. Or did I say the wrong thing?" Dmitri looks over at the rapt line of males across the table.

"Nope, free as a bird these days. Bjorn is at U of M, back in the snow. He likes it. I don't. We're over."

"I've got about hour between classes at 10. How's ten sound?"

The next day came after I spent a sleepless night. What the hell, can't sleep, might as well study. Can't let it get out though. Ruin my image.

I got my wake-up brew and cooled my jets for over half an hour when he sauntered in. I watched as he walked through the room. Damn, he's hot. Too bad he's family. I wish I had a nickel for every time Dad told me 'Family does not marry family, Jeanne. Marriage with a member of the family is a giant no-no—which makes dating pointless. Why'd I have to be born into this family? Sucks living lies, living alone.

"I don't suppose you're here because you have good news to share. Am I right?"

"Deed you are, Auntie."

I punched his shoulder and hissed. "Thought we weren't supposed to get out of character, Hotshot."

"Sorry, Jeanne Bond." I could kill Dad for sharing that little tidbit with the others. Of course, he'd never actually die, but I'd feel better.

"Are we done? I don't get guys, no matter how old they are–and you sure as hell qualify as old–always have a sense of humor like a ten-year-old."

"Ok, truce," he said, holding up his hands and getting serious. "This is the deal. That Walt guy you don't like, the weirdo friend of Rob's?"

Like how many Walts did he think I knew? "What about him?"

"Ricky's minions **see Rob's hidden dark side of his personality—the dark, borderline psycho, buried deep now—thanks to your efforts.** His stepfather's abuse developed this aspect of his character and the after effects of ostracism shows on his face. The tendency might be innate, but they're not sure. Your efforts, your friendship with him, buried this

237

part and kept the darkness at bay. Anyway, this Walt is a sociopath, no kidding, shows no remorse— charming as hell and dangerous as a snake. Somehow, he zeroed in on Rob and has been doing all he can to bring the nastiness to the surface.

"This butt-wipe grew up with the World Church of the Creator and introduced our subject to Resistance Records. He pulled out all the stops to feed our boy his racist and anti-Semitic views, full on hate mongering. He's been trying to get him to join Youth for Western Civilization. Walt's dangerous—helped get a chapter for these bottom-feeders on campus."

"I've never heard of them. Should I have? Guess I'm out of the loop for sure. Studying too much, probably." I said smugly.

Dmitri stared at me, disbelief plastered on his face. "Oh, I'm sure excess studying would be the reason. How dumb do you think I am? Or maybe you spend too much time here with a mob of Bruins. To continue—YWC's been around a lot longer back east so set up a better organization."

I socked him, but he ignored me.

"Some guy named Tansido, Tanfreeto, something like that, acted as their out front guy. This is a nasty group of bigots."

"How come this is the first I learned about the…what is it, Youth for Western Nations?"

"Civilization, Nation, same difference——white guys good, anyone else doesn't count."

"You didn't answer my question, Dmi—Steve."

"My guess—this slimeball attended one of the supremacy camps, learned techniques about how to recruit, how to identify potential, and similar garbage. I suspect he took a couple of courses from McDonald, that professor from Long Beach."

How much double talk and delay does he expect me to take?

Dmitri caught the exasperation on my face and started checking off points on his fingers. "They approach a group like wolves surround a herd of deer to pick out the weak ones. The volunteers look for obvious loners, the ones who are grateful when they are included. The wolf pack separates their victim from the herd and makes their kill on the lone animal. These jokers entice their target by becoming their best buddies. They dangle being an insider in front of them; feed their insecurities with phony notions of superiority. They concentrate on individuals with talents or skills to exploit for their cause. With Rob, Walt pulled out all stops. He gradually isolated him from your influence with a bunch of racist, sexist garbage about male superiority. Classic siren wail of the WASP male."

What a forehead slapper. How could I be so oblivious not to wonder why suddenly Rob was 'busy  so often? Dad wouldn't have missed the signs. Well, they wanted a first-timer,

"Jeanne Bond seems more like Jeanne Blond," I shook my head. "What do we need to do?"

"Sergei is swinging by headquarters for the latest and will be meeting us here. He didn't want to 'go young  yet. I realize he's having too much fun being SuperDoc. Gives him access to the most current cutting-edge research, He's hung up on finding out why we are what we are. He knows I like being a twenty-something anyway."

"I'm kind of glad. Having Dad still being Dad, I mean."

He nodded and asked, "When are you free tomorrow? He and Ricky must  live in the Dad camp and thought face to face time important as well."

"More like he still doesn't trust e-mail or anything much coming out of a computer, for that matter. It's super he'll be here, though. When is he due in? LAX or Burbank?"

"Burbank. I'm picking him up around noon. US Air through Phoenix."

"OK, I'm coming along, too. Screw Epistemology."

"Atta girl, Auntie. That's what I like to see, a dedicated student."

### Teleconference

I stood on tiptoes and gave Dad a big hug when he emerged from security. He looked beat. He whispered in my ear, "Always wonderful to be with you, Love."

Dmitri/Steve picked up Dad's carry-on, and we marched in step toward an exit. "I hope you arranged for a rental car, Sergei. I don't think I could tolerate another minute on the MTA."

"No sympathy from me, Grandson. Little did I realize when I rode horseback across the steppes that one day I'd endure greater hardships in travel. My saddlebags got better care in the eighteenth century from the horses than airline passengers' bags do from today's luggage handlers. I shudder when I think of the treatment of my luggage. I admit flying first class for the Clinic spoils me, but even then—remind me next time to not turn down Ricky's offer to ride on Air Blue Talon."

Dmitri laughed. "Point well taken, Sergei. What about the rental car?"

"Yes, Indolent Grandson, I arranged for a vehicle. I booked something they call an Escapade…or some kind of car starting with an e..."

"Well done, Sergei. Ricky should be paying hardship bonuses if we have to rely on public transportation in this country. When I catch a gig in Europe or China, I've got a much easier time getting around."

"Like you did in Stalingrad?" popped out unbidden from my mouth.

"Right, Auntie, sure thing."

Dad glanced over at me with that's "nothing-to-make-light-of" look. I shrugged.

We swung by the rental car counter, did the paperwork, and Dmitri scooped up the keys. "Sorry, Sergei, riding in the back seat with you piloting our vehicle on the local freeway is an experience I'd rather not repeat. Where to?"

"The Hotel Palomar."

"Ah, life among the mucky-mucks. Another one of those Papa-perks again, Sergei?"

"Someone on staff at HQ made the reservation."

I don't think the elevator door closed completely when Dmitri/Steve motioned for us to wait. He glanced up and down the hallway before he took the key and opened the suite. Bending down, he pulled out a super-strange electronic device, which resembled a miniature metal detector—one of the weird ones geeks used on the beach to find coins. As he entered, he stepped to one side and held the instrument in front of him.

"I wonder if you realize how ridiculous you look, Dmitri. What do you think you're doing? Monitoring gravity or magnetics?"

"Making sure no one else will listen when I set up the teleconferencing with Ricky, Karl, and the others."

"You think someone bugged the room? Come on! When did you move to Paranoia City?"

"Probably not bugged, but checking for listening devices is S.O.P for a Blue Talon operation these days. With our current scope of activities, we can't be too careful."

I glanced over at Dad with a questioning raise of my eyebrows while we cooled our heels in the hallway. "They're doing this routinely. We've lost some short-timers, good agents working for us, over a compromised mission. One of your brothers needed a reanimation and putting someone new in place was a hell of a mess for the rest of the team. "

"You'd know all this if you ever bothered to listen at minion school," Dmitri added as he motioned for us to come in.

"Like you do, Dmitri."

I touched my forehead and bowed in a crude imitation of the Turkish gesture of submission. Dad had demonstrated it for me when he spoke of his time there. "Carry on, all-powerful-one, I await your command."

"As well ye might, insignificant underling," he said with a grin.

"Must I always become a referee for children when you two are together? Were I not armed with the knowledge that several hundred years separated your ages, I would take both of you for less than ten."

I wish I could tell if Dmitri's putting on a show. I hope not. I can joke around and have fun with him. He seems like the brother I never had. Well, I do, but….

"Sorry, Sergei." His face slipped into a serious expression. "Dealing with something as insubstantial as the possible influence of a fudoer intimidates me. I always seemed more at ease with a sword in my hand and a live enemy in front of me. Ricky's gurus seem to do a fine job with spotting trends, but none counteract or encourage those who do. They always leave the hard work to us. They hung Auntie here up to dry in a major way. First timer, no training, working against the worse potential outcome we've come across in a long time. Blue or no Blue, this sucks."

Wow. He sure seems worried. He's seemed so like someone close to my age a few seconds before.

243

"I understand your frustration. Being a doctor for centuries, I've relied on identifying symptoms and trying one thing, and another hoping for a cure. Although the cause of the malady remained unknown, the patient was real. The result of treatment usually appeared in a day or two. Now we are dealing with a patient who appears alive and well, but who may in the future cause hurt and illness in others unless we intervene.

"We must identify the most appropriate surgery to excise the evil and avert a probable event not yet happened. We won't find out how well we've done for years to come. Friedrich tells me the computer should be able to identify a treatment to achieve the best result. As for me—I suffer the same overwhelming sense of incompetence I experienced when I tried to help my wife Frieda fight cholera."

The room fell silent, "Dad, you always tell me the best place to start is at the beginning. We won't succeed unless we begin."

"When did you get so wise, Love?"

We all jumped at the sound of a knock at the suite door. Dmitri shrugged and headed in that direction to answer, grabbed the knob. "Yes?"

"Your delivery, Sir. The manager held the package at the front desk until you arrived."

Dmitri in his role as penniless college student glanced over at Dad who reached in his pocket and pulled out a fistful of bills, "Just put the box on the desk, son. Thank you."

After the bellman left, Dmitri said, "I'm betting this contains what I need to set up the teleconference. Should take a half hour or so. Sergei, if you'll let Ricky know we'll be up and starting the session soon."

The clear skepticism on Dad's face completely conveyed very well what he thought of teleconferencing. After signing up for several on-line classes, I wouldn't argue much with him. I grew up connected, but Dad lived 300 years before he encountered his first PC. Perhaps I'm a Luddite type, too. Face to face often worked better when something big came down.

"Of course," was all he said in response.

Dmitri is almost as old as Dad is, and he's into technology. Go figure.

Once Dmitri completed his set-up, he established the session. We were the last to log on. Dmitri and Karl spent a good half hour fiddle farting around to get the webcam angles right so each person appeared normal. Dmitri threw me a glance, and I rolled my eyes in sympathy. We both understood the display was a concession to Papa. I was used to texting and news a la Facebook or the new super-secure Blue site. A few shared documents ahead of time would handle most of our agenda. No matter. If Papa wanted faces, faces he would get.

One by one, the faces greeted us: Ricky, Tina, Karl head computer guy and his assistant Wang Po, Amelia. Wang Po, a great something of Tina's, and Amelia, a psychiatrist connected to Dad's Polish family somehow. All told, counting Karl in the mountain, representatives from five countries took part. My on-line classes usually enrolled at least this many. No big deal.

Ricky's voice boomed across the room. Dmitri adjusted the volume as he said, "I think we are all present. HW has proposed three different options are on the table for us to consider. We're not married to any of them. Jeanne, you'll need to be our peer gauge here, tell us which one would seem most appropriate."

"Sure, Ricky," I said, astonished at being signaled out this way.

No one was less surprised than I was when the next three hours passed with the discussion dominated by the representatives from anywhere other than where the 'subject lived. The input from Dad, Dmitri or me, except for an occasional nod or shake of the head appeared ignored. My screen went out of focus, and no one except Dmitri noticed—and then only after I threw a paper clip at him to catch his attention.

Karl rambled on and on with his charts, trends, and influencing factors. Wang Po didn't add much although his charts seemed slicker. Tina and Amelia cooed on over the psychological profiles of Rob and Walt, pure psychobabble to my public affairs mind-set. Their suggestions, albeit reached by earnest discussion and consensus seemed, in a word, lame. Everyone came up with a variation of 'get Walt away from Rob'. Things should work out. Garbage—although the one where Karl would plant an arrest warrant with the local PD appealed to me. A lot. Not playing fair, true, but Walt was such a shit.

Dad spoke up. Ah, Papa speaks—everyone listens.

"I seem to remember when we began this session; Jeanne would provide knowledgeable observations on the alternatives."

"Oh, of course, Papa. You're right. Have you anything to add, Jeanne?"

Add? Since when did prime quality feedback like mine become an add?

So I told them. "I think they're all crap, even if seeing Walt in a cell has a certain allure for me, You don't think because he's gone, the bogus warped ideas he planted in Rob's mind would vanish as well, do you? You, the family with all the memories, the memory you call your ace in the hole? Isn't the whole purpose of propaganda to change the minds of the listener? What were you thinking?"

I loved it. The silence, Prolonging the gloat session, although satisfying, did little to accomplish what we needed to do. I gave Ricky credit for gracefully eating his humble pie. "Do you have an alternate plan to suggest, Jeanne? Something more workable?"

I did. "I think you are looking at this in exactly the opposite way you should. Everything you've come up with revolves around getting Walt out of his life. We need to get Rob out of Walt's life. If Rob got too friendly with a person of color or joined in a cause like equal rights—something frowned on by Walt's brand of Aryan zealots—he'd drop Rob like some kind of psychedelic toad. If Walt excluded him from what's going on, Rob should begin to question everything he fed to him.

"Dad, could you use some of your medical contacts to get Rob an internship in a racially-mixed organization. My guess—Walt would throw a snit fit and treat the place and everything it stood for like a garbage dump. Meanwhile, Dmitri and I work on hooking him up with a girl. We make sure we counter every snide white supremacist remark with a rational one. We're both short-timers at UCLA, not in your sense, but literally. One quarter left. I know Rob applied for a joint degree at Stanford. I got early acceptance at law school. Fake something for Steve…" I smirk at Dmitri "because I doubt he'd make the cut without your intervention. Although an internship in, say Africa or some kind of health study maybe would be better for Rob."

"Now you understand why she's drawn the assignment," Dad said quietly, his shirt buttons near to popping off with pride.

When the last screen flicked to black, Dad leaned over and gave me a hug. "Did I ever tell you how proud I am of you?"

"Phew," said Dmitri, "Like her head's not big enough already, All right, hot shot, you got us into this. I hope you're ready with more than just what if's."

I tried to resist making a comeback, but in the end, "I don't see you jumping up to volunteer. Who do you think has been walking point with Rob since high school, huh?"

### Checkmate

Once Ricky's minions e-mailed me a confirmation that Stanford accepted Rob for their PH.D. program, Dad suggested I volunteer to check on my "subject."

"Surprise him, Love. Show me how your powers of observation have improved."

This was the part I hated most—playing Blue Talon spy. As usual, the condition of Rob's off-campus apartment would offend a pig—books, chip crumbs, dirty dishes covered every flat surface. I admit he kept the area around his computer tidy, but the rest of the place would never pass a health inspection. This time the spying didn't bother me as much, Dad's stamp of approval made a big difference.

When I strolled in, Walt sat slouched in the overstuffed brown relic Rob bought from the Goodwill. My "subject" sat sideways on the couch, an open textbook on the floor next to him. Besides the remains of lunch—lunches?—I spotted some brochures and reprints from Youth for Western Civilization. The headlines blurred at this distance, but I didn't need to guess what they said, only wondered how nasty on a scale of one through disgusting they might be.

"Hey, Rob," I said, giving him a neighborly social hug and ignoring Walt. "How's it going, my man?"

"Oh, Jeanne, I'm glad you stopped by. You'll never guess what came in the mail this noon."

"Come on, give it up. You know I suck at guessing."

"Ok, I'll give you a hint. Seems we might be neighbors for a few more years."

I tried for a I confused look, allowed comprehension to show, and at last squealed, "You got accepted in the doc program at the Farm, didn't you? Oh, how awesome is that? Congrats, buddy."

"They accepted you a long time ago, so…"

"Hey, only for Law School. My dad says anyone who bullshits well enough can get into law. Everybody knows how competitive getting into the Nano program is. Good for you. How about we celebrate—go to that dive where Brewco used to be for some wings and harmonize with the Karaoke. Adding a few UCLA grads will up the class of students at Stanford, big time."

"Works for me. Want to join us, Walt?"

"We shouldn't," he snarls, shooting me a dirty look. "We gotta lotta work to do here."

"One night off won't matter. Jeanne and I need to celebrate. Come on."

"Maybe next time."

Ha—Like that would happen. "I think there are four or five Bruins headed north next fall. Let's face it; Stanford is lucky getting the pick of the litter like us."

"Karaoke would be cool," Rob said, surprising the hell out of me. He's got a beautiful voice, but a person so pathologically shy doesn't perform in public very often.


This place seemed like my second home, cheap drinks, big screen TV, and Bruins. Since we arrived in SoCal, I periodically dragged Rob along, part of my make-Rob-less-of-a-geek plan. We found every inch of the place packed. I scanned the dark interior where most of the action took place. My eyes adjusted to the light, and I spotted the others in a corner. I wriggled us through the crowd to the table with two empty chairs. "Hey, Rob, do you remember my old friend Steve? I don't think he'd mind if his table."

I sat down and make myself comfortable before they could say no. Not that I expected one. This meeting was pre-planned.

"Yeah, I guess," he said in a doubtful tone.

Across the table sat Steve/Dmitri and one of the most gorgeous girls—sorry, women, I'm not a teenager any more—I've ever set eyes on next to him. Her tawny skin was flawless, snappy black eyes tilted under a mound of coal black hair. What she was like below the waist wasn't visible, but any guy I know would kill to have her top half. The two of them made a striking couple, and, if I hadn't arranged for both of them to join us, I'd be impressed. Both were family members with Neela coming from the South African branch. If her mix of every ethnic element in that part of the world always ended up this awesome, I chose the wrong parents.

"Hi, Jeanne. Neela, Jeanne is the grade school friend I told you about."

We did the introduction thing all around. Rob glued his eyes on Neela. Despite the crap Walt fed him on racial purity, he couldn't take his eyes off the "mongrel." He hung on her every word. I imagine someone that hot lived with male adulation every day so for her to even notice such an insignificant was remarkable. Man, did she play him. Like a bloody harp. Neela rocked her part in Phase One of the Kick Walt to the Curb plan. I glanced at Steve/Dmitri, and we exchanged a visual high five. We were off and running.

"Long Islands all round?"

Subsequent Long Islands later, even watered down, as usual, gave us all a buzz. We shouted over the din. A loud "I don't believe it!" cut into the meaningless conversation I carry on with the DDG hunk behind me.

"You don't buy into what?"

"Did you know Neela was headed for the Farm?"

"No, when did you get your acceptance. I thought I'd ferreted out all of us headed that way."

"Just today," she answered in her not quite British South African accent.

"Me, too," from Rob, "would you believe it?"

Of course, I would. I was responsible for this part of the Retake Rob task force. Introduction of possible significant other with geographic proximity factored in.

"This is so exciting," she said "Being accepted into my first choice grad program, meeting Rob, and finding out we both will be in the Bioengineering school. A trifecta!"

The next morning, post-LI-Teas, didn't seem too trifecterish. My head pounded and the stomach agreed, insisting I'd been a bad person. Thank heaven for the Blue and twice thanks for the demonstration. The aftermath from last night's violence would leave a supply floating around for me. During what I call my morning run, I spent time searching for the ultimate hangover cure. I inhaled the rays the way Dad taught me. Moderation always, he said. I would need to pay it forward. At this minute, only one thought crossed my mind, I don't care how many boring lives I suffer through if don't have to deal with the after-effects of too much booze.

Last week as the final planks of the S.W.O. phase fell into place. I was flying high— too high apparently. At our final breakdown session, Dad pulled me aside and reminded me in no uncertain way family business was always family business. "Jeanne, Love. I won't diminish your success so far." And then he did. "You must remember, what we do today is the cherry piled on top of a whole mound of ice cream made of Blue Talon experience and resources. Public pride is never acceptable."

Hoo boy. He was right, of course, but couldn't I catch a break? Would one little pat on the back be too much?


Phase II of the plan involved a valuable, but to Walt a distasteful, summer internship for Rob. Phase III meant growing the love buds at Stanford with Phase IV, of course, Rob, matched with Neela, walking the sunny side and saving the world from death and disease. I'd heard the stories about Dad and Dmitri, even Ricky, fighting in battles, all kinds of exciting things. Heroes. I get to be a yenta. What good is having multiple lives if you can't be Princess Leia?

Ricky and the minions did the heavy lifting for Phase II. They set up a summer research slot at Mt. Sinai med center for an on-going study on Gauchers syndrome. How perfect was that? A Jewish hospital site for a study of a disease striking people of Jewish descent. I "find out" when Rob rang me and asked me out for coffee. "Ok, but it'll cost you. Starbucks this time, buddy."

When he didn't object, I zoomed in to take advantage of his state of mind. Usually, he was cheaper than dirt.

"Jeanne, my adviser just gave me a heads up on an internship. The position pays well and would look wonderful on my resume, but…"

"But what, Champ? You can handle it, Mr. All-A's this quarter."

"That's not it, Jeanne." He twisted in his chair, head down. "The problem is Walt. I blurted out something about Dr. DeMente's tip, and he lost it. Told me I was an idiot even to think about spending time with those people. Disgusting was the word he used."

"What's his problem?"

"The place, the people, they're…Jewish, well mostly anyway."

"And?"

"So he thinks we're better than they are."

"Rob, to quote a great man, 'Are you nuts'? What a perfect door-opener. Big gold star on your resume. Who cares if it has six, not five points? And, you might even learn something. I'd tell him to fuck off and mind his own business." Not a word I use often, but sometimes duty calls.

He went silent, and I recognized the conflicting emotions on his face. In the end, I guess my opinion as an old friend trumped those of new assholes. "You're right, Jeanne. I'm going to accept. I'd be crazy not to. About a hundred others in the department would jump at the chance."

"Right you are, Neighbor."

Ah, it felt good. One small step toward rationality, one giant kick in the ass to bigotry.

I called Dad when I got back to the dorm. Ricky's report could wait—Dad was my partner. Him I needed to update.

"Hi, Dad. I wanted you to be the one to tell Ricky my plan worked—that your first timer scored a goal, big time. Dmitri and I got the wedge slammed in between Rob and the a— e Walt. I'll give Ricky a little credit. His minions pulled strings and set up the deal with Mt. Sinai, but we did the heavy blocking."

"I've told him all along I had the best partner."

I basked for a few seconds in his praise up to the time he added, "Being part of the family doesn't always give this much satisfaction. You need to remember this for those times when your mission doesn't go as well."

If I were younger, I'd have whined, "Daaad." Being older, I grew sober and fell silent. Why was I born into this family?

### *Blue Talon speaks and Sergei Listens*

### *Sergei's Phone Rings Again*

Jeanne's call had been welcome. Of all my children, my relationship with her was the closest. Being a single parent forged a bond I'd not experienced with any of the children of my other families. I was happy to do her boasting for her when I called Ricky.

The result was later in the spring, Friedrich and Valentina seized the opportunity for an uninvited face to face with me at my home in Minnesota. Jeanne's spring break began two days hence, and Ricky somewhat sheepishly apologized for barging in.

"Papa, I'm sorry for showing up without an invitation. And, yes, I do remember agreeing meetings in Minnesota would be scheduled ahead of time."

My face must have reflected my displeasure because he held up one hand with the palm toward me so he could continue, "If we didn't consider a 'pre-meeting meeting' before Jeanne gets home, we wouldn't be here. We need to talk about Jeanne—and her…her unorthodox methods."

Under his breath, he added, "and her attitude."

I chose to pretend I didn't hear that last mutter.

"You have no one to blame for this besides yourself, Friedrich. You and your sister pushed me to accelerate her into active service—long before she should have, in my opinion."

"Believe me, Papa, we know. Boy, do we know! She's handled the subject well, but getting into the same room as her ego at this point is proving difficult."

I laughed. "Sometimes you get more than you bargain for, Son. I think you can count on brash females from now on. The demure damsel is a person of the past."

256

Valentina spoke up to support her brother. "We're here to humor you and your … uh … distrust of computer communication. We appreciate the fact you don't throw your weight around insisting on a face to face instead of teleconferencing every time. No IT operator at headquarters would set up a session without clearing it first with you. The respect you command often causes the partners assigned to you to end up less useful. Your reputation impresses them too much—makes them too much in awe and afraid to contradict you," she added in a wry tone. "Ricky needs to be careful who he assigns to you."

"Believe me, Papa, your current partner never presented us the problem of being too awed," my son added.

I pursed my lips and said nothing but conceded to myself their point was valid.

"Ricky, Papa realizes we didn't have much choice. Dmitri is the only one who can slip into an apparent age—and even he makes a mess of anything younger than his twenties. Most of us can look the part, but not play the role. We remember too much. We're disinclined to be teenagers. Given a choice, most of us lean towards staying thirty-something when we choose to "young" ourselves after a reanimation. You hang in your forties if you can. I assume you do this to bolster confidence in you as a kind old doctor."

"I don't argue," Ricky said, "but after all those years of failing to stave off one bad mess after another by not detecting a probable crisis soon enough, we succeed—by using a first-timer less experienced than anyone since your own first time. Now her know-it-all attitude adds salt to the wound. Good thing the family has doctors, frankly, a psychiatrist would be more useful. The worse thing is realizing I might have been exactly the same when I was at the same age, a would-be attorney with a smart mouth."

I stared at him noncommittal. A glint of a smile hovered on my lips.

"Papa, was I such a pile of *Kuhscheiße* when I was at the university in Berlin?

"From the stories I've heard, I was lucky I hadn't met you yet," Valentina commented.

"Jeanne is 100% self-confidence. She's the first modern woman born to me. Her predecessor, Mayta, was a baby boomer. This one expects to succeed and is blind to many of the barriers women like Mayta used to battle. She's a definite preview of what we can expect from our future female children."

"I'm not sure the world is ready for too many Jeannes."

"Okay—what happened to make you show up now? You were lucky I was home. I out in to take a vacation while Jeanne's home. This will most likely be our last chance to travel together as father and daughter."

"You keep up on the progress of her assignment since we talked, I assume?"

I nod, but say nothing.

"Thank you for reminding her to file her reports. Blue Talon has benefitted from her law study. Every report reads like a brief. Our involvement with Rob seems on course. Rob's contact with Walt and others in YWC appears to be at an end. Karl still monitors his internet browsing and reports the subject seldom logs onto questionable sites. I'm sensing the convenient relationship with Neela fast deepening into something closer to a full-blown affair. Neela seems genuinely taken by him. Convenient for us."

"I agree. Jeanne and I ate dinner with them after the last parents' weekend. I suspect the spark between them to be more than we'd expect from an operative acting the part on an assignment. Perhaps the attraction is a fellow scientist thing. That's my take anyway. Mayta would call him an old soul, hooking with a kindred spirit. Or some such nonsense. The current daughter's idea is, as she puts it, 'O M G like I can't believe someone as hot as Neela would actually be attracted to Rob the Nerd.

"I imagine in her mind he's still the geeky boy down the street," Valentina said.

"Umm, maybe. We three shared a fascinating dinner conversation. They tried to include me as they described what they study, their experiments, how their work might apply to society. I must admit, I toyed with the idea of studying the same area in my next life. "

Neither commented on my next life plans. Their eyes glaze over when I pontificate on my search for to what we are.

Instead, they shared the events bringing them to Minnesota slush. "To answer your question. We've got two issues—one immediate and the other longer term, A month or two ago Rob published a short piece in one of the professional journals covering breakthroughs in bioengineering. Viewed one way, this was quite an accomplishment for someone still in school. Feather in his cap, but another take would be he created an additional thorn in our side. The article touched on his experiments for using Nanos as a tool for genetic issues. Publication acted like smoke signals for the eugenic nut-cases and guess who showed up in Palo Alto?"

"You're kidding, the same schmuck we dealt with earlier?"

His eyes widened at the word I used before he answered me.

"Karl tracked his contact attempt from Rob's emails. Jeanne's been out of the loop about what we've set up on our end. She doesn't realize we monitor his emails, so say nothing, So far Rob hasn't responded."

"And?"

"The nature of Rob's work makes him attractive to other nutcases with an agenda like Walt's. Our psychological profile indicates Rob is still susceptible. He doesn't have what he needs to go it alone. We will need more closely monitor and guide him for the near future. The inner 'blackness  we detected which triggers Jeanne's involvement diminished, but did not disappear. If Neela agrees to a long-term commitment, we should be able to keep him on track. His gift for good is too valuable to risk, and Neela would be in the best possible position to bring out his potential. That said, the more volatile aspect is, how will Jeanne accept handing the baton to someone else? To making Neela lead?"

"Indeed. You pursue this course, I assume, because Neela and Rob's pairing gelled because of their shared profession?"

"Correct. No attorney worth a damn would want to waste time hanging around a lab."

"Not a charitable thing to say, Friedrich."

He nodded, and I understood the meaning behind the gentle jibe, maintaining credibility in a close enough relationship to make a difference. Her matchmaking solution worked her out of a job.

"The toughest part of this—I intend to ask her to attend classes at HQ."

"A bit cowardly, Son, to come here so you can use me as a referee."

"Discretion and valor, Papa."

"I'm sensing additional concerns. Out with it, children."

The two exchanged glances. She straightened her shoulders and took a deep breath before she floated a trial balloon on her theory.

"You and I share misgivings about the real worth of computer-generated data. Some at HQ shared my concerns over some hints of a trend in less than explainable actions.

For example, we shared a concern about why Walt sought out our boy. He showed up out of the blue. Not our kind of Blue, randomly. What attracted him to Rob? He'd never met him. We believe we've unearthed a possible answer in the vast piles of metadata we mine. The way the computer team explained the significance, the lengths they go to refine and enhance current search engines and index programs for easy manipulation designed to make the calculations. We're afraid we uncovered evidence another such system exists—one seeking ends differencing from ours. Ricky isn't on the same page, but..."

"You two lifted the whole idea from some crappy science fiction novel. Science fiction is, after all, fiction."

"Not so, little brother. No more a lame sci-fi idea than a computer center housed in a mountain. Buck Rogers  ray gun isn't too different from today's Taser... and don't ask me who Buck Rogers is. You well know although Jeanne might not. He's well before her time."

She paused, one corner of her mouth threatening a smile, before continuing her argument. "Bunkers exist for the President to run to in case of an attack, a safe secured place to continue to run the government. Reality, Ricky, not some writer's imagination."

"You mean a balancing force?" I asked, ignoring the bickering.

"Perhaps I'm sensing something in the shadows when nothing is there, but what if we are right?"

"Tina, this is too metaphysical for me. If such a network exists, as sophisticated as ours, we would know," Friedrich blurted out.

"These tales of shadowy organizations floated around since I escaped my Ottoman master. Evil cabals, which exist in literature, exist in real life as well, in organized crime

261

or terrorist groups for example. Even Sherlock Holmes had his Dr. Moriarity. To consider an opposing rival exists is frightening, but I don't believe you can discount the possibility, Friedrich. Why not sic your minions, as Jeanne would say, on the problem?"

"The good news, Papa, at least in my opinion, is every long-lived we track down is part of our family. We are a product of the Blue. They seem to be mortals motivated by hatred," Valentina added.

I tilted my head one-way then the other. "I suppose we should have anticipated this discovery. The Blue obliges us to provide a counterpoint to the unsavory elements in our world and, in return, gives us life and health. If the rules of physics about equal and opposite reactions follow – leaving out the metaphysical, Friedrich – the opposite—shall we call it red?—likely harms rather than heals a user."

My son stared at me, disbelief written on his face. The question "Are you buying into this drivel "as clear as if he'd spoken aloud.

I was about to reply when I caught the sound of a car pulling up in the driveway. Jeanne's home. She will not be happy. I think I may enjoy her reaction to Friedrich and Valentina's unannounced visit. The Uh oh, what's going on? Face as she walked through the front door dragging her carry-on was a clue.

"We're in the kitchen, Love," I called out.

### *Jeanne's Bittersweet Homecoming?*

Waaay too many cars out front. I grew suspicious as soon as I walked in. Dad called out when he heard the door open. "We're in the kitchen, Love."

We're? Who we?

Until then I'd been looking forward to a chance to raid the refrigerator. I was starving. No food, no blankets, and two hours late. A typical flight home. Now, when I caught sight of two extra people at the table a reverse déjà vu set in. The last time these two appeared unannounced at my house, they'd derailed my life and screwed up everything important to me back then. What now? Why did they show up here again? Another cock and bull story about the world ending? Did someone find another Mayan calendar predicting the end of time?

"Hi, Dad. What's up?" I said with a fake smile.

"These two want to schedule a session. I told them this had better be important because my almost-attorney daughter was coming home, and we had a joint vacation trip planned. Whatever they wanted to talk about had to be brief."

Dad paused to give me a hug, a tight hug before he went on, "You know I'm not comfortable with telegabbing."

I reached up and kissed him on the forehead, working hard to mask my irritation. Is it too bloody much to let us spend a week of father-daughter time?

"Good for you," I said to Dad, turned to Ricky and asked," Aren't weekly reports enough for you?"

His involuntary wince came close to making my day. Satisfying. So, so satisfying. "What's your point here, Big Brother?"

"Jeanne, everyone says your reports are top-notch. You've impressed HQ with how well you've handled the subject, although your unorthodox methods make a few … uneasy … on occasion."

*Nice doublespeak, Ricky.*

"You've devoted more time to your mission than most operatives. Most work undercover for shorter periods, deal with the immediate issue, mitigate or stop a crime or other objective, then returns to his or her current home. An agent might stay undercover for a decade or two, but I am not aware of any who devoted over half their life to a single project. Uncertainty still exists as to the outcome of your mission, and monitoring appears to be long term."

"A couple of decades is longer than I've been on this gig, Ricky. If you intend to be flattering, thank you, you didn't. If Dad put the same percentage of his life in, how long would that be? Two hundred plus years? Did you forget I'm a first-timer?'

Ricky glanced over at Dad from whom he seemed to expect some backup. Dad sat back, and seemed to; quite enjoy Ricky's discomfort.

"Look, Big Brother, Director, Head Cheese, whatever, I'm a little pissed to find you in Minnesota. Even if I were a normal kid, this break might be one of the last times I'll be home. We've made plans for father-daughter time. Maybe once, perhaps twice more, after that, no doubt you'll make sure  I'm  only here as a visitor."

I sensed rather than heard Dad's quick intake of breath and realized his emotional reaction when I was 'called to duty  so young. I was too mature for my age after Mom died, and my assignment rasped up the process even more. In one day, I ceased to be a daughter and became a partner, a co-worker, like his other children and grandchildren did before me. From his long-lived perspective, the short eight-or-ten-year span should seem minute, but in his heart, not so. How many times did he grapple with another sudden void in his life? How many times might I also experience a similar emptiness with my own children? Our eyes met, and we communicated without saying a word.

"We won't stay long, Jeanne, Just tonight and most of the day tomorrow, We plan a teleconference in the morning, we four, Neela, Dmitri, Karl, and Amelia, perhaps one or two more. I'd appreciate some help in setting up here if you don't mind."

I did, but I nodded.

Dad stood up, stretched a little. "Are you hungry? I stocked up on sandwich stuff. I find the conversation is always more civil when food is nearby. Don't think for a minute because a few years separate your births, I find tabletop bickering any more acceptable I did under the Czar or in the Kaiser in Berlin. I've got lifetimes of experience chiding children."

We had to laugh. How many lifetimes beside the one I contributed did this table represent? How many in the family? I gave up. *Too many to waste my young brain cells on.*

"Truce, duly noted, Papa," Ricky put in.

We spent the rest of the day in a pleasant way, bringing each other up to date, ignoring the elephant named Rob lurking in the background.


The next morning, Tina rose early, but my body clock still ran on Pacific Time. A hint of chocolate in the scent of fresh-brewed coffee and the aroma of pastries baking rousted me not too long after. I'd just poured my second cup when the phone rang. Karl was on the line to tell us he was ready on his end if we were good to go. Last night Ricky and I did an equipment crosscheck to make the system was working. Dad made a point of avoiding the den while we installed the computer and communication network.

"We're good here, Karl. I'll get the others together. Let Ricky do his thing."

Ricky began his pompous chairperson of the board act. Did all German-born men like to hear themselves talk as much as he did? I needed to ask Dad if any other of his kids or grandkids were born in Germany.

"Good morning, everyone, or whatever time shows on your clock now. To bring you up to speed, let me share a couple of items with you. Jeanne and Neela know the first one already. And thank you Neela, for staying up with us. I hope you are enjoying your visit at home?"

"No problem, Esteemed Uncle," she replied in that precious ever-so-formal South African accent.

"Some weeks ago, Walt popped up in California again. The agent we'd assigned to surveil him reported he'd tried on multiple occasions to re-establish contact with Rob. We were aware because we'd assigned one of our short-timers with the task of monitoring Walt after he left campus. Although this might seem the height of paranoia, this time our caution proved well advised. Her report outlined how Walt tracked him live and on the net—emailing, IM-ing, Snapchat, Facebook—all that.

Finally, he convinced our subject to meet for coffee in a "for-old-times" guise. Fed him a line about how he 'just happened to be" in the area on business, and a buddy told me you were at the farm, etc. etc.."

Hmm, when did Rob become "our" subject, not "Jeanne's" subject?

"Yeah, Yeah, the usual Walt bullshit. Your point, Ricky?"

He ignored me, and spoke to the others. "We notified Jeanne of Walt's activities. She was able to distract Rob by asking  his input on a scientific patent law case she needed to analyze, totally bogus, but intriguing, even flattering, for Rob. At the same time, Neela found … uh … other ways to distract him. Walt was able to convince Rob to meet. Walt spun a tale about his company setting up a lab for research in the same area. Talked up how Rob's doctoral paper would make him a natural fit. Rob came home excited about the opportunity."

"Naturally, his boss authorized Walt only to hire one person. So Sorry—no position for me. Could my Indian mother or black grandfather possibly be a factor?" Neela said, tongue firmly in check but her distaste showed through nonetheless.

"Not likely, Neela. You're too beautiful for them, and they don't want any competition," someone said.

*Must be Dmitri.*

"Eugenics seemed to be central to the thinking of Walt's crowd, Rob's work fit right in," I said. "If they lock in an exclusive on his discoveries, they'd be skidded to create the master race again, if you want to believe some a-holes."

"Fortunately another development occurred, of which Walt was unaware. Can you fill us in, Neela?"

She held up her left hand, fingers dangling, and a ring flashed on her finger. "I assume you meant this, Ricky?" Seeing a nod, she added, "As of the Friday before break, I have a new piece of jewelry. Rob proposed, and I accepted. We we're planning a wedding as soon as I get back. I wanted to let my parents know first."

I squealed. No other way to react to an announcement like that. "You're getting married? You realize this means I'm a real honest to goodness yenta?"

Everyone offered her congratulations. Privately I wondered what in the world she was thinking. Marriage to the king of the geeks? Then I realized Ricky was talking again.

"Neela agreed to run point on our surveillance of the subject, seeing as she'll be with him at any rate. Jeanne, Dmitri, would this be agreeable to you?"

Agreeable? Not to have to trail Rob for the rest of his life? Are you kidding? Aloud I answered, "If you think it best." Gag me. Total suck up, but a lingering thought like "so I'd agree the plan not 100% goofy'—but once the wedding is over, the natural thing would be for Dmitri and me to fade into the sunset. You'll be keeping me in the loop in case I need to come back in, right?"

Total silence and pot full of sidelong glances. Pretty obvious they set me up. Oh, well.

"Jeanne, honey, I want you as my maid of honor, and Rob is planning to ask 'Steve to be his best man," Neela said, filling the void.

"Well, hot damn," Dmitri/Steve said.

"Sergei agreed he'd stay on as Neela's advisor in a more limited way."

*Dad was staying in and I was out? So much for thank you, Jeanne, you've done a great job.*

"I want to stay on at the Clinic until I age out," Dad put in.

"Dmitri, I'll give you the summer off to relax and brush up on your Farsi. Let your beard grow. We need someone in Iran."

Dmitri's fired, too.

"Sounds interesting. How old do I need to become?"

"For this one, I'd say forty to forty-five."

"Not my favorite age, but I'll deal with it."

"Now Jeanne. You've been talking about going on walk-about...or at least that's where your friends will think you are. Papa and I agreed you'd benefit from at least six months at Blue School. We heaped more responsibility on you without providing you any of the tools others in the organization receive as a matter of routine."

"You're not serious. You want me to spend half a year in your bloody cave?"

I glanced over at Dad. He nodded.

"Traitor," I accused.

### Blue School- An Enrollee and a Visitor

Even though I bore responsibility for the Blue-fated lives of my children's and their children's, the sad weight descending on me as a father with an obligation to insist his child to do something "good for you" seemed worse. The hurt in her eyes when I agreed she must attend Blue School was a persistent memory. I clung to the hope our rift would be repairable. I wondered if any other of my children felt betrayed as Jeanne had.

Today I was a guest at Blue School. I watched Jeanne through the one-way glass. Ricky had been discrete with his surveillance—inside the classroom, the window appeared to be part of an elaborate world map. I kept meaning to ask Friedrich why none of the maps showed through the glass. No need. He'd built in a peephole for observers, a meter and half-square peep. Karl, paranoid as he was, placed enough monitoring devises in this place to make one unnecessary, making Friedrich's spy spot a whimsy.

Jeanne had lobbied me to dissuade "The Bossman," as everyone here calls my son, to cancel … and if cancellation were impossible to delay … her coming. "Dad, I can't abandon Rob. He and I have gotten tight. I don't mind Neela being lead. She'll be spending more time with him, but what if something comes up with that louse Walt again? Rob trusts me—besides I've spent over twenty years in school and need a break. It's not fair." She didn't fool me, or anyone else. She didn't want to be here at all. So much, she would use Rob as a ploy. "Dad, I don't belong here."

When she failed, she settled for finagling as long a delay as possible. Friedrich granted her three months.

I tried to intercede on her behalf, but Friedrich's response had been, "Papa, I want her in class before the winter sets in. Sometimes the road leading up to HQ is snowbound, and I don't think I could deal with her complaining about the cold, the snow, and what she calls 'the bloody cave."

Trapped in a place she didn't want to be, her attitude shown bright and clear. Jeanne always sat in the back of the room pretending to ignore the lecture or exhibits in front of her. I saw through her act. She didn't mind being a celebrity—the only one in the room who'd already completed an assignment—but her notoriety seemed a small consolation for spending hours and days with young kids in their teens. I observed when her chin always rose slightly when an interesting topic came up. Her shoulders straightened if a family member showed up at HQ for a debriefing or for research into the case background before beginning a new assignment.

Ricky insisted family members meet the classes. After such a session, Jeanne would stay to press the visitors to share more about their missions. Friedrich insisted they stress how the skills taught in the school would assist with an assignment. Jeanne didn't buy in and considered the propaganda kid stuff. She avoided spending time with her fellow students whom she considered too 'juvenile.

Jeanne excelled at cornering the visiting agent for a chat and proved not many bested her in natural interrogation skills. She found out more about what they'd done than they intended to share. Despite herself, she admitted to me so many generations mixed together was "Cool, but don't you say anything to the Bossman."

"Why can't I like, you know, tag along with a couple of the guys? I'd learn a lot more than sitting in this silly classroom."

Friedrich walked up behind us and shared his frustration, "Papa, she's never shown a hint of interest at their lectures. If she's doing more than going through the motions in her classes, I'd be surprised."

Jeanne shrugged. Her unvoiced answer was plain.

Not surprise for me—even as a toddler, she tried to control everything. I sympathized with Friedrich. "She hadn't changed, Son. When she was a small child drilling me with questions if she were interested in something and complaining constantly. If she weren't, she'd ask, "How much farther, Dad? When will we get there? Why can't I?'"

He shook his head. "She's got her own mind, for sure. She hits me up every opportunity that comes up to leave. 'Ricky, either let me get on with my life or give me an assignment. Send someone along to brainwash me. I don't want to waste time in this bloody cave. Come on, Ricky. I've got no social life…everyone's family, I haven't had a decent beer since I got here and no time for much else. I outgrew Mac and Cheese a decade ago. Have a heart.'—Papa, she never lets up.'"

Jeanne gave me a half-smile of triumph.


Unlike Jeanne, I enjoyed my time at Blue Talon headquarters–cave or not. Besides the regular students, HQ hosted a floating population of parents, agents between assignments or there for advanced training. The job of maintaining the Archives chronicling Family and Blue Talon history rotated among family members. For me, every visit was a trip down memory lane, for others, a way to learn how another family member confronted a similar situation.

Friedrich set up a "Welcome" sign in the cave lobby where his assistant listed the names of visitors. Whenever my sons, daughters, or grandchildren were there and learned I was on site, they sought me out for 'Papa time'. Multiple greats of my family grabbed the opportunity to meet each other and spend time with me. Valentina accused me of rubbing my nostalgia itch with every visit. As usual, more correct than not, she understood better me than most. Her lives spanned nearly as much time as my own.

I recognized my children and grandchildren who looked much as they had when I "died." The apparent age I preferred might be older than they remembered, but my face was still the one they had loved and respected. These chance meetings away from short-time-life allowed us to shed the identity we were using outside. Hidden in the mountain, we were free to be ourselves. Ourselves as we were when we lived as a family, like any short-lived family. On the outside, they'd ignore me or introduce me as 'an old friend  or 'some kind of cousin', which allowed them to stay in the character they played in their current assignment.

No one counted on seeing a particular member of the family, me included. Comings and goings to the cave were erratic, often clandestine. Many were 'dead  in their prior life. Friedrich often gave me a few hours advance notice of arrivals, but not yesterday. My son showed something of a prankster and kept the identity of this visitor a secret.


When I spotted her entering the dining hall, I dropped my cup, and the pieces clattered across the floor. The newcomer was Gizela, the light of my life in Krakow. She had come half running into the room seeking me. Since that long ago day when I slipped into the forest and left my loved ones in the safety of a cave, we had not seen each other.

273

Time and distance seemed to conspire to keep us from one another. She seldom came to North America, and in all those years, we never were at the same place at the same time.

She ran up to me and threw her arms around my neck crying "TaTa, TaTa" in the archaic Polish dialect we shared. I held her out to take in all of her, my beautiful daughter. Sons I loved, but the daughters I worshiped.

"Moja córka! Gizela, you are all grown up and so beautiful." I held her out to look at her.

"TaTa," she said in voice and manner so like Jeanne's, "Hundreds of years have passed. Of course, I grew up. Many times in fact."

I felt silly. Her life paralleled my own. Still, for me, the years seemed not so long. "Fathers never expect their daughters to grow up, Angel. We hope to have our little girls forever."

She laughed and pulled me down beside her. "Sit. Sit. Let me get us both a fresh glass of tea."

Putting down the glass she'd fetched, she pulled up the chair next to me. "No more Pan Doktor Kowalski. Friedrich told me. Now you are the renowned Doctor Peter McCormick, consultant to the Mayer Foundation. So much change always, so much the same, is it not?"

I nodded, and we sat silent for a moment or two, each remembering. "Did you know Alek and I partnered on an assignment during the days of Gorbachev, during perestroika and glasnost. We needed to maintain our cover identities, but one evening we slipped away and talked as father and son. Far too short a time  because, as  he was about to tell what happened the day I died,  to share with me how you fared in the cave outside Krakow, a local hotshot swooped in and scooped us up to handle the emergency of the hour."

"I know, I know. He told me. We had similar encounters."

"Let's let the past couple centuries wait until and what happened after we left Krakow." She agreed and began.


"'After you and Alek left the cave, Mama told us we must gather branches to build a fire at the back of the cave near a vent which would take up the smoke and not reveal our presence. Pawel and I gathered leaves as well to cover the rock floor, which was freezing cold and hard. We huddled in the rear and spoke in whispers in case any soldiers came nearby. We heard voices and cowered in fear until Mama said, 'That voice is Alek's.'

"Soon after, he returned to the cave carrying a pouch, worried and upset and said, "Papa will go to buy food and blankets. He would not let me go, said I must stay and take care of you."

"Ooh, I feel so safe now," Pawel, said. Alek turned and boxed his ear, the same way you would do when one makes such a remark.'"

I smiled. Unthinkable today, but fathers did such things back then.

"'Mama and Alek murmured in low voices near the cave opening. I could tell Mama was worried. When they joined us, their forced smiles didn't fool me. Pawel sensed something was wrong as well. He started to cry burying his face in Mama's lap. I put my head down, glared at Alek, and made a motion at the entrance. 'What did you say to upset Mama so?'

"He joined me outside. Tata left to go find food and check to see if we are safe to go home. I begged to go with him, but he said, "No." He wouldn't let me come with him, even though I begged. He gave me a huge bag of money in case....

'What good is money out here, Alek?'

'He tried to stall, but when he finally came out with Tata said, 'If I don't come back, follow this path.' He pointed to the opening where it began. 'The path will connect with the road going to Warsaw. The money in this bag will care for your needs. Seek your Grandfather there.'"


"I remember, felt Alek's arms again as we embraced when we parted. I experienced once more the sense of loss and impotence I suffered for a long time after I left.

Oh, TaTa, for a long time we waited and waited, and, still, you did not come. We were so cold and didn't dare light a fire big enough to warm us. Mama's big cloak helped keep us warm, but we all huddled together to share the warmth of our bodies.

We lived on berries and roots for the first few days. When we ventured out, we found the path led to a road leading to some small villages. I convinced Alek and Mama to let each of us carry only a few coins and hide the rest nearby every time we entered a hamlet. If someone tried to rob us, we wouldn't lose all. We took a chance many times when we needed to replenish our food supply. The farther north we went, we more relaxed we became because the local innkeeper told us he seldom saw soldiers.

In Ostroweic, we located a cobbler to repair our shoes. While he worked on them, we stayed and enjoyed our first real meal. We could wash our clothing with warm water when we found a secluded pond where we might stay out of sight. We must have arrived emaciated to Warsaw, judging from Grandmama's expression when we appeared at her front door. Mama tried to hire a carriage to take us to Grandfather's, but no one would stop for us, seeing only a dirty ragged fatherless family."

"Did anyone try to … to hurt you? I stammered, fearing Bozena or Gizela might have fallen prey to men preying on women.

"No, Papa, Alek and I took turns standing guard at night and, if we heard a sound, we hid."

I relaxed. This worry tortured me in the decades since. Their safety was my first unvoiced concern when I regained life and at night thereafter haunted my sleep.

"Were you happy in Warsaw? Did your first life turn out to be a good one?"

"Alek and I … adjusted. Being young helps, Tata. Mama missed you until the day she died. She loved you so much." She paused, and silence hung in the air.

"And the Blue?" I asked, voicing my other concern. "I meant to tell you all the following day, to warn you what might happen and how to best use what it gives you. I never had the opportunity and lost my chance when I lay dead, bleeding on the field. I have lived with the regret of failing my responsibility."

"When Alek turned eighteen, he returned to Krakow for the university. Mama insisted she honor your wish that I should received an education. Grandfather was reluctant, but, in the end, he agreed. For me to pursue my studies, I needed to leave Poland and go to Paris where women studied in salons. The only other alternative, the convent where at least the nuns learned to read and write had no appeal. When Alek graduated in law, he came west to join me.

The Blue, the thing we called Fairy Fire, brought Alek to my Paris home. He realized I had lived with the fire, too, and came seeking my help. He struggled—fighting with it did to him. Remember Tata, I saw the fairy fire as good and magical. I was content in the bluish mist. Alek feared the Blue, took every contact as a negative thing—an enemy to fear and fight. I viewed the Blue like a friend and seemed to realize what I needed  and what might be required of me."

She looked up at me, and then said, "Some years later, Alek and Friedrich shared their similar experiences, the sleeplessness, the arrogance, and the rest. Friedrich credits you with getting him back on track. With Alek, the task fell to me."

I hung my head in shame and regret and could say nothing. When I tried, four dainty fingers gently touched my arm. "I'm sure you didn't choose to deliberately die simply to spite the two of us."

My head shot up, and my eyes drifted toward her. She tried hard to hide the smile tugging at her lips, without success I realized, "No, I've never often had the luxury of setting the day of my death. I sensed when I had overstayed without aging in a community that's different. One simply younged again and began another life. Dying seemed easier, granted, more painful, but with less need to long for the life left. You would be there and then…not."

"I agree. I died twice. Those we leave behind mourn, but the grief lacking the rancor of abandonment."

"And the reanimation?"

"My most difficult happened when I awoke sealed in a crypt, a cold and damp one, almost impossible to escape. They'd dressed me in my party best, a frock not suitable for prying open a casket behind a heavy mausoleum door in the middle of winter."

The picture she painted, the unreality and the familiarity of it made me chuckle. A woebegone sound without mirth. " The one near Krakow was the worst, shook me to my core. My body hurt in every cell, and I was frantic to find you, but my body would not obey me. I ignored the pain, arose as soon as I was able, and ran to the cave. I soon realized you left long before, and I had no idea how long before, only that I had lost you."

We stood. In a single motion, locked in an embrace at being once again together.

"Hey, Dad, who's the girlfriend?" peeled out from behind me.

I turned and extended one arm toward the familiar voice. "Gizela, meet your youngest sister, Jeanne. Jeanne, meet Gizela, your sister and my daughter from my life in Krakow."

"You're Alek's same rung sister, aren't you?"

Gizela nodded, and I decided not to comment on Jeanne's growing use of family lingo and knowledge of family history. They extended their hands, then abandoned the empty gesture and hugged each other.

"We have lots to talk about, Gizela. Compare notes about Dad?"

I answered Gisela's questioning stare. "She insists on using today's word for Papa. I believe she does because she's not into treating me with the respect I so deserve." I ducked the not so gentle punch she aimed at me.

"Dad, I'm getting out on bail. Ricky's  seen reason and come round to let me be Maid of Honor for Rob and Neela, providing you go with me."

"You … you're the Maid of Honor at my granddaughter's wedding?" Gizela asked.

We stared at her.

### Family Wedding

The sun broke free of the clouds moments before we boarded the Blue Talon Gulfstream for Neela and Rob's wedding. We'd all gone to bed early the night before because Ricky had ordered the shuttle for three in the morning, claiming he wanted an inconspicuous pre-dawn take-off for an unfiled flight. Lucky for us,  this airplane tolerated a short runway and a low ceiling, and we took off on schedule. Ricky stayed behind because Rob might wonder why a total stranger showed up. Neela thought bringing the Bossman in this early might pose too much of a risk. Fair enough—great, in fact. Like I'd mind a week away from his prying eyes.

"Papa. I don't want you wasting time flying commercial," he said as we left HQ. "Taking the company plane will get you there and back much faster. We have much to discuss when you return."

Dad seemed a little puzzled at his remark but nodded, "I'm sorry you won't be joining us, Son. So many in the family will be there."

"Duty calls," Ricky said before he turned to me, seeming to realize I stood next to Dad. "You're in luck. The airstrip is dry, which gives our pilot more wiggle room on takeoff. You should be able to make it in three hops going through Buenos Aires. One week, Jeanne. One week, no more, and I want your butt back in the classroom."

I wrinkled my nose but didn't risk a comeback. Secretly I considered myself lucky, considering his attitude when I informed him a Maid of Honor must not miss the ceremony. I was dying to find out what Gizela meant about Neela being her granddaughter, but everything at dinner last night revolved around Dad being with not one, not two, but three of his daughters. He found nothing odd with a hundred or two hundred year age difference between us.

We clambered up the gangway, and I glanced around when we boarded the plane, "Wow, no problem getting used to this."

Wide reclining seats, a dining table for six, large screen TV, fully stocked bar qualified as a long way from the economy class I was familiar with flying home for holidays. A flight attendant greeted us as we took our seats, "Welcome aboard. My name is Cozette. I'll be with you to Cape Town. Breakfast should be ready for you in a minute. The ground crew is finishing the refueling and putting goodies on board."

Blue Talon has flight attendants?

She acted totally perky, although why a family member would ever want this job escaped me. I suspected she was a short-lived without a clue. Her tone changed to respectful, "Sir, when you are comfortable and settled, the pilot would like to speak with you."

Dad seemed somewhat perplexed but smiled as he followed her forward. I never could manage cheerful after a pre-dawn wake-up call, but Dad didn't consider early rising a problem. He followed the flight attendant forward with a smile. I heard a gasp and two male voices. Dad called back, "Jeanne, Gizela. You need to come up here, too."

Our eyes met, and two sets of eyebrows rose at the same time. This family similarity thing was getting spooky. Our gestures, our expressions, even our voices seemed the same. Dad stepped out of the cabin followed by a young man. From the looks of him, he had to be family. Obvious if you know what to look for, and by now, I did. I could tell Dad was excited. "Gizela, I'm not sure if you've met Michael before?" She shook her head.

"I'm sure Jeanne hasn't. Michael is my son, born after I returned from the Second war. Your brother."

Whatever happened to knowing your own family? Every time I turn around, another sister or brother pops up. No more only child for me. Darn it!

Gizela and I glanced at each other, hug or shake hands? Same thought, same time. Michael cut to the chase and pulled us both into a huge bear hug. He seemed about my age, but I estimated he must be at least 70 or 75. "What are the chances?" he said. "I seldom cross paths with any of the really old folks, except Tina over there, and Dad, of course."

"Not too old to take you on, youngster," she said deadpan. Tina was hitching a ride as far as Buenos Aires. The geeks in IT had ferreted out a possible new family member. She was heading south to check out their lead.

"I wasn't often able to spend much time with Dad after I was 'shot down  in 'Nam," Michael said making air quotes around the shot down. "He 'died  a few years after I returned. Ricky assigned a couple of cases to me. I liked being in the crime unit, but I always loved flying more, so when Ricky suggested I be the Blue Talon cab driver, I jumped at the chance. I take on short jobs in crime from time to time."

"Dad, how many more are you going to spring on me?"

His eyes flew up as he brought each to mind, "Alek, he's on Gisela's rung, Hilde, she's on Friedrich's."

"She's the doctor lady, right?"

"Uh huh, Andrew and George I think are back in Ontario. They're together and Suzi."

"She's with me," Michael said,

"Five more? All my life I think I have no brothers or sisters, now I end up with a total of …" I counted on my fingers, "of nine. You have ten kids?"

"More, Love. Ten living kids. Not so many if you figure in an age spread of around three hundred years. The Blue trait doesn't appear for everyone. Some are short-timers. Remember our talk before you got your assignment? How the signs of being aware of the Blue begin to evidence with the onset of adolescence?"

I didn't, but I nodded. He expected me to.

Just then a guy poked his head in the hatch, "We're topped off, Captain. You're good to go."

"Ok, Cozette. I guess we're off. Let's get the steps up and be on our way."

She made a pointed gesture to the seat and seat belts. Safety stuff even with Air Blue Talon. Something wrong with that. Would suck having to reanimate with every bone broken though.

Airborne at 20,000 feet and the four sat around the table over breakfast when I ask, "You're Neela's grandmother? How come she told me about you?"

"I am her grandmother, and she is an Afrikaner. My husband followed the gold in the late nineteenth century, and my son arrived after the first Boer War. He married a beautiful Indian woman, although one of her grandmothers was tribal. Neela came along in 1912. I left South Africa in 1938 to go to Poland. For some reason, I'd grown nostalgic for the land of my birth. Not the wisest decision I ever made I found out later. The Germans invaded shortly after I arrived."

"Nineteen twelve? She's that old, she seems …. oh…she younged."

"Exactly."

"As far as the short-timers invited are concerned, I'm her aunt from Canada."

My head spun trying to get the generations and the people to make any sense. I wonder if we ever have family reunions. Dad must have read my thoughts, "I can't remember an occasion when so many of my children were together. Makes me happy. What a wonderful an opportunity for some to get acquainted, especially with the family spread out so much."

I heard another voice behind, "I can't recall the last time I spent any time with more than one on my same rung. What a trip!"

I whirled peering in all directions, Michael. "Who's flying the plane?"

"Auto-pilot, first-timer. Won't need to take the throttle for a couple of hours. I rigged the panel to email me if there is a problem."

The rest of the flight proved uneventful, as did the wedding. Neela was beautiful… Rob was nervous as hell. To my surprise, I maneuvered down the aisle in stiletto heels, somewhat of a miracle.

Neela's father and "step-mother" threw a wonderful party, blending traditions from many cultures. They had rented a hall at one of the Winelands estates. Beautiful setting— the vines at sunset. The ceremony came off without a hitch. Some guy from the family who was a judge performed the ceremony, and Rob gave Neela his grandmother's ring. I sniffled—figuring a sniff or two appropriate. After all, I was responsible for them being together.

Rob's side of the hall was almost empty, a contrast with the overflow of Neela's many friends and relations. "I'd rather have empty seats than have my stepfather attend. I'd like to have Mom, but she wouldn't come without him," Rob told me. "You and your dad are enough family."

He flattered me, but behind the scenes, Neela made sure Walt and his crowd never got a hint of their wedding plans to show up and ruin the celebration. Michael showed up billed as a distant cousin from Chicago. The locals had zero ideas of the city's location, so naming this as his hometown worked well. The week passed as a blur of booze and family members.

As a guy, Michael met all my hunk expectations. Under normal circumstances, I'd jump at the chance to date him, but the darn rule about family not marrying family thing forbidding romantic relationships with someone else in the family scuttled that. Clear to me now we could set up a small city all on our own. Rumors were flying about Blue School—some council or other working on a permissible degree of separation so not all these hot guys would be off limits forever.

He and I sat off to one side once I completed my Maid of Honor duties. We'd clicked, being both from more modern times. We compared notes on our relationship with Dad. Not as many years separated our birthdays as with most of my siblings, allowing for more similarities than I'd found with the earlier born. Family life was far different for them, same father, no technology.

"My home life then was out of Norman Rockwell including the dog. Suzi and I had no complaints on the parent front. Being "shot down" made a huge change in my life that sent me into a downer. Officially I died. No Dad, no Mom, no sister Suzi now, only me with a new name and nothing from my past following me. I started to hit the bottle I was so lost and lonely. When Dad 'died,' he came to visit, as an old friend once, a distant relative other times. We spent a week together the first time. He younged and appeared to be my twin brother. He helped me a lot, to adjust I mean, even now sometimes. The number of occasions he lost his family circle, the number of times I may have to do the same scared, scares me. Up to now, I've never married for that reason—not sure if I'm ready to be hurt that way again."

"Dad said something about losing me too soon when Ricky and Tina came to our house the first time, but I didn't understand what he meant."

"That's right. I forgot. You're the first-timer who pulled an assignment before Blue School, the only one in modern times. How is it going? OK, I guess, or Ricky would not have allowed you to come."

"Some assignment—my 'subject' is out on the dance floor, the groom in the tux. Geeky as he appears, our esteemed leader was … is … convinced Rob represents the greatest threat the world has ever faced. Not him, per se, but his genius, how he handles his intellect, what he might do, what he might discover. Compared to the problems others handle, my efforts seem more like throwing a rock into a pond without making a splash or ripples. No conclusion, no resolution. At best, I'd call the present situation on hold. No clear forecast to indicate if what I did was enough to be successful long-term. If not … best we can do is an educated guess about when or what the … the until might be. I'm off the hook for now. Neela's taken over lead, being married to him and all, making me maybe second-string backup. She's in greater danger if the wrong guys get to him again. Those a-holes pop up over and over anywhere—like a game of whack-a-mole. "

"That sucks. Nothing you can do, but you're still saddled with the worry."

I nodded. "Exactly." We sat and watched the dancers out on the floor in silence.

He stood up and held his hand out to me, "Okay, First-timer, time to take a night off. Have fun and show the Southern contingent what dancing is all about in the new world? They should pick up a thing or two, judging from what I see out there."

"You got it, Bro."

We had a great time. My feet and my head hurt in the morning.

### *Friedrich's News*

Back at Blue School, Jeanne and I headed in different directions—she down to a classroom and I to the lonely room Friedrich called an office. We gave each stout hugs, and I patted her on the back. The joy I'd shared in Cape Town being with so many of my family diminished into sadness as I watched her trudge to the elevator.

I walked the length of the hall, greeting those I met along the way. The executive elevator seemed more like a freight contraption but had the advantage of missing many flights of stairs up. My vague sadness grew into a growing dread of what surely would be the bad news waiting for me.

"Papa," he said, grabbing my shoulder in a manly gesture of greeting. "How was the wedding? Neela and Rob are settled?"

Jeanne would have said, "Way awesome," but I was less inclined to use the current vernacular. "Elegant and entertaining in every way."

"No ... uh ... outsiders?" he asked.

Now I was sure his news would not please me. "None, why do you ask?"

He stood silent for a while, head down. He sighed, and his eyes met mine. "Papa, do you remember how I scoffed at Tina and Amelia's ideas of a shadow organization, one working against Blue Talon. I was wrong," Friedrich said. "A black network exists. That fellow Walt works for them. The situation with Rob, Jeanne's former subject, appears to be not at all secure. I will ask all family members not on assignment to report to H. Everyone needs either fake their death or make up plausible excuses why they must leave their family. We need to dismantle this beast. Our intel showed Walt as a junior level operative. Certain questionable organizations appear to have engineered affiliations

289

in a massive master network. We decided to call this the Cabal until we come up with a better name. Too many times, these groups seemed to anticipate what we would do. Walt courting Rob during the times we had him under observation represents only one example. Their infiltrations of our operations happened too often to blame coincidence.

"To deal with them, we need to find out how. Karl pointed out we could longer trust the integrity of the individual offices because of the numbers of the short-lived we hire to work for us in the criminal division. A few bad apples may possess limited access to our resources. Even limited in this way, we would have no guarantee of a future intrusion."

"Isn't that name you chose a bit melodramatic, Son?"

"I suppose, but Cabal will have to do until we come up with a better one—with luck, we won't have to.

Not a pretty picture, but perhaps the reason the Blue recruited us.

"What measures do you plan to take, and what role would you like me to take? My obligation is to do all I can."

"While you were in Cape Town, those of us at HQ put together a strategy. We have too many operations in play, some long-running, and a few just beginning, to abandon our current projects. Thus, the number of Blue Talon operatives would too few—unless we pull everyone in. Those already deployed on a case will continue, and I expected them to assume the additional duty of uncovering agents working for our opposition."

"You seem to have covered the bases, Friedrich. I am willing, as always, but why did you ask me to come here before I returned to Minnesota?"

"I have asked the IT folks to produce several algorithms to detect aberrant activity both within our offices and at current work sites. My strength is administration. You have a gift for ferreting out trends arrived by other than logical analyses. Few individuals in the world can meld seemingly unrelated activities to show a potential event. You are one of them—plus you have three hundred years of observing how society works. I am hoping using your gut reactions and the logic of binary, we counteract their activities."

I laughed. "I've never thought of myself as some sort of gypsy mystic, although I admit I've had a few lucky guesses, but…"

"Call them what you will, Papa, but you do possess an uncanny ability. Your current cover identity is perfect for you to observe many situations—all we need to do is to place a call for a difficult case."

"What do I look for?"

"Your job is more of an initial diagnosis—an educated guess as to what might be wrong. We've drawn up a preliminary list of criteria for the others."

Then he answered my unspoken question. "Yes, Jeanne will receive her first assignment as a trained operative soon. We're targeting certain operations or organizations, likely allied with or infiltrated by the Cabal. We plan to pair her with an experienced agent and fill her in with detail on both the specific case and the overall alert."

I stared at him. "Friedrich, tell me true. What is the danger level in her primary objective?"

"The objective is to discover if a certain banking operation has mob connections, nothing more."

"Why not send in someone with banking experience?"

"Her partner will, but Jeanne has … uh … certain distinctive advantages we, as men, don't possess." He made a readily interpreted unseemly gesture.

291

I did not respond. There was nothing civil I could say to this.

**Book IV: Beginning the Big Lonely as a Blue Talon Agent**

### *Jeanne's First Mission*

### *The Next Morning*

"Geez, Ricky, get real. Armenian?" Jeanne said. 'You can't expect me to go to classes all day then turn around and spend half the night learning a language almost nobody speaks? Come on—give me a break. some sleep would be nice for a change. Why would anyone want to learn this weird dialect? Guaranteed I'll never find a use for it—plus the alphabet isn't even close writeable. I'll swallow my tongue trying for sounds like half-baked Hebrew spoken on the inhale not the exhale. Tell you what, how about I learn Russian instead? At least people speak that language. Besides, you told me my assignment would be to Blue Talon's crime section, not some international intrigue investigation," Jeanne persisted.

"Papa, has she always been like this?"

"Son, I tried to convince your sister the advantages of knowing multiple languages—especially for anyone part of Blue Talon. She blew me off."

"Dad, that's not fair. I was a kid and didn't know about Blue Talon and all the rest of this mixed-up-mess I inherited…whether I wanted to be part of whatever this is…or not."

"As of today you do, Love. You inhale the Blue. You must assume the responsibility entailed."

"And that gives him the right to run every minute of my life?"

"Jeanne, stop. Stop being unfair to your brother. I understand Friedrich's frustration. He has to handle a difficult and frustrating role, unceasing in its demands. Over the years, we've tried to find another able to take over so he can enjoy a family again. So he can go out on assignments like the rest of us. If I had the right skills, I would, but I don't. Blue

Talon can't afford second-rate handling of his job for long. He's tried to blend family time with running Blue Talon—using techy tricks like the webcam relationship he had with Mark."

"Dad, doesn't anyone understand, more than anything, I want a normal life. Date a guy, go home to visit my dad once in a while. Make friends. Is that so bloody terrible?"

"No, there's nothing I'd like more than for you to be free to live like others your age, but you aren't an average young person. I've struggled and hidden my sadness when Blue Talon took you from me so soon. To whom should I complain? I started this. Worse, Love, my present visit ends soon. I must fly out tomorrow. My leave from the Clinic ends this week, and duty calls for this Super Doc. I believe I'll be able to hold out for a decade or more— stay in my current life and do what I am doing before I must 'die."

"You win, Dad. I'm being a little shit again. Acting like a spoiled kid. Lead on, Legree, I'm yours to command."

"Has she always been such a drama queen?"

"Not always, Friedrich. Only when I asked her to do something she didn't want to do. Right, Love?"

"Dad, you make me sound terrible."

"Uh uh, Jeanne girl. Remember, family does not lie to family," I said with a smile tugging on one corner of my mouth.

"No, but you push the tiny kernel in the middle to the nth, Dad. I'll be up to say goodbye in the morning."

"Gute Nacht, Papa," Friedrich said, turning to give Jeanne time to wipe away her tears.

295

Tomorrow brought a final farewell to her current life, a breaking of the bond between father and daughter. I'd never been able to handle this well. Doubly hard this time because we'd robbed her of so many years of being a normal teenager. Harder yet as she and I had shared a rare one on one relationship. I might be a legend to most of the family, but for her, and for me, I'm just Dad.


In the weak light of early morning, we sat as a glum clump, in the deserted dining room toying with the breakfast—granola, fresh berries, and yogurt that no one touched. I doubted I would taste a thing, even the incredible fruit  they grow in the biosphere.

"Ricky, I meant what I said when I said I'm yours. One favor though, at least tell me why Armenian." Jeanne made a last-ditch effort to extract more information from Friedrich.

"You, Lil Sis, will be a full-time student at Blue U to prepare for your first assignment as a trained Blue Talon operative. I don't intend to give you any time to mope and less to sleep. Count on sitting through early morning intensive sessions to bring you up to speed in banking and money management. What I have in mind is the equivalent of an MBA in finance. Days I expect you to attend the customary training classes required for every family member. Learning to read and write your new language should take up your evenings until bedtime—and, may I add, this is the first of many languages I will expect you to perfect."

"Figures."

He didn't bother to acknowledge her comment. "Once you satisfactorily conclude your coursework and meet the expectations of your instructors, they will assign you a partner in the criminal division."

"When? Why?"

"Hold on, before you get to the where and how. I want you to concentrate on what you learn wit.0.hout any distractions. Stop dwelling on your future assignment. Obsessing only makes you more eager

to "get sprung," as you say. What you learn in the next few months may save your life, if not this life, then a future life."

"The success rate at Blue Talon rises dramatically when the agent doesn't die and we avoid a reanimation and don't require an immediate replacement. If you avoid dying, you'll be able to cling little longer to the friends and family of your current life." Her facial expression told me she understood that I meant the bond between the two of us.

"So if I'm a good girl and study hard, I might make it to my high school reunion or sit down for coffee with a classmate from law school?"

Although I realized her real question had more to do with me, the close relationship of a daughter with the father she always wanted to make proud rather than slamming shots back and forth.

Friedrich matched her in kind, "With luck, you may be in one place long enough to fit in an affair."

"Why so much time preparing? I assume Armenian is not usual, so I  guess I am headed into an existing mess," she replied.

Damn, she catches on quick. Friedrich must have already swallowed his tongue. How could we appear to be honest and upfront yet not tell her too much too soon? I turned my head toward my son to see how he deflected her this time.

"Not too far off, Lil Sis. The IT lab's model is a whiz at analyzing trends. This criminal endeavor is in the early stage, not yet close to critical. We have time, but factoring a better-than-average command of Armenian added a complicating factor."

"Oh, dandy, hot damn, that bloody jargon and computer trend business again. Another save the world thing dressed up with new words. My last experience with what the minions spit out left me with little to show for the time I spent with Rob and I may never know how things turn out."

"You read too much into it. Rob is important, and you made a difference, Lil Sis. The computer model shows with your help Rob appears to have made a genuine turnaround. We won't stop our surveillance, but I am optimistic the change is real. Remember, we measure our life in centuries which means never is an extremely long time for us. Once you have your system clearance, you'll be able to log in and check on him."

A knock at the door caught our attention. "Yes?"

"Can I borrow you for a while, Bossman? Milo, Friedrich's assistant, asked. "I've got several papers I need you to go over before I can move on. When you've got time, I don't mean to interrupt." Clearly, he did, but no matter.

"Jeanne, you need to get to class," he said.

She glanced over at me.

"I'll be fine, Love. The plane will lift off soon. I've been alone before," I said.

She managed a weak smile and headed back to the shuttle.

After she left, Friedrich pulled out his cell and asked Karl, our head computer guru, along with Filip and Annie, the highest-placed family members in the international Blue Talon Crime Division to meet with us in the conference room. Friedrich delayed my plane so I could attend a meeting he'd scheduled with the Blue Talon Directors from Europe and the Americas. I followed my son up the stairs to the bank-worthy paneled room with enough high tech hidden in the walls to make the most particular spook happy.

No short-timers attended HQ meetings. They staff the office for Friedrich, but Blue Talon relied on family members for high-level decisions. Filip came in the prior evening on the same plane now scheduled to deliver me back to Minnesota. Annie spends the majority of her time in the European Division offices in Frankfort, Filip in New York.

Friedrich needed an update on current cases. I assumed his insistence I be included in this face to face was a gentle concession for my preference for people over a computer report, regardless of the pretty charts. Karl and his minions were the backbone of the organization, which Friedrich headed.

If Jeanne ever heard him called the head, she'd ask who the feet are and who the stomach is.

When we got off the elevator at the conference room level, we found them waiting. Kippers and eggs alongside cold beer lay on the sideboard.

"Good afternoon, guys. Not fair, no one told us we'd be eating bait," Friedrich said, wrinkling his nose. Proper pickled herring was ok with him, but not 'these pathetic excuses for seafood.'

They laughed … barely … at his lame joke, but only to humor him.

"Rough night, Uncle?" asked Filip.

"In a way, Papa leaves for his home in Minnesota at noon, and Jeanne was here to see him off and pump me about her upcoming assignment. You know what she is like."

They sat silent for a minute, each no doubt remembering their own separation from the family who raised them. "You're right, Uncle. We always go through a rough time when one of us leaves home for good the first time."

Friedrich shoved aside the sheaf of papers Milo had placed in front of him. "Change in the agenda, folks. I know you all have situations to you want help or input on,—Filip has an environmental case for us to consider, Annie has two drug cases and money laundering cases—but first, we need to talk about the Cabal."

The look the others shot him would have been funny any other time. "Thought you'd blown that crazy idea off, Uncle," said Feliks.

"I was wrong," Friedrich replied.

The expression on the faces of the others was priceless.

### *Building a Dossier*

Friedrich opened the file, giving me an intense, challenging look. "I am compiling a dossier, and you should expect to be playing a part. Soon two lucky agents will experience the pleasure of working with Papa's youngest. I'm smiling just thinking about it. My baby sister is a handful."

"Come on, Uncle, you know you'll miss her."

"Like a rock in my shoe."

"You don't mean that," said Karl.

"No, you're right. I grant she shows incredible potential. She plunged into the family business when she was damn near cold. She worked a case of the most frustrating kind, one with zero current reward. Tina told me she compares her work to throwing a rock into a pond without causing a ripple or a splash. No question she stepped up with little or no training, armed only Papa's tales. But oh, the cost."

Friedrich's focus shifted to me, "We all know Papa relives everything as he tells what his lives were like. With her, dealing with his own reluctance, he seldom reached our early Pinkerton years. When Tina and I came to detail her assignment, we discovered how little Papa covered. Amelia, our psychologist in residence, considers his attitude toward sharing difficult and as less than therapeutic. Perhaps, she is correct. My life would have been much easier if he'd been more forthcoming."

"Son," I began.

"I know, Papa, I know. What's done is done."

"What we've learned over the past years was, while Jeanne looks like us and shares a bond with the founder of our family, her way of thinking is radically different from older members of the family. She and Dmitri run a close race for the size of ego, but she analyzes a problem in a manner I've not seen before. Perhaps being born into a connected world redefined her brain functions. Growing up with the world only a click away, her view on life might seem peculiar to those of us of prior generations. She's as brash and mouthy as anyone I've met, but she loves Papa as much as any of us. No one is more protective of him … how's that for a joke? A first timer playing mother hen to a man with the wisdom of three centuries behind him?"

Under my breath, I muttered, "That's what happens when a child takes on the role of a mother."

"Take what I share today as background," he said leaving no doubt, he heard my inaudible muttered comment and chose to ignore me. "Rumors have hit my desk about an global underworld gang, perhaps with ties to the cabal, conducting operations affecting more than one Blue Talon office. we stumbled on this one. The initial contact seemed out of character for us. The case began when an elderly woman walked into the criminal division of our Los Angeles branch and tried to hire a detective—yes, she called us detectives, Feliks—to investigate why her son killed himself. "Our office manager suggested she contact the police for a more appropriate response. She told him the local precinct cop blew her off and turned her down cold, blunt as hell."

The Sergeant told her, "Suicides are a job for a shrink, not a cop, thank you for stopping by, Ma'am."

"Our LA manager, an OCD, filed a report anyway. Though how this oddity got as far as my desk, I didn't have a clue.""

"And I thought I was bringing in a non-conforming case," Feliks interjected.

"Turned out, the mailroom procedure is to funnel all reports received by HQ to Karl's group for input. Something in the file clicked, felt wrong,  with someone in IT, which spurred her to do a quick background check. She found the woman's son had worked for a major bank in the Los Angeles area. A few more keystrokes brought up data on the bank listing a pot load of questionable transactions. She started a preliminary track  on anonymous cash floating in,  through, and out the same day, including overseas transfers which the law says must be reported. She used a hidden series of electronic transfers to dummy companies, and dug up an Armenian angle."

"'Ok, Bossman, I remember this now," Karl said. "Nell didn't spend much time on research, but enough to suspect something was wrong. She convinced me, considering the bank's practices, the suicide might not be a suicide. 'We owe the mother an answer,' she argued. I agreed ... not our usual thing, but I let her send the report on to you.'"

"Jeanne is fast-tracked on this case. She's learning Armenian, our unique take on techniques, and should complete the equivalent of a Masters in Finance. The perfect candidate, not because of her qualifications, which will mean next to nothing. Being drop-dead gorgeous with a big bust size will with this bunch. Once she's given an Armenian name, and we finish doctoring the records at UCLA and Stanford, she'll move in and her training will take over. We'll get the mother her answers. Maybe get a lot more besides."

"Uncle, you surprise me. You do possess a heart. I'd have never guessed."

"Stifle it, Filip."

I breathed a sigh of relief. How dangerous can work in a bank be? This sounded like the perfect introduction to our organization. Friedrich must have read my mind because he said, "Yes, Papa, I'll keep you up to date on her. "

I smiled.

### *Jeanne Bond Reporting for Duty*

When I crashed at night on my bunk in the corner of the cave I called home, every brain cell in my head was yelling 'Hey, girl, truce already.  Someday, some way,  will get back at Ricky for making me learn in less than six months what the other kids take three full summers of brainwashing at Blue School to cover. Me, he expected top scores at Blue School plus the equivalent of two years in an MBA program while simultaneously learning a language unrelated to any other in the modern world. I came close to going psycho with all his verbal pats on the head, "You're doing great, Sis."

Tonight I shed all my clothes, but some nights I fell into bed wearing everything except my shoes. Well, both shoes. If I got the luxury of a Blue bath to take the edge off,  great— but my evil brother issued strict instructions to his minions to limit how much and how often. "If you take in too much, without the opportunity to lay off the excess productively, you face leaving here addicted. You won't like you and neither will anyone else."

Everyone in HQ spends a week outside periodically to stoke their batteries with Blue and rescue some poor schmuck attacked by muggers or whatever. Lucky them.

I'd dreaded life in a school filled with one-hundred-percent-rule-following-goody-goodies. The one who always said the right thing and ate nothing but healthy. Still, I was surprised to find I wasn't totally bored silly. Easy to explain because no time remained in a day after I finished my one-on-one workout in Armenian. And, at dinner or a break, I discovered the majority at the table had a wicked sense of humor, a dry wit that sometimes required knowledge of a place several centuries old to appreciate. Sometimes I had to hit the web to get their jokes. Not fun feeling dumb.

One afternoon a week I squandered my meager free time to relax, well, not so much relax as work out. Officially, I spent my time in the gym practicing Blue Talon recommended offensive and defensive moves, but just as often, I'd be talking a few fellow slackards into a quick game of basketball. Making a layup gave me as much of a rush as when I played center back in Minnesota. Crikey, high school seemed an eon ago.

I sat in the conference room, nursed my latte, and waited for Ricky and whoever. I hoped my days in purgatory would soon be over—not a sure thing, as the last of my instructors hadn't signed off yet.

I heard the door open, and three filed in, Ricky leading. "Good morning, Jeanne. I understand congratulations are in order. You're official—an actual Blue Talon operative according to your trainers. Get your things packed to leave in two days for an assignment in the Los Angeles area. Feliks and Karl will go over your cover story and drill you on the details so you will react without hesitation. We arranged transport for you and purchased an apartment, a condo, in fact, to make your woman-on-the-way-up role credible. Dmitri will meet you in LA to practice some techniques you'll find useful when assuming a new identity."

"Dmitri will be my partner?" I asked, not daring to hope but knowing Blue Talon agents always work in tandem.

"No, he's got a week before his next posting. Dmitri likes more adrenaline in his work than the task you'll be doing."

"Are Blue Talon agents allowed to ask what they will be doing? I asked, hoping the edge of sarcasm showed bright and clear.

Feliks answered, "Not in general, mostly a voice comes from on high, solemn, and grave.  Blinding light and  stone tablets may accompany delivery of the message."

I broke out laughing along with Ricky and a stranger, clearly part of the family, but I didn't know him. "I don't think we've met," I said to the stranger.

"Hi, I'm Mario. Tina's grandson."

"The earthquake guy?"

"Yup, that's me. I guess we're to be working together. I pulled a stint as a banker in a prior life."

"Banker?" I glanced over at Ricky. What's with you as a banker? Me? Not a chance.

"We more or less backed into this case," Ricky began. "An older woman approached our Los Angeles office asking us to find out why her son committed suicide. Not our usual thing, but something struck a nerve with our local agent, and she did some digging. He found out the deceased worked at an LA bank with some, shall we say, quite unusual business practice—too employees with Armenian names stuck out and raised a red flag."

"Karl's hack shows an even larger concentration of Armenian customers. An Armenian gang called the Avats  operates in the LA basin. According to our sources, they dabble in extortion, fraud, intimidation, and drugs. You two will find out the extent of Avat involvement at the bank and pinpoint the players. If necessary, Jeanne, you'll volunteer to be a liaison between the local criminals and their counterparts in Europe."

I gulped. "How am I supposed to be accomplishing all this?"

"Well, Miss Dadurian, you are the new commercial loan officer. Arkady Kachadorian here is Your Best Community Bank's latest IT support person. Unfortunately for the bank, he speaks only English."

"We won't tell them I spent one of my lives in the region before, considerably before, around the time of the attack by the Turks."

"So why did you torture me forcing me to learn the language?"

"Relax, Partner, because my Armenian is old style, dated, and differs more yet from the dialect spoken by the Diaspora."

My confused expression said I didn't have a clue what a Diaspora might be. "The Diaspora? I asked.

"The ones left after the Turks allegedly massacred thousands fled and spread out all over the globe," he added.

"OK, I guess. Where do you fit in the family?"

"Third rung. Dare I address you so informally, speaking as I am to an exalted first rung," he answered, making the Ottoman gesture of submission Dad showed me once.

"I think we'll get along, Lesser Being. Do I call you Mario or Arkady?"

"Arkady, always, except when everyone is family or in your reports. Staying in character may save your current life someday. Never forget, slipping out of your identity may put short timers involved at risk."

Ricky answered for him. "I'll not spend much time going over details with you now. You will have time to go over the report detailing what we collected to date on the plane. Dmitri will pick both of you up and help you perfect your characters for the next three days. Yes, Mario, I realize you lived different lives for almost a couple centuries, but I want Dmitri to work on the rhythm between the two of you. Jeanne kept her own persona on her last little errand."

If saving the world is a little errand, I wonder what a big errand is?

"What do I call Dmitri? He was Steve last time."

"Steve'll do. Dmitri decided he likes the name and wants to keep using it for another round. I don't much care for Steve, but he'll be living as Steve, not me."


As we walked to the shuttle, I was aware Arkady was an old timer. I'd learned to pick up the signs, the hints of past lives. By now, I remembered to observe the way they stood when someone older or higher rank is present. I caught on real quick, Dad may be God, but Ricky was his prophet. What's that make me? Handmaiden? The big thing was they <u>focused</u>. Nothing with them was ever half-attention. They listened to the speaker, read the complete page. Oh, and they always seem a little stiff, too polite, I guess. I doubt an outsider would notice, but with practice, we recognized each other. When I made the cut, I joined the herd.

"Penny for your thoughts, Partner?"

"Boy, can I tell you're not on your first life, a penny won't get you much these days."

Still, sleep deprived from the drudgery of the past months, I fell asleep almost with the first turn of the wheels. I woke up when the van stops, more alert than I've been for weeks, "I hope Ricky arranged for breakfast. I'm starved."

"Jury's out. I've been flying commercial of late and am leery of any food prepared and offered above 5000 feet."

"Yuk, in economy, you're better to bring your own."

"Hey, Sis, welcome aboard again. You ready for the big time?

"Michael, I'm so glad you're flying us today. Someone told me Blue Talon used two pilots, and I worried your alternate might be in the cockpit today."

"Just me out of here. The other pilot doesn't do as well with this short a take-off. He's using our smaller plane for the most part. Hey, Mario, how're things in London?"

"Hey yourself. Keep London in mind and volunteer if you get a chance. Super place for a posting."

"You're partnered with my Lil Sis for the next one, aren't you?"

"Yup, I drew the short straw."

"You guys think you are so bloody funny. Why don't you try the tour?"

"Did once," Arkady said. "Chicago during the Depression. Didn't last long. Quickest reanimation I ever had."

Holy Moly, get a load of what I get to look forward to.

**The Mission: Shifty Business**

*Your Best Community Bank: A Lie in a Name*

Dad always told me I should never play poker because my tell would give me away every time. He was right—my tattletale left nostril curled on cue when I first walked into the office of Your Best. Think dingy and stale. What a dump! No receptionist in the main lobby to welcome me. The decor fit in with the class three retail shops flanking the place. Not my idea of a bank. Vacant cubbies lined the walls of the room. Not a soul made a move to greet me. The rear office seemed unoccupied, but etched glass high walls in the two adjoining cubicles acted as a barrier to mask anyone inside. I'm underwhelmed, such a welcome. So glad Ricky sent me to this dump. This whole place screams crooked.

I stood near the door where a receptionist ought to sit, but wasn't. I waited. I waiting a long while until a voice from behind me said, "Can I help you?"

Where the hell did he come from? I spun to spot a half-open door revealing stairs going up.

"I hope so, I'm Aida Dadurian. I'm supposed to start today as a Commercial Loan Officer?"65 I said, leaving a hint of a question in my voice when I spoke.

The guy spewed out, "Oh, of course, Ms. Dadurian. The president said you would be in today. Please follow me. The Commercial department is upstairs."

I followed him up to a new world. Thick forest green carpet in a sitting room led to a series of glass-enclosed offices with dark expensive furniture. The exception was the thick glass cage, crammed with rack after rack of computers across one end. I spotted Arkady's blond head at one workstation. My eyes didn't linger, and he didn't look up. Why should he? We'd never met.

311

A short stocky man with olive skin and snapping black eyes came out of the largest and most ornate office. "Good morning, Ms. Dadurian. Welcome. I am Mr. Petrosian, Chief Financial Officer," he said in Armenian, his eyes fixed on my bust line.

What a sicko.

I answered in the same language. He relaxed. I must have passed the first test.

He led me back to a tiny empty square near his own and gestured. "This will be your office. On rare occasions, you may meet with foreigners downstairs." The word he used meant literally not of our people, so I guessed non-Armenian customers. "We reserve this floor for meetings with our friends—fellow Armenians but also the Russians who depend on us."

My head spun. If Ricky was right, I'm facing not just Armenians, but the Russian mob, too. Holy shit, Batman!

"I filed my initial report with HQ. The first line read, "Warning: Nothing of interest to report." The only important thing already shows in a file. They handled important business in Armenian.

What else could I say?

The more I learned what the business was like the less I respected the people involved. Working with them left a nasty taste in my mouth. Ricky would get an earful on my first report.

Take my first meeting, for example.

*Your Best Clients*

When I met my first client face to face, he was everything I'd expected. I never learned the name of the thuggish man in Mr. Petrosian's office. No introductions. "Ms. Dadurian, I'd like you to meet a new customer here at Your Best. He represents Gater Mark, a corporation investing in auto parts stores."

Big Grumpy growled in Armenian, "What's this? What gives you the right to stick me with a woman, Petrosian, isn't our business important enough for you?

The jerk must think either I am deaf or too stupid to understand his mangled version of the language.

Petrosian glanced over at me, seemed nervous, and his voice broke as he replied, "Ms. Dadurian is qualified and speaks fluent Armenian. You may speak freely with her in complete confidence."

A few minutes conversation and only an idiot would believe his "auto parts stores" were nothing more than chop shops. Dandy. I wonder what the guy did before he took up his current 'legitimate  occupation. He doesn't need to do anything to shed Blue—his past activities create an aura of the stuff.

Later the same day, Arkady and I slapped high fives over a drink that night. "Seems to me, you made the cut, First-timer, now all you need to do is stay in character and build a case as new," he made air quotes, "opportunities" come your way.'

"Yeah, that and stay off roofs."

"Is a situation like that comes up, you use the Blue right away. No delay—no big deal, F.T."

Not another lame nickname! What's this? Like freshman hazing only with a First Timer?

313

"How much luck am I going to need with the characters involved with the Armenian Avats? I'm afraid if I can't corral enough Blue, I'm toast. Reanimation or no reanimation, falling off a roof would hurt."

"Use enough of the Blue, you'll confuse them and convincing them to do a swan dive over the side of the building is a snap. They'd do it."

"And that's okay with the Blue?"

"From what I've learned, Papa calls the Blue an inwit, an intelligent conscience. Thank about it—what self-respecting conscience stands by and lets someone be murdered?"

### Business as Usual

The next day two more loan files appeared on my desk, two Armenian ones. My basket never was empty of the other kind. The first proved to be chump change, the other not so much. A two billion dollar request, multiple real estate buildings including several "out of country" properties, in the former Soviet Republic of Armenia no less, and a scattering in the Kurdish area of Turkey. Arkady's old stomping grounds. I wonder what kind of buildings they need on the drug isthmus between Asia and Europe.

By day, I made nice to my Armenian Avats, and in the evenings, Arkady and I worked to trounce their ugly butts. We collaborated on our weekly reports, and called for backup, just like in the TV shows.

"Nothing about this deal checks out, Arkady. I'm not even sure any of the buildings exist. For sure, they don't show up on Google Earth."

"Don't get your butt in a bottle, FT. You have a portal for Karl on your machine, didn't you? "

"Yeah, what do you think? I'm some dummy who didn't know how to?"

"No, for someone who grew up with a mouse in your hand, you're darn touchy. I'll check on the health of our virus. With the portal in place, Karl can download your file and verify the contents before they hide half of the contents in the server. Meanwhile, you need to continue playing the role. We don't want to rouse their suspicion. We don't know everyone involved yet, so we need to keep close."

"Duh."

### Reporting In and a Briefing

I replayed the next few months in my mind recalling the reports I'd submitted with the same advisory until Ricky told me to knock it off. I toyed with using ditto marks but decided not to push my luck. Arkady and I met once a month 'by chance  at an ear-splitting noisy bar down the street. He was able to supply Karl's minions with high-level passwords to give them a backdoor to hack in and establish a listening post.

Like a good lackey, I processed loan packages to Petrosian's satisfaction, but so far, all in the low-rent loan district —a loan on a retail store selling manufacturer's overstocks, a line of credit on a cash-checking outlet. In my opinion, that's a slimy way to earn a living.

The duh-light went on after I'd graduated to handling financing for a three-store mini-strip center. The common thread was how they conducted business at Your Best. Every loan must go out the door with this "special" insurance, even if the borrower had his or her own. "We need a good cover if anything happens," Petrosian told me when I asked. I didn't handle the insurance. When I finished my work-up, I delivered it to the "insurance desk."

None of my clients ever came back and complained about the add-ons to their loan. Why not? Are they afraid of something? I noticed someone added additional pages to my file or inserted an alternative credit report. Your Best only trusted me with the legit business so I handled business loans but almost no real estate loans.

Your Best hid this bogus cost in the payment, clumping them with other nonsense charges, making discovery more difficult for anyone unfamiliar with loan documents. Folks at the bank made money, and the customers seemed all too happy to get a loan at all.

One of the other loan officers told me, "None of our borrowers have sterling credit, but that's ok, we have good collectors."

I'll bet they did!—and maybe creative credit reporting.

The longer I was there, newbie I might be, but the operation smelled. I didn't enjoy sticking someone with an off-brand contract hiding somewhere who knows what offshore. The Blue Talon minions wore their little fingers out doing extensive research to identify all the phony companies the bank dealt with. At quarter end, I got a small, picayune actually, cut on every loan. Now I knew what a bribe felt like.

More inconsistencies surfaced. People stuck with fees for things they didn't need so the bank could up profits seem not so bad. Arkady unearthed other dirty dealings. He told me he was checking into real estate loans, the ones, which seldom crossed my desk.

"I encountered questionable tactics—dirty dealings, profitable ones litter on every step of the way—nice trick," I said. "I don't understand how they're getting away with this racket."

"My guess—they're up to their hips in laundering dirty money. We'll ask the minions find out how and which one of the less-than-savory companies are shells for the Armenian Avats or less reputable gangs abroad," he answered.

"You think we're getting any closer?"

"Do you review your loans from time to time? Or check on something for a borrower?"

"Once in a while. Loan files are like mega-boring."

"Ever found any loans which stay with the bank? Not packaged, peddled, or sold to someone else?"

"Now that you mention it, I remember only one, An Armenian restaurant."

"Karl's geeks need to follow the paper trail and track where the paper goes. Follow the money. An old saying, but still true today. If I'm right, Your Best gets its cash and then some and some poor schmuck takes a bath … or gets foreclosed on."

"Why didn't Karl's minion pick up on the connection when they did the research on the company?"

"'In my opinion, computers and the humans who serve them live in a zero-one world. Lawyers sense when the law and people intersect. Attorneys combine random comments or use something as unlikely as a billboard to trigger an illogical, at least to a computer's way of thinking, thought process, and come up with a winning legal strategy. Bankers often make loans on their 'gut.' Family teaches us to draw on our memories, our experiences in prior lives. Every life we lead adds to an "organic database,"' as Karl would call it, for use in our current life. I've been a banker in another life so I use what I learned the first time around.'"

"What about someone like me, a first timer?"

"We share our lives, our recollections. Papa's stories or Dmitri's wise-ass remarks, for example. We always partner, and no family member ever refused to lend a hand when needed. Or, again to paraphrase our computer guru, we establish an organic peer-to-peer network. Didn't you ever take advantage of the family memory archives?"

"Like I had time to do anything besides study in that bloody cave! What are they?"

"Recordings and videos of every past life in the family history. Cataloged by the person creating the video, language, country, era, occupation, and others I don't recall right now. I came in several times to record. I've used them to search for relevant recollections for insight with an assignment. All of us do. Not all of us were as lucky as you were to get Papa's stories one on one. You must realize we need to rely on more than the Blue to do what we do, don't you?"

I considered what he told me, gave up, and decided to lighten the mood, "Think I should put my "Warning" opening on this week's report?"

He laughed. "Ricky might even get a kick out of it."

We slammed down our beers and put on an exchanging phone numbers act in case someone was watching. We wanted no one to connect the two of us. I pulled out my cell, made like I was checking the time and hurried off. Arkady, I noticed, ordered another beer. Lucky him.

### *Detective Jeanne*

I sighed as I headed to Better Bargains. I planned to reward myself for unearthing something concrete at last. After a short pause,  I sighed again. Now I understand why Blue Talon always uses a dynamic duo. My part was to add a bust line, but Arkady brought experience to the table. Snuffling through the bank computers gave him some advantage, but he connected random facts better and faster than I would. Playing second chair is never my favorite. Time to get my Superchick outfit out of the closet.

I comforted myself with the fact I was able to piece together the last hours of our suicidal banker before he launched himself, or someone launched him on his final flight six stories down from the roof of his apartment building. Mitt, that was his name short for Mittleford, apparently followed the same leads Arkady and I unraveled. He read old loan packages to identify questionable loans. We took turns doing the same thing. Sometimes a drive-by was all we needed. I suspected believing the earth opened up and swallowed the buildings I or some other loan officer gave loans on was an unlikely explanation. More plausible, nothing was ever on the property.

I creeped out when I discovered my mini-office was his mini-office, and I was sitting in a dead man's chair, using his pen, his keyboard. I bought new pens, sanitized everything I thought he might have touched, but I couldn't do anything about the chair. Ick.

When I asked one of the downstairs secretaries if she knew the former occupant of my workspace, she mentioned he came back from the county seat with some documents one day. "He acted strange, secretive you know, and didn't share with anyone. Told me he picked them up for some kind of fancy loan he was putting together for a preferred customer. We don't usually do that, and, anyway, usually the title company or that other place do any searches for us."

"I didn't see anything different about him. He seemed a little up that last week," another told me. "Happy, you know, the way you are when you finally finish a project that's been bugging you."

Justifiably happy, according to the minions, the FBI would recognize some names on his list. Marti seemed to search for the right words before she said, "He got ... odd the last few weeks before ... before he ... you know. Took work home, which he never used to do, ate alone, and checked his phone all the time. He ... um ... fiddled with the thing all the time, even the wall connection. Someone told me he broke up with his girlfriend, but I think he found someone else. He talked about having lunch with her the next day."

Uh-uh. No girlfriend. Mitt was gay. He had an on-again off-again affair with one guy, but nothing serious. His only stable relationship was with his grandmother. His parents were dead in an auto accident. This explained why she was the only one who cared to look for an explanation for the why in his suicide.

Suicide, hell, my money was on someone pushing him. Did his lunch 'date  sell him out or someone kills him because of their meeting? Something he found did him in. The jury was still out, but regardless, if we weren't careful, things could get hairy. We needed to watch our backs.

### *Stepping up to the Big Time: Operational Meeting with the Big Wigs*

I wasn't sleeping well, and that fouled up my day. My subconscious kept gnawing at the Mitt situation. Numbers from loan packages haunted my head, with the opposite effect of sheep. I could have used some reliable sheep to fill my hours of tossing and turning.

My antidote for lack of sleep was braving the LA air to jog every morning. I enjoyed the early quiet before the commute made the neighborhood hum. This time I was running on fumes before my foot hit the front step. The exercise had sapped my Blue, and I needed a refill. I'd passed muster with Mr. Petrosian and got to work a transaction in Armenian. Whoopee, I'd hit the big time. I felt wired all the time and took to sucking on 0.mints.

After my usual half hour run, my uneasiness with Your Best worries had eased. Mindless movements remained my best remedy for stress. I wasn't all that thrilled with some of the after effects though. Sweat trickled down my back as I rounded the corner and arrived at my condo. One benefit of being a member of the family—access to the healing Blue. I partook frequently.

At my door, I reached into my pocket for my key.

"Aida. Oh, Aida."

Dandy, my nosey neighbor from across the court.

"This good-looking older man stopped by your house. He left about ten minutes ago. I told him you were out on your run. He mentioned he'd come back in an hour. He said, "If you don't mind, would you let her know her Uncle Sergei is in town?" So as soon as I spotted you, I hurried right over."

Mrs. Abbott would hurry over anyway. Who needs to feed a watchdog if Mrs. Abbott is around?

"Thank you. I had no idea my uncle was in town." I lied.

Opening the door, I stepped inside  and mouthed "Thank you again," before shutting the door to avoid a lengthy probing discussion with Mrs. Abbott.

I'd hoped Dad might part of the upcoming big-shot meeting. Earlier in the week Arkady and I, along with three outside Blue Talon agents, and the Office Chief who forwarded the unlikely case on to Ricky, received an "invitation" to meet at the family's safe house on Lankershim. The Chapel of the Palms contained a legitimate funeral business, but the sub-basement operated strictly as our undercover headquarters in the LA basin. I'd visited the place once before and left with the impression the facility failed the impressive test. This is only a dingier small version of the cave. You reached the boardroom via the combination embalming room and crematorium. The public somehow seemed less than eager to venture anywhere near the area.

The schedule called for a noon start, which meant I had time for a date with my water pic showerhead and perhaps a bite after. This Wonderful gadget, loaded with the variable jets and massage attachment, made a shower a total experience. Better than my love life, for sure. I didn't dare socialize with the folks at Your Best, and I'd lost contact with Joe the DDG guy who used to live two doors down.

When my doorbell rang, I wrapped my hair in a towed and pulled on my robe to answer.

"Da... Uncle Sergei," I said. Stay in character, Jeanne, never slip out of character, that's what they tell you.

"Aida, my favorite niece," he said, bending to place an uncle-ish kiss on my forehead.

"What a surprise, come in, Uncle Sergei. When did you get in?" I babbled. The nosey Mrs. Abbott peeked out her window. Gotta stay in character. "Come on in."

I shut the door and leaned back against it. "Dad, I didn't expect you... so soon," I ended lamely. I shut up and gave him a big hug. He held me hard and close. My head dropped to his shoulder, and the tears came. "I am so glad you're here. Ricky Lagree says I can't write, call, e-mail, anything. My social life sucks. Only Mitzi and I most nights."

To answer the question in his expression, I explained, "Mitzi is my cat. A Manx with an attitude."

I stepped back and looked at him. His eyes glistened. "Russian men don't cry, huh, Dad?"

He laughed. "Never, Love."

"I worry about you, you know. Are you eating right? Who's cooking for you?"

"The cook is still with me, so you can rest easy, I only have the housekeeper in twice a month though because I'm gone so much."

"Gone where?"

"Just gone—I'm almost never home. I rattle there, too empty. I find excuses to volunteer with the family and add additional consults for the Clinic."

"'Will we ever get to be "partners" again? I still haven't heard if I stay Aida or if I can be Jeanne for a little while more.'"

"Officially, you're still alive. I told the neighbors you landed this great job in Hollywood and are so busy etc. etc... If they don't need Aida, and no posting calling comes up you can handle, maybe a slight chance Ricky will let you come home for a visit."

"I hope so, Dad. I'm like a boat adrift without an anchor. No friends, no father, no fun. That's my life."

"For all of us, Love, every time we're pushed into the unfamiliar and face a possible end of the life we've known."

"Dad, I don't want this life to be over. I'm not that old. I've got friends from school and…"

"I was 16 the first time," he said in a quiet voice. "No family to rely on, no way to realize I would face more years than I could imagine:

I shut up. I was already throwing myself a pity party, and nothing happened yet. Dad threw me a life preserver with his "she's busy in LA" story.

"You win."

Dad was silent for a moment or two and then changed the subject. "Ricky asked me to sit in with the Blue Talon local agents at the meeting today. I am familiar with Armenia. I walked much of the area before … before my master took me to Turkey."

Uh oh, the slave life … time to move on….

"The mortuary is not too far, want to walk? We've got a few minutes. You might as well take advantage of some good weather. Minnesota is usually still cold at this time of year." I said with the smirk folks who've escaped the cold can't hold back.

"Snow's not a problem for me. I've spent a lot of time in snow country, but a walk does sound good. A little exercise to help get the flight kinks out."

We didn't hurry. Someone told me once you won't miss your parents until they are gone and you can't be with them again. I missed my mom like crazy when I was a kid. Now similar sadness swamped me, even though Dad was walking next to me.

When we reached the mortuary and headed downstairs, I was glad no one occupied the embalming table. Nothing like seeing a naked corpse to ruin your day. Our meeting room may not be as luxurious as my first impression. Perhaps the contrast with the adjoining gruesome area made a difference.

"Ricky, hello. I didn't expect you today."

"This case has branched out in a lot of directions. Some familiar faces are showing up too often. Once I get a better handle on what's going on, I'll arrange a teleconference with any others who need to take on a role later. Besides, when Papa is on the list of those coming, I show up and placate his face-to-face preference."

What familiar faces? What's that about?

I laugh, "More likely you want out of your cave, to take in some sunshine and warm weather for a change."

A couple at the table seemed shocked to hear sass directed at the Bossman. What the hell, he's my brother after all. Not some bloody god.

He surprised me, "Perhaps a little. I've been ... uh ... in my office without a break for too long."

Oops, big boo boo, forgot the short-timers don't know about the cave.

Arkady came round the table to shake hands with Dad. "Jeanne, do you know all here? If not, I'll introduce them anyway. Mark Larson is the Office Chief in LA. He brought the case to us; Sam Goldstein's an insurance and banking expert, Marylyn Osbourn, gang activities liaison to the FBI, this is Aida Dadurian, our undercover operative at Your Best Community Bank. Aida adds extensive law and finance expertise to our team on Operation Avats. And you've met Dr. McCormick before

Yeah, like known him all of my life.

I shoved my own file down on the desk and lined the thing up with the others already in place. Mine contained the names written and oral of the principals in my current activities, and a listing of all the properties. I copied most of the pages I figured might be important. I was sweating the whole time. Risky didn't even come close. Should have had Karl run a copy through his portal for Ricky to bring with him. 'Course I didn't know Ricky was coming. I was doing the same thing led the last guy in my space to make like Icarus. He didn't get as high as the sun, but the trip ended the same way. Squish.

Ricky nodded at Mark to chair, and we began. "I will not go over every detail of how we entered this case. I assume you all read the background briefing on the Armenian Avats, part street gang, part sophisticated criminal operators. You may not be aware many of the members are immigrants who retained ties to crime syndicates in their home country. The locals start with petty crime, ripping off credit cards and the like. Because of this case, we now find their repertoire has been much larger and intertwined with money laundering and drugs throughout the Asia Minor corridor. At this point, so many balls are in the air and more than many shells in the game making the players almost interchangeable. Sam, would you fill us in on what you've uncovered thus far?"

"Bear in mind, my findings are preliminary," he began, his voice in a dull monotone.

Why are accountants always so dry? Yawn.

"This sleazeball bunch broke more than their share of state and federal laws. Got to give them credit for being inventive, besides fraud, money laundering, extortion, and intimidation, they've covered the waterfront. I'm surprised they tried this. Most don't dare to practice this form of extortion after a federal court case pulled the rug out from under those who did. I'm of the opinion no legitimate operation would go along, no matter how you chop the meat.

"Apparently Avats and some individuals in the gang own the bank—which is illegal even if we ignored some blatant intimidation. They seem to have concocted a way to collect twice on the arrangement.

"I don't have a handle yet on how many fraudulent deals they've put together, but the borrower always ends up shortchanged. Bad news, considering he or she was the person who actually put up the money to start things rolling. Any money received stayed with the bank, or should I say the Avats?"

I'm yawning for real by now. How does anyone ever get excited about anything involving banking is bad enough?

"What's your recommendation, Sam?"

"Normally I'd recommend going through official channels. However, I'm not sure much good would come from this approach. Bottom-line, this is a matter for Treasury or the FBI. Are we in a position to push the package over to them once we gather more proof, Mr. Kellner?"

"I believe the Blue Talon master contracts with both agencies would cover activities such as this, meaning the ones too grey for the usual government types," Ricky answered.

Mr. Kellner?

"For Treasury, FBI, CIA, we've got long-standing arrangements. State, Defense, and Homeland Security are on a case by case. Most governments have a similar arrangement in countries where we maintain offices."

"The SEC and Treasury need to run point on this," Sam continued,  but I believe the right thing to do is for us to put aside some money for legal help for the poor schmucks Your Best bilked."

"Nothing beyond what you laid out so far?"

"Not from us, although with what we found the FDIC probably would close the place down."

"No loss," I said, "although I hate that some who work there will lose their jobs. They don't seem to have a clue of what is going on—and at least one of them is a single mom."

"Good point, Aida," Arkady added. "There's a couple in IT with little kids as well."

"How hard would it be to find them new jobs with one of the companies we own?" Dad asked. "We've got a lot of slots to fill."

"I'll make sure we get resumes from everyone," Sam said. "How many might have them loaded on Your Best's computer system?"

"Not sure, Sam, not something I spent time on. I'll check and get back to you."

"OK, Marylyn, you're up. "

"Marylyn is my name and gangs are my game," she said with a smile, giving us a hint she intended the line to be a joke. We smiled, sorta.

She and Sam need to work on their jokes. Lame, lame, lame.

"We work with the local police and sheriff on gang-related issues, although the Feds get involved if they can point to RICO. From what Sam said, we'll be working with them. Our usual focus is identifying of current and potential gang members and their confederates."

"Right now we've got two agents undercover with the Avats.   'S as many as I could get in. Harder with the Armenian factor and the need to speak the language. We lost one a while back, and the slot has been tough to fill. I'd put in more, but I need to use only men. Chauvinism is alive and well with Armenians, and the gangs fall right in line. Once we get wind of a planned or robbery or something similar, we leak the news to law officers we trust so they can stop the action. Occasionally, we directly intervene. Don't like risking my men though.

"'We provide the security for neighborhood centers, which gives us an opportunity to learn what's going on without being obvious. We use college kids on an internship to staff our legitimate operation working with a resident "counselor". Our guys are getting good at talking the talk. We try to convince the younger ones to stay in school. When new kids show up, our counselors  sound them out, and if they are leaning to the gang life, we rely on free-lance psychologists who have some unique methods. Not sure of all the details, but they call what they do 'color counseling.'"

Arkady and I glanced at each other. We knew exactly color counseling involved. His shoulders moved up and down infinitesimally. News to him, too.

Marylyn paused with a worried expression on her face, "Something big is going down. Our bad actors are huddling around in the corners. The gang is making a point to keep anyone who's not part of Avats out of the circle. Not sure what Sam has dug up to matches with what I'm picking up on the streets."

Ricky and Dad exchanged glances. I noticed an ever-so-slight nod from Ricky. Hmm.

"Anything to add at this point Arkady? Aida?

"I think my last report detailed how non-reportable, just barely non-reportable mind you, sums were spinning around the globe several times through multiple banks. Difficult to track even though there was an apparent pattern," Arkady volunteered.

"Jeanne?"

"Nothing specific, although I noticed tension in the upper floor. I'm reasonably sure I'm not the target, but not positive. Too many visits from Mr. Petrosian, but perhaps he's getting his jollies looking down my blouse. Although…."

Dad and Ricky exchanged glances again. "Although what, Jeanne?"

"I could swear I say Walt hanging around last week—or someone who who resembles him.'

## *Final Touches*

Ricky got up and paced back and forth at the head of the table. Nothing I hadn't heard before, so I got up and filled two coffee cups and brought one cup to him like a good little first timer.

"Thanks," Dad said, holding out his cup. I ended up filling or refilling a cup for the entire table. I glanced up at Dad and saw what I expected, a hint of a smile curling one side of his mouth. The little smile gave him away. He'd cooked up this waitress-to-the-gods-thing for me. Some partner.

"I work for tips," I said, but they ignored me.

Ricky didn't bother to notice, just kept talking while he pulled out a display board.

Oh no, not a flip chart.

"Perhaps I can shed a little light on where the money has gone. Some at HQ helped me with this show and tell." He hauled out a world map and, so help me I'm serious, a laser pointer.

"The bank is here." He tapped the map. "Most of the money ended up here." He pointed at the area northeast of Turkey. "According to Annie McNabb, -Hmm, he's using short-timer name convention with a last name, interesting- an agent operating in the criminal division in Europe, the cash was used to purchase drugs from Afghanistan, Azerbaijan, and points east. Most concentrated on heroin or opium, but many included marijuana. Their purchases go west into Europe where a multi-billion Euro market exists."

He glanced up, but no one reacted.

Maybe they're as comatose as I am.

"Recent intel leads us to believe maybe a third of the money ends up in Swiss numbered accounts and the balance in Panama or the Caymans. The Swiss are tight-lipped, but the other two do not cooperate at all. We saw this ping-pong path of money flow duplicated when it reached North America."

"No way you can expect us to tackle all that, Bossman," said Mark.

"I agree. We'll must involve Interpol and contact a few known reliable folks in the various governments. Europe does not differ from the Americas. They buy and sell officials, too. The money is too tempting for most. Your question is appropriate, however. What we need is sufficient proof for the agency or the government to which we supply the information. You all realize how dicey the drug end of our operation may become. I don't want agents killed, leaving a kid without a parent."

"Sam, forward what you get to HQ so we can sic the Feds on them. Marylyn, your job is to keep tabs on the gang leaders here. Send reports to HQ as you gather info."

They both nodded.

What else would they do when the Boss gives an order?

"The overseas Armenian connection created a need for undercover operatives, two at least to cover both ends. Arkady already volunteered to leave for Armenia. With luck, his arrival will be timed a week or two before the stuff hits the fan here. Aida speaks fluent Armenian and should be able to cover any Armenian speaking communication. Dr. McCormick also traveled the area previously and will act as a courier for sensitive materials."

"I spent time in the Peace Corps and speak a similar dialect. My consulting work helps keep me current with the language," Dad put in.

All heads nodded, except mine.

Dad's fed me a line like this before. Sit in, bullpucky. I'm not happy. And I have a few things to say to Arkady, too. Hell, I didn't even think to call him Mario anymore. What do they think I am, a little girl to shield? Prejudiced against first-timers?

"I'm not sure I fully understand. I believe what you are saying is I stay here, out of harm's way, and Arkady and the good doctor sally forth with their lances into the heart of drug country? Am I wrong?"

"I don't believe I'd describe the plan in quite that way, but, yes," Ricky said, at least responding with enough grace as to appear uncomfortable.

Give him credit for a politically correct answer.

"I must be missing something. My understanding of Blue Talon procedures called for two agents together—always—one to cover the other's back. Your plan seems to put Arkady, Sergei, and me on solo trips, so what about those backs now?"

You could taste the shock coming from Sam, Mark, and Marilynn. A good agent didn't question the orders of a superior. Didn't happen. Problem was, I had. I stared at Ricky, glanced over at Dad, and caught one corner of Dad's mouth up in a half smile again. He didn't show any shock. I'd bet he predicted my reaction. Even instigated it.

"What we learned since you and Arkady were placed indicates we would  find him more useful in a different role. You both should expect a new partner assigned to you soon."

"What's with soon? Your analysis making us well matched as partners possessing complementary skills was an error? What other 'revised  analyses should I be expecting?"

Dad stepped in as I suspected he would. "Ricky, I believe sending Arkady is the correct move. He is familiar with the land and the culture. He and his new partner have worked a case together before. On the other hand, I once had my partner reassigned, and I understand Aida's uneasiness with no one for backup. I also understand your hesitation in sending her into a culture where they regard women as lesser beings and agree her in-your-face attitude might pose a problem. I suggest she and I share courier duties. She may establish herself as a man-woman, a woman who earns the respect given a man. As a practical matter, to maintain my cover, I cannot always be gone long enough to take care of multiple deliveries. Does that work for you?"

Ricky hesitated, but nodded. "Good suggestion, Doctor."

I realized with ice around my heart the partner Dad spoke of was me. How could I refuse? I didn't buy into the family never says no bit, but I was getting a better idea of how lonely life, lives, might be for our kind, the ones I mentally referred to as the Blue Crew.

"Once Arkady settles into his new undercover identity, I believe the modification in the operation would be appropriate."

"When do I leave?" Arkady asked.

"You'll soon take on a new job, one you can't refuse. I would guess you'd be on a plane with a new passport within a month. OK, unless someone wants to add more, you all know what you need to take care of in your area. You need your input to HQ to be detailed and encrypted. On any development requiring immediate action, you must call using the double relay secure phone. I will assign a person to be on call twenty-four seven. Don't attempt anything alone. I want no one killed. "

Arkady came round the table, peered down at me. "I'll miss you, F.T. I hope we work together again. Only one life and you're damn near as good as I am," he added in a soft tone so others would not overhear.

My punch flew, and he ducked*. "I'm glad you aren't leaving today. I hope we partner up again in a future life," I whispered.

"You heard what Ricky said about not trying to be a hero. I've gotten a bad feeling. Your Walt remark threw me. I thought we were done with that schmuck. Why didn't you tell me you thought you recognized him when you first saw him?"

"I'm not one to scare up ghosts if I'm not sure. I won't do something dumb, Arkady, okay?"

"Promise me if things get hot, you call for back-up?"

I nodded. "Okay, but I think you're making too much of this."

"Hmm, maybe. Okay, then. Ricky wants time with me, so catch you at work tomorrow? I'll still be around for a few days."

I nodded and peered around for Dad. He was over by the coffee machine. I strolled over, "Latte addict."

"My secret is out," he said in mock dismay.

"Lunch?"

"Sounds good. You're the one familiar with the places around here."

We said our goodbyes and slipped out at intervals so as not to attract attention. Dad and I walked down Lankershim and turned into a wonderful Caribbean place I'd found a few months ago. The smell of spicy pepper pot filled the place. We sat down by the window. "Thanks, Dad. I appreciate you going to bat for me."

"I told Ricky you would not be meek and go along when he shared with me what he planned to do. You are no eighteenth-century salon grand dame. "Be prepared for fireworks," I said. He should have known than to answer, "No she's part of the family and will do what we expect." After all, you spend six months at Blue School with him."

"So he already knew about the alternative?"

"No, I sprung my idea on him."

"I'm glad. I was so pissed he thought he could push me off in a corner."

"No surprise to me, Love. Don't forget, I lived with you for a long time."

"I wish you didn't need to leave so soon. I think I could pull off treating you as Uncle Sergei for a while."

"I'm supposed to deliver a paper at a medical convention which begins tomorrow. A colleague roped me into dinner tonight with the president of the local association."

"So you take off after lunch?"

"Once we get back to your condo, and I retrieve my rental car, yes."

Dad and I walked back to where he parked. We didn't hurry. Neither of us wanted the visit to end. "Any news from Neela lately?" I asked. "Did she say how Rob is doing? Our lives seemed so tangled up together for so long; I don't feel right letting him go. I worry about him sometimes though. I mother-henned him for a long time. Will Neela spot his little quirks, which signal something's up? I know until I finish this assignment, I'm not supposed to contact them...." I trailed off.

"Neela and I talk every couple weeks. I'm still active on the case on the periphery, as you know. Both are working in research at Cedar Sinai.  Rob's abilities and insight impress Neela, but what you shared makes her aware he's too open to outside influence."

"Well, if it's kosher, greet them for me. Tell Rob I think of him every time I go for karaoke. He'll understand."

"What's the story?"

"Rob and I were celebrating getting admitted to grad school at Stanford. I doubt he ever sang in public later, but that night he took the mike. I put Neela and him together for the first time there."

"Young love."

"Umm."

Being a long-lifer sucks. Can't get together with old friends or call your dad. Once you're in the Blue, you're becking-and-calling for Blue Talon.

We walked another couple of blocks, and Dad asked, "What's on your mind, Love. You're preoccupied. Not your usual hundred words a minute self."

"This life sucks, Dad. When do I get to do something I want to do? Does Blue Talon ever give you time off? I don't see you. I'm losing a partner I like, and he's good. The way this lecher keeps looking down my blouse and treating me like meat make me up to here with Armenians. Even the language is sexist."

"The family short-changed you. Back-to-back assignments, the first one before you completed your training. Without an on-site partner, once Arkady leaves for Armenia. I understand your frustration. Your time will come. Blue Talon made few demands on me as you were growing up. Stay safe, Jeanne, don't let your guard down. Cultivate a little paranoia, and your current life should last longer. We can meet again at HQ."

"Do you ever spend time with … your children outside the cave? Like take a vacation with your grandchildren or drop in on a…daughter?"

"Most often not—Blue Talon demands on me do not allow me to do things like that when they are living a second life with a new identity."

"Is everyone in the family lonely? Always being on the outside? Never being who you really are?"

"Not always, more for some, less for some."

"You are a master of ambiguity, Dad. Your car is the green one?" He nodded.

"Time for a cup of coffee before you go?"

"Not this time, Love."

I watched him as he drove out. I picked up the newspaper delivered after we left and went inside. Mitzi greeted me with a meow. The "I'm-hungry-what-kept-you meow," I picked her up and put my cheek against her soft fur. "If all my lives suck as much as this one, Mitzi, I'm resigning."

## *Work, Sleep, Eat*

In the three weeks after the briefing, I divided my waking hours between work, sleep, TV, and my morning run—with an occasional movie or bar fly night thrown in. In no time at all, sleep jumped to the top of my favorite list. When I was sleeping, I didn't need to think about my future life, lives. Let my subconscious deal with that stuff. I remembered Dad telling me how he longed for death in one of his lives. I wondered if he ever tried dying of boredom

The IT nerds and a few from the second floor planned to take Arkady out for drinks on his last day. Wowee. I could scarcely contain my excitement about a night out with the geeks. I decided to go anyway—in part because I hated he was leaving, in part because a night out even being part of nerd central would be better than watching more re-runs. In the meantime, my about-to-be-former partner and I planned to meet tonight "by accident" at the closest watering hole. His idea.

I played the surprise encounter ploy to the hilt when I walked in the sleazy bar down the street. "Arkady, what a surprise. I sure didn't think I'd run into you—what with your leaving and all. You  here for a date?"

"No, more like my wine gene required treatment."

"Funny," I said, "ever thought about a career in stand-up?"

"There's a booth open, care to join me?"

"Aida, did you process a big package this week?  he asked after we'd secured a semi-private place to talk. "With a guy named Abe Savon? Not sure what company name he might have used."

"Yeah, wasn't much of a loan, but Petrosian sure gave Savon the royal treatment."

"He's the big cheese of the local Avat's. One nasty piece of work. No doubt, your boss was shitting his pants having to deal with him. Not that he's got a choice if he wanted to stay healthy."

"As far as I am concerned, he was, and is, a total slimeball. He practically dove into my blouse."

"Yesterday I overheard him talking with Petrosian and one of his gang members. Your name came up several times which makes me very uneasy. Petrosian seemed to be back peddling and shaking his head. I didn't like the sound of it. You need to be careful, F.T. Take a taxi home, keep your door locked."

"You're scaring me, Arkady. Do you think they've made us?"

"I meant to scare you. I'm not crazy about leaving before your new partner shows up. Any news about who you're the lucky guy might be?"

"Not a whisper."

"Ricky needs to get his act together. I may be scaring up ghosts where none exists, but no family member acts alone on an assignment. His Raunchiness might only be planning to have sex with you, but if not ... to be safe, I'm adding my concerns onto this week's report..."

We reached a tacit agreement to drop the subject and enjoy a couple of glasses of top-drawer wine and some bar food. I relaxed and was in a good mood when I left for the parking garage to retrieve my car.

Once I left the street and neared my Hot Pink Fusion, I grew uneasy, peering into the dark. All that scary talk from Arkady. Silly. No one else was around, but my footfalls seemed loud in the deserted ramp. While I fiddled with my purse fishing for my keys, I sensed rather than heard someone behind me. An arm circled my throat, and something hard hit my head. "You're getting yours, Bitch."

Half-unconscious, aware I'd been picked up and thrown over someone's shoulder. Whoever he was, he stunk. Stale beer, garlic, and cigarettes. I gagged but still could press the silent alarm on my phone alerting Arkady. I guess I must have lost consciousness at that point because the last thing I remembered another man saying, "Take her up the elevator, Ando. Six floors should do the trick. Interfering bitch."

His voice was familiar, belonged to someone who didn't belong here. More like a voice from my past, I wasn't sure, but this guy sounded … like Walt.

Hitting the ground after a six-story fall hurt. Hurt a lot. Those bastards had little imagination. They did the same thing before. Hot damn I hurt. I can't move. Is that blood trickling down the side of my face? This is so weird. Like I'm in a whirlpool, slipping down into … not water. How did it get so dark?

The me part of me hovered nearby—a spectator to what was happening. Somehow, I sensed Arkady nearby, even as some old guy zipped up a black bag around me. With a stunning sudden awareness, I realized I must be dead. Yucky, Yuck, and Yuck. This sack reeks of mold and something else I don't want to identify. Guess I get to find out if this reanimation thing is for real. What a lousy way to end an evening.

Oh no, who'll take care of Mitzi?

### Not Alive, but Not Dead

"Paging Dr. McCormick. Paging Dr. Peter McCormick. Please come to the Main Desk. Dr. Peter McCormick."

By the third announcement, I realized the page was for me. In my experience, a page in an unfamiliar place was never good news. My stomach churned. I swallowed, squared my shoulders, and headed toward the lobby. From the main assembly hall, I needed to take the escalator down three flights. My mood sank at each successive floor.

"I'm Dr. McCormick. You have a message for me?"

The clerk punched keys before he answered, "Ah yes, a Mario called and left a number for you. Said it was an emergency.

"Did he say anything else?"

"Just to call him at 212.555.2323. He's waiting for your call."

"Thank you."

"No problem."

I made my way to an out-of-the-way corner and placed the call. "Hello, Mario. What's wrong?"

"Bad news, Sergei. Some scum murdered Jeanne. I called Magda and asked her to claim the body because I'm still undercover for another week. No sense confirming any suspicions they may have already. I'm afraid they made the connection with Jeanne—how I have no idea."

I sagged back against the chair. "Were you there? Did you see what happened, Mario?"

"About the same time I heard police sirens down the block, the silent alarm in my pocket signaled a call for help from Jeanne. I almost ran into the fire truck someone called to cover the emergency as I tracked her signal to the scene. I pushed through the crowd and saw Jeanne's body, broken and bleeding on the street. I caught the beat cop who told me they'd already sent the ambulance a message to arrange for a transfer to a hearse to take the body to the coroner. They'd verified the jumper was dead. A doctor on the street called the TOD. They're talking suicide."

"No way would she have jumped, Mario."

"'Sergei, you know that, and I know that, but… Anyway, with nothing else to do, I pulled out his cell phone, punched in a speed dial number, and got Ricky on the line. Told him, "Ricky, sorry to get you out of bed. The Avats got Aida."'

"He didn't believe me, but I continued, "Yes, I'm sure the Avats did this. How do I know? I'd wager a goodly sum on them being at the bottom of this. The bastards threw her off a roof. Same as before, Seems too coincidental for me, Coincidences never are random, isn't that what they teach the kids at Blue School?"

I tilted my head back imagining the worst. "Was she…?"

Mario didn't answer, but in an effort to distract me, he continued to recount his conversation with Friedrich.

"'I told Ricky, "The only thing I need is help dealing with the coroner. Who's the closest long-lifer I can call to go to the morgue to claim the remains. Not fair for a first-timer to reanimate on the slab. If they do an autopsy, healing and reanimation take longer. Not to mention, someone waking up on the table scares the hell out of the attendant. He suggested Magda."'

"Magda? Isn't she living as Maria Escobar in Oxnard?"

"That's the one. I asked Ricky for her phone number saying her cell would be best. He gave me both numbers. I thanked him and hung up. I wanted to let you know what had happened as soon as I could. Jeanne told me you were presenting again at the Westin this week, but I wasn't looking forward to this call."

As a doctor, I well knew of the normal procedure in cases like this. "I need to get to the coroners as soon as possible."

"Sergei, Magda knows she will need to refuse an autopsy citing religious reasons. The coroner may insist on the procedure due to the nature of the death, however."

"Mein Gott, Mario. I left her only a couple of weeks ago."

"I'm sorry, Sergei. She had time to send a signal so I saw her before … the transport left."

"How will Magda identify her?"

"I told her to ask for Jeanne McCormick. Someone must have informed the Avats she wasn't who she said she was, so no real harm done on that score now. If Magda can't convince them to suspend the autopsy, her father Dr. McCormick should."

"I'll take a cab now, Mario. Thank you for your help. I've got to be with her, help her through reanimation. This will be her first time. In my experience, a violent death always seems harder to undo."

### *Claiming the Body*

"My name is Dr. Peter McCormick. I received word they delivered my daughter here. A fall, my nephew told me."

"Dr. Angus is with the remains. Another family member…"

"Requested no autopsy. I concur. I will accompany the body to Chapel of the Palms," I said dabbing the attendant in a short bath of Blue in case he needed further convincing. The pathologist needed more, but I prevailed—insuring no ugly y-incision would mar her torso, although that was not the reason I gave. I played the religion card again.

"I'm with you now, Love; we'll bring you through together. You've depleted your store of Blue. I'll give you what I have until we reach the Palms."

I sat next to her, held her cold hand, and shared the rest of the Blue remaining after my encounter with the attendants. I hoped enough awareness remained in her to hear my voice. She'll need a safe house in an area where the Blue is easier to retrieve. I palpated her body gently, and my worry over her condition grew. Two hundred plus years of medical training served me well as I diagnosed the extent of her injuries. I hope x-rays prove me wrong. I doubt if any unbroken bone remains in her body. Her internal injuries and the skull and brain damage won't be easy to heal. My poor child.

My experience with violent death left me with little doubt she faced obstacles for a successful reanimation. When I underwent the process, I suffered alone, on a battlefield or lying in muck. Compared to her shattered body, my injuries were minor, through shots or a clean blade thrust. During my bouts of reanimation, once the Blue neared me, I would begin to feel again, to heal. At the same time, I endured incredible pain while the energy siphoned death out from my corpse. Rivers of razors, streams of fire filled me for hours, days, I don't know how long. Regaining my life force took most of the energy in the Blue, the healing less because the wounds were straightforward.

The first time, when I arose in my boyhood body, I needed to establish a new life on my own. With subsequent reanimations, the sporadic healing of the Blue left the patient dealing with the pain from a wound  lingering for months.

Her rebirth would not be the first over which I presided. In the trenches, on violent streets, near unspeakable atrocities, I brought the long-lived back from the in-between, the not-death-but-not-life stage. I wiped their brows, eased their pain with gentle applications of Blue, and massaged their stiffened muscles. All were family but never this child. She, the other half of this life's family. Will I be able to ease her pain, facilitate her healing, offer the comfort she will need once awareness returns. She will face extreme suffering with such a battered body. I must spare my use of the Blue—use small amounts each time to heal and coax her back to consciousness. I chuckled. As much for my protection as hers. I'd never be able to be near her if she younged back to being a teenager again after so little time living like an adult.

*Cold, cold, so cold.*

One spot of warm only. On my hand. Why?

"We're just about at Chapel of the Palms, Doctor," the driver of the hearse said. "We'll be taking her through the rear and into the embalming room, if that's ok?"

"I assume this is routine?"

"Yes, I unwrap the body first, and then place it on the table. Once I get a signature, I take off."

"Fine. I'll want to talk to the mortician and my … uh … my colleague will meet me soon."

"I'm sorry for your loss, Doctor. Family members seldom ride with me, and sometimes I forget my package was a person. Someone loved."

"Thank you."

He wheeled in the long black bag on the gurney and eased the sagging shape over onto the stainless steel table. After he unzipped the sack revealing the ill-used contents, turning, he half saluted. "The mortician should be along soon."

I bobbed my head in response and sat down beside my Jeanne, my youngest.

How long I sat was a mystery, perhaps I dozed or fell into a trancelike state because the sound of a door closing startled me. I heard Ricky's voice. "Papa, I came as fast as I could. I lifted off soon after Mario's call."

"Friedrich, if Jeanne were conscious, she'd be at you, complaining how unfair this is."

"No doubt. That one has never shy about saying what she's thinking, that one. How bad is she?"

"Bad, Friedrich. Few of my patients have been worse. X-rays may reveal more."

"Papa, except once in the Great War, I've never faced reanimation after a violent death. I'd just age out; leave when others noticed I'd younged. The time I did, I don't remember with any fondness."

"Three times I visited in-between, bit never entered as broken as she is now."

"What do we need to do?"

"First, I want an MRI, A necessity to discover how serious the damage to soft tissue and the boney portions of her body might be. I believe I can call in a favor from a colleague at Sinai Cedars. When the results are complete, I'll have a better idea of how long and how intense our treatment must be. I'd appreciate a couple of others with me to help harvest the Blue. Does Blue Talon keep a safe house in a high crime area?"

"We own one south of Tucson; the Sonoran drug route goes close by along the ridges. You'd be about an hour from the airport we use in LA to the one in Arizona."

"You know the family properties. If you believe this one is the most suitable, I'm fine with that."

"I need to work with Karl to notify family members to assist you. The partner works on a reanimation, but Mario must leave for Armenia in the morning. I'll be damned if I let these animals get away with this, and one way is to freeze their product and money coming in from the area. Operation Avats will be our first priority for us from now on. Our agents are so pissed off. If a long-lived finds one of the bastards, they'll find themselves encouraged to do a swan dive off the nearest tall building."

"Agreed," I said my tone grim.

"Once he finds out about her, I won't be able to keep Dmitri away. He'll love stealing the Blue and banging the brains of the local traffickers."

"Are any of her classmates from Blue School between assignments?"

"I'll check. A desert hunt and being around a reawakening should be an opportunity for them to learn, an eye-opener anyway. I don't believe finding volunteers will be a problem, Papa."

I stopped talking and turned back to Jeanne. I was silent for a long time and was barely aware of Friedrich's departure. I rubbed her arm between my thumb and forefinger, up and down, and started when I realized I was humming a lullaby her mother and I used to sing to her when she was a baby.

### Grim Recollection

Our pilot touched down at the isolated Arizona airstrip, an asphalt runway surrounded by the saguaro-studded desert. Blue Talon used the strip near Tucson as an entry to the Southwest. An ambulance waited for us at the small Quonset hut that doubled as a terminal. At the main highway, we turned south to Tupac , the location of the safe house. Considering the nondescript adobe exterior, the plush interior struck me as more impressive. I asked the ambulance driver to put Jeanne in the rear bedroom. I didn't detect a pulse, but no rigor had presented—a good sign.

The doorbell sounded, and I heard the front door open. A rough-dressed Mexican peasant strolled in, "Buenos Tardes, Seňor Sergei," the disheveled person greeted me. "I was to be in the area and thought I'd stop by."

Typical Dmitri. Worried and still a wise ass.

"Thank you for coming. You're the first, but I expect Friedrich."

"'Kidding aside, I really was in the neighborhood. My current mission involved monitoring drugs shipped north by the Mexican cartel. I've been traveling with a herd of mules, the two-legged sort. They buy passage into the 'Promised Land  by hauling "product" to market on their backs. When the Colombian cartels in Cali and Medellin tanked and the drug kingpins found Florida too hot, our neighbors took over the trade. I'm supposed to guide the poor bastards to the delivery site then kill them once the drugs landed in 'safe  hands the US side of the border. Unofficially, I Blued them, burned the cartel crap, and put the mules on a train east. Their chances to continue living improved elsewhere."'

"You have Blue to spare?"

"S why I'm here. I hear my old partner is in trouble. How could I stay away?"

"She's bad, Dmitri. Internal injuries, massive bone damage, head fractured so I assume brain trauma."

"Bastards!"

"We need to treat her gradually. Not only for the injuries but to protect ourselves. If we aren't careful, we might young her back to childhood. She wouldn't  appreciate a rerun."

Dmitri laughed, "Right you are, Sergei. Where is she?"

"Backroom."

I watched my grandson stare down at the still form. We both realized she would live again, but in the hours or minutes before reanimation, death always appeared supreme.

"Heart first, Dmitri. Then legs."

He sailed a puff of Blue with care, aiming toward her chest. He waved his fingers up and down like an orchestra conductor and directed the spiral of Blue haze to slide down and sink into her body. Again the same movements, then once more. I took her wrist. Faint, discernible, but only a doctor's fingers would detect the feeble movement.

"A pulse, Dmitri."

He broke out in a huge smile. He gave me a thumbs up and moved Blue down to her legs. A thin haze enveloped them and faded. He glanced over at me with a question.

I answered, "Not much more now. Give her time to stabilize."

"Good, I'm tapped out. I'll be back after I bash a bad guy."

"Have you eaten?"

"Depends on what you've got here. I've eaten enough rice and beans for several lifetimes."

"Not sure. Let's let her rest and check out the kitchen."

I opened the cabinets and the refrigerator. Well stocked. Ricky's usual efficiency. "You're good to go, Dmitri. Pretty much anything you like."

"I'll make myself a couple of sandwiches I can tote, something to drink as long as it's alcoholic, and I'll be gone."

"Don't see any vodka, Grandson."

"No civilized drinking for me here. Oh well. I guess I settle for cerveza."

### *Time Heals All*

In the next few days, I sat by her bedside as others filled and emptied the other bedrooms. No hesitation. No reservation. My family accepted the call to assist. My sons Michael and Friedrich, daughters Valentina and Hilde, students from her class at Blue School. A constant stream of persons coming and going. Leaving to hunt the Blue m and returning to move Jeanne's reanimation forward little by little. Hilde took over my vigil on occasion to let me sleep, fitful as my hours in bed might be. She was my only daughter to pursue medicine making me confident Jeanne was in safe hands. Well-tended for the time, I, too, must leave to seek the Blue for me and for my youngest.

With a sandwich and ample water, I climbed the desolate rocky sides of the mountain and followed the trails of trash to a drug-ring night-stay location. My stock of Blue seemed depleted. I inhaled of the dark intense rays lingering at the site. The energy filled me and armed me against violence. To lull the suspicions of the small circle of exhausted men and women clustered near the fire while I crept in closer, I took a page from Dmitri's playbook and 'suggested  they burn the drugs. Once I discovered the man in charge, I hosed him in Blue. When he reached the level of suggestibility I wanted, I ordered him to escort the party to a train or bus station, purchase tickets for them, and forget they ever existed. To be sure, in the event the suggestion faded, I insisted he try every effort to protect them until they leave. Blue Talon experience proved specific instructions stayed longer in the memory.

One week passed and another, my days seemed a blur of hellos and goodbyes every time one of my kin arrived and then departed to their current life. The sense of outrage at Jeanne's treatment was universal. To our minds, death in war, death in an accident, death by drowning might be excusable. The wanton murder of an unarmed person in an ambush was not. Family spines collectively stiffened.

Filip, Talon head for the Americas, arrived early to go over details of the local drug running with Dmitri, but not before, he slipped in beside me and gave my shoulders a squeeze. "This one sucks, Papa," he said. "First timers should age out, not have to go through reanimation."

No, they shouldn't, "I agreed. "She's older than I was the first time, but we grew up faster back then."

## *Report from Arkady*

"Didn't we though?" he said before turning to join Friedrich. My son took advantage of the gathering to devise a strategy to deal with the current problem. I wasn't an active participant, but from where I sat near Jeanne's bed, their conversation was clear and audible. Beside Friedrich, I recognized, Dmitri's voice joined by Filip's deep bass. The buzz grew louder. Friedrich asked, "Ok, have we got a good connection for you?"

"Figures, he's got the entire world on alert and logged in. He loves these on-line meetings."

"When I got the call from Marilyn telling me the Avats murdered her undercover agent. She and another agent liberated the tapes from the garage. Clear enough once we identified who threw Jeanne off the rooftop. I reviewed what she sent and recognized one standing beside her. Walt, the YWC racist clown who tried to recruit Rob to the dark side—Jeanne's earlier suspicions were correct, but too late. Somehow, one of the gang caught on to Marilyn's surveillance team. I'd told her if things got hot to call for back-up. When I heard from her, I arranged for the company plane to take me and two of my kick-ass family agents to LA. None of us wanted anyone else dead on this mission."

"Papa, even though these assholes were more than the usual gang punks, but I wasn't worried. The two I brought along with me trained as British SAS. We ready to handle whatever–or whoever–we found. I never saw anyone work a scene like those two. They got in and knocked the gang-bangers inside out. A beautiful operation, they trussed up and hauled both of them off without a sound. And, before you ask, yes, they used the Blue."

"We packed them up in a delivery van and delivered them to a facility north of Granada Hills. Lucky for us, the bastard who masterminded the whole thing was on site. The same asshole we dealt with in southern California. Him, they shipped directly to HQ for questioning. After a day or so, we found out everything. The names of the higher-ups in North America and the big guns in Turkey and Armenia. Turned out we're just a sideshow. They told us any major action takes place where Ricky assigned Arkady."

"I never saw Ricky so focused on a mission before, and not just Ricky, Tina, too. He was all businesslike, efficient, but he made it clear he expected us to treat this undertaking with more urgency, more intensity, more something. Our work wouldn't be a simple snatch and dash. We comprised only a part of a larger operation. No matter, I intended to do my damndest for Jeanne. She was my partner, after all."

"We got lucky, and Arkady was in the right place at the right time. He represented our best chance to get the names of the others farther up the line in the drug and money laundering syndicate. Getting him back with the two we needed to interrogate was a logistical nightmare. They went from oxcart to wagon, to train, boat, and plane. "Tell you what Ricky. That trip was like reliving all my lives. After that oxcart ride, I'll take civilization any day."

The group laughed, and I smiled with them, but the smile disappeared as the discussion continued.

"Much as I hate to admit this—Tina and Amelia were right all along, and I was wrong," Friedrich said. "A black network exists. The two Arkady brought in held a rank high enough on the food chain to point us at a bigger and more spread out organization and their attached vermin. All family members not on a current assignment are about to be on one.

357

Everyone needs to die or make up plausible excuses to leave their family, at least for a while, to work on this."

"Certain organizations seem to have engineered an affiliation with a kind of master network. Walt's band of racists is only one of a dozen. We'll call this the Cabal until we come up with a better name. Too many times, they seemed to expect what we would be doing. They infiltrated and profited too often to blame coincidence. We needed to find out how. Karl pointed out we could longer trust the integrity of the individual offices because of the numbers of the short-lived we hire to work for us in the criminal division. A few bad apples may possess limited access to our resources. Even limited this doesn't make for a pretty picture."

Not a pretty picture, but perhaps the reason the Blue recruited us.

I stared down at the unmoving form of my daughter. The prospect was daunting. If I had known when I died the first time what I've learned since, would I have married knowing my children must follow the same path as I, be forced to live life after life and suffer the joys and sorrows of centuries? Indeed, did I ever have a choice? Will we be able to fulfill the mission given us by the Blue? Can we make a difference in a world constantly inventing new horrors? I hope so for my children's sake. For Jeanne's sake. I hope so.

## On the Mend

Jeanne's body mended more daily, but I insisted she remained unconscious until the brain injury healed. Ricky sent a portable CereTom head cat scanner. Although bulky and heavy, the scanner fit  inside a panel truck. I chose to leave the device in the van, to bring Jeanne to the vehicle for scanning. Mountain and Mohammad, so to speak. Better anyway, as no adequate shielding existed in the old adobe.

The room grew pin-drop silent when I unfolded the paper showing the results of the first scan.

"You want me to read it to you, Sergei? Dmitri asked.

"No, I need to find out for myself." My fingers trembled and the printout rustled. I don't want her living life her next life unable to care for herself, unable to make her own decisions. She'll be better one day, of course. Her limitations would not be for forever, but for how long? I had no experience with such severe brain damage as she suffered. Would our efforts be enough? Would the Blue heal her unseen injuries?

"I'm not sure how much more we can use with her without making her as young as when the Blue first appeared to her."

I scanned the paper, read the results in fear. I looked up at my anxious family and wordlessly thrust the paper out to them to read. Overcome, I placed my hands around my head, and rested my elbows on my knees. What if I'm misinterpreting the slice readings?

Hilde took the paper from my hand, glanced over the entries with her practiced eye. "She'll be fine, Papa. Some temporary problems with short-term memory, hesitation in her step on the left side, which is treatable even in a short-lived. After we add a bit more Blue, she should be fine."

The room cheered and rushed me. We clung to each other, relief mixed with pride. Safe now for my girl to wake up, I breathed deep.

"You send her the Blue, Papa." "Yes, Yes, Papa should," they urged.

Still fearing the worst, I delayed, examined her. Our treatment appeared effective, younger, yes, but not so much she resembled a child, nor, I thought, a proper teenager. More like an youthful adult. She might even be pleased.

I bent over and kissed her forehead. "Time to wake up, little girl. Time for School."

Then I bathed her in Blue once more. Everyone held his or her breath, until, infinitesimally, she stirred. Her movements grew stronger, and she yawned, threw her arms out in a stretch.

Turning her head, she said, "Dad, what are you doing here? Why aren't you at the clinic? Who are all these people with you? Who's taking care of Mitzi?"

I sagged, my face contorted, and I couldn't speak. My eyes were moist, and I turned away.

"Dad," she said, "Remember, Russian men don't cry."

Her voice was halting and hoarse, but my Jeanne was Jeanne still. Without doubt.

**Epilogue**

I had prescribed recuperation time back in Minnesota for my youngest. A decision now open to question. My ears hurt. Jeanne had set the volume of her music at a level only a trifle less than intolerable.

Still, the noise was a readymade excuse to leave the room when the distinctive signal of HQ sounded. Jeanne bolted over to the computer. "Arkady…Mario, whatever in hell I'm supposed to call you now. I'm so glad you're ok. I suppose Ricky told you I was off my game for a while. I hope I didn't miss all the action … I didn't, right?"

I kept one ear peeled. What would she try to, as she puts it, "get sprung."

"Don't think so, F.T. Ricky's got a bug up his behind though. He's treating Your Best more than a simple drug and money dump scheme. You may get more use out of your Armenian yet. You sure you're all back together? From what they told me, my impression was your condition leaned more to taking a wide detour, not some little side-track."

She glanced in my direction with an accusing expression. "Dad exaggerates, Mario. What about you? Did you find your assignment in Armenia just too exciting?"

"You can be glad you stayed home all warm and cozy. I froze my ass hiking across a bunch of nothing. We did what we came to do, just like the Mounties in Canada. I'm sure they'll fill you in. What's new with you?"

"For the time being, I'm stuck here in Arizona. Ricky wanted me back at HQ, but Dad told him, "No way until she's stronger. He's touting something about being more back together before taking on anything new. He's been overprotective and doctorish, but, on the bright side, we've shared super father-daughter time. Ricky even relented and let me chat with Rob and Neela. Neela told me things were quiet on the "Rob Front." I touched base with some of my old Bruin buddies and tipped a few with one who lives down this way, but, I'm ready for something new. Turns out I'm as much of an adrenaline junky as the rest of the family."

"Good for you, F.T., I understand you two have kept busy entertaining a bunch of visitors—Dmitri, Hilde…."

"Sure, they all visited while I was asleep! When I woke up, they all took off. 'S been Dad and I since then. "

I heard a break in her voice before she continued.

"I want to be doing something constructive, Arkady. I don't feel so much like an outsider now. I understand I am part of a big family, an extraordinary unique family, and what being a member means. The whole reanimation thing made me realize we share memories, a common goal, and the Blue. According to the grapevine, the geek squad has turned the memory recordings into virtual reality situations so we can experience the same memory with its maker. Doesn't this sound cool?"

I didn't catch Mario's reply when I entered the room and said, "The phone call was Ricky. Looks like you'll get your wish, Jeanne Bond."

"What, what was that name you called her?" Mario/Arkady demanded from the screen.

"Don't you dare, Dad. I mean it, don't you dare!"

www.ingramcontent.com/pod-product-compliance
Lightning Source LLC
Chambersburg PA
CBHW032042050726
47590CB00001B/91